A MODERN TREASURY OF
GREAT DETECTIVE
AND MURDER MYSTERIES

A MODERN TREASURY OF GREAT DETECTIVE AND MURDER MYSTERIES

Edited by Ed Gorman

Carroll & Graf Publishers, Inc.
New York

First Carroll & Graf edition 1994
First Carroll & Graf paperback edition 1997

Carroll & Graf Publishers, Inc.
260 Fifth Avenue
New York, NY 10001

Library of Congress Cataloging-in-Publication Data

A modern treasury of great detective and murder mysteries / edited by
   Ed Gorman. — 1st paperback ed.
      p.   cm.
   ISBN 0-7867-0378-4
   1. Detective and mystery stories. American.   I. Gorman, Edward.
[PS648.D4M64   1997]
813'.087208054—dc21   86-36791
                                                                  CIP

Manufactured in the United States of America

Contents

INTRODUCTION
BY JON L. BREEN

Some people will always insist, first, that the good old days were better, and, second, that there is nothing new under the sun. If you claim that the last twenty-five years have brought an unprecedented renaissance to the field of crime and mystery fiction, that the real Golden Age is right now, they will haul out some heavy ammunition to challenge you. And as long as consideration is confined to individual titles and authors, the advocate of the past will be able to make a case.

There is probably no single book so original in its theme, approach, or subject matter that an enthusiast with a pack-rat memory can't reach back to the twenties or thirties or forties to cite something roughly comparable. And if someone asks you, where is there a writer today who is the equal of Hammett or Chandler or Sayers or Christie or Queen or Carr or Stout or Tey or Allingham or Armstrong or any of the other crime/mystery/suspense icons, you might have to grudgingly admit that in their particular specialties, those great individuals will never be equalled. But as soon as you start comparing the whole field of the last couple of decades with that of any other period of time, the amazing breadth and depth of the present-day output is overwhelming.

What has happened to transform the field of crime and suspense fiction in the last quarter century? Though the old traditions are still honored where appropriate, the old constraints have broken down. There is much less emphasis on what can and can't be done in a mystery novel.

In years gone by, even in most mysteries considered tough, violence and gore were muted, as if, in the tradition of Hollywood movies before the sixties, bullets could politely, antiseptically kill without drawing blood or making a hole in the fabric of the victim's clothes. Today, even in some books considered cozy, the odd *fuck* may creep into the dialogue, corpses may evacuate their bowels, and the sleuth may be seen coping with all the same bodily functions as the reader.

We hear a lot today about political correctness, which supposedly constrains writers and others from statements that offend members of an ethnic, religious, or radical group, a gender, or a sexual orientation. Though the phenomenon exists, its pervasiveness has been exaggerated. Compared to any other period, writers of today are more free to depict members of all classes and categories of people as fully human individuals with good features and bad. Would we really like to return to a time when an African American could never be a hero, could never be a villain, could only be comic relief, a bit player, or (in the odd brave liberal offering) a symbol of suffering nobility? Would we prefer a climate where gay people only exist as objects of derisive humor, disgust, or suspicion? Would we be more comfortable if a character's Native American blood would be cited as a proud touch of exoticism but no connection to any kind of tribal culture was suggested? Would we prefer a world where Della Street and Mme. Maigret, admirable as they were, defined the limits of a woman's aspirations?

In the crime fiction field of a quarter century ago, the spy was king— indeed, some claimed that the international espionage thriller, with its determination to hang the fate of the world by a thread in every outing, had forever displaced the musty old detective novel with its quaint focus on single crimes, single deaths. How can a crime against one or two people engage our interest, asked the spy proponents, when we've developed weapons that can take out whole cities with a single push of a button? (It shouldn't take the O.J. Simpson case to tell us what a misreading of human nature that theory was.)

At the same time, the romantic suspense novel or modern gothic was approaching its peak. It was a form that could be magical when practiced by its masters but tired and formulaic in the hands of their imitators. And one of its prime characteristics was an avoidance of clues and detection.

True, many of the great names of the pure detective story were still practicing twenty-five years ago—Ellery Queen, Agatha Christie, John Dickson Carr, Ngaio Marsh, Michael Innes, Helen McCloy, Rex Stout—but most were past their prime and only a few new classicists (Emma Lathen and John Ball, among the American ones) had been recruited to join them. Similarly, though Ross Macdonald was the object of critical acclaim and other established private-eye bylines like Brett Halliday, Richard S. Prather, and Mickey Spillane continued to command a market share, the shamus seemed to be an endangered species. (One of the few major ones to debut in the sixties was Michael Collins's Dan Fortune.)

When the first general mystery fanzines, *The Armchair Detective* and *The Mystery Lover's* [later *Reader's*] *Newsletter,* began to appear in the late sixties, the emphasis of the articles, letters, and even book reviews was on the old classics, with relatively little attention paid to a somewhat depressed current market. When I conducted a poll of the ten favorite novels and twelve favorite authors for *TAD* (results published in the February 1973 issue), the most recent novel among the top vote-getters (Josephine Tey's *The Daughter of Time*) was over twenty years old and the living writers in the top sixteen had all debuted in the forties or earlier, with John D. MacDonald the contemporary having least seniority. Freeman Wills Crofts, now forgotten by all but a few long-memoried specialists, had seven different book titles nominated by participants.

Though it may have seemed both classical and hardboiled detection were on the ropes in the sixties and early seventies, there was at least one strong clue to their continued viability. With their last books, Agatha Christie and Ross Macdonald began to join spy specialists like John Le Carré, Ian Fleming, and Len Deighton on the bestseller lists. The growing preponderance of crime fiction writers on such lists, which has steadily increased right up to the present, demonstrates both the strength of genre fiction and the relative weakness of mainstream fiction. Many writers of considerable literary talent, turned off by the lessened reader interest and the decreased emphasis on pure storytelling in so-called serious fiction, have turned to popular genres where they could deliver an intriguing plot and still make serious statements about humanity and society.

Through the seventies, eighties, and early nineties, these were some of the developments in American crime fiction:

1) The private eye made a strong comeback with the introduction of such characters as Bill Pronzini's Nameless, Loren D. Estleman's Amos Walker, Robert B. Parker's Spenser, Joe Gores's Daniel Kearny Associates, and Lawrence Block's Matt Scudder, plus a new group of female operatives—Maxine O'Callaghan's Delilah West, Marcia Muller's Sharon McCone, Sue Grafton's Kinsey Millhone, Sara Paretsky's V. I. Warshawski, and Linda Barnes's Carlotta Carlyle.

2) The pure detective story was given a new lease on life by writers who could observe its rules of fair play while satisfying the other demands of the market. Some of them were William L. DeAndrea, James Yaffe, Herbert Resnicow, Susan Dunlap, Sharyn McCrumb, Nancy Pickard, and Jane Haddam (Orania Popazoglou).

3) Women writers, always a strong presence in the field, seized a share of the market more closely proportional to their representation among the readership.

4) Crime fiction, once a contemporary form almost by definition, began to mine the past for fresh backgrounds and viewpoints. Prominent American writers of historical mysteries included Elizabeth Peters (a.k.a. Barbara Michaels), Max Allan Collins, and James Sherburne.

5) A field whose gestures toward multiculturalism hadn't extended much beyond Earl Derr Biggers's well-intended but much-maligned Charlie Chan now had more and more sleuths of varied ethnicity and, even more amazingly, sexual preference. See, for example, the works of Barbara Neely, Walter Mosley, Joseph Hansen, Katharine V. Forrest, Eleanor Taylor Bland, Manuel Ramos, and Tony Hillerman.

6) Mystery-story elements were used more and more frequently by mainstream writers, even those who did not enter the field overtly, among them Joyce Carol Oates, Don DeLillo, E. L. Doctorow, Norman Mailer, and Diane Johnson.

5) Social, sexual, religious, and political issues, once considered outside the realm of escapist popular fiction, were explored in a way previously unprecedented.

6) Lines dividing popular genres were crossed, as bestselling writers like Stephen King, Peter Straub, Dean R. Koontz, William Peter Blatty, and Michael Crichton drew elements from various categories.

7) Through conventions like the annual Bouchercon and its specialized or regional equivalents, periodicals like *The Armchair Detective* and *Mystery Scene*, and a growing number of fan publications, the American mystery field developed an expanded sense of community coincident with the unprecedented volume of new titles being published.

In the early 1980's, I took a hiatus from regular book reviewing, partly because I felt I was becoming a slave to the new, that I didn't have enough chance to delve into the vintage mysteries that lined my walls. They are still there; I still rediscover them periodically; and if you ask me to name the greatest mystery byline of them all, I will still say Ellery Queen without the slightest hesitation. But as the new books pour in at a delightful if overwhelming rate, in a volume no mortal could possibly keep up with, nearly all of them better written and more readable than the average standard of the thirties or forties, I realize I may never retreat again. Present-day crime fiction is where I want to be as a writer and a reader.

Somewhere there's a John D. MacDonald quote to the effect that the only mystery novelist who could be accused of writing real literature was Margaret Millar.

After writing a few routine early novels, Millar went on to do work that was singularly her own, and to make the traditional mystery novel something far more complex and serious than it ever had been before.

Millar's writing came of age in the fifties and sixties. Her turf was Southern California, and wealthy Southern California at that, and in her concerns and prose one hears the voice of that generation that came to maturity during WW II—fascinated with wealth and power, yet ultimately undone by them, too, at least in spiritual ways.

In many respects, Millar and Dorothy B. Hughes were mystery's first mainstream novelists, preparing the way for several women who would appear twenty years later, notably Ruth Rendell.

The saddest aspect of Maggie's long career—she was not enamored of the name Margaret—was that she never found the wide public acceptance she deserved. I've never been sure why. Her stories and books are perfect reflections of their times, and rendered with great wit, poignance, and grace.

The following story is a fine example.

The People Across the Canyon
MARGARET MILLAR

The first time the Bortons realized that someone had moved into the new house across the canyon was one night in May when they saw the rectangular light of a television set shining in the picture window. Marion Borton knew it had to happen eventually, but that didn't make it any easier to accept the idea of neighbors in a part of the country she and Paul had come to consider exclusively their own.

1

They had discovered the site, had bought six acres, and built the house over the objections of the bank, which didn't like to lend money on unimproved property, and of their friends who thought the Bortons were foolish to move so far out of town. Now other people were discovering the spot, and here and there through the eucalyptus trees and the live oaks, Marion could see half-finished houses.

But it was the house directly across the canyon that bothered her most; she had been dreading this moment ever since the site had been bulldozed the previous summer.

"There goes our privacy." Marion went over and snapped off the television set, a sign to Paul that she had something on her mind which she wanted to transfer to his. The transference, intended to halve the problem, often merely doubled it.

"Well, let's have it," Paul said, trying to conceal his annoyance.

"Have what?"

"Stop kidding around. You don't usually cut off Perry Mason in the middle of a sentence."

"All I said was, there goes our privacy."

"We have plenty left," Paul said.

"You know how sounds carry across the canyon."

"I don't hear any sounds."

"You will. They probably have ten or twelve children and a howling dog and a sports car."

"A couple of children wouldn't be so bad—at least, Cathy would have someone to play with."

Cathy was eight, in bed now, and ostensibly asleep, with the night light on and her bedroom door open just a crack.

"She has plenty of playmates at school," Marion said, pulling the drapes across the window so that she wouldn't have to look at the exasperating rectangle of light across the canyon. "Her teacher tells me Cathy gets along with everyone and never causes any trouble. You talk as if she's deprived or something."

"It would be nice if she had more interests, more children of her own age around."

"A lot of things would be nice *if*. I've done my best."

Paul knew it was true. He'd heard her issue dozens of weekend invitations to Cathy's schoolmates. Few of them came to anything. The mothers offered various excuses: poison oak, snakes, mosquitoes in the creek at the bottom of the canyon, the distance of the house from town in case something happened and a doctor was needed in a hurry . . . these excuses, sincere and valid as they were, embittered Marion. *"For heaven's sake, you'd think we lived on the moon or in the middle of a jungle."*

"I guess a couple of children would be all right," Marion said. "But please, no sports car."

"I'm afraid that's out of our hands."

"Actually, they might even be quite *nice* people."

"Why not? Most people are."

Both Marion and Paul had the comfortable feeling that something had been settled, though neither was quite sure what. Paul went over and turned the television set back on. As he had suspected, it was the doorman who'd killed the nightclub owner with a baseball bat, not the blonde dancer or her young husband or the jealous singer.

It was the following Monday that Cathy started to run away.

Marion, ironing in the kitchen and watching a quiz program on the portable set Paul had given her for Christmas, heard the school bus groan to a stop at the top of the driveway. She waited for the front door to open and Cathy to announce in her high thin voice, "I'm home, Mommy."

The door didn't open.

From the kitchen window Marion saw the yellow bus round the sharp curve of the hill like a circus cage full of wild captive children screaming for release.

Marion waited until the end of the program, trying to convince herself that another bus had been added to the route and would come along shortly, or that Cathy had decided to stop off at a friend's house and would telephone any minute. But no other bus appeared, and the telephone remained silent.

Marion changed into her hiking boots and started off down the canyon, avoiding the scratchy clumps of chapparal and the creepers of poison oak that looked like loganberry vines.

She found Cathy sitting in the middle of the little bridge that Paul had made across the creek out of two fallen eucalyptus trees. Cathy's short plump legs hung over the logs until they almost touched the water. She was absolutely motionless, her face hidden by a straw curtain of hair. Then a single frog croaked a warning of Marion's presence and Cathy responded to the sound as if she was more intimate with nature than adults were, and more alert to its subtle communications of danger.

She stood up quickly, brushing off the back of her dress and drawing aside the curtain of hair to reveal eyes as blue as the periwinkles that hugged the banks of the creek.

"Cathy."

"I was only counting waterbugs while I was waiting. Forty-one."

"Waiting for what?"

"The ten or twelve children, and the dog."

"What ten or twelve chil—" Marion stopped. "I see. You were listening the other night when we thought you were asleep."

"I wasn't listening," Cathy said righteously. "My ears were hearing."

Marion restrained a smile. "Then I wish you'd tell those ears of yours to hear properly. I didn't say the new neighbors had ten or twelve children, I said they *might* have. Actually, it's very unlikely. Not many families are that big these days."

"Do you have to be old to have a big family?"

"Well, you certainly can't be very young."

"I bet people with big families have station wagons so they have room for all the children."

"The lucky ones do."

Cathy stared down at the thin flow of water carrying fat little minnows down to the sea. Finally she said, "They're too young, and their car is too small."

In spite of her aversion to having new neighbors, Marion felt a quickening of interest. "Have you seen them?"

But the little girl seemed deaf, lost in a water world of minnows and dragonflies and tadpoles.

"I asked you a question, Cathy. Did you see the people who just moved in?"

"Yes."

"When?"

"Before you came. Their name is Smith."

"How do you know that?"

"I went up to the house to look at things and they said, hello, little girl, what's your name? And I said, Cathy, what's yours? And they said Smith. Then they drove off in the little car."

"You're not supposed to go poking around other people's houses," Marion said brusquely. "And while we're at it, you're not supposed to go anywhere after school without first telling me where you're going and when you'll be back. You know that perfectly well. Now why didn't you come in and report to me after you got off the school bus?"

"I didn't want to."

"That's not a satisfactory answer."

Satisfactory or not, it was the only answer Cathy had. She looked at her mother in silence, then she turned and darted back up the hill to her own house.

After a time Marion followed her, exasperated and a little confused. She hated to punish the child, but she knew she couldn't ignore the matter entirely—it was much too serious. While she gave Cathy her graham crackers and orange juice, she told her, reasonably and kindly, that she would have to stay in her room the following day after school by way of learning a lesson.

That night, after Cathy had been tucked in bed, Marion related the incident to Paul. He seemed to take a less serious view of it than Marion, a fact of which the listening child became well aware.

"I'm glad she'd getting acquainted with the new people," Paul said. "It shows a certain degree of poise I didn't think she had. She's always been so shy."

"You're surely not condoning her running off without telling me?"

"She didn't run far. All kids do things like that once in a while."

"We don't want to spoil her."

"Cathy's always been so obedient I think she has *us* spoiled. Who knows, she might even teach us a thing or two about going out and making new friends." He realized, from past experience, that this was a very touchy subject. Marion had her house, her garden, her television sets; she didn't seem to want any more of the world than these, and she resented any implication that they were not enough. To ward off an argument he added, "You've done a good job with Cathy. Stop worrying . . . Smith, their name is?"

"Yes."

"Actually, I think it's an excellent sign that Cathy's getting acquainted."

At three the next afternoon the yellow circus cage arrived, released one captive, and rumbled on its way.

"I'm home, Mommy."

"Good girl."

Marion felt guilty at the sight of her: the child had been cooped up in school all day, the weather was so warm and lovely, and besides Paul hadn't thought the incident of the previous afternoon too important.

"I know what," Marion suggested, "let's you and I go down to the creek and count waterbugs."

The offer was a sacrifice for Marion because her favorite quiz program was on and she liked to answer the questions along with the contestants. "How about that?"

Cathy knew all about the quiz program; she'd seen it a hundred times, had watched the moving mouths claim her mother's eyes and ears and mind. "I counted the waterbugs yesterday."

"Well, minnows, then."

"You'll scare them away."

"Oh, will I?" Marion laughed self-consciously, rather relieved that Cathy had refused her offer and was clearly and definitely a little guilty about the relief. "Don't you scare them?"

"No. They think I'm another minnow because they're used to me."

"Maybe they could get used to me, too."

"I don't think so."

When Cathy went off down the canyon by herself Marion realized, in a vaguely disturbing way, that the child had politely but firmly rejected her mother's company. It wasn't until dinner time that she found out the reason why.

"The Smiths," Cathy said, "have an Austin-Healey."

Cathy, like most girls, had never shown any interest in cars, and her glib use of the name moved her parents to laughter.

The laughter encouraged Cathy to elaborate. "An Austin-Healey makes a lot of noise—like Daddy's lawn mower."

"I don't think the company would appreciate a commercial from you, young lady," Paul said. "Are the Smiths all moved in?"

"Oh, yes. I helped them."

"Is that a fact? And how did you help them?"

"I sang two songs. And then we danced and danced."

Paul looked half pleased, half puzzled. It wasn't like Cathy to perform willingly in front of people. During the last Christmas concert at the school she'd left the stage in tears and hidden in the cloak room . . . Well, maybe her shyness was only a phase and she was finally getting over it.

"They must be very nice people," he said, "to take time out from getting settled in a new house to play games with a little girl."

Cathy shook her head. "It wasn't games. It was real dancing—like on Ed Sullivan."

"As good as that, eh?" Paul said, smiling. "Tell me about it."

"Mrs. Smith is a nightclub dancer."

Paul's smile faded, and a pulse began to beat in his left temple like a small misplaced heart. "Oh? You're sure about that, Cathy?"

"Yes."

"And what does Mr. Smith do?"

"He's a baseball player."

"You mean that's what he does for a living?" Marion asked. "He doesn't work in an office like Daddy?"

"No, he just plays baseball. He always wears a baseball cap."

"I see. What position does he play on the team?" Paul's voice was low.

Cathy looked blank.

"Everybody on a ball team has a special thing to do. What does Mr. Smith do?"

"He's a batter."

"A batter, eh? Well, that's nice. Did he tell you this?"

"Yes."

"Cathy," Paul said, "I know you wouldn't deliberately lie to me, but sometimes you get your facts a little mixed up."

He went on in this vein for some time but Cathy's story remained unshaken: Mrs. Smith was a nightclub dancer, Mr. Smith a professional baseball player, they loved children, and they never watched television.

"That, at least, must be a lie," Marion said to Paul later when she saw the rectangular light of the television set shining in the Smiths' picture window. "As for the rest of it, there isn't a night club within fifty miles, or a professional ball club within two hundred."

"She probably misunderstood. It's quite possible that at one time Mrs. Smith was a dancer of sorts and that he played a little baseball."

Cathy, in bed and teetering dizzily on the brink of sleep, wondered if she should tell her parents about the Smiths' child—the one who didn't go to school.

She didn't tell them; Marion found out for herself the next morning after Paul and Cathy had gone. When she pulled back the drapes in the living room and opened the windows she heard the sharp slam of a screen door from across the canyon and saw a small child come out on the patio of the new house. At that distance she couldn't tell whether it was a boy or a girl. Whichever it was, the child was quiet and well behaved; only the occasional slam of the door shook the warm, windless day.

The presence of the child, and the fact that Cathy hadn't mentioned it, gnawed at Marion's mind all day. She questioned Cathy about it as soon as she came home.

"You didn't tell me the Smiths have a child."

"No."

"Why not?"

"I don't know why not."

"Is it a boy or a girl?"

"Girl."

"How old?"

Cathy thought it over carefully, frowning up at the ceiling. "About ten."

"Doesn't she go to school?"

"No."

"Why not?"

"She doesn't want to."

"That's not a very good reason."

"It is her reason," Cathy said flatly. "Can I go out to play now?"

"I'm not sure you should. You look a little feverish. Come here and let me feel your forehead."

Cathy's forehead was cool and moist, but her cheeks and the bridge of her nose were very pink, almost as if she'd been sunburned.

"You'd better stay inside," Marion said, "and watch some cartoons."

"I don't like cartoons."

"You used to."

"I like real people."

She means the Smiths, of course, Marion thought as her mouth tightened. "People who dance and play baseball all the time?"

If the sarcasm had any effect on Cathy she didn't show it. After waiting until Marion had become engrossed in her quiz program, Cathy lined up all her dolls in her room and gave a concert for them, to thunderous applause.

"Where are your old Navy binoculars?" Marion asked Paul when she was getting ready for bed.

"Oh, somewhere in the sea chest, I imagine. Why?"

"I want them."

"Not thinking of spying on the neighbors, are you?"

"I'm thinking of just that," Marion said grimly.

The next morning, as soon as she saw the Smith child come out on the patio, Marion went downstairs to the storage room to search through the sea chest. She located the binoculars and was in the act of dusting them off when the telephone started to ring in the living room. She hurried upstairs and said breathlessly, "Hello?"

"Mrs. Borton?"

"Yes."

"This is Miss Park speaking, Cathy's teacher."

Marion had met Miss Park several times at P.T.A. meetings and report-card conferences. She was a large, ruddy-faced, and unfailingly cheerful young woman—the kind, as Paul said, you wouldn't want to live with but who'd be nice to have around in an emergency. "How are you, Miss Park?"

"Oh, fine, thank you, Mrs. Borton. I meant to call you yesterday but things were a bit out of hand around here, and I knew there was no great hurry to check on Cathy; she's such a well-behaved little girl."

Even Miss Park's loud, jovial voice couldn't cover up the ominous sound of the word *check*. "I don't think I quite understand. Why should you check on Cathy?"

"Purely routine. The school doctor and the health department like to keep records of how many cases of measles or flu or chicken pox are going the rounds. Right now it looks like the season for mumps. Is Cathy all right?"

"She seemed a little feverish yesterday afternoon when she got home from school, but she acted perfectly normal when she left this morning."

Miss Park's silence was so protracted that Marion became painfully conscious of things she wouldn't otherwise have noticed—the weight of the binoculars in her lap, the thud of her own heartbeat in her ears. Across the canyon the Smith child was playing quietly and alone on the patio. *There is definitely something the matter with that girl,* Marion thought. *Perhaps I'd better not let Cathy go over there any more, she's so imitative.* "Miss Park, are you still on the line? Hello? Hello—"

"I'm here," Miss Park's voice seemed fainter than usual, and less positive. "What time did Cathy leave the house this morning?"

"Eight, as usual."

"Did she take the school bus?"

"Of course. She always does."

"Did you see her get on?"

"I kissed her goodbye at the front door," Marion said. "What's this all about, Miss Park?"

"Cathy hasn't been at school for two days, Mrs. Borton."

"Why, that's absurd, impossible! You must be mistaken." But even as she was speaking the words, Marion was raising the binoculars to her eyes: the little girl on the Smiths' patio had a straw curtain of hair and eyes as blue as the periwinkles along the creek banks.

"Mrs. Borton, I'm not likely to be mistaken about which of my children are in class or not."

"No. No, you're—you're not mistaken, Miss Park. I can see Cathy from here—she's over at the neighbor's house."

"Good. That's a load off my mind."

"Off yours, yes," Marion said. "Not mine."

"Now we mustn't become excited, Mrs. Borton. Don't make too much of this incident before we've had a chance to confer. Suppose you come and talk to me during my lunch hour and bring Cathy along. We'll all have a friendly chat."

But it soon became apparent, even to the optimistic Miss Park, that Cathy didn't intend to take part in any friendly chat. She stood by the window in the classroom, blank-eyed, mute, unresponsive to the simplest questions, refusing to be drawn into any conversation even about her favorite topic, the Smiths. Miss Park finally decided to send Cathy out to play in the schoolyard while she talked to Marion alone.

"Obviously," Miss Park said, enunciating the word very distinctly because it was one of her favorites, "obviously, Cathy's got a crush on this young couple and has concocted a fantasy about belonging to them."

"It's not so obvious what my husband and I are going to do about it."

"Live through it, the same as other parents. Crushes like this are common at Cathy's age. Sometimes the object is a person, a whole family, even a horse. And, of course, to Cathy a nightclub dancer and a baseball player must seem very glamorous indeed. Tell me, Mrs. Borton, does she watch television a great deal?"

Marion stiffened. "No more than any other child."

Oh, dear, Miss Park thought sadly, *they all do it; the most confirmed addicts are always the most defensive.* "I just wondered," she said. "Cathy likes to sing to herself and I've never heard such a repertoire of television commercials."

"She picks things up very fast."

"Yes. Yes, she does indeed." Miss Park studied her hands, which were always a little pale from chalk dust and were even paler now because she was angry—at the child for deceiving her, at Mrs. Borton for brushing aside the television issue, at herself for not preventing, or at least anticipating, the current situation, and perhaps most of all at the Smiths who ought to have known better than to allow a child to hang around their house when she should obviously be in school.

"Don't put too much pressure on Cathy about this," she said finally, "until I talk the matter over with the school psychologist. By the way, have you met the Smiths, Mrs. Borton?"

"Not yet," Marion said grimly. "But believe me, I intend to."

"Yes, I think it would be a good idea for you to talk to them and make it clear that they're not to encourage Cathy in this fantasy."

The meeting came sooner than Marion expected.

She waited at the school until classes were dismissed, then she took Cathy into town to do some shopping. She had parked the car and she and Cathy were standing hand in hand at a corner waiting for a traffic light to change; Marion was worried and impatient, Cathy still silent, unresisting, inert, as she had been ever since Marion had called her home from the Smiths' patio.

Suddenly Marion felt the child's hand tighten in a spasm of excitement. Cathy's face had turned so pink it looked ready to explode and with her free hand she was waving violently at two people in a small cream-colored sports car—a very pretty young woman with blonde hair in the driver's seat, and beside her a young man wearing a wide friendly grin and a baseball cap. They both waved back at Cathy just before the lights changed and then the car roared through the intersection.

"The Smiths," Cathy shouted, jumping up and down in a frenzy. "That was the Smiths."

"Sssh, not so loud. People will—"

"But it was the *Smiths*!"

"Hurry up before the light changes."

The child didn't hear. She stood as if rooted to the curb, staring after the cream-colored car.

With a little grunt of impatience Marion picked her up, carried her across the road, and let her down quite roughly on the other side. "There. If you're going to act like a baby, I'll carry you like a baby."

"I saw the Smiths!"

"All right. What are you so excited about? It's not very unusual to meet someone in town whom you know."

"It's unusual to meet *them*."

"Why?"

"Because it is." The color was fading from Cathy's cheeks, but her eyes still looked bedazzled, quite as if they'd seen a miracle.

"I'm sure they're very unique people," Marion said coldly. "Nevertheless they must stop for groceries like everyone else."

Cathy's answer was a slight shake of her head and a whisper heard only by herself: "No, they don't, never."

When Paul came home from work Cathy was sent to play in the front yard while Marion explained matters to him. He listened with increasing irritation—not so much at Cathy's actions but at the manner in which Marion and Miss Park had handled things. There was too much talking, he said, and too little acting.

"The way you women beat around the bush instead of tackling the situation directly, meeting it head-on—fantasy life. Fantasy life, my foot! Now we're going over to the Smiths right this minute and talk to them and that will be that. End of fantasy. Period.''

"We'd better wait until after dinner. Cathy missed her lunch.''

Throughout the meal Cathy was pale and quiet. She ate nothing and spoke only when asked a direct question; but inside herself the conversation was very lively, the dinner a banquet with dancing, and afterward a wild, windy ride in the roofless car . . .

Although the footpath through the canyon provided a shorter route to the Smiths' house, the Bortons decided to go more formally, by car, and to take Cathy with them. Cathy, told to comb her hair and wash her face, protested: "I don't want to go over there.''

"Why not?'' Paul said. "You were so anxious to spend time with them that you played hooky for two days. Why don't you want to see them now?''

"Because they're not there.''

"How do you know?''

"Mrs. Smith told me this morning that they wouldn't be home tonight because she's putting on a show.''

"Indeed?'' Paul said grim faced. "Just where does she put on these shows of hers?''

"And Mr. Smith has to play baseball. And after that they're going to see a friend in the hospital who has leukemia.''

"Leukemia, eh?'' He didn't have to ask how Cathy had found out about such a thing; he'd watched a semidocumentary dealing with it a couple of nights ago. Cathy was supposed to have been sleeping.

"I wonder,'' he said to Marion when Cathy went to comb her hair, "just how many 'facts' about the Smiths have been borrowed from television.''

"Well, I know for myself that they drive a sports car, and Mr. Smith was wearing a baseball cap. And they're both young and good-looking. Young and good-looking enough,'' she added wryly, "to make me feel—well, a little jealous.''

"Jealous?''

"Cathy would rather belong to them than to us. It makes me wonder if it's something the Smiths have or something the Bortons don't have.''

"Ask her.''

"I can't very well—''

"Then I will, dammit,'' Paul said. And he did.

Cathy merely looked at him innocently. "I don't know. I don't know what you mean.''

"Then listen again. Why did you pretend that you were the Smiths' little girl?"

"They asked me to be. They asked me to go with them."

"They actually said, Cathy, will you be our little girl?"

"Yes."

"Well, by heaven, I'll put an end to this nonsense," Paul said, and strode out to the car.

It was twilight when they reached the Smiths' house by way of the narrow, hilly road. The moon, just appearing above the horizon, was on the wane, a chunk bitten out of its side by some giant jaw. A warm dry wind, blowing down the mountain from the desert beyond, carried the sweet scent of pittosporum.

The Smiths' house was dark, and both the front door and the garage were locked. Out of defiance or desperation, Paul pressed the door chime anyway, several times. All three of them could hear it ringing inside, and it seemed to Marion to echo very curiously—as if the carpets and drapes were too thin to muffle the sound vibrations. She would have liked to peer in through the windows and see for herself, but the venetian blinds were closed.

"What's their furniture like?" she asked Cathy.

"Like everybody's."

"I mean, is it new? Does Mrs. Smith tell you not to put your feet on it?"

"No, she never tells me that," Cathy said truthfully. "I want to go home now. I'm tired."

It was while she was putting Cathy to bed that Marion heard Paul call to her from the living room in an urgent voice, "Marion, come here a minute."

She found him standing motionless in the middle of the room, staring across the canyon at the Smiths' place. The rectangular light of the Smiths' television set was shining in the picture window of the room that opened onto the patio at the back of the Smiths' house.

"Either they've come home within the past few minutes," he said, "or they were there all the time. My guess is that they were home when we went over, but they didn't want to see us, so they just doused the lights and pretended to be out. Well, it won't work! Come on, we're going back."

"I can't leave Cathy alone. She's already got her pajamas on."

"Put a bathrobe on her and bring her along. This has gone beyond the point of observing such niceties as correct attire."

"Don't you think we should wait until tomorrow?"

"Hurry up and stop arguing with me."

Cathy, protesting that she was tired and that the Smiths weren't home anyway, was bundled into a bathrobe and carried to the car.

"They're home all right," Paul said. "And by heaven they'd better answer the door this time or I'll break it down."

"That's an absurd way to talk in front of a child," Marion said coldly. "She has enough ideas without hearing—"

"Absurd is it? Wait and see."

Cathy, listening from the back seat, smiled sleepily. She knew how to get in without breaking anything: ever since the house had been built, the real estate man who'd been trying to sell it always hid the key on a nail underneath the window box.

The second trip seemed a nightmarish imitation of the first: the same moon hung in the sky but it looked smaller now, and paler. The scent of pittosporum was funereally sweet, and the hollow sound of the chimes from inside the house was like the echo in an empty tomb.

"They must be crazy to think they can get away with a trick like this twice in one night," Paul shouted. "Come on, we're going around to the back."

Marion looked a little frightened. "I don't like trespassing on someone else's property."

"They trespassed on our property first."

He glanced down at Cathy. Her eyes were half closed and her face was pearly in the moonlight. He pressed her hand to reassure her that everything was going to be all right and that his anger wasn't directed at her, but she drew away from him and started down the path that led to the back of the house.

Paul clicked on his flashlight and followed her, moving slowly along the unfamiliar terrain. By the time he turned the corner of the house and reached the patio, Cathy was out of sight.

"Cathy," he called. "Where are you? Come back here!"

Marion was looking at him accusingly. "You upset her with that silly threat about breaking down the door. She's probably on her way home through the canyon."

"I'd better go after her."

"She's less likely to get hurt than you are. She knows every inch of the way. Besides, you came here to break down the doors. All right, start breaking."

But there was no need to break down anything. The back door opened as soon as Paul rapped on it with his knuckles, and he almost fell into the room.

It was empty except for a small girl wearing a blue bathrobe that matched her eyes.

Paul said, "Cathy. Cathy, what are you doing here?"

Marion stood with her hand pressed to her mouth to stifle the scream that was rising in her throat. There were no Smiths. The people in the sports car whom Cathy had waved at were just strangers responding to the friendly greeting of a child—had Cathy seen them before, on a previous trip to town? The television set was no more than a contraption rigged up by Cathy herself—an orange crate and an old mirror that caught and reflected the rays of the moon.

In front of it Cathy was standing, facing her own image. "Hello, Mrs. Smith. Here I am, all ready to go."

"Cathy," Marion said in a voice that sounded torn by claws. "What do you see in that mirror?"

"It's not a mirror. It's a television set."

"What—what program are you watching?"

"It's not a program, silly. It's real. It's the Smiths. I'm going away with them to dance and play baseball."

"There are no Smiths," Paul bellowed. "Will you get that through your head? *There are no Smiths!*"

"Yes, there are. I see them."

Marion knelt on the floor beside the child. "Listen to me, Cathy. This is a mirror—only a mirror. It came from Daddy's old bureau and I had it put away in the storage room. That's where you found it, isn't it? And you brought it here and decided to pretend it was a television set, isn't that right? But it's really just a mirror, and the people in it are us—you and Mommy and Daddy."

But even as she looked at her own reflection, Marion saw it beginning to change. She was growing younger, prettier; her hair was becoming lighter and her cotton suit was changing into a dancing dress. And beside her in the mirror, Paul was turning into a stranger, a laughing-eyed young man wearing a baseball cap.

"I'm ready to go now, Mr. Smith," Cathy said, and suddenly all three of them, the Smiths and their little girl, began walking away in the mirror. In a few moments they were no bigger than matchsticks—and then the three of them disappeared, and there was only the moonlight in the glass.

"Cathy," Marion cried. "Come back, Cathy! Please come back!"

Propped up against the door like a dummy, Paul imagined he could hear above his wife's cries the mocking muted roar of a sports car.

Probably no contemporary crime novelist carries on the tradition of Raymond Chandler better than Loren Estleman. In prose as imposing and impressive as Chandler's own, Estleman has turned Detroit into his own version of Chandler's La La Land, charging the air with the same kind of angry poetry and rueful social observation. He has also written a group of historical novels about Detroit, books many consider to be his finest work.

Bodyguards Shoot Second
LOREN D. ESTLEMAN

1

"A. Walker Investigations."

"Amos Walker?"

The voice on the other end of the line was male and youthful, one of those that don't change from the time they crack until the time they quake. I said, "This is he."

"Huh?"

"Grammar," I said. "It gets me business in Grosse Pointe. But not lately. Who's speaking?"

"This is Martin Cole. I'm Billy Dickerson's road manager."

"Okay."

"No, really."

"I believe you, Mr. Martin. How can I make your life easier?"

"Cole. Martin's my first name. Art Cradshaw recommended you. He said you were the best man for what you do in Detroit."

"Sweet of him. But he still owes me for the credit check I ran for his company six months ago."

"That's hardly my business. I need a man."

I parked the receiver in the hollow of my shoulder and lit a Winston. "Walker?"

"I'm here. You need a man."

"The man I need doesn't pick his teeth with his thumbnail and can wear a dinner jacket without looking as if he was strapped in waiting for the current, but doesn't worry about popping a seam when he has to push somebody's face in. He's a good enough shot to light a match at thirty paces on no notice, but he carries himself as if he thought the butt of a gun would spoil the lines of his suit. He can swear and spit when called upon but in polite conversation wouldn't split an infinitive at knifepoint."

I said, "I wish you'd let me know when you find him. I could use someone like that in the investigation business."

"According to Art Cradshaw you're that man."

"I don't own a dinner jacket, Mr. Dickerson."

"Cole. Dickerson's the man I represent. The jacket's no problem. We have a tailor traveling with us and he'll fix you up in a day."

"I didn't know tailors traveled. But then I don't know any tailors. What business are you and Mr. Dickerson in?"

Pause. "You're kidding, right?"

"Probably not. I don't have a sense of humor."

"Billy Dickerson. The singer. Rock and Country. He's opening at the Royal Tower in Dearborn tomorrow night. Don't tell me you've never heard of him."

"My musical appreciation stops around nineteen sixty-two. What sort of work do you have in mind for this cross between Richard Gere and the Incredible Hulk?"

"Protection. Billy's regular bodyguard has disappeared and he can't leave his suite here at the Tower without someone to stand between him and his adoring fans. Too much adoration can be fatal."

"I don't do that kind of work, Mr. Cole. Bodyguards shoot second. If at all."

"We're paying a thousand. For the week."

I hesitated. Habit. Then: "My daily's two-fifty. That comes to seventeen-fifty for seven days."

"We'll go that."

"Can't do it, Mr. Cole. I'm sitting on retainer for a local union just now. They could call me anytime. Try Ned Eccles on Michigan; security's his specialty. Infinitives don't last too long around him, but he's hard and fast and he knows how to tie a bow.''

"I don't know. Art said you were the guy to call.''

"Cradshaw's in the tool design business. He doesn't know a body-guard from a right cross.''

"I thought you guys never turned down a job.''

I said, "It's not a thing I'd care to get good at. Tell Ned I sent you.''

"Will he give me a discount?''

"No. But he might give me one next time I farm something out to him.'' I wished him good luck and we were through talking to each other.

The union rep didn't call that day or the next, just as he hadn't called for a week, not since the day I'd accepted his retainer. Meanwhile I was laying in a hundred and a half every twenty-four hours just for playing solitaire within reach of the telephone. I closed the office at five and drove home. It was November. The city was stone-colored under a gray sky and in the air was the raw-iron smell that comes just before a snow.

Out of long habit I flipped on the television set the minute I got in the door and went into the kitchen, stripping off my jacket and tie as I went. When I came out opening a can of beer the picture had come on but not the sound and I was looking at a studio shot of Ned Eccles' fleshy moustached face.

"... died three hours later at Detroit Receiving Hospital,'' came on the announcer's voice, too loud. I jumped and turned down the volume. Now they were showing film of a lean young man in a gold lamé jumpsuit unzipped to his pelvis and stringy blond hair to his shoulders striding down a stage runway, shouting song lyrics into a hand mike while the crowd jammed up against the footlights screamed. The announcer continued.

"Dickerson, shown here during his last appearance at the Royal Tower two years ago, was shoved out of the line of fire by a member of his entourage after the first shot and was unharmed. The slain body-guard has been identified as Edward Eccles, forty-five, a Detroit private investigator with a background in personal security. Police have no leads as yet to the man who fired the shots.'' After a short pause during which the camera focused on the announcer's grave face, he turned his head and smiled. "How are the Tigers doing, Steve?''

I changed channels. There was a commercial for a women's hygiene product on the next local station and a guy in a chef's hat showing how to make cheese gooey on the last. I turned off the set and sipped beer and thought. The telephone interrupted my thinking.

"Walker?"

"Yeah."

"This is Carol Greene. You heard?"

Carol Greene was Ned Eccles' business partner. I said, "I just caught a piece of it. What happened?"

"Not on the phone. Can you come to Ned's office?"

"What for?"

"I'll tell you when you get here." After a beat: "You owe Ned. You got him killed."

"Don't hang that on me, Carol. I just made a referral. He didn't have to take the job. Give me twenty minutes." I hung up and retrieved my tie and jacket.

2

Eccles Investigations and Security worked out of a storefront off Cadillac Square, with an oak railing separating Carol's desk in front from Ned's in back and a lot of framed photographs on the walls of Ned shaking hands with the mayor and the governor and various presidential candidates whose faces remained vaguely familiar long after their names were faded on old baled ballots. The place had a friendly, informal, unfussy look that had set its owners back at least three grand. The basement vault where the firm's files were kept had cost more than the building. I went through a swinging gate in the railing to Ned's desk where Carol was supporting herself on her small angular fists.

"Give some guys twenty minutes and they'll take forty," she greeted.

"The rush hour got me by the throat. You look the same as always."

"Don't start." She put the cigarette she was holding between thumb and forefinger to her lips, bit off some smoke, and tipped it down her throat in a series of short, jerky movements like a bird bolting grain. She was a small, wiry woman in a man's flannel shirt and jeans with gray-streaked blond hair cut very short and unadorned glasses with under-slung bows. She had been Ned Eccles' junior partner for ten years. Whatever else she might have been to him wasn't my business today or ever.

"How much do you know about what happened to Ned?" she asked.

"Just that he was killed. Apparently by someone trying to get Billy Dickerson."

She nodded jerkily, ate some more cigarette, ground it out in a glass ashtray full of butts on the desk. "Dickerson stopped to sign an autograph in front of the service elevator on the way up to his suite at the Royal Tower. Ned had told him to avoid the lobby. He'd told him not to stop for anyone either, but I guess Billy-boy didn't hear that part. The guy ducked Ned and stuck a pad in Dickerson's hand and while Dickerson was getting out a pen he pulled a piece. Ned saw it and got between them just in time to get his guts drilled. That was about noon. He spent the afternoon dying. I just got back from the hospital."

Her eyes were a little red behind the cheaters. I said, "Who saw this?"

"Dickerson's manager, Martin Cole. Dickerson. Some gofer, Phil something. I talked to them at the hospital. While they were busy getting the Music Man out of the way of the bullets the gunny lit out through the rear entrance. Six feet, a hundred and eighty, thirties, balding. Dark zipper jacket. That's as good as it gets. The croakers dug two thirty-eight slugs out of Ned's insides."

"Say anything before he died?"

She shook her head, firing up a fresh cigarette from a butane lighter whose flame leaped halfway to the ceiling. "Outside of cussing a blue streak. That why you turned Cole down? You had dope on the shoot?"

"I was in the clutch when he called."

"Yeah."

I said, "Ned and I didn't get along, that's yesterday's news. We had different ideas about how the investigating business should be run. But I didn't put him in front of those bullets."

"Yeah. I guess not." She tossed the cold lighter atop a stack of Manila file folders on the desk. Then she looked at me. "I'll go your full rate to look into Ned's death."

"Ned's death was an accident."

"Maybe. Either way you get paid."

"You've got a license."

"I make out the books, trace an occasional skip. That's all I've done for ten years. Ned was the detective. You do this kind of thing all the time."

"Wrong. Mostly I look for missing persons."

"The guy who killed Ned is missing."

"He's cop meat," I said. "Save your money and let them do their job."

"Cops. First Monday of every month I hand an envelope to our department pipeline, a night captain. A thing like that can shake your faith. You still in the clutch?''

I nodded. "Retainer. I sit by the telephone.''

"You've got an answering service to do that. Look, I won't beg you.'' She made a face and killed the butt, smoked only a third down. "I know everyone thought I was sleeping with Ned, including that slut of a wife of his, who should know about that kind of thing. I haven't cared what people thought of me since my senior prom. For the record, though, I wasn't. He was my friend and my partner and I have to do this one thing for him before I can go back to what I was doing. If you won't take the job I'll find someone else. The Yellow Pages are lousy with plastic badges.''

"I'll look into it. Courtesy rate, two hundred a day and expenses. Couple of days should tell if I'm wasting your money.''

She wrote out a check for five hundred dollars and gave it to me. "That should see you through. If it doesn't, come back here. With an itemized list of expenses. No whiskey.''

"You keep the books, all right.'' I folded the check and stuck it in my wallet. "One question. Don't hit me with the desk when I ask it.''

"Ask.''

"Did you ever know Ned to be the kind of bodyguard who would throw himself between a gun and its target, even if the target was the person he was guarding?''

"No,'' she said quickly. "No, I didn't know him to be that kind of a bodyguard.''

"Neither did I.''

3

I cashed the check at my bank, deposited all but a hundred of it, and drove the four miles to Dearborn. The sky was low and the heater took ten minutes to chase the chill out of the upholstery. I parked in the lot behind the Royal Tower. A uniformed cop stopped me at the main entrance to the hotel. "Excuse me, sir, but are you a guest here?''

"No, I'm here to see someone.''

"No one goes in without a room key, sorry. We had some excitement here earlier.''

I handed him one of my cards. "Would you see that Martin Cole gets that? He's with Billy Dickerson. It's important."

The cop called over another uniform, gave him the card, and told him to take it up. Ten minutes later the second officer returned. "Lieutenant says okay." To me: "Three-oh-six."

More uniforms and a group of men in suits greeted me in the hall when I stepped off the elevator. One of the latter was an inch shorter than I but half again as broad through the shoulders. It would have been a long time since he had gone through a doorway any way but sideways. His skin was pale to the point of translucence, almost albino, but his eyes were blue. He combed his short blond hair forward over a retreating widow's peak.

"Walker? I'm Gritch, homicide lieutenant with the Dearborn Police." He flashed his badge in a leather folder. "Cole says to let you through, but we got to check you for weapons."

"I'm not carrying," I said, but stood for the frisk by a black officer with hands like Ping-Pong paddles. Gritch meanwhile looked through the credentials in my wallet. He handed it back.

"Okay. We got to play it tight. The description of the guy that tried to kill Dickerson fits you as good as it fits a thousand other guys in this town."

"Anything new?" I put the crease back in my topcoat.

"Now, would I be earning your tax dollars if I answered that, after going to so much trouble to keep the public off the premises?"

"Nothing new," I said. "I thought so. Where's three-oh-six?"

"Right in front of you, Sherlock." He stepped away from it.

Before I could knock, the door was opened by a young man in shirtsleeves and stockinged feet. His hair was brown and wavy and combed behind his ears, his face clean-shaven, and his eyes as lifelike as two stones. He had a nine-millimeter automatic pistol in his right hand.

"Let him in, Phil."

The man who spoke was smaller than Lieutenant Gritch but not so small as Carol Greene, with a great mane of styled black hair and a drooping moustache and aviator's glasses with rose-tinted lenses. He wore a dark European-looking jacket with narrow lapels and a pinched waist over yellow-and-red checked pants. His shoes were brown leather with tassels, and he had a yellow silk scarf knotted at his throat. "Walker, is it? I'm Martin Cole. Decent of you to stop in."

At first glance, Cole was as youthful as his voice, but there were hairline fissures around his eyes and pouches at the corners of his mouth that his moustache couldn't hide. I took the moist warm hand he offered and entered the suite. The room was plushly carpeted and furnished as a living room, with a sofa and easy chairs, but folding metal chairs had been added. Cole caught me looking at them.

"For the press," he said. "We're holding a conference as soon as the police finish downstairs. Billy Dickerson, Amos Walker."

I looked at the man seated on the end of the sofa with a small barrel glass of copper-colored liquid in one hand. In person he was older and not so lean as he appeared on television. His skin was grayish against the long open collar of his white jumpsuit, and a distinct roll showed over his wide brown tooled-leather belt with an ornate gold buckle. His long yellow hair was thinning at the temples. He glanced at me, drank from his glass, and looked at Cole. "He the best you could do?"

"Walker came on his own, Billy," the manager said. Quickly he introduced the man with the gun as Phil Scabarda.

I said, "He must have a permit for that or he wouldn't be waving it around with the cops so close. That doesn't mean he can point it at me."

Cole gestured at the young man, who hesitated, then hung the pistol on a clip on the back of his belt. "Phil is Billy's driver and companion. These days that requires courses in racing and weaponry."

"Ned Eccles' partner hired me to look into the shooting," I said. "I appreciate your seeing me."

"Ah. I thought maybe you wanted his job after all. I'd rather hoped."

"You've got police protection now. What happened in front of the service elevator?"

"Well, we were standing there waiting for the doors to open when this guy came out from behind the elevator and asked Billy for his autograph. As soon as he got rid of the pad he pulled a gun from under his jacket. Eccles stepped in and took both bullets."

"Was Eccles armed?"

Cole nodded. "A revolver of some kind. I don't know from guns. It was still in his shoulder holster when the police came. There wasn't time to get it out."

"What was Phil doing while all this was going on?"

"Hustling Billy out of the way, with me. Meanwhile the guy got away." He gave me the same description he'd given Carol.

"If he was after Dickerson, why'd he leave without scratching him?"

"He panicked. Those shots were very loud in that enclosed space. As it was he barely got out before the place was jammed with gawkers."

"What happened to the pad?"

"Pad?"

"The pad he handed Dickerson for his autograph. Fingerprints."

"I guess Billy dropped it in the scramble. Some souvenir hunter has it by now."

I got out a cigarette and tapped it on the back of my left hand. "Anyone threaten Dickerson's life lately?"

"The police asked that. He gets his share of hate mail like every other big-name entertainer. They don't like his hair or his singing or his politics. That kind of letter is usually scribbled in Crayola on ruled paper with the lines an inch apart. I called Billy's secretary in L.A. to go through the files and send the most likely ones by air express for the police to look at. But she throws most of them away."

"What's the story on this bodyguard that disappeared?"

"Henry?" Carefully plucked eyebrows slid above the tinted glasses. "Forget him. He was a drunk and he got to wandering just when we needed him most. Flying in from L.A. day before yesterday we changed planes in Denver and he was missing when we boarded for Detroit. Probably found himself a bar and he's drying out in some drunk tank by now. If he hadn't ducked out we'd have fired him soon anyway. He was worse than no protection at all."

"Full name and description." I got out my notebook and pencil.

"Henry Bliss. About your height, a little over six feet. Two hundred pounds, sandy hair, fair complexion. Forty. Let's see, he had a white scar about an inch long on the right side of his jaw. Dropped his guard, he said. Don't waste your time with him. He was just an ex-pug with a taste for booze."

"It's my client's time. Any reason why someone would want to kill Dickerson? Besides his hair and his singing and his politics?"

"Celebrities make good clay pigeons. They're easier to get at than politicians, but you can become just as famous shooting them."

"Everyone's famous today. It's almost worth it to get an obscure person's autograph." I flipped the notebook shut. "Can I reach you here if something turns up?"

"We're booked downstairs for two weeks."

"Except for tonight."

"We're opening tonight as scheduled. Look, you can tell Ned's partner how sorry we are, but—"

"The show must go on."

Cole smiled thinly. "An ancient tradition with a solid mercenary base. No one likes giving refunds."

"Thanks, Mr. Cole. You'll be hearing from me."

"You know," he said, "I can't help thinking that had you been on the job, things would have gone differently today."

"Probably not. Ned knew his business. Your boy's alive. That's what you paid for."

As I closed the door behind me, Lieutenant Gritch came away from his crew next to the elevator. "What'd you get?" he demanded.

"Now, would I be earning my client's money if I answered that, after going to so much trouble to keep the cops out of my pockets?"

His pale face flushed for a moment. Then the color faded and he showed his eyeteeth in a gargoyle's grin, nodding. "Okay. I guess I bought that. We'll trade. You go."

I told him what I'd learned. He went on nodding.

"That's what we got. There's nothing in that autograph pad. Even if it had liftable prints, which nothing like that ever does, they'd have someone else's all over them by now. We Telexed this Henry Bliss's name and description to Denver. It won't buy zilch. This one's local and sloppy. If we get the guy at all it'll be because somebody unzipped his big yap. Give me a pro any time. These amateurs are a blank order."

"What makes him an amateur?"

"You mean besides he got the wrong guy? The gun. We frisked the service area and the parking lot and the alley next door. No gun. A pro would've used a piece without a history and then dumped it. He wouldn't take a chance on being picked up for CCW. You got a reference?"

The change of subjects threw me for a second. Then I gave him John Alderdyce's name in Detroit Homicide. He had a uniform write down the name in his notebook.

"Okay, we'll check you out. You know what the penalty is for interfering with a murder investigation."

"Something short of electrocution," I said. "In this state, anyway."

"Then I won't waste breath warning you off this one. You get anything—anything—you know where to come." He handed me one of his cards.

I gave him one of mine. "If you ever have a rug that needs looking under."

"I'd sooner put my gun in my mouth," he said. But he stuck the card in his pocket.

4

The sun had gone down, sucking all the heat out of the air. It still smelled like snow. On my way home I stopped at the main branch of the Detroit Public Library on Woodward, where I knew the security guard. I spotted him a ten to let me in after closing and browsed through the out-of-town directories until I found a list of detective agencies in Denver and copied some likelies into my notebook.

Colorado is two hours behind Michigan. Calling long-distance from home I found most of the offices still open. The first two I called didn't believe in courtesy rates. The third took down the information I had on Henry Bliss the wandering bodyguard and said they'd get back to me. I hung up and dialed my service for messages. I had a message. I got the union executive I was working for at home. He had a tail job for me, a shop steward suspected of pocketing membership dues.

"What am I looking for?" I asked.

"Where he goes with the money." The executive's tone was as smooth as ice. No lead pipes across his throat like in the old days. "He's not depositing it and he's not investing it. Follow him until it changes hands. Get pictures."

The job would start in the morning. I took down the necessary information, pegged the receiver, slid a TV tray into the oven, and mixed myself a drink while it was heating up. I felt like a pretty, empty-headed girl with two dates for Saturday night.

In the morning after breakfast I rang up Barry Stackpole at the Detroit *News*. While waiting for him to answer I watched the snow floating down outside the window turn brown before it reached the ground.

"Amos the famous shamus," said Barry, after I'd announced myself. "What can I do for you this lovely morning?"

"You must be in St. Tropez. I need a name on a pro heavyweight." I described Ned Eccles' killer. Barry wrote a syndicated column on organized crime and had a national reputation and an artificial leg to show for it.

"Offhand I could name twenty that would fit," he said. "Local?"

"Maybe. More likely he was recruited from somewhere else."

"Make that a hundred. I can get a list to your office by special messenger this afternoon. What's the hit?"

"A P.I. named Eccles. You wouldn't know him. He ate that lead that was meant for Billy Dickerson yesterday."

"That was a hit?"

"I don't know. But the cops are following the amateur theory and that leaves this way open. I step on fewer official toes."

"When did you get religion?"

"I'm duplicating them on one thing, a previous bodyguard that got himself lost out West. The cops don't put much faith in it. I wouldn't be earning my fee if all I did was sniff their coattails. What's this list going to run me?"

"A fifth of Teacher's."

"Just one?"

"I'm cutting back. Hang tight."

After he broke the connection I called my service and asked them to page me if Denver called. Then I dug my little pen-size beeper out of a drawer full of spent cartridges and illegible notes to myself and clipped it to my belt and went to work for the union.

The shop steward lived a boring life. I tailed his Buick from his home in Redford Township to the GM Tech Center in Warren where he worked, picked him up again when he and two fellow workers walked downtown for lunch, ate in a booth across the restaurant from their table, and followed them back to work. One of the other guys got the tab. My guy took care of the tip. On my way out I glanced at the bills on the table. Two singles. He wasn't throwing the stuff away, that was sure.

During the long gray period before quitting time I found a public booth within sight of the Buick in the parking lot and called my service. There were no messages from Denver or anywhere else. I had the girl page me to see if the beeper was working. It was.

I followed the steward home, parked next to the curb for two hours waiting to see if he came out again, and when he didn't I started the engine and drove to the office. Opening the unlocked door of my little waiting room I smelled cop. The door to my private office, which I kept locked when I'm not in it, was standing open. I went through it and found Gritch sitting behind my desk looking at a sheet of typing paper. His skin wasn't any more colorful and he looked like a billboard with the window at his back. My Scotch bottle and one of my pony glasses stood on the desk, the glass half full.

"Pour one for me." I hung up my hat and coat.

He got the other glass out of the file drawer and filled it. His eyes didn't move from the paper in his left hand. "You got better taste in liquor than you do in locks," he said, leveling off his own glass.

"I'm working. I wasn't when I bought the lock." I put down my drink in one installment and waited for the heat to rise.

"This is quite a list you got. Packy Davis, yeah. Benny Boom-Boom Bohannen, sure. Lester Adams, don't know him." His voice trailed off, but his lips kept moving. Finally he laid the sheet on the desk and sat back in my swivel-shrieker and took a drink, looking at me for the first time. "It isn't quite up to date. Couple of those guys are pulling hard time. Two are dead, and one might as well be, he's got more tubes sticking out of him than a subway terminal."

"You know lists. They get old just while you're typing them up." I bought a refill.

"Some smart kid in a uniform brought it while I was sitting for you. I gave him a quarter and he looked like I bit his hand. Who sent it?"

"A friend. You wouldn't know him. He respects locks."

His marblelike face didn't move. He'd heard worse. "This to do with the Eccles burn?"

I said nothing. Drank.

"Yeah, Alderdyce said you could shut up like an oyster. I called him. We had quite a conversation about you. Want to know what else he said?"

"No, I want to know what brings you to my office when everyone else's office who has any brains is closed."

"Your client won't answer her phone. Her office is closed too, but it's been closed all day and her home isn't listed. And you're harder to get hold of than an eel with sunburn. I didn't feel like talking to the girl at your service. She sounds like my aunt that tells fortunes. I got to find out if there was any connection between Eccles and Henry Bliss, Dickerson's old bodyguard."

A little chill chased the whisky-warmth up my spine, like a drop of cold water running uphill. "How come?"

"No reason. Except the Denver Police fished a floater out of the South Platte this morning, with two holes in the back of its skull. We got the Telex two hours ago. The stiff fits Bliss's description down to the scar on his chin."

5

I struck a match, cracking the long silence, and touched the flame to a Winston. Gritch watched me. He said:

"Dunked stiffs surface after three days. That puts him in the river just about the time Dickerson and Cole and their boy Phil noticed him missing."

"Meaning?" I flipped the dead match into the ashtray on the desk and cocked a hip up on one corner, blowing smoke out my nostrils.

"Meaning maybe yesterday's try on Dickerson, if that's what it was, wasn't a backyard job after all. Meaning maybe the same guy that dusted Bliss dusted Eccles. Meaning that seeing as how the two hits were a thousand miles apart and seeing as how the guy that did it didn't leave tracks either time, he's pro after all."

"Slugs match up?"

He shook his fair head without taking his eyes off my face. "Nothing on that yet. But they won't. Major leaguers never use the same piece twice. What I want to know—"

"You said they didn't take their pieces away with them either."

"What I want to know," he went on, "is how it happens I come here looking to talk to you and your client about Eccles' being a mechanic's job and find a list of mechanics all typed up nice and neat before I'm here five minutes."

"Just touching all the bases," I said. "Like you. You didn't send a flyer to Denver looking for some local nut that doesn't like loud music."

"That's it, huh."

I said it was it. He sipped some more Scotch, made a face, rubbed a spot at the arch of his ribcage, and set the glass down. I never knew a cop that didn't have something wrong with his back or his stomach. He said, "Well, I got to talk to Carol Greene."

"I'll set up a meet. What makes it Bliss and Eccles were connected?"

"Nothing. But if it's Dickerson this guy was after, he's a worse shot than I ever heard of."

"Why make the bodyguards targets?"

"That's what I want to ask the Green woman." He got up, rubbing the spot. The hound's-tooth overcoat he had on was missing a few teeth. "Set it up. Today. I get off at eight."

"How'd Dickerson do last night?"

He opened the door to the outer office. "Capacity crowd. But he don't have the stuff he had when the wife was a fan. When no one shot at him they left disappointed."

He went out. I listened to the hallway door hiss shut behind him against the pressure of the pneumatic device. Thinking.

6

I finished the cigarette and pulled the telephone over and dialed Carol's number. She answered on the third ring.

"Lieutenant Gritch wants to talk to you," I told her, after the preliminaries. "You're better off seeing him at Headquarters. That way you can leave when you want to."

"I already talked to him once. What is it this time?" Her tone was slurred. I'd forgotten she was an alcoholic. I told her about Bliss. After a pause she said, "Ned never mentioned him. I'd know if they ever did business."

"Tell Gritch that."

"You got anything yet?"

"A shadow of a daydream of an idea. I'll let you know. Take a cab to Dearborn."

Next I got the Denver P.I. on the telephone. He said he was still working on the description I'd given him of Henry Bliss. I told him that was all wrapped up and I'd send him a check. Then I called Barry Stackpole.

"That list all right?" he asked.

"A little out of date, according to the cops. I may not need it. Who's on the entertainment desk today?"

"Jed Dutt. I still get my Teacher's, right?"

"If you switch me over to Dutt I'll even throw in a bottle of tonic water."

"Don't be blasphemous." He put me on hold.

"Dutt," announced a rusty old wheeze thirty seconds later.

"My name's Walker," I said. "I'm investigating the attempt on Billy Dickerson's life yesterday. I have a question for you."

"Shoot."

"Very funny," I said.

"Sorry."

I asked him the question. His answer was the first time I got more than one word out of him. I thanked him and broke the connection. The telephone rang while my hand was still on the receiver. It was the man from the union.

"I'm still working on it," I told him. "No money changed hands today."

He said, "Keep an eye on him. He isn't swallowing it or burying it in the basement. I made some inquiries and found out the house across the street is for rent. Maybe you ought to move in."

"Round-the-clock surveillance costs money."

"Name a figure."

I named one. He said, "Can you move in tomorrow?"

I said that was short notice. He said, "Your retainer buys us that right. Shall I make the rental arrangements?"

"I'll let you know," I said.

I smoked a cigarette, looking at the blonde in the bikini on the calendar on the wall opposite the desk. Then I ground out the stub and made one more call. It took a while. When it was finished I got up and unpegged my hat and coat. Before going out I got the Smith & Wesson out of the top drawer of the desk and checked it for cartridges and snapped the holster onto the back of my belt under my jacket. I hate forcing a case.

7

No cops stopped me on my way into the Royal Tower this time, no one was waiting to frisk me when I stepped off the elevator on the third floor. I felt neglected. I rapped on 306.

"What do you want?"

I grinned at Phil. There was no reflection at all in his flat dark eyes. The automatic pistol was a growth in his fist. "This is for the grown-ups," I said. "Any around?"

"You got a lot of smart mouth."

"That makes one of us."

"Phil, who is it?"

The voice was Martin Cole's. It sounded rushed and breathless.

"That snooper," answered Phil, his eyes still on me.

"Tell him to come back later."

"You heard." The man with the gun smiled without opening his lips, like a cat.

A sudden scuffling noise erupted from inside the room. Someone grunted. A lamp turned over with a thud, slinging lariats of shadow up one wall. Phil turned his head and I chopped downward with the edge of my left hand, striking his wrist at the break. He cursed and the gun dropped from his grip. When he stooped to catch it I brought my right fist scooping up, catching him on the point of the chin and closing his mouth with a loud clop. I stepped back to give him room to fall. He used it.

I got the automatic out from under his unconscious body and stepped over him holding it in my sore right hand. I'd barked the knuckles on his obelisk jaw. It was a wasted entrance. Nobody was paying me any attention.

Billy Dickerson, naked but for a pair of blue jockey shorts with his pale belly hanging over the top, was on his knees on the floor astraddle a scarcely more dapper-looking Martin Cole. The manager's tailored jacket was torn and his neatly styled hair hung cockeyed over his left ear. It was the first I knew he wore a wig. Dickerson was holding a shiny steel straight-razor a foot from Cole's throat and Cole had both hands on the singer's wrist trying to keep it there. Dickerson's eyes bulged and his lips were skinned back from long white teeth in a depraved rictus. His breath whistled. Through his own teeth Cole said, "Phil, give me a hand."

Phil wasn't listening. I took two steps forward and swept the butt of the automatic across the base of Dickerson's skull. The singer whimpered and sagged. Falling, the edge of the razor nicked Cole's cheek. It bled.

A floor lamp had been toppled against a chair. I straightened it and adjusted the shade.

"Most people watch television this time of the evening," I said.

The manager paused in the midst of pushing himself free to look at me. Automatically a hand went up and righted his wig. Then he finished rolling the singer's body off his and got up on his knees, listening with head cocked. A drop of blood landed on Dickerson's naked chest with a plop. The manager sat back on his heels. "He's breathing. You hit him damn hard."

"Pistol-whipping isn't an exact science. What happened?"

"D.T.'s. Bad trip. Maybe a combination of the two. He usually doesn't get this violent. When he does, Phil's usually there to get a grip on him and tie him up till it's over." He glanced toward the man lying in the open doorway, "Jeez, what'd you do, kill him?"

"It'd take more than an uppercut to do that. How long's he been like this?"

"Who, Billy? Couple of years. The last few months, though, he's been getting worse. The drugs pump him up for his performances, the booze brings him back down afterwards. But lately it's been affecting his music."

"Not just lately," I said. "It's been doing that for the past year anyway. That's how long attendance at his concerts has been falling off, according to the entertainment writer I spoke to at the *News*."

He had picked up his tinted eyeglasses from the floor and was polishing them with a clean corner of the silk handkerchief he had been using to staunch the trickle of blood from his cut cheek. He stopped polishing and put them on. "Your friend's mistaken. We're sold out."

"They came to see if history would repeat itself and someone would make a new try on Dickerson. Just as you hoped they would."

"Explain."

"First get your hands away from your body."

He smiled. The expression reminded me of Phil's cat's-grin. "If I were armed, do you think I'd have wrestled Billy for that razor barehanded?"

"You would have. He's too valuable to kill. Get 'em up."

He raised his hands to shoulder level. I unholstered my .38 and put the nine-millimeter in my topcoat pocket. Go with the weapon you know.

"There was no hit man," I said, "not attempt on your boy's life. The man you intended to get killed got killed. It was going to be Henry Bliss, but in Denver something went wrong and you had to dump him without trumpets. What did he do, find out what you had planned for him and threaten to go to the law?"

He was still smiling. "You're out of it, Walker. If there was no hit man, who killed Ned Eccles?"

"I'm coming to that. You've got a lot of money tied up in Dickerson, but he's depreciating property. I'm guessing, but I'd say a man with your expensive tastes has a lot of debts, maybe to some people it's not advisable to have a lot of debts with. So you figured to squeeze one more good season out of your client and get out from under. Attempted assassination is box office. A body gives it that authentic touch. After disposing of Bliss you shopped around. I looked pretty good. Security isn't my specialty, my reflexes might not be embarrassingly fast. Also I'm single, with no attachments, no one to demand too thorough an investigation into my death. But I turned you down. Ned Eccles wasn't as good. He was married. But his marriage was sour—you'd have found that out through questioning, as keeping secrets was not one of Ned's specialties—and being an experienced shield he'd have been looking for trouble from outside, not from his employers.

"I called Art Cradshaw a little while ago. That was a mistake, Cole, saying he recommended me. He wasted some of my time being evasive, but when he found out I wasn't dunning him for what he owes me he was willing to talk. He remembered especially how pleased you were to learn I have no family."

Dickerson stirred and groaned. His manager ignored him. Cole wasn't smiling now. I went on.

"What'd you do, promise to cut Phil in on the increased revenue, or just pay him a flat fee to ventilate the bodyguard?"

"Now I know you're out of it. If Phil shot him, where's the gun? His is a nine-millimeter. Eccles was shot with a thirty-eight."

"You were right in front of the service elevator. One of you stepped inside and ditched it. Probably Phil, who was more reliable than Dickerson and tall enough to push open one of the panels on top of the car and stash it there. The cops had no reason to look there, because they were after a phantom hit man who made his escape through the back door."

"You're just talking, Walker. None of it's any good."

"The gun is," I said. "I think you have it hidden somewhere in this suite. The cops will find it. They've been sticking too close to you since the shooting for you to have had a chance to get rid of it. Until now, that is. Where are they?"

"I pulled them off."

The voice was new. I jumped and swung around, bringing the gun with me. I was pointing it at Lieutenant Gritch. He was holding his own service revolver at hip level. Phil lay quietly as ever on the floor between us.

"Put it away," Gritch said patiently. "I don't want to add threatening a police officer to the charge of interfering in an official investigation. Too much paperwork."

I leathered the Smith & Wesson. "You pulled them off why?"

"To give Cole and Scabarda here breathing space. I didn't have enough to get a warrant to search the suite. I had a plainclothes detail in the lobby and near the back entrance ready to follow them until they tried to ditch the piece. Imagine my surprise when one of my men called in to say he saw you going up to the third floor.''

''You knew?''

He said, ''I'm a detective. You private guys forget that sometimes. I had to think who stood the most to gain from two dead bodyguards. What tipped you?''

''Cole's story of what happened downstairs. Ned Eccles wouldn't have stopped a bullet meant for his mother. But it didn't mean anything until you said what you did in my office about Dickerson's fans paying to see him get killed.''

''Yeah, that's when it hit me too.''

''Couple of Sherlocks,'' I said.

And then the muzzle of Gritch's revolver flamed and the report shook the room and if there had been a mirror handy I'd have seen my hair turn white in that instant. The wind of his bullet plucked at my coat. Someone grunted and I turned again and looked at Cole kneeling on the floor, gripping his bloody right wrist in his left hand. A small automatic gleamed on the carpet between him and Billy Dickerson, the King of Country Rock.

''Circus shooting,'' Gritch said, disgusted. ''If my captain asks, I was aiming for the chest. I got suspended once for getting fancy. Oh, your client's waiting out in the parking lot, shamus. I was questioning her when the call came in. Couldn't talk her out of going. Three sheets to the wind she's still one tough broad. You better see her before she comes up here.''

''Yeah,'' I agreed. ''She might kick Cole's head in.''

''Guess I'll be able to get that warrant now. You going to be handy for a statement?''

I wrote the address of the shop steward's house in Redford Township on the back of a card and gave it to him. ''Don't try to reach me there. I'll be staying in the place across the street for a while starting tomorrow.''

''How long?''

''Indefinitely.''

''I got a sister-in-law trying to get out of Redford,'' he said. ''I feel sorry for you.''

''Like hell you do.''

He grinned for the first time since I knew him.

I'm not sure that Tony Hillerman would like to be called beloved, but few mystery writers seem to inspire, among readers and publishing people alike, the warm feelings Tony does.

He is an original, very much reflective of the biases and beliefs of his generation, but in many respects he's outside our time—there's a mythic feeling to his novels of Navajo life. They loom in the fables our parents used to tell us, vivid, colorful, complete in themselves.

For all his popularity, one has the feeling that his run on the international bestseller lists has only begun.

Chee's Witch
TONY HILLERMAN

Snow is so important to the Eskimos they have nine nouns to describe its variations. Corporal Jimmy Chee of the Navajo Tribal Police had heard that as an anthropology student at the University of New Mexico. He remembered it now because he was thinking of all the words you need in Navajo to account for the many forms of witchcraft. The word Old Woman Tso had used was "anti'l," which is the ultimate sort, the absolute worst. And so, in fact, was the deed that seemed to have been done. Murder, apparently. Mutilation, certainly, if Old Woman Tso had her facts right. And then, if one believed all the mythology of witchery told among the fifty clans who comprised The People, there must also be cannibalism, incest, even necrophilia.

On the radio in Chee's pickup truck, the voice of the young Navajo reading a Gallup used-car commercial was replaced by Willie Nelson singing of trouble and a worried mind. The ballad fit Chee's mood. He was tired. He was thirsty. He was sticky with sweat. He was worried. His pickup jolted along the ruts in a windless heat, leaving a white fog of dust to mark its winding passage across the Rainbow Plateau. The truck was gray with it. So was Jimmy Chee. Since sunrise he had covered maybe 200 miles of half-graded gravel and unmarked wagon tracks of the Arizona-Utah-New Mexico border country. Routine at first—a check into a witch story at the Tsossie hogan north of Teec Nos Pos to stop trouble before it started. Routine and logical. A bitter winter, a sandstorm spring, a summer of rainless, desiccating heat. Hopes dying, things going wrong, anger growing, and then the witch gossip. The logical. A bitter winter, a sandstorm spring, a summer awry. The trouble at the summer hogan of the Tsossies was a sick child and a water well that had turned alkaline—nothing unexpected. But you didn't expect such a specific witch. The skin-walker, the Tsossies agreed, was The City Navajo, the man who had come to live in one of the government houses at Kayenta. Why the City Navajo? Because everybody knew he was a witch. Where had they heard that, the first time? The People who came to the trading post at Mexican Water said it. And so Chee had driven westward over Tohache Wash, past Red Mesa and Rabbit Ears to Mexican Water. He had spent hours on the shady porch giving those who came to buy, and to fill their water barrels, and to visit, a chance to know who he was until finally they might risk talking about witchcraft to a stranger. They were Mud Clan, and Many Goats People, and Standing Rock Clan—foreign to Chee's own Slow Talking People—but finally some of them talked a little.

A witch was at work on the Rainbow Plateau. Adeline Etcitty's mare had foaled a two-headed colt. Hosteen Musket had seen the witch. He'd seen a man walk into a grove of cottonwoods, but when he got there an owl flew away. Rudolph Bisti's boys lost three rams while driving their flocks up into the Chuska high pastures, and when they found the bodies, the huge tracks of a werewolf were all around them. The daughter of Rosemary Nashibitti had seen a big dog bothering her horses and had shot at it with her .22 and the dog had turned into a man wearing a wolfskin and had fled, half running, half flying. The old man they called Afraid of His Horses had heard the sound of the witch on the roof of his winter hogan, and saw the dirt falling through the smoke hole as the skinwalker tried to throw in his corpse powder. The next morning the old man had followed the tracks of the Navajo Wolf for a mile, hoping to kill him. But the tracks had faded away. There was nothing very unusual in the stories, except their number and the recurring hints that City Navajo was the witch. But then came what Chee hadn't expected. The witch had killed a man.

The police dispatcher at Window Rock had been interrupting Willie

Nelson with an occasional blurted message. Now she spoke directly to Chee. He acknowledged. She asked his location.

"About fifteen miles south of Dennehotso," Chee said. "Homeward bound for Tuba City. Dirty, thirsty, hungry, and tired."

"I have a message."

"Tuba City," Chee repeated, "which I hope to reach in about two hours, just in time to avoid running up a lot of overtime for which I never get paid."

"The message is FBI Agent Wells needs to contact you. Can you make a meeting at Kayenta Holiday Inn at eight P.M.?"

"What's it about?" Chee asked. The dispatcher's name was Virgie Endecheenie, and she had a very pretty voice and the first time Chee had met her at the Window Rock headquarters of the Navajo Tribal Police he had been instantly smitten. Unfortunately, Virgie was a born-into Salt Cedar Clan, which was the clan of Chee's father, which put an instant end to that. Even thinking about it would violate the complex incest taboo of the Navajos.

"Nothing on what it's about," Virgie said, her voice strictly business. "It just says confirm meeting and place with Chee or obtain alternate time."

"Any first name on Wells?" Chee asked. The only FBI Wells he knew was Jake Wells. He hoped it wouldn't be Jake.

"Negative on the first name," Virgie said.

"All right," Chee said. "I'll be there."

The road tilted downward now into the vast barrens of erosion that the Navajos call Beautiful Valley. Far to the west, the edge of the sun dipped behind a cloud—one of the line of thunderheads forming in the evening heat over the San Francisco Peaks and the Coconino Rim. The Hopis had been holding their Niman Kachina dances, calling the clouds to come and bless them.

Chee reached Kayenta just a little late. It was early twilight and the clouds had risen black against the sunset. The breeze brought the faint smells that rising humidity carry across desert country—the perfume of sage, creosote brush, and dust. The desk clerk said that Wells was in room 284 and the first name was Jake. Chee no longer cared. Jake Wells was abrasive, but he was also smart. He had the best record in the special FBI Academy class Chee had attended, a quick, tough intelligence. Chee could tolerate the man's personality for a while to learn what Wells could make of his witchcraft puzzle.

"It's unlocked," Wells said. "Come on in." He was propped against the padded headboard of the bed, shirt off, shoes on, glass in hand. He glanced at Chee and then back at the television set. He was as tall as Chee remembered, and the eyes were just as blue. He waved the glass at Chee without looking away from the set. "Mix yourself one," he said, nodding toward a bottle beside the sink in the dressing alcove.

"How you doing, Jake?" Chee asked.

Now the blue eyes re-examined Chee. The question in them abruptly went away. "Yeah," Wells said. "You were the one at the Academy." He eased himself up on his left elbow and extended a hand. "Jake Wells," he said.

Chee shook the hand. "Chee," he said.

Wells shifted his weight again and handed Chee his glass. "Pour me a little more while you're at it," he said, "and turn down the sound."

Chee turned down the sound.

"About thirty percent booze," Wells demonstrated the proportion with his hands. "This is your district then. You're in charge around Kayenta? Window Rock said I should talk to you. They said you were out chasing around in the desert today. What are you working on?"

"Nothing much," Chee said. He ran a glass of water, drinking it thirstily. His face in the mirror was dirty—the lines around mouth and eyes whitish with dust. The sticker on the glass reminded guests that the laws of the Navajo Tribal Council prohibited possession of alcoholic beverages on the reservation. He refilled his own glass with water and mixed Wells's drink. "As a matter of fact, I'm working on a witch-craft case."

"Witchcraft?" Wells laughed. "Really?" He took the drink from Chee and examined it. "How does it work? Spells and like that?"

"Not exactly," Chee said. "It depends. A few years ago a little girl got sick down near Burnt Water. Her dad killed three people with a shotgun. He said they blew corpse powder on his daughter and made her sick."

Wells was watching him. "The kind of crime where you have the insanity plea."

"Sometimes," Chee said. "Whatever you have, witch talk makes you nervous. It happens more when you have a bad year like this. You hear it and you try to find out what's starting it before things get worse."

"So you're not really expecting to find a witch?"

"Usually not," Chee said.

"Usually?"

"Judge for yourself," Chee said. "I'll tell you what I've picked up today. You tell me what to make of it. Have time?"

Wells shrugged. "What I really want to talk about is a guy named Simon Begay." He looked quizzically at Chee. "You heard the name?"

"Yes," Chee said.

"Well, shit," Wells said. "You shouldn't have. What do you know about him?"

"Showed up maybe three months ago. Moved into one of those U.S. Public Health Service houses over by the Kayenta clinic. Stranger. Keeps to himself. From off the reservation somewhere. I figured you federals put him here to keep him out of sight."

Wells frowned. "How long you known about him?"

"Quite a while," Chee said. He'd known about Begay within a week after his arrival.

"He's a witness," Wells said. "They broke a car-theft operation in Los Angeles. Big deal. National connections. One of those where they have hired hands picking up expensive models and they drive 'em right on the ship and off-load in South America. This Begay is one of the hired hands. Nobody much. Criminal record going all the way back to juvenile, but all nickel-and-dime stuff. I gather he saw some things that help tie some big boys into the crime, so Justice made a deal with him."

"And they hide him out here until the trial?"

Something apparently showed in the tone of the question. "If you want to hide an apple, you drop it in with the other apples," Wells said. "What better place?"

Chee had been looking at Wells's shoes, which were glossy with polish. Now he examined his own boots, which were not. But he was thinking of Justice Department stupidity. The appearance of any new human in a country as empty as the Navajo Reservation provoked instant interest. If the stranger was a Navajo, there were instant questions. What was his clan? Who was his mother? What was his father's clan? Who were his relatives? The City Navajo had no answers to any of these crucial questions. He was (as Chee had been repeatedly told) unfriendly. It was quickly guessed that he was a "relocation Navajo," born to one of those hundreds of Navajo families that the federal government had tried to re-establish forty years ago in Chicago, Los Angeles, and other urban centers. He was a stranger. In a year of witches, he would certainly be suspected. Chee sat looking at his boots, wondering if that was the only basis for the charge that City Navajo was a skinwalker. Or had someone seen something? Had someone seen the murder?

"The thing about apples is they don't gossip," Chee said.

"You hear gossip about Begay?" Wells was sitting up now, his feet on the floor.

"Sure," Chee said. "I hear he's a witch."

Wells produced a pro-forma chuckle. "Tell me about it," he said.

Chee knew exactly how he wanted to tell it. Wells would have to wait a while before he came to the part about Begay. "The Eskimos have nine nouns for snow," Chee began. He told Wells about the variety of witchcraft on the reservations and its environs: about frenzy witchcraft, used for sexual conquests, of witchery distortions, of curing ceremonials, of the exotic two-heart witchcraft of the Hopi Fog Clan, of the Zuni Sorcery Fraternity, of the Navajo "chindi," which is more like a ghost than a witch, and finally of the Navajo Wolf, the anti'l witchcraft, the werewolves who pervert every taboo of the Navajo Way and use corpse powder to kill their victims.

Wells rattled the ice in his glass and glanced at his watch.

"To get to the part about your Begay," Chee said, "about two months ago we started picking up witch gossip. Nothing much, and you expect it during a drought. Lately it got to be more than usual." He described some of the tales and how uneasiness and dread had spread across the plateau. He described what he had learned today, the Tsossie's naming City Navajo as the witch, his trip to Mexican Water, of learning there that the witch had killed a man.

"They said it happened in the spring—couple of months ago. They told me the ones who knew about it were the Tso outfit." The talk of murder, Chee noticed, had revived Wells's interest. "I went up there," he continued, "and found the old woman who runs the outfit. Emma Tso. She told me her son-in-law had been out looking for some sheep, and smelled something, and found the body under some chamiso brush in a dry wash. A witch had killed him."

"How—"

Chee cut off the question. "I asked her how he knew it was a witch killing. She said the hands were stretched out like this." Chee extended his hands, palms up. "They were flayed. The skin was cut off the palms and fingers."

Wells raised his eyebrows.

"That's what the witch uses to make corpse powder," Chee explained. "They take the skin that has the whorls and ridges of the individual personality—the skin from the palms and the finger pads, and the soles of the feet. They take that, and the skin from the glans of the penis, and the small bones where the neck joins the skull, and they dry it, and pulverize it, and use it as poison."

"You're going to get to Begay any minute now," Wells said. "That right?"

"We got to him," Chee said. "He's the one they think is the witch. He's the City Navajo."

"I thought you were going to say that," Wells said. He rubbed the back of his hand across one blue eye. "City Navajo. Is it that obvious?"

"Yes," Chee said. "And then he's a stranger. People suspect strangers."

"Were they coming around him? Accusing him? Any threats? Anything like that, you think?"

"It wouldn't work that way—not unless somebody had someone in their family killed. The way you deal with a witch is hire a singer and hold a special kind of curing ceremony. That turns the witchcraft around and kills the witch."

Wells made an impatient gesture. "Whatever," he said. "I think something has made this Begay spooky." He stared into his glass, communing with the bourbon. "I don't know."

"Something unusual about the way he's acting?"

"Hell of it is I don't know how he usually acts. This wasn't my case. The agent who worked him retired or some damn thing, so I got stuck with being the delivery man." He shifted his eyes from glass to Chee. "But if it was me, and I was holed up here waiting, and the guy came along who was going to take me home again, then I'd be glad to see him. Happy to have it over with. All that."

"He wasn't?"

Wells shook his head. "Seemed edgy. Maybe that's natural, though. He's going to make trouble for some hard people."

"I'd be nervous," Chee said.

"I guess it doesn't matter much anyway," Wells said. "He's small potatoes. The guy who's handling it now in the U.S. Attorney's Office said it must have been a toss-up whether to fool with him at all. He said the assistant who handled it decided to hide him out just to be on the safe side."

"Begay doesn't know much?"

"I guess not. That, and they've got better witnesses."

"So why worry?"

Wells laughed. "I bring this sucker back and they put him on the witness stand and he answers all the questions with I don't know and it makes the USDA look like a horse's ass. When a U.S. attorney looks like that, he finds an FBI agent to blame it on." He yawned. "Therefore," he said through the yawn, "I want to ask you what you think.

This is your territory. You are the officer in charge. Is it your opinion that someone got to my witness?''

Chee let the question hang. He spent a fraction of a second reaching the answer, which was they could have if they wanted to try. Then he thought about the real reason Wells had kept him working late without a meal or a shower. Two sentences in Wells's report. One would note that the possibility the witness had been approached had been checked with the local Navajo Police. The next would report whatever Chee said next. Wells would have followed Federal Rule One—Protect Your Ass.

Chee shrugged. ''You want to hear the rest of my witchcraft business?''

Wells put his drink on the lamp table and untied his shoes. ''Does it bear on this?''

''Who knows? Anyway there's not much left. I'll let you decide. The point is we had already picked up this corpse Emma Tso's son-in-law found. Somebody had reported it weeks ago. It had been collected, and taken in for an autopsy. The word we got on the body was Navajo male in his thirties probably. No identification on him.''

''How was this bird killed?''

''No sign of foul play,'' Chee said. ''By the time the body was brought in, decay and the scavengers hadn't left a lot. Mostly bone and gristle, I guess. This was a long time after Emma Tso's son-in-law saw him.''

''So why do they think Begay killed him?'' Wells removed his second shoe and headed for the bathroom.

Chee picked up the telephone and dialed the Kayenta clinic. He got the night supervisor and waited while the supervisor dug out the file. Wells came out of the bathroom with his toothbrush. Chee covered the mouthpiece. ''I'm having them read me the autopsy report,'' Chee explained. Wilson began brushing his teeth at the sink in the dressing alcove. The voice of the night supervisor droned into Chee's ear.

''That all?'' Chee asked. ''Nothing added on? No identity yet? Still no cause?''

''That's him,'' the voice said.

''How about shoes?'' Chee asked. ''He have shoes on?''

''Just a sec,'' the voice said. ''Yep. Size 10D. And a hat, and . . .''

''No mention of the neck or skull, right? I didn't miss that? No bones missing?''

Silence. ''Nothing about neck or skull bones.''

''Ah,'' Chee said. ''Fine. I thank you.'' He felt great. He felt wonderful. Finally things had clicked into place. The witch was exorcised. "Jake," he said. "Let me tell you a little more about my witch case."

Wells was rinsing his mouth. He spit out the water and looked at Chee, amused. "I didn't think of this before," Wells said, "but you really don't have a witch problem. If you leave that corpse a death by natural causes, there's no case to work. If you decide it's a homicide, you don't have jurisdiction anyway. Homicide on an Indian reservation, FBI has jurisdiction." Wells grinned. "We'll come in and find your witch for you."

Chee looked at his boots, which were still dusty. His appetite had left him, as it usually did an hour or so after he missed a meal. He still hungered for a bath. He picked up his hat and pushed himself to his feet.

"I'll go home now," he said. "The only thing you don't know about the witch case is what I just got from the autopsy report. The corpse had his shoes on and no bones were missing from the base of the skull."

Chee opened the door and stood in it, looking back. Wells was taking his pajamas out of his suitcase. "So what advice do you have for me? What can you tell me about my witch case?"

"To tell the absolute truth, Chee, I'm not into witches," Wells said. "Haven't been since I was a boy."

"But we don't really have a witch case now," Chee said. He spoke earnestly. "The shoes were still on, so the skin wasn't taken from the soles of his feet. No bones missing from the neck. You need those to make corpse powder."

Wells was pulling his undershirt over his head. Chee hurried.

"What we have now is another little puzzle," Chee said. "If you're not collecting stuff for corpse powder, why cut the skin off this guy's hands?"

"I'm going to take a shower," Wells said. "Got to get my Begay back to LA tomorrow."

Outside the temperature had dropped. The air moved softly from the west, carrying the smell of rain. Over the Utah border, over the Coconino Rim, over the Rainbow Plateau, lightning flickered and glowed. The storm had formed. The storm was moving. The sky was black with it. Chee stood in the darkness, listening to the mutter of thunder, inhaling the perfume, exulting in it.

He climbed into the truck and started it. How had they set it up, and why? Perhaps the FBI agent who knew Begay had been ready to retire. Perhaps an accident had been arranged. Getting rid of the assistant prosecutor who knew the witness would have been even simpler—a matter of hiring him away from the government job. That left no one who knew this minor witness was not Simon Begay. And who was he? Probably they had other Navajos from the Los Angeles community stealing cars for them. Perhaps that's what had suggested the scheme. To most white men all Navajos looked pretty much alike, just as in his first years at college all Chee had seen in white men was pink skin, freckles, and light-colored eyes. And what would the impostor say? Chee grinned. He'd say whatever was necessary to cast doubt on the prosecution, to cast the fatal "reasonable doubt," to make—as Wells had put it—the U.S. District Attorney look like a horse's ass.

Chee drove into the rain twenty miles west of Kayenta. Huge, cold drops drummed on the pickup roof and turned the highway into a ribbon of water. Tomorrow the backcountry roads would be impassable. As soon as they dried and the washouts had been repaired, he'd go back to the Tsossie hogan, and the Tso place, and to all the other places from which the word would quickly spread. He'd tell the people that the witch was in custody of the FBI and was gone forever from the Rainbow Plateau.

Bob's career has spanned six decades. Think about all that has happened in that time and you'll realize how singular his career has been. Of course he wrote *Psycho*, but he's also written half a dozen novels just as good, and he's shown an equal talent for the short story. "Water's Edge" is included here because it helps mark the transition from the hardboiled crime story of the fifties and sixties into the quiet revolution of the seventies. This is a beautifully structured and paced story, and should be studied carefully by all readers who also have a hankering to be writers.

Water's Edge
ROBERT BLOCH

The fly-specked lettering on the window read *The Bright Spot Restaurant*. The sign overhead urged *Eat*.

He wasn't hungry, and the place didn't look especially attractive, but he went inside anyway.

It was a counter joint with a single row of hard-backed booths lining one wall. A half dozen customers squatted on stools at the end of the counter, near the door. He walked past them and slid onto a stool at the far end.

There he sat, staring at the three waitresses. None of them looked right to him, but he had to take a chance. He waited until one of the women approached him.

"Yours, mister?"

"Coke."

She brought it to him and set the glass down. He pretended to be studying the menu and talked without looking up at her.

"Say, does a Mrs. Helen Krauss work here?"

"I'm Helen Krauss."

He lifted his eyes. What kind of a switch was this, anyway? He remembered the way Mike used to talk about her, night after night. "She's a tall blonde, but stacked. Looks a lot like that dame who plays the dumb blonde on television—what's-her-name—you know the one I mean. But she's no dope, not Helen. And boy, when it comes to loving. . . ."

After that, his descriptions would become anatomically intricate, but all intricacies had been carefully filed in memory.

He examined those files now, but nothing in them corresponded to what he saw before him.

This woman was tall, but there all resemblance ended. She must have tipped the scales at one-sixty, at least, and her hair was a dull, mousy brown. She wore glasses, too. Behind the thick lenses, her faded blue eyes peered stolidly at him.

She must have realized he was staring, and he knew he had to talk fast. "I'm looking for a Helen Krauss who used to live over in Norton Center. She was married to a man named Mike."

The stolid eyes blinked. "That's me. So what's this all about?"

"I got a message for you from your husband."

"Mike? He's dead."

"I know. I was with him when he died. Just before, anyway. I'm Rusty Connors. We were cell-mates for two years."

Her expression didn't change, but her voice dropped to a whisper. "What's the message?"

He glanced around. "I can't talk here. What time do you get off?"

"Seven-thirty."

"Good. Meet you outside?"

She hesitated. "Make it down at the corner, across the street. There's a park, you know?"

He nodded, rose and left without looking back.

This wasn't what he had expected—not after the things Mike had told him about his wife. When he bought his ticket for Hainesville, he had had other ideas in mind. It would have been nice to find this hot, good-looking blond widow of Mike's and, maybe, combine business with pleasure. He had even thought about the two of them blowing town together, if she was half as nice as Mike said. But that was out, now. He wanted no part of this big, fat, stupid-looking slob with the dull eyes.

Rusty wondered how Mike could have filled him with such a line of bull for two years straight—and then he knew. Two years straight—that was the answer—two years in a bare cell, without a woman. Maybe it had got so that, after a time, Mike believed his own story, that Helen Krauss became beautiful to him. Maybe Mike had gone a little stir-simple before he died, and made up a lot of stuff.

Rusty only hoped Mike had been telling the truth about one thing. He had better have been, because what Mike had told Connors, there in the cell, was what brought him to town. It was this that was making him cut into this rat-race, that had led him to Mike's wife. He hoped Mike had been telling the truth about hiding away the fifty-six thousand dollars.

She met him in the park, and it was dark. That was good, because nobody would notice them together. Besides, he couldn't see her face, and she couldn't see his, and that would make it easier to say what he had to say.

They sat down on a bench behind the bandstand, and he lit a cigarette. Then he remembered that it was important to be pleasant, so he offered the pack to her.

She shook her head. "No thanks—I don't smoke."

"That's right. Mike told me." He paused. "He told me a lot of things about you, Helen."

"He wrote me about you, too. He said you were the best friend he ever had."

"I'd like to think so. Mike was a great guy in my book. None better. He didn't belong in a crummy hole like that."

"He said the same about you."

"Both of us got a bad break, I guess. Me, I was just a kid who didn't know the score. When I got out of Service, I lay around for a while until my dough was gone, and then I took this job in a bookie joint. I never pulled any strong-arm stuff in my life until the night the place was raided.

"The boss handed me this suitcase, full of dough, and told me to get out the back way. And there was this copper, coming at me with a gun. So I hit him over the head with the suitcase. It was just one of those things—I didn't mean to hurt him, even, just wanted to get out. So the copper ends up with a skull-fracture and dies."

"Mike wrote me about that. You had a tough deal."

"So did he, Helen." Rusty used her first name deliberately and let his voice go soft. It was part of the pitch. "Like I said, I just couldn't figure him out. An honest John like him, up and knocking off his best friend in a payroll stickup. And all alone, too. Then getting rid of the body, so they'd never find it. They never did find Pete Taylor, did they?"

"Please! I don't want to talk about it any more."

"I know how you feel." Rusty took her hand. It was plump and sweaty, and it rested in his like a big warm piece of meat But she didn't withdraw it, and he went on talking. "It was just circumstantial evidence that pinned it on him, wasn't it?"

"Somebody saw Mike pick Pete up that afternoon," Helen said. "He'd lost his car keys somewhere, and I guess he thought it would be all right if Mike took him over to the factory with the payroll money. That was all the police needed. They got to him before he could get rid of the bloodstains. Of course, he didn't have an alibi. I swore he was home with me all afternoon. They wouldn't buy that. So he went up for ten years."

"And did two, and died," Rusty said. "But he never told how he got rid of the body. He never told where he put the dough."

He could see her nodding in the dimness. "That's right. I guess they beat him up something awful, but he wouldn't tell them a thing."

Rusty was silent for a moment. Then he took a drag on his cigarette and said, "Did he ever tell you?"

Helen Krauss made a noise in her throat. "What do *you* think? I got out of Norton Center because I couldn't stand the way people kept talking about it. I came all the way over here to Hainesville. For two years, I've been working in that lousy hash-house. Does that sound like he told me anything?"

Rusty dropped the cigarette stub on the sidewalk, and its little red eye winked up at him. He stared at the eye as he spoke.

"What would you do if you found that money, Helen? Would you turn it over to the cops?"

She made the noise in her throat again. "What for? To say, 'Thank you,' for putting Mike away and killing him? That's what they did, they killed him. Pneumonia, they told me—I know about their pneumonia! They let him rot in that cell, didn't they?"

"The croaker said it was just flu. I put up such a stink over it, they finally took him down to the Infirmary."

"Well, *I* say they killed him. And *I* say he paid for that money with his life. I'm his widow—it's mine."

"Ours," said Rusty.

Her fingers tightened, and her nails dug into his palms. "He told you where he hid it? Is that it?"

"Just a little. Before they took him away. He was dying, and couldn't talk much. But I heard enough to give me a pretty good hunch. I figured, if I came here when I got out and talked to you, we could put things together and find the dough. Fifty-six gees, he said—even if we split it, that's still a lot of money."

"Why are you cutting me in on it, if you know where it is?" There was an edge of sudden suspicion in her voice, and he sensed it, met it head-on.

"Because, like I told you, he didn't say enough. We'd have to figure out what it means, and then do some hunting. I'm a stranger around here, and people might get suspicious if they saw me snooping. But if you helped, maybe there wouldn't be any need to snoop. Maybe we could go right to it."

"Business deal, is that it?"

Rusty stared at the glowing cigarette butt again. Its red eye winked back at him.

"Not *all* business, Helen. You know how it was with Mike and me. He talked about you all the time. After a while, I got the funniest feeling, like I already knew you—knew you as well as Mike. I wanted to know you better."

He kept his voice down, and he felt her nails against his palm. Suddenly his hand returned the pressure, and his voice broke. "Helen, I don't know, maybe I'm screwy, but I was over two years in that hole. Two years without a woman, you got any idea what that means to a guy?"

"It's been over two years for me, too."

He put his arms around her, forced his lips to hers. It didn't take much forcing. "You got a room?" he whispered.

"Yes, Rusty—I've got a room."

They rose, clinging together. Before moving away, he took a last look at the little winking red eye and crushed it out under his foot.

Another winking red eye burned in the bedroom, and he held the cigarette to one side in his hand so as to keep the light away. He didn't want her to see the disgust in his face.

Maybe she was sleeping now. He hoped so, because it gave him time to think.

So far, everything was working out. Everything *had* to work out, this time. Because before, there had always been foul-ups, somewhere along the line.

Grabbing the satchel full of dough, when the cops raided the bookie joint, had seemed like a good idea at the time. He had thought he could lam out the back door before anyone noticed in the confusion. But he had fouled that one up himself, and landed in stir.

Getting buddy-buddy with that little jerk Mike had been another good idea. It hadn't been long before he knew everything about the payroll caper—everything except where Mike had stashed the loot. Mike never *would* talk about that. It wasn't until he took sick that Rusty could handle him without anybody getting wise. He had made sure Mike was real sick before he put real pressure on.

Even then, the lousy fink hadn't come across—Rusty must have half-killed him, right there in the cell. Maybe he'd overdone it, because all he got out of him was the one sentence before the guards showed up.

For a while there, he had wondered if the little quiz show was going to kick back on him. If Mike had pulled out of it, he'd have talked. But Mike hadn't pulled out of it—he had died in the Infirmary before morning, and they had said it was the pneumonia that did it.

So Rusty was safe—and Rusty could make plans.

Up till now, his plans were going through okay. He had never applied for parole—believing it better to sweat out another six months, so he could go free without anybody hanging onto his tail. When they sprung him, he had taken the first bus to Hainesville. He knew where to go because Mike had told him about Helen working in this restaurant.

He hadn't been conning her as to his need for her in the deal. He needed her all right. He needed help, needed her to front for him, so he wouldn't have to look around on his own and arouse curiosity when he asked questions of strangers. That part was straight enough.

But, all along, he had believed what Mike told him about Helen—that she was a good-looking doll, the kind of dame you read about in the paperback books. He had coked himself up on the idea of finding the dough *and* going away with her, of having a real ball.

Well, that part was out.

He made a face in the darkness as he remembered the clammy fat of her, the wheezing and the panting and the clutching. No, he couldn't take much more of that. But he had to go through with it, it was part of the plan. He needed her on his side, and that was the best way to keep her in line.

But now he'd have to decide on the next move. If they found the dough, how could he be sure of her, once they made the split? He didn't want to be tied to this kitchen mechanic, and there had to be a way.

"Darling, are you awake?"

Her voice! And calling him "darling." He shuddered, then controlled himself.

"Yeah." He doused the cigarette in an ash tray.

"Do you feel like talking now?"

"Sure."

"I thought maybe we'd better make plans."

"That's what I like, a practical dame." He forced a smile into his voice. "You're right, baby. The sooner we get to work the better." He sat up and turned to her. "Let's start at the beginning—with what Mike told me, before he died. He said they'd never find the money, they couldn't—because Pete still had it."

For a moment Helen Krauss was silent. Then she said, "Is that all?"

"*All?* What more do you want? It's plain as the nose on your face, isn't it? The dough is hidden with Pete Taylor's body."

He could feel Helen's breath on his shoulder. "Never mind the nose on my face," she said. "I know where that is. But for two years, all the cops in the county haven't been able to find Pete Taylor's body." She sighed. "I thought you really had something, but I guess I was wrong. I should of known."

Rusty grabbed her by the shoulders. "Don't *talk* like that! We've got the answer we need. All we got to do now is figure where to look."

"*Sure.* Real easy!" Her tone dripped sarcasm.

"Think back, now. Where did the cops look?"

"Well, they searched our place, of course. We were living in a rented house, but that didn't stop them. They tore up the whole joint, including the cellar. No dice there."

"Where else?"

"The sheriff's department had men out for a month, searching the woods around Norton's Center. They covered all the old barns and deserted farmhouses too, places like that. They even dragged the lake. Pete Taylor was a bachelor—he had a little shack in town and one out at the lake, too. They ripped them both apart. Nothing doing."

Rusty was silent. "How much time did Mike have between picking up Pete and coming back home again?"

"About three hours."

"Hell, then he couldn't have gone very far, could he? The body must be hid near town."

"That's just how the police figured. I tell you, they did a job. They dug up the ditches, drained the quarry. It was no use."

"Well, there's got to be an answer somewhere. Let's try another angle. Pete Taylor and your husband were pals, right?"

"Yes. Ever since we got married, Mike was thick with him. They got along great together."

"What did they do? I mean, did they drink, play cards or what?"

"Mike wasn't much on the sauce. Mostly, they just hunted and fished. Like I say, Pete Taylor had this shack out at the lake."

"Is that near Norton's Center?"

"About three miles out." Helen sounded impatient. "I know what you're thinking, but it's no good. I tell you, they dug things up all around there. They even ripped out the floorboards and stuff like that."

"What about sheds, boathouses?"

"Pete Taylor didn't have anything else on his property. When Mike and him went fishing, they borrowed a boat from the neighbors down the line." She sighed again. "Don't think I haven't tried to figure it out. For two years, I've figured, and there just isn't any answer."

Rusty found another cigarette and lit it. "For fifty-six grand, there's got to be an answer," he said. "What happened the day Pete Taylor was killed? Maybe there's something you forgot about."

"I don't know what happened, really. I was at home, and Mike had the day off, so he went downtown to bum around."

"Did he say anything before he left? Was he nervous? Did he act funny?"

"No—I don't think he had anything planned, if that's what you mean. I think it was just one of those things—he found himself in the car with Pete Taylor and all this money, and he just decided to do it.

"Well, they figured it was all planned in advance. They said he knew it was payroll day, and how Pete always went to the bank in his car and got the money in cash. Old Man Huggins at the factory was a queer duck, and he liked to pay that way. Anyway, they say Pete went into the bank, and Mike must have been waiting in the parking lot behind.

"They think he sneaked over and stole Pete's car keys, so, when he came out with the guard, Pete couldn't get started. Mike waited until the guard left, then walked over and noticed Pete, as if it was an accident he happened to be there, and asked what the trouble was.

"Something like that must have happened, because the guy in the parking lot said they talked, and then Pete got into Mike's car and they drove off together. That's all they know, until Mike came home alone almost three hours later."

Rusty nodded. "He came home to you, in the car, alone. What did he say?"

"Nothing much. There wasn't time, I guess. Because the squad car pulled up about two minutes after he got in the house."

"So fast? Who tipped them off?"

"Well, naturally the factory got worried when Pete never showed with the payroll. So Old Man Huggins called the bank, and the bank checked with the cashier and the guard, and somebody went out and asked around in the parking lot. The attendant told about how Pete had left in Mike's car. So they came around here, looking for him.''

"Did he put up any struggle?"

"No. He never even said a word. They just took him away. He was in the bathroom, washing up."

"Much dirt on him?" Rusty asked.

"Just his hands, is all. They never found anything they could check up on in their laboratories, or whatever. His shoes were muddy, I think. There was a big fuss because his gun was missing. That was the worst part, his taking the gun with him. They never found it, of course, but they knew he'd owned one, and it was gone. He said he'd lost it months beforehand but they didn't believe him.''

"Did *you?*"

"I don't know."

"Anything else?"

"Well, he had a cut on his hand. It was bleeding a little when he came in. I noticed it and asked him about it. He was halfway upstairs, and he said something about rats. Later in court, he told them he'd caught his hand in the window-glass, and that's why there was blood in the car. One of the windows was cracked. They analyzed the blood, it wasn't his type. It checked with Pete Taylor's blood-type record.''

Rusty took a deep drag. "But he didn't tell you that when he came home. He said a big rat bit him.''

"No—he just said something about rats, I couldn't make out what. In court, the doctor testified he'd gone upstairs and cut his hand open with a razor. They found his razor on the washstand and it was bloody.''

"Wait a minute," Rusty said slowly. "He started to tell you something about rats. Then he went upstairs and opened up his hand with a razor. Now its beginning to make sense, don't you see? A rat *did* bite him, maybe when he was getting rid of the body. But if anyone knew that, they'd look for the body some place where there were rats. So he covered up by opening the wound with his razor.''

"Maybe so," Helen Krauss said. "But where does that leave us? Are we going to have to search every place with rats in it around Norton's Center?''

"I hope not," Rusty answered. "I hate the damned things. They give me the creeps. Used to see them in the Service, big fat things hanging around the docks. . . .'' He snapped his fingers. "Just a second. You say, when Pete and Mike went fishing, they borrowed a boat from the neighbors. Where did the neighbors keep their boat?''

"They had a boathouse."

"Did the cops search there?"

"I don't know—I guess so."

"Maybe they didn't search good enough. Were the neighbors on the property that day?"

"No."

"Are you sure?"

"Sure enough. They were a city couple from Chicago, name of Thomason. Two weeks before the payroll robbery, they got themselves killed in an auto accident on the way home."

"So nobody was around at all, and Mike knew it."

"That's right." Helen's voice was suddenly hoarse. "It was too late in the season anyway, just like now. The lake was deserted. Do you think . . . ?"

"Who's living in the neighbors' place now?" Rusty asked.

"No one, the last I heard. They didn't have any kids, and the real estate man couldn't sell it. Pete Taylor's place is vacant, too. Same reason."

"It adds up—adds up to fifty-six thousand dollars, if I'm right. When could we go?"

"Tomorrow, if you like. It's my day off. We can use my car. Oh, darling, I'm so excited!"

She didn't have to tell him. He could feel it, feel her as she came into his arms. Once more, he had to force himself, had to keep thinking about something else, so that he wouldn't betray how he felt.

He had to keep thinking about the money, and about what he'd do after they found it. He needed the right answer, fast.

He was still thinking when she lay back, and then she suddenly surprised him by asking, "What are you thinking about, darling?"

He opened his mouth and the truth popped out. "The money," he said. "All that money. Twenty-eight gees apiece."

"Does it have to be apiece, darling?"

He hesitated—and then the right answer came. "Of course not—not unless you want it that way." And it wouldn't be. It was still fifty-six thousand, and it would be his after they found it.

All he had to do was rub her out.

If Rusty had any doubts about going through with it, they vanished the next day. He spent the morning and afternoon with her in her room, because he had to. There was no sense in letting them be seen together here in town or anywhere around the lake area.

So he forced himself to stall her, and there was only one way to do that. By the time twilight came, he would have killed her anyway, money or no money, just to be rid of her stinking fat body.

How could Mike have ever figured she was good-looking? He'd never know, any more than he'd ever known what had gone on in the little jerk's head when he suddenly decided to knock off his best friend and steal the dough.

But that wasn't important now—the important thing was to find that black metal box.

Around four o'clock he slipped downstairs and walked around the block. In ten minutes, she picked him up at the corner in her car.

It was a good hour's drive to the lake. She took a detour around Norton Center, and they approached the lake shore by a gravel road. He wanted her to cut the lights, but she said there was no need, because nobody was there anyway. As they scanned the shore Rusty could see she was telling the truth—the lake was dark, deserted, in the early November night.

They parked behind Pete Taylor's shack. At sight of it, Rusty realized that the body couldn't possibly be hidden there. The little rickety structure wouldn't have concealed a dead fly for long. Helen got a flashlight from the car. "I suppose you want to go straight to the boathouse," she said. "It's down this way, to the left. Be careful—the path is slippery."

It was treacherous going in the darkness. Rusty followed her, wondering if now was the time. He could pick up a rock and bash her head in while she had her back to him.

No, he decided, better wait. First see if the dough was there, see if he could find a good place to leave her body. There must be a good place—Mike had found one.

The boathouse stood behind a little pier running out into the lake. Rusty tugged at the door. It was padlocked. "Stand back," he said. He picked up a stone from the bank. The lock was flimsy, rusty with disuse. It broke easily and fell to the ground.

He took the flashlight from her, opened the door and peered in. The beam swept the interior, piercing the darkness. But it wasn't total darkness. Rusty saw the glow of a hundred little red cigarette butts winking up at him, like eyes.

Then, he realized, they *were* eyes.

"Rats," he said. "Come on, don't be afraid. Looks like our hunch was right."

Helen moved behind him, and she wasn't afraid. But he had really been talking to himself. He didn't like rats. He was glad when the rodents scattered and disappeared before the flashlight's beam. The sound of footsteps sent them scampering off into the corners, into their burrows beneath the boathouse floor.

The floor! Rusty sent the beam downward. It was concrete, of course. And underneath . . . ?

"Damn it!" he said. "They *must* have been here."

They had—because the once-solid concrete floor was rubble. The pick-axes of the sheriff's men had done a thorough job. "I *told* you," Helen Krauss sighed. "They looked everywhere."

Rusty swept the room with light. There was no boat, nothing stored in corners. The beam bounced off bare walls.

He raised it to the flat roof of the ceiling and caught only the reflection of mica from tar-paper insulation.

"It's no use," Helen told him. "It couldn't be this easy."

"There's still the house," Rusty said. "Come on."

He turned and walked out of the place, glad to get away from the rank, fetid animal odor. He turned the flashlight toward the roof.

Then he stopped. "Notice anything?" he said.

"What?"

"The roof. It's higher than the ceiling."

"So what?"

"There could be space up there," Rusty said.

"Yes, but . . ."

"Listen."

She was silent—both of them were silent. In the silence, they could hear the emerging sound. It sounded at first like the patter of rain on the roof, but it wasn't raining, and it wasn't coming from the roof. It was coming from directly underneath—the sound of tiny, scurrying feet between roof and ceiling. The rats were there. The rats and what else?

"Come on," he muttered.

"Where are you going?"

"Up to the house—to find a ladder."

He didn't have to break in, and that was fine. There was a ladder in the shed, and he carried it back. Helen discovered a crowbar. She held the flashlight while he propped the ladder against the wall and climbed up. The crowbar pried off the tar-paper in strips. It came away easily, ripping out from the few nails. Apparently the stuff had been applied in a hurry. A man with only a few hours to work in has to do a fast job.

Underneath the tar-paper, Rusty found timbers. Now the crowbar really came in handy. The boards groaned in anguish, and there were other squeaking sounds as the rats fled down into the cracks along the side walls. Rusty was glad they fled, otherwise he'd never have had the guts to crawl up there through the opening in the boards and look around. Helen handed him the flashlight, and he used it.

He didn't have to look very far.

The black metal box was sitting there right in front of him. Beyond it lay the thing.

Rusty knew it was Pete Taylor, because it had to be, but there was no way of identification. There wasn't a shred of clothing left, or a shred of flesh, either. The rats had picked him clean, picked him down to the bones. All that was left was a skeleton—a skeleton and a black metal box.

Rusty clawed the box closer, opened it. He saw the bills, bulging in stacks. He smelled the money, smelled it even above the sickening fetor. It smelled good, it smelled of perfume and tenderloin steak and the leathery seat-cover aroma of a shiny new car.

"Find anything?" Helen called. Her voice was trembling.

"Yes," he answered, and his voice was trembling just a little too. "I've got it. Hold the ladder, I'm coming down now."

He was coming down now, and that meant it was time—time to act. He handed her the crowbar and the flashlight, but kept his fingers on the side of the black metal box. He wanted to carry that himself. Then, when he put it down on the floor, and she bent over to look at it, he could pick up a piece of concrete rubble and let her have it.

It was going to be easy. He had everything figured out in advance—everything except the part about handing her the crowbar.

That's what she used to hit him with when he got to the bottom of the ladder. . . .

He must have been out for ten minutes, at least. Anyway, it was long enough for her to find the rope somewhere. Maybe she had kept it in the car. Wherever she got it, she knew how to use it. His wrists and ankles hurt almost as much as the back of his head, where the blood was starting to congeal.

He opened his mouth and discovered that it did no good. She had gagged him tightly with a handkerchief. All he could do was lie there in the rubble on the boathouse floor and watch her pick up the black metal box.

She opened it and laughed.

The flashlight was lying on the floor. In its beam, he could see her face quite plainly. She had taken off her glasses, and he discovered the lenses lying shattered on the floor.

Helen Krauss saw what he was staring at and laughed again.

"I don't need those things any more," she told him. "I never did. It was all part of the act, like letting my hair go black and putting on all this weight. For two years now, I've put on this dumb slob routine, just so nobody'd notice me. When I leave town, nobody's going to pay any attention either. Sometimes it's smart to play dumb, you know?"

Rusty made noises underneath the gag. She thought that was funny, too.

"I suppose you're finally beginning to figure it out," she said. "Mike never meant to pull off any payroll job. Pete Taylor and I had been cheating on him for six months, and he had just begun to suspect. I don't know who told him, or what they said.

"He never said anything to me about it beforehand—just went downtown with his gun to find Pete and kill him. Maybe he meant to kill me too. He never even thought about the money at the time. All he knew was that it would be easy to pick Pete up on payroll day.

"I guess he knocked Pete out and drove him down here, and Pete came to before he died and kept saying he was innocent. At least, Mike told me that much when he did come back.

"I never got a chance to ask where he'd taken Pete or what he'd done with the money. The first thing I did, when Mike came home and said what he'd done, was to cover up for myself. I swore it was all a pack of lies, that Pete and I hadn't done anything wrong. I told him we'd take the money and go away together. I was still selling him on that when the cops came.

"I guess he believed me—because he never cracked during the trial. But I didn't get a chance again to ask where he hid the dough. He couldn't write me from prison, because they censor all the mail. So my only out was to wait—wait until he came back, or someone else came. And that's how it worked out."

Rusty tried to say something, but the gag was too tight.

"Why did I conk you one? For the same reason you were going to conk me. Don't try to deny it—that's what you intended to do, wasn't it? I know the way creeps like you think." Her voice was soft.

She smiled down at him. "I know how you get to thinking when you're a prisoner—because I've been a prisoner myself, for two years— a prisoner in this big body of mine. I've sweated it out for that money, and now I'm leaving. I'm leaving here, leaving the dumb waitress prison I made for myself. I'm going to shed forty pounds and bleach my hair again and go back to being the old Helen Krauss—with fifty-six grand to live it up with.''

Rusty tried just once more. All that came out was a gurgle. ''Don't worry,'' she said, ''they won't find me. And they won't find you for a long, long time. I'm putting that lock back on the door when I go. Besides, there's nothing to tie the two of us together. It's clean as a whistle.''

She turned, and then Rusty stopped gurgling. He hunched forward and kicked out with his bound feet. They caught her right across the back of the knees, and she went down. Rusty rolled across the rubble and raised his feet from the ground, like a flail. They came down on her stomach, and she let out a gasp.

She fell against the boathouse door, and it slammed shut, her own body tight against it. Randy began to kick at her face. In a moment the flashlight rolled off into the rubble and went out, so he kicked in the direction of the gasps. After a while, the moaning stopped, and it was silent in the boathouse.

He listened for her breathing and heard no sound. He rolled over to her and pressed his face against something warm and wet. He shivered and drew back, then pressed again. The unbattered area of her flesh was cold.

He rolled over to the side and tried to free his hands. He worked the rope-ends against the jagged edges of rubble, hoping to feel the strands fray and part. His wrists bled, but the rope held. Her body was wedged against the door, holding it shut—holding him here in the rank darkness.

Rusty knew he had to move her, had to get the door open fast. He had to get out of here. He began to butt his head against her, trying to move her—but she was too solid, too heavy, to budge. He banged into the money box and tried to gurgle at her from under the gag, tried to tell her that she must get up and let them out, that they were both in prison together now, and the money didn't matter. It was all a mistake, he hadn't meant to hurt her or anyone, he just wanted to get out.

But he didn't get out.

After a little while, the rats came back.

There are at least two Sharyn McCrumbs, one who writes darkly poetic books about the New South and the Old South intersecting, and one who writes witty and occasionally nasty comedies about how most of us leave something to be desired as human beings.

Sharyn writes nimbly, gracefully, yet with a style always appropriate to the subject matter. Her infamous novel about science fiction conventions, *Bimbos of the Death Sun*, reads like a collaboration between Dorothy Parker and Donald Westlake.

On some occasions, you see both Sharyn McCrumbs evident in the same piece of fiction—the arch social critic and the forgiving poet. As here.

A Predatory Woman
SHARYN McCRUMB

"She looks a proper murderess, doesn't she?" said Ernie Sleaford, tapping the photo of a bleached blonde. His face bore that derisive grin he reserved for the "puir doggies," his term for unattractive women.

With a self-conscious part of her own more professionally lightened hair, Jackie Duncan nodded. Because she was twenty-seven and petite, she had never been the object of Ernie's derision. When he shouted at her, it was for more professional reasons—a missed photo opportunity or a bit of careless reporting. She picked up the unappealing photograph. "She looks quite tough. One wonders that children would have trusted her in the first place."

"What did they know, poor lambs? We never had a woman like our Erma before, had we?"

Jackie studied the picture, wondering if the face were truly evil, or if their knowledge of its possessor had colored the likeness. Whether or not it was a cruel face, it was certainly a plain one. Erma Bradley

61

had dumpling features with gooseberry eyes, and that look of sullen defensiveness that plain women often have in anticipation of slights to come.

Ernie had marked the photo *Page One*. It was not the sort of female face that usually appeared in the pages of *Stellar*, a tabloid known for its daily photo of Princess Diana, and for its bosomy beauties on page three. A beefy woman with a thatch of badly bleached hair had to earn her way into the tabloids, which Erma Bradley certainly had. Convicted of four child murders in 1966, she was serving a life sentence in Holloway Prison in north London.

Gone, but not forgotten. Because she was Britain's only female serial killer, the tabloids kept her memory green with frequent stories about her, all accompanied by that menacing 1965 photo of the scowling, just-arrested Erma. Most of the recent articles about her didn't even attempt to be plausible: *Erma Bradley: Hitler's Illegitimate Daughter; Children's Ghosts Seen Outside Erma's Cell*; and, the October favorite, *Is Erma Bradley a Vampire?* That last one was perhaps the most apt, because it acknowledged the fact that the public hardly thought of her as a real person anymore; she was just another addition to the pantheon of monsters, taking her place alongside Frankenstein, Dracula, and another overrated criminal, Guy Fawkes. Thinking up new excuses to use the old Erma picture was Ernie Sleaford's specialty. Erma's face was always good for a sales boost.

Jackie Duncan had never done an Erma story. Jackie had been four years old at the time of the infamous trial, and later, with the crimes solved and the killers locked away, the case had never particularly interested her. "I thought it was her boyfriend, Sean Hardie, who actually did the killing," she said, frowning to remember to details of the case.

Stellar's editor sneered at her question. "Hardie? I never thought he had a patch on Erma for toughness. Look at him now. He's completely mental, in a prison hospital, making no more sense than a vegetable marrow. That's how you *ought* to be with the lives of four kids on your conscience. But not our Erma! Got her university degree by telly, didn't she? Learned to talk posh in the cage? And now a bunch of bloody do-gooders have got her out!"

Jackie, who had almost tuned out this tirade as she contemplated her new shade of nail varnish, stared at him with renewed interest. "I hadn't heard that, Sleaford! Are you sure it isn't another of your fairy tales?" She grinned. "*Erma Bradley, Bride of Prince Edward?* That was my favorite."

Ernie had the grace to blush at the reminder of his last Erma headline, but he remained solemn. "S'truth, Jackie. I had it on the quiet from a screw in Holloway. She's getting out next week."

"Go on! It would have been on every news show in Britain by now! Banner headlines in the *Guardian*. Questions asked in the House."

"The prison officials are keeping it dark. They don't want Erma to be pestered by the likes of us upon her release. She wants to be let alone." He smirked. "I had to pay dear for this bit of information, I can tell you."

Jackie smiled. "Poor mean Ernie! Where do I come into it, then?"

"Can't you guess?"

"I think so. You want Erma's own story, no matter what."

"Well, we can write that ourselves in any case. I have Paul working on that already. What I really need is a new picture, Jackie. The old cow hasn't let herself be photographed in twenty years. Wants her privacy, does our Erma. I think *Stellar*'s readers would like to take a butcher's at what Erma Bradley looks like today, don't you?"

"So they don't hire her as the nanny." Jackie let him finish laughing before she turned the conversation round to money.

The cell was beginning to look the way it had when she first arrived. Newly swept and curtainless, it was a ten-by-six-foot rectangle containing a bed, a cupboard, a table and a chair, a wooden wash basin, a plastic bowl and jug, and a bucket. Gone were the posters and the photos of home. Her books were stowed away in a Marks & Spencers shopping bag.

Ruthie, whose small, sharp features earned her the nickname Minx, was sitting on the edge of the bed, watching her pack. "Taking the lot, are you?" she asked cheerfully.

The thin dark woman stared at the array of items on the table. "I suppose not," she said, scowling. She held up a tin of green tooth powder. "Here. D'you want this, then?"

The Minx shrugged and reached for it. "Why not? After all, you're getting out, and I've a few years to go. Will you write to me when you're on the outside?"

"You know that isn't permitted."

The younger woman giggled. "As if that ever stopped you." She reached for another of the items on the bed. "How about your Christmas soap? You can get more on the outside, you know."

She handed it over. "I shan't want freesia soap ever again."

"Taking your posters, love? Anyone would think you'd be sick of them by now."

"I am. I've promised them to Senga." She set the rolled-up posters on the bed beside Ruthie, and picked up a small framed photograph. "Do you want this, then, Minx?"

The little blonde's eyes widened at the sight of the grainy snapshot of a scowling man. "Christ! It's Sean, isn't it? Put it away. I'll be glad when you've taken that out of here."

Erma Bradley smiled and tucked the photograph in among her clothes. "I shall keep this."

Jackie Duncan seldom wore her best silk suit when she conducted interviews, but this time she felt that it would help to look both glamorous and prosperous. Her blond hair, shingled into a stylish bob, revealed shell-shaped earrings of real gold, and her calf leather handbag and shoes were an expensive matched set. It wasn't at all the way a working *Stellar* reporter usually dressed, but it lent Jackie an air of authority and professionalism that she needed in order to profit from this interview.

She looked around the shabby conference room, wondering if Erma Bradley had ever been there, and, if so, where she had sat. In preparation for the new assignment, Jackie had read everything she could find on the Bradley case: the melodramatic book by the BBC journalist; the measured prose of the prosecuting attorney; and a host of articles from more reliable newspapers than *Stellar*. She had begun to be interested in Erma Bradley and her deadly lover, Sean Hardie: *the couple who slays together stays together?* The analyses of the case had made much of the evidence and horror at the thought of child murder, but they had been at a loss to provide motive, and they had been reticent about details of the killings themselves. There was a book in that, and it would earn a fortune for whoever could get the material to write it. Jackie intended to find out more than she had uncovered, but first she had to find Erma Bradley.

Her Sloan Ranger outfit had charmed the old cats in the prison office into letting her in to pursue the story in the first place. The story they thought she was after. Jackie glanced at herself in the mirror. Very useful for impressive old sahibs, this posh outfit. Besides, she thought, why not give the prison birds a bit of a fashion show?

The six inmates, dressed in shapeless outfits of polyester, sprawled in their chairs and stared at her with no apparent interest. One of them was reading a Barbara Cartland novel.

"Hello, girls!" said Jackie in her best nursing home voice. She was used to jollying up old ladies for feature stories, and she decided that this couldn't be much different. "Did they tell you what I'm here for?"

More blank stares, until a heavyset redhead asked, "You ever do it with a woman?"

Jackie ignored her. "I'm here to do a story about what it's like in prison. Here's your chance to complain, if there are things you want changed."

Grudgingly then, they began to talk about the food, and the illogical, unbending rules that governed every part of their lives. The tension eased as they talked, and she could tell that they were becoming more willing to confide in her. Jackie scribbled a few cursory notes to keep them talking. Finally one of them said that she missed her children: Jackie's cue.

As if on impulse, she put down her notepad. "Children!" she said breathlessly. "That reminds me! Wasn't Erma Bradley a prisoner here?"

They glanced at each other. "So?" said the dull-eyed woman with unwashed hair.

A ferrety blonde, who seemed more taken by Jackie's glamour than the older ones, answered eagerly, "I knew her! We were best friends!"

"To say the least, Minx," said the frowsy embezzler from Croyden.

Jackie didn't have to feign interest anymore. "Really?" she said to the one called Minx. "I'd be terrified! What was she like!"

They all began to talk about Erma now.

"A bit reserved," said one. "She never knew who she could trust, because of her rep, you know. A lot of us here have kids of our own, so there was feeling against her. In the kitchen, they used to spit in her food before they took it to her. And sometimes, new girls would go at her to prove they were tough."

"That must have taken nerve!" cried Jackie. "I've seen her pictures!"

"Oh, she didn't look like that anymore!" said Minx. "She'd let her hair go back to its natural dark color, and she was much smaller. Not bad, really. She must have lost fifty pounds since the trial days!"

"Do you have a snapshot of her?" asked Jackie, still doing her best impression of breathless and impressed.

The redhead laid a meaty hand on Minx's shoulder. "Just a minute. What are you really here for?"

Jackie took a deep breath. "I need to find Erma Bradley. Can you help me? I'll pay you."

A few minutes later, Jackie was saying a simpering goodbye to the warden, telling her that she'd have to come back in a few days for a follow-up. She had until then to come up with a way to smuggle in two bottles of Glenlivet: the price on Erma Bradley's head. Ernie would probably make her pay for the liquor out of her own pocket. It would serve him right if she got a good book deal out of it on the side.

The flat could have used a coat of paint, and some better quality furniture, but that could wait. She was used to shabbiness. What she liked best about it was its high ceiling and the big casement window overlooking the moors. From that window you could see nothing but hills and heather and sky; no roads, no houses, no people. After twenty-four years in the beehive of a women's prison, the solitude was blissful. She spent hours each day just staring out that window, knowing that she could walk on the moors whenever she liked, without guards or passes or physical restraints.

Erma Bradley tried to remember if she had ever been alone before. She had lived in a tiny flat with her mother until she finished O levels, and then, when she'd taken the secretarial job at Hadlands, there had been Sean. She had gone into prison at the age of twenty-three, an end to even the right to privacy. She could remember no time when she could have had solitude, to get to know her own likes and dislikes. She had gone from Mum's shadow to Sean's. She kept his picture, and her mother's, not out of love, but as a reminder of the prisons she had endured before Holloway.

Now she was learning that she liked plants, and the music of Sibelius. She liked things to be clean, too. She wondered if she could paint the flat by herself. It would never look clean until she covered those dingy green walls.

She reminded herself that she could have had a house, *if*. If she had given up some of that solitude. Sell your story to a book publisher; sell the film rights to this movie company. Keith, her long-suffering attorney, dutifully passed along all the offers for her consideration. The world seemed willing to throw money at her, but all she wanted was for it to go away. The dowdy but slender Miss Emily Kay, newborn at forty-seven, would manage on her own, with tinned food and second-hand furniture, while the pack of journalists went baying after Erma Bradley, who didn't exist anymore. She wanted solitude. She never thought about those terrible months with Sean, the things they did together. For twenty-four years she had not let herself remember any of it.

Jackie Duncan looked up at the gracefully ornamented stone building, carved into apartments for working-class people. The builders in that gentler age had worked leaf designs into the stonework framing the windows, and they had set gargoyles at a corner of each roof. Jackie made a mental note of this useful detail; yet another monster has been added to the building.

In the worn but genteel hallway, Jackie checked the names on mailboxes to make sure that her information was correct. There it was: E. Kay. She hurried up the stairs with only a moment's thought to the change in herself these past few weeks. When Ernie first gave her the assignment, she might have been fearful of confronting a murderess, or she might have gone upstairs with the camera poised to take the shot just as Erma Bradley opened her door, and then she would have fled. But now she was as anxious to meet the woman as she could be to interview a famous film star. More so, because this celebrity was hers alone. She had not even told Ernie that she had found Erma. This was her show, not *Stellar*'s. Without another thought about what she would say, Jackie knocked at the lair of the beast.

After a few moments, the door opened partway, and a small dark-haired woman peered nervously out at her. The woman was thin, and dressed in a simple green jumper and skirt. She was no longer the brassy blonde of the 'sixties. But the eyes were the same. The face was still Erma Bradley's.

Jackie was brisk. "May I come in, Miss *Kay*? You wouldn't want me to pound on your door calling our your real name, would you?"

The woman fell back and let her enter. "I suppose it wouldn't help to tell you that you're mistaken?" No trace remained of her Midlands accent. She spoke in quiet, cultured tones.

"Not a hope. I swotted for weeks to find you, dear."

"Couldn't you just leave me alone?"

Jackie sat down on the threadbare brown sofa and smiled up at her hostess. "I suppose I could arrange it. I could, for instance, *not* tell the BBC, the tabloids, and the rest of the world what you look like, and where you are."

The woman looked down at her ringless hands. "I haven't any money," she said.

"Oh, but you're worth a packet all the same, aren't you? In all the years you've been locked up, you never said anything except, *I didn't do it,* which is rubbish, because the world knows you did. You taped the Doyle boy's killing on a bloody tape recorder!"

The woman hung her head for a moment, turning away. "What do you want?" she said at last, sitting in the chair by the sofa.

Jackie Duncan touched the other woman's arm. *"I want you to tell me about it."*

"No. I can't. I've forgotten."

"No, you haven't. Nobody could. And that's the book the world wants to read. Not this mealymouthed rubbish the others have written about you. I want you to tell me ever single detail, all the way through. That's the book I want to write." She took a deep breath, and forced a smile. "And in exchange, I'll keep your identity and whereabouts a secret, the way Ursula Bloom did when she interviewed Crippen's mistress in the 'fifties."

Erma Bradley shrugged. "I don't read crime stories," she said.

The light had faded from the big window facing the moors. On the scarred pine table a tape recorder was running, and in the deepening shadows, Erma Bradley's voice rose and fell with weary resignation, punctuated by Jackie's eager questions.

"I don't know," she said again.

"Come on. Think about it. Have a biscuit while you think. Sean didn't have sex with the Allen girl, but did he make love to *you* afterwards? Do you think he got an erection while he was doing the strangling?"

A pause. "I didn't look."

"But you made love after he killed her?"

"Yes."

"On the same bed?"

"But later. A few hours later. After we had taken away the body. It was Sean's bedroom, you see. It's where we always slept."

"Did you picture the child's ghost watching you do it?"

"I was twenty-two. He said— He used to get me drunk—and I—"

"Oh, come on, Erma. There's no bloody jury here. Just tell me if it turned you on to watch Sean throttling kids. When he did it, were both of you naked, or just him?"

"Please, I—Please!"

"All right, Erma. I can have the BBC here in time for the wake-up news."

"Just him."

An hour later. "Do stop sniveling, Erma. You lived through it once, didn't you? What's the harm in talking about it? They can't try you again. Now come on, dear, answer the question."

"Yes. The little boy—Brian Doyle—he was quite brave, really. Kept saying he had to take care of his mum, because she was divorced now, and asking us to let him go. He was only eight, and quite small. He even offered to fight us if we'd untie him. When Sean was getting the masking tape out of the cupboard, I went up to him, and I whispered to him to let the boy go, but he ..."

"There you go again, Erma. Now, I've got to shut the machine off again while you get hold of yourself."

She was alone now. At last, the reporter woman was gone. Just before eleven, she had scooped up her notes and her tape recorder, and the photos of the dead children she had brought from the photo archives, and she'd gone away, promising to return in a few days to "put the finishing touches on the interview." The dates and places and forensic details she could get from the other sources, she'd said.

The reporter had gone, and the room was empty, but Miss Emily Kay wasn't alone anymore. Now Erma Bradley had got in as well.

She knew, though, that no other journalists would come. This one, Jackie, would keep her secret well enough, but only to ensure the exclusivity of her own book. Other than that, Miss Emily Kay would be allowed to enjoy her freedom in the shabby little room overlooking the moors. But it wasn't a pleasant retreat any longer, now that she wasn't alone. Erma had brought the ghosts back with her.

Somehow the events of twenty-five years ago had become more real when she told them than when she lived them. It had been so confused back then. Sean drank a lot, and he liked her to keep him company in that. And it happened so quickly the first time, and then there was no turning back. But she never let herself think about it. It was Sean's doing, she would tell herself, and then part of her mind would close right down, and she would turn her attention to something else. At the trial, she had thought about the hatred that she could almost touch, flaring at her from nearly everyone in the courtroom. She couldn't think then, for if she broke down, they would win. They never put her on the stand. She answered no questions, except to say when a microphone was thrust in her face, *I didn't do it*. And then later in prison there were adjustments to make, and bad times with the other inmates to be faced. She didn't need a lot of sentiment dragging her down as well. *I didn't do it* came to have a truth for her: it meant, I am no longer the somebody who did that. I am small, and thin, and well-spoken. The ugly, ungainly monster is gone.

But now she had testified. Her own voice had conjured up the images of Sarah Allen calling out for her mother, and of Brian Doyle, offering to sell his bike to ransom himself, for his mum's sake. The hatchet-faced blonde, who had told them to shut up, who had held them down ... she was here. And she was going to live here, too, with the sounds of weeping, and the screams. And every tread on the stair would be Sean, bringing home another little lad for a wee visit.

I didn't do it, she whispered. And it had come to have another meaning. *I didn't do it*. Stop Sean Hardie from hurting them. Go to the police. Apologize to the parents during the years in prison. Kill myself from the shame of it. *I didn't do it*, she whispered again. *But I should have.*

Ernie Sleaford was more deferential to her now. When he heard about the new book, and the size of her advance, he realized that she was a player, and he had begun to treat her with a new deference. He had even offered her a raise, in case she was thinking of quitting. But she wasn't going to quit. She quite enjoyed her work. Besides, it was so amusing now to see him stand up for her when she came into his grubby little office.

"We'll need a picture for the front page, love," he said in his most civil tones. "Would you mind if Denny took your picture, or is there one you'd rather use?"

Jackie shrugged. "Let him take one. I just had my hair done. So I make the front page as well?"

"Oh yes. We're devoting the whole page to Erma Bradley's suicide, and we want a sidebar of your piece: *I Was the Last to See the Monster Alive*. It will make a nice contrast. Your picture beside pudding-faced Erma."

"I thought she looked all right for forty-seven. Didn't the picture I got turn out all right?"

Ernie looked shocked. "We're not using that one, Jackie. We want to remember her the way she *was*. A vicious ugly beastie in contrast to a pure young thing like yourself. Sort of a moral statement, like."

The cliché is that the eighties belonged to female writers. And while that's true, there's a slightly patronizing air to that surmise—as if they were let through the gates only because it was Their Turn. As Linda Barnes and a dozen others proved, most of the women were Let In on the basis of sheer merit. Linda is a modernist in nearly every respect. While some of her plotting comes from the mysteries of other eras, her dialogue, pacing, and sardonic comments are definitely of the eighties and nineties.

Lucky Penny
LINDA BARNES

Lieutenant Mooney made me dish it all out for the record. He's a good cop, if such an animal exists. We used to work the same shift before I decided—wrongly—that there was room for a lady P.I. in this town. Who knows? With this case under my belt, maybe business'll take a 180-degree spin, and I can quit driving a hack.

See, I've already written the official report for Mooney and the cops, but the kind of stuff they wanted: date, place, and time, cold as ice and submitted in triplicate, doesn't even start to tell the tale. So I'm doing it over again, my way.

Don't worry, Mooney. I'm not gonna file this one.

The Thayler case was still splattered across the front page of the *Boston Globe*. I'd soaked it up with my midnight coffee and was puzzling it out—my cab on automatic pilot, my mind on crime—when the mad tea party began.

"Take your next right, sister. Then pull over, and douse the lights. Quick!"

I heard the bastard all right, but it must have taken me thirty seconds or so to react. Something hard rapped on the cab's dividing shield. I didn't bother turning around. I hate staring down gun barrels.

I said, "Jimmy Cagney, right? No, your voice is too high. Let me guess, don't tell me—"

"Shut up!"

"*Kill* the lights, *turn off* the lights, okay. But *douse* the lights? You've been tuning in too many old gangster flicks."

"I hate a mouthy broad," the guy snarled. I kid you not.

"*Broad*," I said. "Christ! *Broad?* You trying to grow hair on your balls?"

"Look, I mean it, lady!"

"*Lady's* better. Now you wanna vacate my cab and go rob a phone booth?" My heart was beating like a tin drum, but I didn't let my voice shake, and all the time I was gabbing at him, I kept trying to catch his face in the mirror. He must have been crouching way back on the passenger side. I could't see a damn thing.

"I want all your dough," he said.

Who can you trust? This guy was a spiffy dresser: charcoal-gray three-piece suit and rep tie, no less. And picked up in front on the swank Copley Plaza. I looked like I needed the bucks more than he did, and I'm no charity case. A woman can make good tips driving a hack in Boston. Oh, she's gotta take precautions, all right. When you can't smell a disaster fare from thirty feet, it's time to quit. I pride myself on my judgment. I'm careful. I always know where the police check-points are, so I can roll my cab past and flash the old lights if a guy starts acting up. This dude fooled me cold.

I was ripped. Not only had I been conned, I had a considerable wad to give away. It was near the end of the shift, and like I said, I do all right. I've got a lot of regulars. Once you see me, you don't forget me—or my cab.

It's gorgeous. Part of my inheritance. A '59 Chevy, shiny as new, kept on blocks in a heated garage by the proverbial dotty old lady. It's the pits of the design world. Glossy blue with those giant chromium fins. Restrained decor: just the phone number and a few gilt curlicues on the door. I was afraid all my old pals at the police department would pull me over for minor traffic violations if I went whole hog and painted "Carlotta's Cab" in ornate script on the hood. Some do it anyway.

So where the hell were all the cops now? Where are they when you need 'em?

He told me to shove the cash through that little hole they leave for the passenger to pass the fare forward. I told him he had it backwards. He didn't laugh. I shoved bills.

"Now the change," the guy said. Can you imagine the nerve?

I must have cast my eyes up to heaven. I do that a lot these days.

"I mean it." He rapped the plastic shield with the shiny barrel of his gun. I checked it out this time. Funny how big a little .22 looks when it's pointed just right.

I fished in my pockets for change, emptied them.

"Is that all?"

"You want the gold cap on my left front molar?" I said.

"Turn around," the guy barked. "Keep both hands on the steering wheel. High."

I heard jingling, then a quick intake of breath.

"Okay," the crook said, sounding happy as a clam. "I'm gonna take my leave—"

"Good. Don't call this cab again."

"Listen!" The gun tapped. "You cool it here for ten minutes. And I mean frozen. Don't twitch. Don't blow your nose. Then take off."

"Gee, thanks."

"Thank *you*," he said politely. The door slammed.

At times like that, you just feel ridiculous. You *know* the guy isn't going to hang around, waiting to see whether you're big on insubordination. *But*, he might. And who wants to tangle with a .22 slug? I rate pretty high on insubordination. That's why I messed up as a cop. I figured I'd give him two minutes to get lost. Meantime I listened.

Not much traffic goes by those little streets on Beacon Hill at one o'clock on a Wednesday morn. Too residential. So I could hear the guy's footsteps tap along the pavement. About ten steps back, he stopped. Was he the one in a million who'd wait to see if I turned around? I heard a funny kind of whooshing noise. Not loud enough to make me jump, and anything much louder than the ticking of my watch would have put me through the roof. Then the footsteps patted on, straight back and out of hearing.

One minute more. The only saving grace of the situation was the location: District One. That's Mooney's district. Nice guy to talk to.

I took a deep breath, hoping it would have an encore, and pivoted quickly, keeping my head low. Makes you feel stupid when you do that and there's no one around.

I got out and strolled to the corner, stuck my head around a building kind of cautiously. Nothing, of course.

I backtracked. Ten steps, then whoosh. Along the sidewalk stood one of those new "Keep Beacon Hill Beautiful" trash cans, the kind with the swinging lid. I gave it a shove as I passed. I could just as easily have kicked it; I was in that kind of funk.

Whoosh, it said, just as pretty as could be.

Breaking into one of those trash cans is probably tougher than busting into your local bank vault. Since I didn't even have a dime left to fiddle the screws on the lid, I was forced to deface city property. I got the damn thing open and dumped the contents on somebody's front lawn, smack in the middle of a circle of light from one of those snooty Beacon Hill gas streetlamps.

Halfway through the whiskey bottles, wadded napkins, and beer cans, I made my discovery. I was doing a thorough search. If you're going to stink like garbage anyway, why leave anything untouched, right? So I was opening all the brown bags—you know, the good old brown lunch-and-bottle bags—looking for a clue. My most valuable find so far had been the moldy rind of a bologna sandwich. Then I hit it big: one neatly creased bag stuffed full of cash.

To say I was stunned is to entirely underestimate how I felt as I crouched there, knee-deep in garbage, my jaw hanging wide. I don't know what I'd expected to find. Maybe the guy's gloves. Or his hat, if he'd wanted to get rid of it fast in order to melt back into anonymity. I pawed through the rest of the debris. My change was gone.

I was so befuddled I left the trash right on the front lawn. There's probably still a warrant out for my arrest.

District One Headquarters is off the beaten path, over on New Sudbury Street. I would have called first, if I'd had a dime.

One of the few things I'd enjoyed about being a cop was gabbing with Mooney. I like driving a cab better, but, face it, most of my fares aren't scintillating conversationalists. The Red Sox and the weather usually covers it. Talking to Mooney was so much fun, I wouldn't even consider dating him. Lots of guys are good at sex, but conversation—now there's an art form.

Mooney, all six-foot-four, 240 linebacker pounds of him, gave me the glad eye when I waltzed in. He hasn't given up trying. Keeps telling me he talks even better in bed.

"Nice hat," was all he said, his big fingers pecking at the typewriter keys.

I took it off and shook out my hair. I wear an old slouch cap when I drive to keep people from saying the inevitable. One jerk even misquoted Yeats at me: "Only God, my dear, could love you for yourself alone and not your long red hair." Since I'm seated when I drive, he missed the chance to ask me how the weather is up here. I'm six-one in my stocking feet and skinny enough to make every inch count twice. I've got a wide forehead, green eyes, and a pointy chin. If you want to be nice about my nose, you say it's got character.

Thirty's still hovering in my future. It's part of Mooney's past.

I told him I had a robbery to report and his dark eyes steered me to a chair. He leaned back and took a puff of one of his low-tar cigarettes. He can't quite give 'em up, but he feels guilty as hell about 'em.

When I got to the part about the bag in the trash, Mooney lost his sense of humor. He crushed a half-smoked butt in a crowded ashtray.

"Know why you never made it as a cop?" he said.

"Didn't brown-nose enough."

"You got no sense of proportion! Always going after crack-pot stuff!"

"Christ, Mooney, aren't you interested? Some guy heists a cab, at gunpoint, then tosses the money. Aren't you the least bit *intrigued*?"

"I'm a cop, Ms. Carlyle. I've got to be more than intrigued. I've got murders, bank robberies, assaults—"

"Well, excuse me. I'm just a poor citizen reporting a crime. Trying to help—"

"Want to help, Carlotta? Go away." He stared at the sheet of paper in the typewriter and lit another cigarette. "Or dig me up something on the Thayler case."

"You working that sucker?"

"Wish to hell I wasn't."

I could see his point. It's tough enough trying to solve any murder, but when your victim is *the* Jennifer (Mrs. Justin) Thayler, wife of the famed Harvard Law prof, and the society reporters are breathing down your neck along with the usual crime-beat scribblers, you got a special kind of problem.

"So who did it?" I asked.

Mooney put his size twelves up on his desk. "Colonel Mustard in the library with the candlestick! How the hell do I know? Some scumbag housebreaker. The lady of the house interrupted his haul. Probably didn't mean to hit her that hard. He must have freaked when he saw all the blood, 'cause he left some of the ritziest stereo equipment this side of heaven, plus enough silverware to blind your average hophead. He snatched most of old man Thayler's goddam idiot artworks, collections, collectibles—whatever the hell you call 'em—which ought to set him up for the next few hundred years, if he's smart enough to get rid of them."

"Alarm system?"

"Yeah, they had one. Looks like Mrs. Thayler forgot to turn it on. According to the maid, she had a habit of forgetting just about anything after a martini or three."

"Think the maid's in on it?"

"Christ, Carlotta. There you go again. No witnesses. No fingerprints. Servants asleep. Husband asleep. We've got word out to all the fences here and in New York that we want this guy. The pawnbrokers know the stuff's hot. We're checking out known art thieves and shady museums—"

"Well, don't let me keep you from your serious business," I said, getting up to go. "I'll give you the collar when I find out who robbed my cab."

"Sure," he said. His fingers started playing with the typewriter again.

"Wanna bet on it?" Betting's an old custom with Mooney and me.

"I'm not gonna take the few piddling bucks you earn with that ridiculous car."

"Right you are, boy. I'm gonna take the money the city pays you to be unimaginative! Fifty bucks I nail him within the week."

Mooney hates to be called "boy." He hates to be called "unimaginative." I hate to hear my car called "ridiculous." We shook hands on the deal. Hard.

Chinatown's about the only chunk of Boston that's alive after midnight. I headed over to Yee Hong's for a bowl of wonton soup.

The service was the usual low-key, slow-motion routine. I used a newspaper as a shield; if you're really involved in the *Wall Street Journal*, the casual male may think twice before deciding he's the answer to your prayers. But I didn't read a single stock quote. I tugged at strands of my hair, a bad habit of mine. Why would somebody rob me and then toss the money away?

Solution Number One: He didn't. The trash bin was some mob drop, and the money I'd found in the trash had absolutely nothing to do with the money filched from my cab. Except that it was the same amount—and that was too big a coincidence for me to swallow.

Two: The cash I'd found was counterfeit and this was a clever way of getting it into circulation. Nah. Too baroque entirely. How the hell would the guy know I was the pawing-through-the-trash type?

Three: It was a training session. Some fool had used me to perfect his robbery technique. Couldn't he learn from TV like the rest of the crooks?

Four: It was a frat hazing. Robbing a hack at gunpoint isn't exactly in the same league as swallowing goldfish.

I closed my eyes.

My face came to a fortunate halt about an inch above a bowl of steaming broth. That's when I decided to pack it in and head for home. Wonton soup is lousy for the complexion.

I checked out the log I keep in the Chevy, totaled my fares: $4.82 missing, all in change. A very reasonable robbery.

By the time I got home, the sleepiness had passed. You know how it is: one moment you're yawning, the next your eyes won't close. Usually happens when my head hits the pillow; this time I didn't even make it that far. What woke me up was the idea that my robber hadn't meant to steal a thing. Maybe he'd left me something instead. You know, something hot, cleverly concealed. Something he could pick up in a few weeks, after things cooled off.

I went over that backseat with a vengeance, but I didn't find anything besides old Kleenex and bent paperclips. My brainstorm wasn't too clever after all. I mean, if the guy wanted to use my cab as a hiding place, why advertise by pulling a five-and-dime robbery?

I sat in the driver's seat, tugged my hair, and stewed. What did I have to go on? The memory of a nervous thief who talked like a B movie and stole only change. Maybe a mad toll-booth collector.

I live in a Cambridge dump. In any other city, I couldn't sell the damned thing if I wanted to. Here, I turn real estate agents away daily. The key to my home's value is the fact that I can hoof it to Harvard Square in five minutes. It's a seller's market for tarpaper shacks within walking distance of the Square. Under a hundred thou only if the plumbing's outside.

It took me a while to get in the door. I've got about five locks on it. Neighborhood's popular with thieves as well as gentry. I'm neither. I inherited the house from my weird Aunt Bea, all paid for. I consider the property taxes my rent, and the rent's getting steeper all the time.

I slammed my log down on the dining room table. I've got rooms galore in that old house, rent a couple of them to Harvard students. I've got my own office on the second floor, but I do most of my work at the dining room table. I like the view of the refrigerator.

I started over from square one. I called Gloria. She's the late-night dispatcher for the Independent Taxi Owners Association. I've never seen her, but her voice is as smooth as mink oil and I'll bet we get a lot of calls from guys who just want to hear her say she'll pick 'em up in five minutes.

"Gloria, it's Carlotta."

"Hi, babe. You been pretty popular today."

"Was I popular at one-thirty-five this morning?"

"Huh?"

"I picked up a fare in front of the Copley Plaza at one-thirty-five. Did you hand that one out to all comers or did you give it to me solo?"

"Just a sec." I could hear her charming the pants off some caller in the background. Then she got back to me.

"I just gave him to you, babe. He asked for the lady in the '59 Chevy. Not a lot of those on the road."

"Thanks, Gloria."

"Trouble" she asked.

"Is mah middle name," I twanged. We both laughed and I hung up before she got a chance to cross-examine me.

So. The robber wanted my cab. I wished I'd concentrated on his face instead of his snazzy clothes. Maybe it was somebody I knew, some jokester in mid-prank. I killed that idea; I don't know anybody who'd pull a stunt like that, at gun-point and all. I don't want to know anybody like that.

Why rob my cab, then toss the dough?

I pondered sudden religious conversion. Discarded it. Maybe my robber was some perpetual screwup who'd ditched the cash by mistake.

Or . . . maybe he got exactly what he wanted. Maybe he desperately desired my change.

Why?

Because my change was special, valuable beyond its $4.82 replacement cost.

So how would somebody know my change was valuable?

Because he'd given it to me himself, earlier in the day.

"Not bad," I said out loud. "Not bad." It was the kind of reasoning they'd bounced me off the police force for, what my so-called superiors termed the "fevered product of an overimaginative mind." I leapt at it because it was the only explanation I could think of. I do like life to make some sort of sense.

I pored over my log. I keep pretty good notes: where I pick up a fare, where I drop him, whether he's a hailer or a radio call.

First, I ruled out all the women. That made the task slightly less impossible: sixteen suspects down from thirty-five. Then I yanked my hair and stared at the blank white porcelain of the refrigerator door. Got up and made myself a sandwich: ham, Swiss cheese, salami, lettuce and tomato, on rye. Ate it. Stared at the porcelain some more until the suspects started coming into focus.

Five of the guys were just plain fat and one was decidedly on the hefty side; I'd felt like telling them all to walk. Might do them some good, might bring on a heart attack. I crossed them all out. Making a thin person look plump is hard enough; it's damn near impossible to make a fatty look thin.

Then I considered my regulars: Jonah Ashley's a tiny blond southern gent; muscle-bound "just-call-me-Harold" at Long-fellow Place; Dr. Homewood getting his daily ferry from Beth Israel to MGH; Marvin of the gay bars; and Professor Dickerman, Harvard's answer to Berkeley's sixties radicals.

I crossed them all off. I could see Dickerman holding up the First Filthy Capitalist Bank, or disobeying civilly at Seabrook, even blowing up an oil company or two. But my mind boggled at the thought of the great liberal Dickerman robbing some poor cabbie. It would be like Robin Hood joining the sheriff of Nottingham on some particularly rotten peasant swindle. Then they'd both rape Maid Marian and go off pals together.

Dickerman *was* a lousy tipper. That ought to be a crime.

So what did I have? Eleven out of sixteen guys cleared without leaving my chair. Me and Sherlock Holmes, the famous armchair detectives.

I'm stubborn; that was one of my good cop traits. I stared at that log till my eyes bugged out. I remembered two of the five pretty easily; they were handsome and I'm far from blind. The first had one of those elegant bony faces and far-apart eyes. He was taller than my bandit. I'd ceased eyeballing him when I noticed the ring on his left hand; I never fuss with the married kind. The other one was built, a weight lifter. Not an Arnold Schwarzenegger extremist, but built. I think I'd have noticed that bod on my bandit. Like I said, I'm not blind.

That left three.

Okay. I closed my eyes. Who had I picked up at the Hyatt on Memorial Drive? Yeah, that was the salesman guy, the one who looked so uncomfortable that I'd figured he'd been hoping to ask his cabbie for a few pointers concerning the best skirt-chasing areas in our fair city. Too low a voice. Too broad in the beam.

The log said I'd picked up a hailer at Kenmore Square when I'd let out the salesman. Ah, yes, a talker. The weather, mostly. Don't you think it's dangerous for you to be driving a cab? Yeah, I remembered him, all right: a fatherly type, clasping a briefcase, heading to the financial district. Too old.

Down to one. I was exhausted but not the least bit sleepy. All I had to do was remember who I'd picked up on Beacon near Charles. A hailer. Before five o'clock, which was fine by me because I wanted to be long gone before rush hour gridlocked the city. I'd gotten onto Storrow and taken him along the river into Newton Center. Dropped him off at the Bay Bank Middlesex, right before closing time. It was coming back. Little nervous guy. Pegged him as an accountant when I'd let him out at the bank. Measly, undernourished soul. Skinny as a rail, stooped, with pits left from teenage acne.

Shit. I let my head sink down onto the dining room table when I realized what I'd done. I'd ruled them all out, every one. So much for my brilliant deductive powers.

I retired to my bedroom, disgusted. Not only had I lost $4.82 in assorted alloy metals, I was going to lose fifty dollars to Mooney. I stared at myself in the mirror, but what I was really seeing was the round hole at the end of a .22, held in a neat, gloved hand.

Somehow, the gloves made me feel better. I'd remembered another detail about my piggy-bank robber. I consulted the mirror and kept the recall going. A hat. The guy wore a hat. Not like my cap, but like a hat out of a forties gangster flick. I had one of those: I'm a sucker for hats. I plunked it on my head, jamming my hair up underneath—and I drew in my breath sharply.

A shoulder-padded jacket, a slim build, a low slouched hat. Gloves. Boots with enough heel to click as he walked away. Voice? High. Breathy, almost whispered. Not unpleasant. Accentless. No Boston *r*.

I had a man's jacket and a couple of ties in my closet. Don't ask. They may have dated from as far back as my ex-husband, but not necessarily so. I slipped into the jacket, knotted the tie, tilted the hat down over one eye.

I'd have trouble pulling it off. I'm skinny, but my build is decidedly female. Still, I wondered—enough to traipse back downstairs, pull a chicken leg out of the fridge, go back to the log, and review the feminine possibilities. Good thing I did.

Everything clicked. One lady fit the bill exactly: mannish walk and clothes, tall for a woman. And I was in luck. While I'd picked her up in Harvard Square, I'd dropped her at a real address, a house in Brookline: 782 Mason Terrace, at the top of Corey Hill.

JoJo's garage opens at seven. That gave me a big two hours to sleep. I took my beloved car in for some repair work it really didn't need yet and sweet-talked JoJo into giving me a loaner. I needed a hack, but not mine. Only trouble with that Chevy is it's too damn conspicuous.

I figured I'd lose way more than fifty bucks staking out Mason Terrace. I also figured it would be worth it to see old Mooney's face.

She was regular as clockwork, a dream to tail. Eight-thirty-seven every morning, she got a ride to the Square with a next-door neighbor. Took a cab home at five-fifteen. A working woman. Well, she couldn't make much of a living from robbing hacks and dumping the loot in the garbage.

I was damn curious by now. I knew as soon as I looked her over that she was the one, but she seemed so blah, so *normal*. She must have been five-seven or -eight, but the way she stooped, she didn't look tall. Her hair was long and brown with a lot of blond in it, the kind of hair that would have been terrific loose and wild, like a horse's mane. She tied it back with a scarf. A brown scarf. She wore suits. Brown suits. She had a tiny nose, brown eyes under pale eyebrows, a sharp chin. I never saw her smile. Maybe what she needed was a shrink, not a session with Mooney. Maybe she'd done it for the excitement. God knows, if I had her routine, her job, I'd probably be dressing up like King Kong and assaulting skyscrapers.

See, I followed her to work. It wasn't even tricky. She trudged the same path, went in the same entrance to Harvard Yard, probably walked the same number of steps every morning. Her name was Marcia Heidegger and she was a secretary in the admissions office of the college of fine arts.

I got friendly with one of her coworkers.

There was this guy typing away like mad at a desk in her office. I could just see him from the side window. He had grad student written all over his face. Longish wispy hair. Gold-rimmed glasses. Serious. Given to deep sighs and bright velour V necks. Probably writing his thesis on "Courtly Love and the Theories of Chrétien de Troyes."

I latched onto him at Bailey's the day after I'd tracked Lady Heidegger to her Harvard lair.

Too bad Roger was so short. Most short guys find it hard to believe that I'm really trying to pick them up. They look for ulterior motives. Not the Napoleon type of short guy; he assumes I've been waiting years for a chance to dance with a guy who doesn't have to bend to stare down my cleavage. But Roger was no Napoleon. So I had to engineer things a little.

I got into line ahead of him and ordered, after long deliberation, a BLT on toast. While the guy made it up and shoved it on a plate with three measly potato chips and a silver of pickle you could barely see, I searched through my wallet, opened my change purse, counted out silver, got to $1.60 on the last five pennies. The counterman sang out, "That'll be a buck eighty-five." I pawed through my pockets, found a nickel, two pennies. The line was growing restive. I concentrated on looking like a damsel in need of a knight, a tough task for a woman over six feet.

Roger (I didn't know he was Roger then) smiled ruefully and passed over a quarter. I was effusive in my thanks. I sat at a table for two, and when he'd gotten his tray (ham-and-cheese and a strawberry ice cream soda), I motioned him into my extra chair.

He was a sweetie. Sitting down, he forgot the difference in our height, and decided I might be someone he could talk to. I encouraged him. I hung shamelessly on his every word. A Harvard man, imagine that. We got around slowly, ever so slowly, to his work at the admissions. What kind of people did he work with? Were they congenial? What was the atmosphere like? Was it a big office? How many people? Men? Women? Any soulmates? Readers? Or just, you know, office people?

According to him, every soul he worked with was brain dead. I interrupted a stream of complaint with "Gee, I know somebody who works for Harvard. I wonder if you know her."

"It's a big place," he said, hoping to avoid the whole endless business.

"I met her at a party. Always meant to look her up." I searched through my bag, found a scrap of paper and pretended to read Marcia Heidegger's name off it.

"Marcia? Geez, I work with Marcia. Same office."

"Do you think she likes her work? I mean I got some strange vibes from her," I said. I actually said "strange vibes" and he didn't laugh his head off. People in the Square say things like that and other people take them seriously.

His face got conspiratorial, of all things, and he leaned closer to me.

"You want it, I bet you could get Marcia's job."

"You mean it?" What a compliment—a place for me among the brain dead.

"She's gonna get fired if she doesn't snap out of it."

"Snap out of what?"

"It was bad enough working with her when she first came over. She's one of those crazy neat people, can't stand to see papers lying on a desktop, you know? She almost threw out the first chapter of my thesis!"

I made a suitably horrified noise and he went on.

"Well, you know, about Marcia, it's kind of tragic. She doesn't talk about it."

But he was dying to.

"Yes?" I said, as if he needed egging on.

He lowered his voice. "She used to work for Justin Thayler over at the law school, that guy in the news, whose wife got killed. You know, her work hasn't been worth shit since it happened. She's always on the phone, talking real soft, hanging up if anybody comes in the room. I mean, you'd think she was in love with the guy or something, the way she. . . ."

I don't remember what I said. For all I know, I may have volunteered to type his thesis. But I got rid of him somehow and then I scooted around the corner of Church Street and found a pay phone and dialed Mooney.

"Don't tell me," he said. "Somebody mugged you, but they only took your trading stamps."

"I have just one question for you, Moon."

"I accept. A June wedding, but I'll have to break it to Mother gently."

"Tell me what kind of junk Justin Thayler collected."

I could hear him breathing into the phone.

"Just tell me," I said, "for curiosity's sake."

"You onto something, Carlotta?"

"I'm curious, Mooney. And you're not the only source of information in the world."

"Thayler collected Roman stuff. Antiques. And I mean old. Artifacts, statues—"

"Coins?"

"Whole mess of them."

"Thanks."

"Carlotta—"

I never did find out what he was about to say because I hung up. Rude, I know. But I had things to do. And it was better Mooney shouldn't know what they were, because they came under the heading of illegal activities.

When I knocked at the front door of the Mason Terrace house at 10:00 A.M. the next day, I was dressed in dark slacks, a white blouse, and my old police department hat. I looked very much like the guy who reads your gas meter. I've never heard of anyone being arrested for impersonating the gasman. I've never heard of anyone really giving the gasman a second look. He fades into the background and that's exactly what I wanted to do.

I knew Marcia Heidegger wouldn't be home for hours. Old reliable had left for the Square at her usual time, precise to the minute. but I wasn't 100 percent sure Marcia lived alone. Hence the gasman. I could knock on the door and check it out.

Those Brookline neighborhoods kill me. Act sneaky and the neighbors call the cops in twenty seconds, but walk right up to the front door, knock, talk to yourself while you're sticking a shim in the crack of the door, let yourself in, and nobody does a thing. Boldness is all.

The place wasn't bad. Three rooms, kitchen and bath, light and airy. Marcia was incredibly organized, obsessively neat, which meant I had to keep track of where everything was and put it back just so. There was no clutter in the woman's life. The smell of coffee and toast lingered, but if she'd eaten breakfast, she'd already washed, dried, and put away the dishes. The morning paper had been read and tossed in the trash. The mail was sorted in one of those plastic accordion files. I mean, she folded her underwear like origami.

Now coins are hard to look for. They're small; you can hide 'em anywhere. So this search took me one hell of a long time. Nine out of ten women hide things that are dear to them in the bedroom. They keep their finest jewelry closest to the bed, sometimes in the nightstand, sometimes right under the mattress. That's where I started.

Marcia had a jewelry box on top of her dresser. I felt like hiding it for her. She had some nice stuff and a burglar could have made quite a haul with no effort.

The next favorite place for women to stash valuables is the kitchen. I sifted through her flour. I removed every Kellogg's Rice Krispy from the giant economy-sized box—and returned it. I went though her place like no burglar ever will. When I say thorough, I mean thorough.

I found four odd things. A neatly squared pile of clippings from the *Globe* and the *Herald*, all the articles about the Thayler killing. A manila envelope containing five different safe-deposit-box keys. A Tupperware container full of superstitious junk, good luck charms mostly, the kind of stuff I'd never have associated with a straight-arrow like Marcia: rabbits' feet galore, a little leather bag on a string that looked like some kind of voodoo charm, a pendant in the shape of a cross surmounted by a hook, and, I swear to God, a pack of worn tarot cards. Oh, yes, and a .22 automatic, looking a lot less threatening stuck in an ice cube tray. I took the bullets; the loaded gun threatened a defenseless box of Breyers' mint chocolate-chip ice cream.

I left everything else just the way I'd found it and went home. And tugged my hair. And stewed. And brooded. And ate half the stuff in the refrigerator, I kid you not.

At about one in the morning, it all made blinding, crystal-clear sense.

The next afternoon, at five-fifteen, I made sure I was the cabbie who picked up Marcia Heidegger in Harvard Square. Now cabstands have the most rigid protocol since Queen Victoria; you do not grab a fare out of turn or your fellow cabbies are definitely not amused. There was nothing for it but bribing the ranks. This bet with Mooney was costing me plenty.

I got her. She swung open the door and gave the Mason Terrace number. I grunted, kept my face turned front, and took off.

Some people really watch where you're going in a cab, scared to death you'll take them a block out of their way and squeeze them for an extra nickel. Others just lean back and dream. She was a dreamer, thank God. I was almost at District One Headquarters before she woke up.

"Excuse me," she said, polite as ever, "that's Mason Terrace in *Brookline*."

"Take the next right, pull over, and douse your lights," I said in a low Bogart voice. My imitation was not that good, but it got the point across. Her eyes widened and she made an instinctive grab for the door handle.

"Don't try it, lady," I Bogied on. "You think I'm dumb enough to take you in alone? There's a cop car behind us, just waiting for you to make a move."

Her hand froze. She was a sap for movie dialogue.

"Where's the cop?" was all she said on the way up to Mooney's office.

"What cop?"

"The one following us."

"You have touching faith in our law-enforcement system," I said.

She tried to bolt, I kid you not. I've had experience with runners a lot trickier than Marcia. I grabbed her in approved cop hold number three and marched her into Mooney's office.

He actually stopped typing and raised an eyebrow, an expression of great shock for Mooney.

"Citizen's arrest," I said.

"Charges?"

"Petty theft. Commission of a felony using a firearm." I rattled off a few more charges, using the numbers I remembered from cop school.

"This woman is crazy," Marcia Heidegger said with all the dignity she could muster.

"Search her," I said. "Get a matron in here. I want my four dollars and eighty-two cents back."

Mooney looked like he agreed with Marcia's opinion of my mental state. He said, "Wait up, Carlotta. You'd have to be able to identify that four dollars and eighty-two cents as yours. Can you do that? Quarters are quarters. Dimes are dimes."

"One of the coins she took was quite unusual," I said. "I'm sure I'd be able to identify it."

"Do you have any objection to displaying the change in your purse?" Mooney said to Marcia. He got me mad the way he said it, like he was humoring an idiot.

"Of course not," old Marcia said, cool as a frozen daquiri.

"That's because she's stashed it somewhere else, Mooney," I said patiently. "She used to keep it in her purse, see. But then she goofed. She handed it over to a cabbie in her change. She should have just let it go, but she panicked because it was worth a pile and she was just baby-sitting it for someone else. So when she got it back, she hid it somewhere. Like in her shoe. Didn't you ever carry your lucky penny in your shoe?"

"No," Mooney said. "Now, Miss—"

"Heidegger," I said clearly. "Marcia Heidegger. She used to work at Harvard Law School." I wanted to see if Mooney picked up on it, but he didn't. He went on: "This can be taken care of with a minimum of fuss. If you'll agree to be searched by—"

"I want to see my lawyer," she said.

"For four dollars and eighty-two cents?" he said.

"It'll cost you more than that to get your lawyer up here."

"Do I get my phone call or not?"

Mooney shrugged wearily and wrote up the charge sheet. Called a cop to take her to the phone.

He got Jo Ann, which was good. Under cover of our old-friend-long-time-no-see greetings, I whispered in her ear.

"You'll find it fifty well spent," I said to Mooney when we were alone.

Jo Ann came back, shoving Marcia slightly ahead of her. She plunked her prisoner down in one of Mooney's hard wooden chairs and turned to me, grinning from ear to ear.

"Got it?" I said. "Good for you."

"What's going on?" Mooney said.

"She got real clumsy on the way to the pay phone," Jo Ann said. "Practically fell on the floor. Got up with her right hand clenched tight. When we got to the phone, I offered to drop her dime for her. She wanted to do it herself. I insisted and she got clumsy again. Somehow this coin got kicked clear across the floor."

She held it up. The coin could have been a dime, except the color was off: warm, rosy gold instead of dead silver. How I missed it the first time around I'll never know.

"What the hell is that?" Mooney said.

"What kind of coins were in Justin Thayler's collection?" I asked. "Roman?"

Marcia jumped out of the chair, snapped her bag open, and drew out her little .22. I kid you not. She was closest to Mooney and she just stepped up to him and rested it above his left ear. He swallowed, didn't say a word. I never realized how prominent his Adam's apple was. Jo Ann froze, hand on her holster.

Good old reliable, methodical Marcia. Why, I said to myself, *why* pick today of all days to trot your gun out of the freezer? Did you read bad luck in your tarot cards? Then I had a truly rotten thought. What if she had two guns? What if the disarmed .22 was still staring down the mint chocolate-chip ice cream?

"Give it back," Marcia said. She held out one hand, made an impatient waving motion.

"Hey, you don't need it, Marcia," I said. "You've got plenty more. In all those safe deposit boxes."

"I'm going to count to five—" she began.

"Were you in on the murder from day one? You know, from the planning stages?" I asked. I kept my voice low, but it echoed off the walls of Mooney's tiny office. The hum of everyday activity kept going in the main room. Nobody noticed the little gun in the well-dressed lady's hand. "Or did you just do your beau a favor and hide the loot after he iced his wife? In order to back up his burglary tale? I mean, if Justin Thayler really wanted to marry you, there is such a thing as divorce. Or was old Jennifer the one with the bucks?"

"I want that coin," she said softly. "Then I want the two of you"— she motioned to Jo Ann and me—"to sit down facing that wall. If you yell, or do anything before I'm out of the building, I'll shoot this gentleman. He's coming with me."

"Come on, Marcia," I said, "put it down, I mean, look at you. A week ago you just wanted Thayler's coin back. You didn't want to rob my cab, right? You just didn't know how else to get your good luck charm back with no questions asked. You didn't do it for money, right? You did it for love. You were so straight you threw away the cash. Now here you are with a gun pointed at a cop—''

"Shut up!"

I took a deep breath and said, "You haven't got the style, Marcia. Your gun's not even loaded."

Mooney didn't relax a hair. Sometimes I think the guy hasn't ever believed a word I've said to him. But Marcia got shook. She pulled the barrel away from Mooney's skull and peered at it with a puzzled frown. Jo Ann and I both tackled her before she got a chance to pull the trigger. I twisted the gun out of her hand. I was almost afraid to look inside. Mooney stared at me and I felt my mouth go dry and a trickle of sweat worm its way down my back.

I looked.

No bullets. My heart stopped fibrillating, and Mooney actually cracked a smile in my direction.

So that's all. I sure hope Mooney will spread the word around that I helped him nail Thayler. And I think he will; he's a fair kind of guy. Maybe it'll get me a case or two. Driving a cab is hard on the backside, you know?

Ed Hoch may be one of only two or three people on the entire planet who make their living writing short fiction. He produces two and sometimes three stories per month, month in month out, published in worldwide editions of *Ellery Queen Mystery Magazine* and various anthologies—and there's nobody quite like him. He works in a variety of forms, styles, and voices, always eager to try some new twist or turn or variation on what first appears to be a familiar tale. This is one of his most remarkable stories.

Second Chance
EDWARD D. HOCH

Their meeting was one of those bizarre things that happen only in real life. Carol Rome was home from her assembly-line job at Revco with the beginning of an autumn cold, running just enough of a fever to prefer the quiet warmth of her apartment to the constant chatter of her co-workers. She'd heard the door buzzer sound once but decided to ignore it. What was the point of being sick in bed if you had to get up and answer the door?

She had almost drifted back into sleep when she became aware of some scrapings at the apartment door. Then, with a loud snap that brought her fully awake, the door sprang open. Through the bedroom door she saw a tall, dark-haired young man enter quietly and close the jimmied door behind him. He looked to be in his late twenties, not much older than Carol herself, and he carried a black attaché case in one hand. The iron crowbar in his other hand had no doubt come out of it.

The telephone was next to the bed and Carol considered the possibility of dialing for help before he became aware of her. She was just reaching for the phone when he glanced into the bedroom and saw her.

89

"Well—what have we here?"

"Get out or I'll scream," she said.

He merely smiled, and she was all too aware that he was still holding the crowbar. "You wouldn't do that," he said. "I'm not going to hurt you." His face relaxed into a grin. "That is, not unless you'd like me to."

"Get out!" she repeated.

"You should get a stronger lock on that door. In this old building they're awfully easy to pop open."

She was becoming really afraid now, perhaps because he wasn't. "Look, my purse is on the dresser. There's about twenty dollars in it. That's all I've got."

He continued grinning at her, making no move toward the purse. "You're sort of cute-looking, you know. What're you doing home in bed in the middle of the day? Are you sick?"

"Yes."

"Too bad. I buzzed first. If you'd answered the door I'd have said I was an insurance claims adjuster looking for somebody else. That's why I'm dressed up, with the attaché case and all. I wouldn't have come in if I'd known you were home." The grin widened. "But I'm glad I did."

She took a deep breath and lunged for the telephone.

He was faster. He dropped the crowbar and grabbed her, pulling her half out of the bed until they tumbled together to the floor in a tangle of sheets and blankets.

His name was Tony Loder and he'd been ripping off apartments for the past two years. He didn't need the money for a drug habit, he was quick to inform her. He just liked it better than working for a living.

"Aren't you afraid I'll call the cops?" she asked, rising to get a cigarette from her purse.

"I guess you'd have done that already if you were going to."

"Yes," she agreed. "I guess I would have."

"What about you? How come you're living alone?"

"My former roommate moved in with a guy from the plant. Besides, I like living alone." She sneezed and reached for a Kleenex. "I hope you don't catch my cold."

"I don't worry about colds." He was staring at her with the same intensity as when he'd first discovered her in the bed. "Do you have a man around?"

"Not right now. I was married once, five years ago."

"What happened?"

"He was dull. He wanted to buy a house in the suburbs and raise kids. I don't think I could live like that. As soon as I realized it, I got out."

"What do you do at this plant? Anything connected with money? Are you in the bookkeeping department?"

Carol laughed. "Sorry. I'm on an assembly line with twenty-three other girls. We run wire-wrap machines. Do you know what they are?"

"I don't want to know. It sounds too much like work."

"I'll bet you do as much work breaking into places as I do working on the line."

"It'd be a lot easier if I had a partner, that's for sure."

"How come?"

He shrugged, "I could do different things. I wouldn't have to jimmy doors for a living."

He left her after an hour or so, promising to phone. And he did, the following evening. She began seeing him almost every night. There was something exciting about having a burglar for a lover, something that kept her emotions charged all during the day. It was a life worlds apart from the dull, plodding existence she'd known during her brief marriage to Roy. Listening to Tony's exploits, she was like a child hearing fairy tales for the very first time.

"I almost bought it today," he'd say, rubbing the back of her neck as he sipped the martini she'd prepared for him. "An old lady came home too soon and caught me in her house. I'd phoned to tell her I was from the social-security office and she had to come down about some mix-up. Old ladies living alone always swallow that one. But after she left the house it started to drizzle and she came back for her umbrella."

"What'd you do? You didn't hurt her, did you?"

"I had to give her a shove on my way out and she fell down, but she wasn't hurt bad. I could hear her screaming at me all the way down the block."

In the morning paper Carol read that the elderly woman had suffered a broken hip in the fall, and for a moment she felt sick. That evening she confronted Tony.

"It wouldn't have happened if I had a lookout to honk the horn when the old lady came back. I didn't *want* to hurt her!"

She believed him and calmed down a little. "A lookout?"

"How about it, babe? You could do it."

"*Me?*"

"Why not?"

"No, thanks! I'm not going to end up in prison with you! I like my freedom too much."

She was cool to him the rest of the evening and he said no more about it.

When he phoned the following evening she told him she was sick and refused to see him. She spent a long time thinking about the old woman with the broken hip and even considered sending flowers to the hospital. But in the end she did nothing, and a few days later she saw Tony Loder again. Nothing more was said about the old woman or his need for a lookout, and he no longer told her his detailed stories of the day's activities. She was almost afraid to hear them now.

Around the end of October, half the girls on her production line were laid off, including Carol. Standing in line at the unemployment office she thought about the bleak Christmas season ahead, and about Tony's offer. It meant money, and more than that it meant excitement she'd dreamed of but never really experienced.

That night she asked him, "Do you still want a partner?"

The first few times were easy.

She sat in the car across the street from the house he was hitting, waiting to tap the horn if anyone approached.

No one did, and for doing nothing he gave her a quarter of his take. It amounted to $595 the first week—more than she'd earned in a month on the production line.

Once during the second week Carol honked the horn when a homeowner returned unexpectedly from a shopping trip. Then she circled the block and picked Tony up. He was out of breath but smiling. "Got some jewelry that looks good," he told her. "A good haul."

"Sometime I want to go in with you, Tony. Into the house with you."

"Huh?"

"I mean it! I get bored sitting in the car."

He thought about that. "Maybe we'll try it sometime."

His voice lacked conviction but that night she pestered him until he agreed. The following morning they tried an apartment house together, going back to his old crowbar routine. She worked well at his side, but the haul was far less than in private homes.

"Let me try one on my own," she said that night.

"It's too dangerous. You're not ready."

"I'm as ready as I'll ever be. Were you ready the first time you went into a house alone?"

"That was different."

"Why? Because you're a man and I'm a woman?"

He had no answer to that. The next morning they cruised the suburbs until they found a corner house with a woman in the front yard raking leaves. "Pull into the side street and drop me off," Carol said. "She'll have the door unlocked and her purse just sitting around somewhere."

"What if someone's home?"

She shook her head. "Her husband's at work and the kids are at school. Wait down the block for me till I signal you."

"All right, but just take cash. No credit cards. That way if you're grabbed coming out it's your word against hers."

She got out of the car halfway down the block and walked back toward the corner house, feeling the bright November sunshine on her face. She was wearing slacks and a sweater, and her hands were empty. The money, if she found any, would go into her panties.

The woman was still in the front yard raking leaves, with the corner of the house shielding Carol's approach. The side door was unlocked as she'd expected, and she entered quietly. It was even easier than she expected—a big black purse sat in plain view on the kitchen table. She crossed quickly to it and removed the wallet inside, sliding out the bills and returning the wallet to the purse. She moved to the living room doorway to check on the woman through the front window, and had an unexpected bit of luck. There was a man's worn wallet on top of the television set. She pulled the bills from it and added them to the others.

Only then did she realize the wallet meant there was probably a man in the house.

She started back through the kitchen and was just going out the door when an attractive red-haired man appeared, coming up the steps from the basement. "What are you doing here?" he demanded.

She fought down the urge to panic and run. He could easily overtake her, or get the license number of Tony's car. "Is this the place that's giving away the free kittens?" she asked calmly.

"Kittens? We don't have any kittens here."

She edged toward the door. "I know it's one of these houses."

"There are no new kittens in the neighborhood. How come you opened the door?"

Carol ignored his question. "Is that your wife raking leaves? Maybe she knows about them." She hurried outside and down the steps, walking purposefully toward the front yard.

The woman was still raking and she didn't even look in their direction as Tony pulled up and Carol jumped into the car. "My God, there was a man in the house! Let's get out of here!"

"Is he after you?"

"He will be as soon as he checks his wallet. I told him I was looking for free kittens."

Tony chuckled and patted her knee. "You're learning fast." He turned the car down another side street to make certain they weren't being followed. "How much did you get?"

She thumbed quickly through the bills. "Forty-five from her purse and fifty-three from his wallet. Not bad for a few minutes' work."

"From now on you get half of everything," he decided. "You're a full partner."

His words made her feel good, made her feel that maybe she'd found her place in life at last.

With the coming of winter they moved their operations downtown to the office buildings. "I don't like leaving footprints in the snow," Tony said.

Large offices occupying whole floors were the best, because Carol could walk through them during lunch hours virtually unnoticed. Mostly she looked for cash in purses or desk drawers. If anyone questioned her, she always said she was there for a job interview. Once Tony dressed as a repairman and walked off with an IBM typewriter, but both agreed that was too risky to try again. "We've got to stick to cash," he decided. "Typewriters are too clumsy if someone starts chasing you."

But after a few weeks of it Carol said, "I'm tired of going through desk drawers for dimes and quarters. Let's go south for the winter, where there isn't any snow to show footprints."

They didn't go far south but they did go to New York. They found an apartment in the West Village and contacted some friends of Tony. "You'll like Sam and Basil," he assured Carol. "They're brothers. I met them in prison."

Somehow the words stunned Carol. "You never told me you were in prison."

"You never asked. It's no big secret."

"What were you in for?"

"Breaking and entering. I only served seven months."

"Here in New York?"

"Yeah. Three years ago. And I haven't been arrested since, in case you're wondering. That was just bad luck."

She said no more about it, but after meeting Sam and Basil Briggs in a Second Avenue bar she was filled with further misgivings. Sam was the older of the brothers, a burly blond-haired man of about Tony's age. Both he and the slim, dark-haired Basil seemed hyped up, full of unnatural energy. "Are they on heroin?" she asked Tony when they were alone for a moment.

"No, of course not! Maybe they took a little speed or something."

"I don't like it."

"Just stay cool."

Basil went off to make a phone call and Sam Briggs returned to the table alone. He ran his eyes over the turtleneck sweater Carol was wearing and asked Tony, "How about it? Want to make some money?"

"Sure. Doing what?"

"A little work in midtown."

"Not the park."

"No, no—what do you take us for? Hell, I'd be afraid to go in the park at night myself! I was thinking of Madison Avenue. The classy area."

Tony glanced at Carol. "We've been working as a team."

"You can still work as a team. She can finger our targets."

"What is all this?" Carol asked. The bar had grown suddenly noisy and they had to lean their heads together to be heard.

"Most guys get hit when they're all alone, on some side street at two in the morning," Sam explained, eyeing her sweater again as he spoke. "But I got a spot picked out right on Madison. We hit middle-aged guys walking with their wives earlier in the evening—nine, ten o'clock."

"Hit them?" Carol asked.

"Roll them, take their wallets. And their wives' purses. We're gone before they know what happened!"

"Aren't there a lot of people on Madison Avenue at that time of night?"

"Not as many as you'd think. I got a perfect corner picked out— there's an empty restaurant there and when the offices close down it's fairly dim."

"What do I have to do?"

"Go halfway down the block, pretending to windowshop or wait for a date, and watch for a likely prospect. If a couple come by talking, listen to what they're saying. If they sound right, just point your finger and we do the rest.''

Carol was silent for a moment. ''There won't be knives or anything, will there?''

''Hell, no! What do you take us for?''

She turned to Tony. ''Do you want me to?''

''We've got to live on something.''

''All right,'' she decided. ''Let's do it.''

Two nights later, on an evening when the weather had turned unusually mild, Carol and Tony met the Briggs brothers at the corner of Madison and 59th. Carol was wearing a knit cap to hide her hair and a matching scarf to muffle the lower part of her face.

''It's just after nine,'' Sam Briggs told her. ''Look for couples with shopping bags, maybe coming from Bloomingdale's, tourists heading back to their hotels. If the man has both hands full it's easiest for us.''

The three men hovered near the corner, glancing into the empty restaurant as if surprised to find it closed. Carol walked up the block toward Park Avenue, letting one man pass who was carrying only a newspaper. She'd been strolling back and forth about five minutes when she spotted a couple, crossing Park in her direction. The man, stocky and middle-aged, carried a shopping bag in his left hand and a briefcase in his right. The woman, obviously his wife, carried a tote bag along with her purse.

Carol followed discreetly along behind them, listening to their conversation until she was certain they weren't police decoys. About fifty feet from the corner, she signaled a finger at them. When the couple reached Tony and the Briggs brothers at the corner, Sam Briggs walked up to the man and asked for a match. Before the man and woman realized what was happening, Sam punched the man in the face, knocking him backward into Basil's arms. Tony grabbed the woman as she started to scream and yanked the purse from her hand. Basil had pinned the man's arms while Sam went for his wallet.

Then, throwing the man to the sidewalk, they scattered in opposite directions. Carol, walking quickly back to Park Avenue, ducked into the lobby of a hotel and pretended to use the pay phone near the door.

The whole thing had taken less than a minute.

They tried again three nights later in almost the same location. This time the man tried to fight back and Sam Briggs gave him a vicious punch in the stomach. The first time they'd gotten $214 plus some credit cards they'd promptly discarded. The second time they realized less—only $67 from the man and $16 from the woman.

"Everybody carries credit cards now," Sam Briggs complained later over drinks in his Village apartment. "What good are credit cards to us? By the next day the computer knows they're stolen."

"Let's go after something big," his younger brother suggested.

"Like what—a bank?"

"Count me out," Carol said, afraid they might be serious. "I'm having nothing to do with guns."

She went to the kitchen to make some coffee and she could hear Tony speaking in a low tone while she was gone. Later back at their own place, he started in on her. "You got this thing about guns and knives, but sometimes they can actually *prevent* violence."

"Oh yeah? How?"

"Remember that first time you went into a house alone? Remember how the man came up from the basement and surprised you? Suppose he hadn't believed your story about the kittens. Suppose he'd grabbed you and you'd picked up a kitchen knife to defend yourself. You might have killed him. But if you'd been carrying a weapon he wouldn't have grabbed you in the first place."

"I don't buy that sort of logic, Tony."

"Look, you saw Sam Briggs punch that guy tonight. You're part of it! Suppose there's some internal bleeding and the guy dies. The simple act of carrying a gun or knife isn't all that much worse than what we're doing already."

"It's worse in the eyes of the law."

He sighed and tried again. "Look, Carol, Sam and Basil have an idea that can make us a lot of money all at once. We won't have to go around mugging people on the street corners. The thing is foolproof, but we need you to hold a gun on two people for about ten minutes."

"In a bank?"

"No, not in a bank. This is far safer than a bank."

"Why can't you do it without me?"

"We need a woman to get in the place before they're suspicious."

"Where?"

"I want Sam to tell you. It's his plan."

"I don't like that man, Tony. I don't like the way he looks at me."

"Oh, Sam's all right. He's a little rough at times."

"He's a criminal!"

"We're all criminals, Carol," Tony reminded her.

She took a deep breath. "I've never thought of myself as one," she admitted. "Maybe because I've never been arrested."

"How about it? One big job and we can live like normal people for a change."

"Maybe I don't want to live like a normal person, Tony. I guess I've always been bored by normal people. I was married to one once, and it bored the hell out of me."

He put his arms around her. "How about it? One big job? I promise it won't be boring. You'll never be bored with me."

"One big job . . ." She remembered them saying that in the movies, and they always walked into a police trap. But this wasn't the movies, and she knew she'd go along with whatever they wanted of her. She'd go along with it because Tony Loder had made her feel like a real person and not just a cog in some insensitive machine.

The plan was simple.

Sir Herbert Miles, the wealthy and successful British actor, maintained a luxury apartment with his wife on Central Park South. They were going to rob him of cash and jewelry, using Carol to penetrate the elaborate security precautions in the building's lobby. "You see," Sam Briggs explained, sketching a rough diagram on a sheet of paper, "they have a guard at a desk just inside the door. He monitors the elevators and hallways with a bank of closed-circuit TV screens. And nobody gets by him unless they're a resident or a guest who's expected."

"Then how do I get by?"

"There's a night elevator operator as added security, and from eleven o'clock on he sells the following morning's newspapers. All you do is walk through the revolving doors about eleven-fifteen and ask the man on the desk if you can buy a copy of *The Times*. He'll say sure and send you back to the elevator operator. That's when you take out your gun and cover them both. Make them lie on the floor. We come through the door, take the elevator up to the penthouse, and rob Miles and his wife. In ten minutes we're back downstairs. You stay in the lobby the whole time."

"Why can't we just tie up the two guards and leave them?"

"Because another resident might come in and find them while we're all upstairs. This way if anyone else arrives you cover them with the gun too."

"I couldn't bring myself to shoot anyone."

"You don't have to shoot anyone. Just hold the gun and they'll behave. Nobody wants to get shot."

Sam gave her a .38 revolver of the sort detectives carried on television. It held five bullets and he showed her how to load and fire it. "That's all you need," he said.

"Will you all have guns too?"

"Sure, but nobody'll need to use them."

That night, in bed with Tony, she started to tremble and he held her tight. "It's going to be all right," he whispered reassuringly.

She was a long way from the assembly line at Revco.

The uniformed guard glanced up from his newspaper as she entered. Behind him a half-dozen TV screens flickered their closed-circuit images. "Can I help you, ma'am?"

"Someone said you sold tomorrow's *Times* here."

He nodded and motioned around the corner. "The elevator man has some."

She walked down two steps and saw the second uniformed man already folding a paper to hand it to her. The gun came out of her purse. "Not a sound!" she warned.

The man behind the desk turned toward her and she shifted the pistol to bring him into range. "You too—get down here and lie on the floor! Quickly!"

"This building is robbery-proof, girlie. You won't get away with it."

"We'll see. Both of you stay down there. Don't even lift your heads or I'll shoot!"

As soon as they saw the empty desk, Tony and the Briggs brothers came through the revolving door. They were wearing stocking masks, and she wasn't too happy about being bare-faced. Still, the knit cap and scarf helped hide her features. "Ten minutes," Tony said as he went by her.

She watched the floor numbers as the elevator rose, keeping the gun steady on the two guards. "Who are they after?" the elevator man asked.

"Shut up!"

Eight long minutes later she saw the elevator start down from the top floor. No one else had entered the lobby and she was thankful for that. When the elevator stopped, Sam Briggs was the fist one off, carrying a bulging plastic trash bag in one hand. The other two were behind him. "Let's go!" he told her.

"Don't follow us," she warned the two guards. "Stay on the floor!" Then, as she backed toward the door, she asked Tony, "How'd it go?"

"Great! No trouble."

Basil had left the car on one of the secondary roads in Central Park, with a phony television press card on the windshield in case anyone got curious. They broke onto Central Park South, running across toward the low park wall. Carol was in the middle of the street when she heard a shouted command.

"Police! Stop or we'll shoot!"

At the same instant she saw the police cars, realized both ends of the street were blocked off. "The guard must have pushed a silent alarm," Tony gasped at her side. "Forget the car and run for it!"

She heard a shot and turned to see Basil with his gun out. Then there were three more shots close together and he spun around and went down in the street.

She kept running, afraid to look back.

There were more shots, and the stone wall of the park was before her. She went over it fast, her legs scraping against the rough stone. Tony was somewhere behind her and she turned to look for him.

"Run!" he screamed at her. "Run!"

She saw the blood on his face, saw him reaching out for her as he ran toward the wall, then his whole body shuddered and he went down hard.

She ran on, deep into the park, until the breath was torn from her lungs in pulse-pounding gasps and she sank to the frozen earth and started to cry.

God! Oh, God!

Tony was hit, probably dead. And the others too.

After a long time she picked herself up and after walking for what seemed hours she managed to reach Fifth Avenue, at 66th Street. She hailed a taxi and took it downtown, getting out a block from the apartment in case the police tried to trace her later. She circled the block twice on foot, mingling with the late strollers, until she felt it was safe to go in. Then she collapsed onto the bed and pulled the blankets tight around her, trying not to think.

She must have lain there an hour or longer before she heard a gentle knock on the door. Her first thought was the police, but they'd be less timid. She got up and listened at the door. The knocking came again and she could hear breathing on the other side of the door. "Who is it?" she asked softly.

"Me!"

"Tony!" She threw off the bolt and opened the door.

It was Sam Briggs. "Let me in!"

"I—"

He pushed her aside and closed the door after him. "I thought they got you too."

"No."

"Basil and Tony are both dead. The cops were right on my tail but I lost them in the park."

"You can't stay here," she said. "I want to be alone."

"Come on! There's only the two of us left now. Tony's dead!"

She turned away from him. "What about the money?"

"I dropped the bag when I was running. I had to save my skin!"

She didn't know whether to believe him, but it didn't really matter. "You'll have to go," she repeated. "You can't stay here."

"I'm afraid to go back to my place. They'll be looking for me."

"I'm sorry."

"To hell with you! I'm staying!"

She walked casually over to her coat and slipped the pistol from the pocket. Pointing it at him, she said, "Get out, Sam."

His eyes widened. "Hell, Carol, we're partners! I always liked you, from the first time I saw you."

"I was Tony's partner, not yours. Get out!" The gun was steady in her hand.

He smiled. "You wouldn't use that."

"Wouldn't I?" In that instant she wanted to. She wanted to squeeze the trigger and wipe the smile off his face for good. He had caused Tony's death and now he was standing grinning at her.

But he was right about the gun. She wanted to use it, but she couldn't.

"You can sleep on the couch," she told him. "Just for tonight." She went into the bedroom and closed the door, taking the gun with her.

In the morning he was still asleep as she dressed quickly and left the apartment. She bought a paper at the corner store and read about the robbery: "ACTOR'S PENTHOUSE ROBBED AT GUNPOINT—POLICE SLAY TWO FLEEING SCENE." The dead were identified as Tony Loder and Basil Briggs, both convicts.

She put the paper down.

So that was Tony's epitaph, after all the things he'd been. Not lover, nor dreamer, not even thief. Only ex-convict.

She started reading again. The police were seeking Sam Briggs, brother of the slain man, and an unidentified woman, who were believed to have fled with an estimated $80,000 in cash and jewelry.

So Sam had lied about dropping the bag. He had it stashed somewhere, probably in a locker at the bus station.

She thought about going back to the apartment and confronting him, pointing the gun at him again and demanding a share for her and Tony.

But Tony was dead, and she'd shown Sam last night that she wouldn't use the gun.

She went to a phone booth and dialed the police. When a gruff voice answered she said, "You're looking for Sam Briggs in connection with last night's robbery. If you hurry you can find him at this address."

After that she took the subway to the Port Authority Terminal on Eighth Avenue and caught the next bus home.

They were hiring again at Revco and they took her back without question. She had her old spot on the assembly line, with many of the same girls, and when they asked where she'd been she only smiled and said, "Around."

She learned from the New York papers that Sam Briggs had been arrested and the loot recovered. The unidentified woman wasn't mentioned. Even if Sam had given them her names, he didn't know where she came from. After a month she stopped worrying about being found. Instead, she felt that by some miracle she had been given a second chance.

For a time she was happy at work, and she thought of Tony only at night. But with the coming of spring, boredom set in once again. The routine of the assembly line began to get her down. She tried going out drinking with the other women on Friday nights but it didn't help. There was nothing in their bickering conversations or the half-hungry glances of their male friends to interest Carol.

One morning in May she phoned in sick, then dressed in a dark sweater and jeans and went out for a drive.

She parked near an apartment house in a better section of town and walked through the unguarded lobby. An inner door had to be opened with a key or by a buzzer from one of the apartments. She pressed three or four numbers until someone buzzed the door open, then took the elevator to the third floor. Tony had told her once never to go up too high, in case she had to run down the fire stairs.

She used the knocker on a door chosen at random and nobody answered. Taking a plastic credit card from the pocket of her jeans, she used it on the bolt the way Tony had shown her. She was lucky. There was no chain, no Fox lock. In a moment she was inside the apartment.

It was tastefully furnished in a masculine manner, with an expensive TV-stereo combination and a few original paintings. She saw a desk and crossed to it.

"Hello there," a male voice said.

She whirled around, tensed on the balls of her feet, and saw a man standing there in his robe. His dark hair was beginning to go grey, but his face still had a boyish quality. He was smiling at her. "This is my first encounter with a real live burglar. Are they all as pretty as you?"

"I'm no burglar," she said, talking fast. "I must have gotten the wrong apartment." She turned and started for the door.

"Not just yet!"

"What?"

"I want you to stay a bit, talk to me."

She was reminded of that day last year when she'd been home in bed. "Are you sick?"

"Only unemployed. I lost my job last month. It's sort of lonely being unemployed. I'd find it interesting to talk with a burglar. Maybe I can pick up a few pointers."

She moved a step closer. "Are you going to call the police?"

"I'd have done that already if I was going to."

"Yes," she agreed. "I suppose you would have."

She sat down in a chair facing him.

"Tell me what it's like breaking into apartments. Is it exciting? Can you actually make money at it?"

"It's like nothing clsc in the world," she said.

He smiled again and suddenly she knew that this was her real second chance, now, with this man whose name she didn't even know.

And maybe this time it wouldn't end the same way.

It would be easy to pigeonhole Linda Grant's novels as representative of this or that trend, but in truth they are very much informed by a very singular muse, one all Linda's own.

Her books are entertaining, exciting, sometimes feisty, and always wise in the way they look at people. She is one of the best, and the public at large is just now acknowledging this fact.

Last Rite
LINDA GRANT

Monday

Somewhere around thirty-five the future shrinks, and you realize you won't live forever. Not long after that you begin to look at old people with newfound interest. I was between those two points when my aunt Janet broke her hip and summoned me to her bedside to solve a murder.

Janet is not one of my favorite people. Timid and rather querulous, she is the sort who gives old women a bad name. Show her a rose; she'll notice the aphids. I try not to blame her. Hannah Sayler couldn't have been an easy mother to have, God knows she wasn't even an easy grandmother. The Chinese bound their daughters' feet; Hannah bound their spirits.

My dad and his brother escaped somehow. They got all the humor, the life, and spirit in the family, leaving Janet to peek behind the closed door for imagined dangers and sit in thin-lipped judgment of the many forms of human frailty. She's fond of commenting on the deficiencies of women like myself who don't know their place and can't seem to settle down with a husband and children; and after twelve years, she still regards my decision to become a private investigator as a passing whim that will go away when I grow up. Janet and I don't have a whole lot to talk about.

I hadn't seen Janet in years, despite my mother's urgings, and I knew I ought to feel guilty but I didn't. She lived at Laurel Heights, which my mother informed me was not an old folks home but a retirement community. It looked like a high-rise apartment house to me, the only noticeable difference being that the average age of the tenants was around seventy.

Janet was in the nursing wing, a modern one-story building connected to the main building by a corridor from the lobby. The decor was the same in the two buildings, but the difference was apparent as soon as you stepped through the connecting door.

The nursing wing had that unmistakable institutional feel to it. It could have been a hospital or psych ward, but it was not a place you went by choice. A middle-aged woman in a white uniform sat behind a large semicircular desk. She looked up from the clipboard on which she was writing and seemed surprised to see me.

"Can I help you?" she asked.

"I've come to see Janet Thomas," I said. "I'm her niece."

"Oh, visitors usually come through the front door," she said in a tone I remembered from my third-grade teacher. "You'll need to sign in at the front desk."

She allowed me to walk unsupervised from her station to the front desk, though I had a feeling she was keeping an eye on me all the way. The front desk was next to a large sunny room where about twenty women and a couple of men sat in a circle of wheelchairs while an impossibly cheerful blonde woman read to them from the newspaper.

A white card in the doorway proclaimed in large print, "Current Events—2:00." Some of the audience listened and appeared to understand; others looked like they'd been parked there for a nap. One woman who seemed at least a hundred and ten was slumped forward in her chair with her mouth hanging open. The man next to her stared into space, his face a complete blank.

I don't much like to think about old age, especially now that I realize it might happen to me, so I hurried off to Janet's room as quickly as I could.

She was sitting up in bed in a room that was split exactly in half. Each half had a bed, nightstand, chair, and television set. The half near the window was furnished in heavy mahogany pieces from a bedroom set. Janet's half was strictly institutional modern.

Janet was heavier than I remembered her, and her face was a mass of tiny wrinkles. The skin on the back of her hands was so thin it looked like it might tear. She's twelve years older than my dad, and she's been old since I was a kid. But then anyone over thirty is old to a child.

I was prepared to make small talk. Janet was not. She got to the point immediately. "We don't have long before my roommate gets back from therapy. I don't want anyone to know I suspect anything."

Oh boy, I thought, galloping paranoia.

She must have read my thoughts on my face because she said quite sharply, "I am here because I broke my hip, Catherine, not because there's anything wrong with my mind."

She proceeded to prove her point by giving me a clear and detailed explanation of why she believed that the woman across the hall, Mary Norton, had been the victim of foul play. Mary had suffered a massive stroke six weeks earlier and had never regained consciousness. Two weeks ago on a Thursday morning, the nurse who checked her room found her dead. Cause of death was determined to be heart failure.

It was a perfectly credible cause of death in a woman of seventy-six who had just suffered a massive stroke. The piece that didn't fit was that Janet had heard someone going into Mary's room around two A.M.

"You just don't sleep as well when you get to be my age," she informed me. "That's why they pass out those little orange pills, to help people sleep. I don't take them; I figure I'll be sleeping all the time soon enough."

Without the little orange pills, Janet was awake from one to three most mornings. To entertain herself she reconstructed exactly what was happening outside her room from the sounds that reached her through the partially open door. She could tell who was on duty not only from the sound of their voices but from the things they did; trips to the coffee machine, television programs they watched or music they listened to. She knew the routine of the entire night.

The night that Mary died, that routine was altered. Someone buzzed for the nurse, and he walked down the hall. That wasn't so unusual, but the sound of the door across the hall snapping closed was. Janet explained that Mary's door had a distinctive sound because the spring didn't work quite right and it always closed harder than the other doors.

"In this section, they don't check on us between twelve and seven," she explained. "Down in the infirmary, they check every four hours, but here they let us sleep. So you see there was no reason for anyone to go into Mary's room.''

"Maybe she rang for the nurse," I suggested.

"She was unconscious," Janet reminded me, "and she was alone in the room.''

"Maybe he decided to check on her.''

"He could have, but why did he deny it? I heard them out in the hall the next morning when they found her. The director, Mrs. Hiller, wanted to know exactly where everyone had been and if anyone had gone into her room. Juan was on duty, and he said he hadn't gone in the room. Mrs. Hiller said the other nurses hadn't either.''

Aunt Janet had been reading too many mystery novels, but I couldn't tell her that. I also couldn't tell her that I don't do murders. My clients are banks and big corporations; their problems usually involve employees with sticky fingers or loose lips—embezzlement, creative fraud, industrial espionage—that sort of thing. Murder, I leave to the police.

Janet was not going to accept that, and neither was my mother. I've confronted crooks and even a hired killer, but I wasn't about to take on Janet and my mom. I had no choice but to investigate. It was enough to make me wish that private investigators, like doctors, weren't allowed to work for relatives.

I asked my partner, Jesse, to do the background work. I'd have loved to stick him with the undercover part, but there are limits to what you can ask of a partner and still have one.

I needed to spend time at Laurel Heights, to get to know people there and to become familiar enough that no one would notice me too much. Since Janet regarded my profession as on the wrong side of decent, I could rely on her not to tell anyone about it. She was delighted that I planned to present myself as an English teacher volunteering to teach a class in oral history. In her eyes, it was as close to respectability as I'd come since high school.

Thursday

Jesse didn't get a lot from his official visit to Laurel Heights. The staff was neither more nor less helpful than others we've interviewed. Asking people what they know that might implicate a friend or coworker in a serious crime doesn't endear you to them, but they don't dare misbehave too badly lest you become suspicious of them.

Three nurses had been on duty the night Mary Norton died—Clarence Jones, Juan Morales, and Dorothy Waters. Morales had been at Station A, just down from Janet's room, Jones at Station B down from the infirmary, Waters in the infirmary. The outside doors were locked at nine, and anyone entering after that had to ring the bell and sign in. No one had signed in after eleven. The only keys to the outside doors were kept by the director, Audrey Hiller, and the Chief of Security for the entire Laurel Heights complex.

Mary Norton's body had been discovered by a nurse on the morning shift. The doctor estimated that she'd died between midnight and three A.M. No autopsy had been performed.

Three nurses and one administrator wasn't bad for a list of suspects, especially when you didn't know if you had a crime.

It was a stroke of luck that all three nurses were on the day shift at present. Laurel Heights rotated their staff every week, one week of day duty, one of P.M. shift, and one of night duty. Janet pointed the nurses out to me and gave me her assessment of each of them—two stinkers and one who might be all right.

I met the director, Audrey Hiller, when I volunteered to teach the oral history class. She was a stern-looking woman in her fifties with gray eyes set in a long face that seemed always to wear an expression of mild irritation. She warned me not to expect too much of my students. "Patience is very important with older people," she said. "In some ways it's like working with children."

Tuesday

There were eleven people in the class, all women. Seven came from the regular retirement community, and four from the nursing facility. As I entered the dayroom where the class was to be held, I felt an attack of self-consciousness. I had no idea what to expect from these women. Some looked so old and frail that I wasn't sure they'd be capable of participating. How would I ever get them to function as a class?

I needn't have worried. They all knew each other, and oral history was a large part of their normal conversation. I didn't have to do more than give them some topics and turn on the tape recorder. Even Laura

Mosher, who suffered from Alzheimer's and was often confused about the present, remembered her childhood with startling clarity.

We began with "an event that changed your life" as the topic, and Emma Warren volunteered to go first. She was a large woman who looked like she belonged in a rocker on the front porch of a Kansas farmhouse. Her body was sturdy and solid, but her hands were so gnarled by arthritis that they looked like old wood.

She told of being on her own for the first time in her life when her husband went to war. Her story was a reminder of how much things have changed for women in a generation. She had moved from her father's house to her husband's farm, knowing exactly what was expected of her and fitting herself to that role. War had redefined the rules and brought an unexpected sense of freedom.

I looked down at the back of my hand and noticed the brown spots that looked like large freckles. The woman next to me had the same spots, only larger and far more obvious against the porcelain whiteness of her skin. Grandma Sayler had had the same spots. I hate them.

"By the time Ross came home from the South Pacific, we had a one-year-old daughter who he'd never seen," Emma Warren said. "I remember him holding her and saying, 'I'm glad she's a girl so she'll never have to go to war.' It was a good thing he felt that way since we ended up with five daughters."

The circle of women laughed, none harder than Emma Warren. It was a comfortably female group. All had outlived the men they'd married and in a couple of cases, the children they'd borne. They had come to Laurel Heights to finish out their lives, but they maintained a rebellious vitality that I found endearing. I hoped that when I reached their age I'd still be able to laugh as Emma Warren did.

Beyond the circle of women a small man in a white coat hurried down the hall. His skin was the color of light chocolate, and his black hair was flecked with gray and receded from a smooth expanse of forehead. I recognized him from Jesse's description as Clarence Jones, one of the nurses on duty the night Mary Norton died. I could't see his face, but I knew it probably wore the same slightly anxious look that Jesse had described.

He was a shy man, more comfortable, I suspected, counting pills and filling out schedules than interacting with his elderly patients. He was a hard worker, but a silent one, and he was not very popular with the women.

"A little field mouse, that one," Betty Katzen said.

"He's such an old woman," Emma Warren said, laughing her warm, earthy laugh. They all laughed then, pleased by the idea that Clarence Jones was more an old woman than any of them. I wondered how they'd react if they knew he was a murder suspect.

I could see that across the circle Sarah Meyers was tiring. Her eyes lost their focus and her head drooped. She was still recovering from the stroke that had forced her into a wheelchair six months earlier and the struggle to make herself understood exhausted her quickly.

Aimee Girault also noticed. "Sarah's tired," she said. "Someone must take her back to her room." Aimee understood better than the others the exhausting work of rebuilding a life shattered by stroke. Two years earlier she had suffered a massive stroke that cost her the use of her left arm and leg and exiled her from her comfortable apartment in the Adult Community Building to a shared room in the convalescent hospital.

I went to the nurses' station to find someone to take Sarah to her room. Juan Morales, suspect number two, sat reading a newspaper. He greeted me with a broad smile.

"Sarah, she tired? Sure I take her to her room. She work so hard, that lady. She's a fighter."

He followed me back to the circle and wheeled Sarah off, chatting as he went.

"He's such a nice boy," Emma said. "So friendly."

"He's from El Salvador," another woman said. "He was active in the trade unions. They killed his brother and his uncle, and he had to flee into the countryside. He's always worried they'll deport him. The immigration doesn't accept that's he a political refugee."

"They're Nazis," Aimee said with uncharacteristic bitterness.

When class ended I watched the seven "healthy" members of the group head off down the hall that connected the nursing wing to the rest of Laurel Heights. Beyond the double doors, they stepped into a normal life where privacy and independence were still available, where each had a key to her own apartment, meals could be cooked in her own kitchen, and the day's activities were a matter of choice.

As nursing homes go, Laurel Heights was probably one of the better ones. The lobby was cheerful, the rooms reasonably large, and friends from the adult community were close at hand. But it was a place defined by loss—the loss of health, mobility or mental acuity, of independence and privacy. For some the loss of the past, for all the loss of the future.

With class over, I headed for the director's office. Hiller was attending a conference on geriatric care and would be out all day.

My position as volunteer teacher was a license to snoop. Since Jesse had found no one on the staff willing to cooperate, snooping was all we had left. It's tough to start an investigation from your fallback position.

I let myself into the director's office with a credit card. I'd checked the lock earlier when everyone was occupied with breakfast and found that it was little more than decoration. I don't enjoy this sort of thing. It gives me the same jagged adrenaline surge as a roller coaster ride and there's no one at the switch.

I looked around for someplace to hide if someone decided to check on the office. A door behind the desk opened into a small closet. I hoped I wouldn't need it.

Hiller struck me as the kind of person for whom a sloppy file drawer was a sign of moral turpitude, and as I expected, I found her office organized to the point of compulsiveness, a nice trait in someone whose files you want to search. It took only a few minutes to find the files of the three who had been working the night that Mary Norton died.

Clarence Jones had been employed in the nursing facility for six years. Before that he'd been an attendant in a convalescent hospital in Newark, New Jersey. He was taking courses for a nursing credential.

Juan Morales' file contained a surprise. It indicated that he was a U.S. citizen, raised in Los Angeles. He'd been at the nursing home just over a year. I scanned the file and wondered which of Juan's histories was correct, and why he'd given his employer a different story from the one he'd told the women.

Dorothy Waters' file revealed that she'd worked at Laurel Heights for three years. The listing of previous employment included stints at numerous other nursing facilities and before that jobs in food service.

I hadn't met Waters, but I remembered complaints about her. She was a woman who vacillated between warm good humor and dark moods of rough irritation. Janet complained that you never knew what to expect; one day she was full of laughter and smiles, doing extra favors without being asked; the next she was angry and sullen, snarling at anyone who rang for help and handling patients with a roughness that bordered on abuse. Janet also suspected she was a thief.

There was one letter from the son of a patient who believed Waters was responsible for the disappearance of his mother's watch and silver picture frame. An attached note indicated that results of an investigation of the charges had been inconclusive.

I copied some information from each of the files so that I could check on it later and put them back in the drawer. Then I went looking for Mary Norton's file. It resided in a bottom drawer marked "Deceased.'' I do love organized people. No one would have found anything this easily in my office.

I was opening Mary's file when a sound at the door turned my stomach to stone. I slid the file drawer closed and jumped for the closet. It wasn't much bigger than the average coffin, and there was no place to hide if someone opened the door. My body ran through its embarrassing set of reactions to danger—pounding heart, lump in the throat, icy hands, while I tried to keep my breathing light so I didn't puff like a steam engine.

I don't know who came in or what they did. I heard the office door open, a drawer slide out and then close, and the door snap shut again. When I finally emerged from the closet, the room appeared unchanged. If someone besides Hiller had the key, I didn't want to stick around.

Janet invited me for lunch, but I couldn't face another ten minutes at Laurel Heights. I gave her what I hoped was a satisfactory excuse. Then I headed home, changed my clothes and went for a long, satisfying run.

I've been studying the martial art of aikido for ten years. I usually train on Monday and Wednesday nights and skip Tuesdays, but that night I was at the dojo fifteen minutes early. I partnered with the youngest, strongest black belts and trained hard.

Thursday

Today was Aimee Girault's turn. Her stroke had robbed her of the use of the left side of her body, and her left hand lay stiff and clawlike in her lap. She was a tiny woman, probably no more than five-three in her prime, and age and two years in a wheelchair had shrunk her to the size of a ten-year-old.

While other patients favored sweat suits and house dresses or robes chosen to be easy to put on, Aimee wore dark slacks and a tailored blouse that gave her an air of elegance. I wondered how she disciplined her uncooperative limbs to get them into such clothes.

She was the leader of the nursing facility women. When Sarah Meyers felt too tired to come to class, Aimee fussed over her and cajoled until she came. She could tell us exactly what kind of shape Laura or any of the other Alzheimer patients was in that day. She reminded me of my mom's mother, sweet and kindly, gentle and strong.

The story she told us was anything but sweet or gentle. The topic was still an event that changed your life, and Aimee's event took place during the war. When the Germans swept into France, she was in her early twenties and still living on her family's farm. Her immediate reaction to the occupation was to join the Resistance.

"We put as little as possible in writing," she said, "but sometimes we had to write. Then I was the courier; I rode my bicycle to the next town every week so the Germans got used to seeing me. If there was a message, I carried it tucked in my skirt, under my blouse.

"One week I had something very important so I went one day early. At the bridge outside of town was a new soldier. He stopped me and asked me questions. I acted friendly so he won't get suspicious, but then he started flirting. I said no and tried to get back on my bike, but he grabbed me and pulled me into the woods at the side of the road.

"He was trying to kiss me and putting his hands on me. I broke away to run, but he grabbed me and pushed me to the ground. Later I realized he was going to rape me, but then all I could think of was the paper. He was pulling at my clothes, and I was struggling, and then the paper fell to the ground. When he reached down for it, I knew that we were all dead.

"I looked for some weapon, and there was a rock. I grabbed it and I hit him as hard as I could in the head. He didn't fall, and I hit him again and again. There was blood everywhere, but I couldn't be sure he was dead. He had a knife in his belt so I turned him over and pulled it free, and I cut his throat."

The circle was absolutely still as Aimee looked up at us. I stared at the tiny fragile woman and tried to imagine her slitting the throat of a soldier. She looked around the circle.

"It had to be done," she said.

The group erupted in questions. It was clear that Aimee had never told this story to her friends, but it surprised them far less than it did me. Aimee described how she had hidden the soldier's body and his motorcycle under the bridge and covered the area of the struggle with dry leaves, then sneaked home to change her bloodstained clothes and to get her friends to help her make sure the soldier would never be found.

I stayed for lunch, against my better judgment. I make it a point to avoid places that routinely put their food through a blender. The meal reminded me that there are things worse than dieting.

After lunch I went looking for Dorothy Waters. I found her at the nurses' station. She was complaining loudly to another nurse about one of the patients. "She just don't remember when to go, and she don't ask in time, and then it's oops, all over the place. I seen two-year-olds could do better.''

Just down the hall beyond the desk, one of my students, Sarah Meyers, sat in her wheelchair. Tears ran silently down her face. Rage burned in my throat. I wanted to strangle the insensitive nurse. I went to Sarah, wiped her eyes, and tried to console her.

Then I turned on Waters. "I've seen two-year-olds with more tact," I said to her. "I think Mrs. Meyers would like to be somewhere else," I told the other nurse. "Find out where she'd like to go and take her there." The woman took one look at my face and went to Sarah.

"Who the hell are you?" Waters asked.

"I could be from State Unemployment at the rate you're going."

"What the hell? You threatening me?"

"I *never* threaten," I said. I made no attempt to keep the anger out of my voice.

I watched the belligerence fade to uncertainty. "I didn't mean nothing," she said. "I take good care of Sarah."

I softened my tone. "It might help to remember that inside she has the same feelings you do."

"Who're you to be talking about feelings and telling me what to do?" she demanded.

"I just started recently. I work with the program director," I said, hoping that gave me enough status to command co-operation. "I'll bet it isn't easy taking care of all these folks."

She shook her head. "Half of them are off their heads. They ask for something; you get it; they just keep asking. Can't remember you ever brought it. It's 'Nurse, this' and 'Nurse, that,' till you want to scream. I shoulda stayed in food service."

"It was probably easier," I said, settling into the chair next to her desk.

"Sure was." She looked tired now. "I wanted the night work so I could be home in the day with my granddaughter. Then they started this stupid rotation business. Every week's a different schedule, so's you never get used to it. And I gotta leave the child with a neighbor who got no more sense than she has. I'm here taking care of someone else's parents, can't even take care of my own grandchild."

Anxious to justify herself to me, she poured out her story. I learned more than I wanted to know about her cocaine-addicted daughter, her son in the army, her diabetic mother who could no longer live by herself, and her four-year-old grandchild. She also covered her pinched nerve, gastric ulcer, and various other aches and pains.

I steered her to the subject of Laurel Heights and got a list of grievances against administrators, coworkers, and patients. No single piece of it was relevant to Mary Norton's death, yet taken together it gave me a sense of the frustrating, sometimes infuriating work it is to care for others when no one is caring for you. None of the employees of Laurel Heights would ever sleep in its beds. Their elderly parents had to be kept at home or in cheaper, shabbier facilities where welfare paid the tab. It wasn't hard to see how that could make a person bitter.

The results of the background checks on the three nurses and the director were beginning to come in. So far, we didn't have anything more than a few traffic tickets and a squabble with a neighbor. Jesse had discovered one interesting thing. The contract for Laurel Heights stated that once individuals moved into the community, they would be taken care of for the rest of their lives. There was an extra charge for care in the nursing facility, but residents who ran through their savings were kept on at the home's expense.

"Could provide some incentive to hurry along those who are terminal," Jesse said.

"We're all terminal, Jesse," I said, "and the police frown on hurrying people along."

Tuesday

I arrived fifteen minutes before class to discover that it had been canceled. Betty Katzen, one of the women from the adult community, met me in the lounge and told me that Emma Warren was in intensive care at Providence Hospital. "She always showered first thing in the morning, and she must have fallen then, on Saturday; but most of us were going on a field trip to the Flower Show downtown, so we didn't notice her until dinner time. They think she hit her head when she fell, and by the time they found her, she'd been unconscious for over ten hours."

"Has she regained consciousness?" I asked, afraid to hear the answer.

Betty shook her head. "No, and she isn't going to." She paused to gain control of the tears that threatened to break through. "They've done a brain scan; it's flat." At that she began to sob and I put my arm around her and stopped fighting back my own tears.

It took us several minutes to regain control of ourselves. Betty shook her head as she wiped her eyes. "She's gone. Her body's still there, but Emma's gone."

I found Audrey Hiller, the administrator, in the little room the staff used as a lounge. She confirmed Betty's diagnosis. "There's no brain activity," she said. "She can breathe without a respirator and her heart's strong. They'll bring her back here this afternoon, but there's nothing we can do but feed her. I've seen cases like this where they go on for years."

Dorothy Waters sat nearby reading the paper. She should have been home, but she'd been working double shifts lately. "That woman'd been better off if the fall killed her outright," she said. "Then her soul'd gone to the Lord instead of hanging around this place."

"Dorothy," Audrey Hiller said sharply, "I don't like that kind of talk."

Dorothy nodded sullenly, but her expression suggested that we all knew she was right.

Thursday

I wasn't sure the women would feel like meeting, but Betty Katzen had assured me that they could use something to take their minds off Emma's accident, so I'd told the recreation director to schedule the class.

The lounge was empty when I arrived and the chairs hadn't been set out for class. With a growing sense of unease, I headed for Audrey Hiller's office only to meet her in the hall. She looked surprised to see me, then realized why I was there and apologized for not calling to tell me that class had been canceled. In a tone completely devoid of emotion, she informed me that Emma Warren had died the night before.

I wondered aloud how a woman she had said could "go on for years" had died so quickly. She gave me a glib and unsatisfactory answer and tried to excuse herself. I pretended not to understand. My questions met with something more than resistance. Was it fear?

I stopped by to see Aimee and found her staring out her window.

"I'm so sorry about Emma," I said, feeling the inadequacy of the words.

"We'll miss her," Aimee said, "but she had a full life, and it didn't end too badly." Her bright eyes studied my face. "She wasn't afraid of death, you know," she said.

Like the grandmother she reminded me of, she was more at ease offering comfort than receiving it. How many friends and relatives had she lost, I wondered. She was of an age when those losses become frequent. Did they become any easier for that? Her face was calm, not serene but certainly not grief-wracked. I suspected that she feared death far less than I.

"Her death came so suddenly," I said, searching for a way to ask the questions I needed answers to. "Does it seem at all strange to you?"

Aimee shook her head. "People die for more reasons than the doctors understand, Catherine. She was a vegetable; maybe some part of her wanted to die. You knew her. She was so strong and robust; she'd have hated being stuck in a bed, completely dependent on people."

I nodded and decided not to press matters. It was unfair to arouse fears in Aimee when she had to remain in what might well be a dangerous situation.

I did get Aimee to tell me that Emma had a daughter in Oakland, and I asked the receptionist at Laurel Heights for the address and phone number so that I could express my condolences.

Finding Emma's daughter's house and telling her of my suspicions was a lot harder than convincing her to request an autopsy. She was a nurse, and she knew how easy it is to give a patient the wrong medication.

Monday

The results took a couple of days, and when they came back they didn't make any of us happy. Emma died from a heavy dose of Seconal, the medication that the nursing facility used to help patients sleep. There was no indication of a needle puncture, so they assumed it had been administered in liquid form.

Having the cops called into the case put me in an awkward position. My ex-husband, Dan Walker, is in homicide, so no matter who got the case, it'd be someone who knew I wasn't a school teacher. Dan wasn't going to be thrilled to hear that I was involved. He never likes civilian involvement, and he likes it even less when I'm the civilian.

All the tricks I'd have used on any other cop would be wasted on Dan, so I brought out the heavy guns. I told him everything I knew about the case and asked if he'd object if I remained undercover in order to reassure my parents. Dan gets along with my parents slightly better than I do, but I knew he wouldn't want to deal with them on this any more than I did. Sure enough, he agreed not to blow my cover. In return, he extracted a promise that I would tell him anything I discovered. He did not make a reciprocal offer.

Tuesday

Our next class meeting took place in the middle of the police investigation. Uniformed officers and sober-looking men in dark suits measured and inspected Emma's room and questioned all the employees.

We had the lounge to ourselves, but it was hard to ignore what was going on just outside the door. I was glad that it was Betty Katzen's turn. She had a strong, clear voice that carried well and a calm manner that helped focus the group. Betty was the Hallmark grandmother—slightly stout with an ample lap for grandchildren to crawl into, apple red cheeks, and a full head of thick white hair.

Her story too dealt with an event that changed her life; and like Emma's and Aimee's, it was a war story. Betty had been an army nurse assigned to a hospital in the Philippines, and was evacuated just before the islands were invaded. She was a direct, plain-spoken woman, and her descriptions of some of the things she'd seen made the other women wince.

I was only half listening when the expression of the woman opposite me brought my attention back to the circle. Betty was describing the agonizing decision to let the most seriously injured die in order to be able to treat those who might benefit. "Some of them were so young, and they looked like the kid down the street, but you knew it'd take a team all day to put them back together and even then they probably wouldn't make it. I tried not to look at their faces, just their wounds."

Triage, doing what you must to save the maximum number of lives. I wondered if the Laurel Heights killer thought he or she was practicing triage.

There weren't many questions that day, and the women seemed to feel the same relief I did when I dismissed class. I didn't have a good excuse for hanging around, but no one was paying much attention to me so it didn't matter. I watched the police question not only the nurses but the maintenance man, the delivery people, and the food service workers. The only people they didn't talk to were the patients.

Aimee and Sarah sat in the lounge and chatted. Laura was having a good day and seemed quite lucid if you didn't notice that she repeated herself. They were friends of Emma's; Aimee's room was down the hall from the one where Emma had died, yet no one asked them anything. It was as if they were invisible.

"When you're in a wheelchair people treat you different," Aimee told me. "They think your mind is as weak as your body." Her voice had an uncharacteristic bitterness to it.

"Do you have any suspicions of who the killer might be?" I asked.

All three women shook their heads. "I worry about Juan," Aimee said. "Not because he did anything, but because of the immigration."

I worried about Juan, too, but for other reasons. I'd done some checking and found that the story he told the women was true, which meant that he'd lied on his application. It wouldn't take the police long to discover that he was not a U.S. citizen, and the fact that he was hiding his immigration status might well mean he'd fail a lie detector test.

Unless they found something I'd missed, the police would realize fairly quickly that only the nurses and the administrators with keys had access to the nursing facility. They'd also realize that the same set of nurses had been on duty when Mary and Emma died. Juan was in for a rough time.

I was concerned that the women must feel very threatened with a murderer loose in their midst. I knew Janet was terrified. I started to reassure them that the killer probably wouldn't strike now that the police were investigating, but Aimee just shook her head.

"We're not afraid of dying, Catherine," she said. "There are things far worse than death."

I went back to Laurel Heights at nine that night, just to test the security. Dorothy Waters answered the door, admitted me and had me sign the book. I expressed surprise at finding her there, and she explained that she was subbing for someone else. She acted far less interested in my presence there than I was in hers.

The lounge, so sunny and inviting during the day, was still and empty, a shadowy world of angular shapes. In the hall the doors had been left open, perhaps to protect the patients from deeds best done out of sight.

I walked down the hall, past the room where a frail female voice called out for help. When I'd first heard her pleas three weeks ago. I'd been haunted by them. Now I barely heard them. Past Room 108, which was shared by two men. The one near the door was little more than a skeleton with skin stretched tight over its frame. His mouth hung open as he slept. I had never seen him awake. The other sat in his bed holding the television remote control and flicking through the channels. He never watched anything for more than a few seconds.

I'd gotten used to the days at Laurel Heights; nights were different.

The hall was an empty tunnel under the harsh glare of fluorescent light. Most of the rooms were dark, illuminated only by the pale flickering of a television screen. I could hear snatches of a dozen television shows mixed with other voices, frail and querulous.

A tiny woman with thin gray hair sat in a wheelchair holding a rag doll. Her hands moved constantly, picking at the blanket that covered her lap. She smiled sweetly at me, and said something I didn't understand then held her doll up to show me.

I forced myself to smile back, but it was a pasted-on smile. The messy sludge of emotions coalesced into my old friend, fear. Laurel Heights scared me. Hell, it terrified me. I've faced men with knives and guns and none of it was nearly as frightening as the thought of ending up in this place.

I looked down at the old woman with the rag doll. She'd returned to her own world, her eyes dull but her hands constantly working. I wondered what she'd looked like when she was *my* age. Once she'd been young, probably had her time of love and romance. I wanted to imagine that she'd been frail, that somehow she'd been different from me, but the biographies of my oral history group had robbed me of that comforting thought.

These were not weak women. In their youth they had been daring and resourceful. Emma Warren had run a farm by herself while her husband went to war. Betty Katzen had been among the last Americans out of the Philippines. And Aimee Girault had stood against the Nazi soldiers and risked torture and death only to end her life imprisoned in a wheelchair, betrayed by her own body.

I imagined myself as a resident of this place, with a roommate whose mind was drawing her ever backwards into a final infancy and minimum wage attendants who were at best overworked and at worst brutal. There was no privacy here, strangers stripped off your clothes and bathed your body as if it were an inanimate object to be scrubbed and dried and then returned to its shelf. You shared a room with a person you didn't choose and might very well find objectionable. You ate what you were served or went hungry. You did what you were told or suffered subtle and not so subtle forms of punishment. Prisoners in the county jail were better off; and this was a "good" facility.

My chest was so tight that I could hardly breathe, and the walls seemed to be closing in on me. I simply couldn't stay in the building any longer. Instead of turning down the hall to the infirmary, I headed for the front door.

It took all my self-control to walk through the lobby and out the door. My body wanted desperately to run. Once outside, I took great gulping breaths of air. I leaned against a tree trunk and stared up at the dark, starless sky. The bands around my chest loosened slightly, but I still felt the panic pressing in on me.

I needed to move, to feel my legs swing and my feet meet the ground. I turned to the right and began walking with no destination other than away from Laurel Heights.

I walked for over an hour, more aware of movement than thought, and as I headed back for Laurel Heights, I knew who'd killed Mary and Emma.

Wednesday

Betty Katzen's apartment was on the fifth floor of the main building. She looked surprised to find me at her door.

"Catherine, this is Wednesday, isn't it? We don't have class today."

I asked if I could come in and she ushered me into a living area with a couch and chair upholstered in a bright floral print. "I know who killed Emma," I said.

Her gaze never faltered. "Really."

I nodded and said nothing.

"Why are you telling me?" she asked. "Surely that's information for the police."

"I guess I wanted to hear about it from you first."

She sighed. "You're not really a teacher, are you?"

"No," I said. "I'm a private investigator."

She nodded. "Aimee wondered about you. You were always watching. You were different from the other volunteers." She paused. "We knew we'd have to do something, of course, if they arrested one of the nurses. But we hoped they wouldn't have enough evidence to accuse anyone."

"And you knew they'd never think of you."

"A bunch of sweet old ladies. Never."

"How long has this been going on?" I asked.

"It started four years ago. A friend, Clair Meltzor, got Alzheimer's. It went very fast, and she was beyond us before we knew how bad it was. We watched as she deteriorated, first her mind, then her body. It was awful.

"She used up all her money. She'd wanted to give her granddaughter something for college, but it all went for nursing. We were all horrified that it could happen to us. That was when we got the idea. No one wanted to be a vegetable, and no one wanted to end up with the mind of a two-year-old. Pain doesn't scare any of us so much, but being like Claire was at the end that we couldn't face. You probably think we're cowards."

I shook my head. "I think you're among the bravest people I know."

"Aimee is, and Sarah. When Aimee came out of that stroke, she couldn't even roll over. She works every day just to be able to feed herself or hold a book. I've seen her so tired she can't reach up to wipe the tears from her face. But how did you figure it out?"

"I spent some time in the nursing wing last night and got a healthy case of claustrophobia. It made me start to think about how it was for Aimee and the others. Then I realized that there was one door to the nursing facility that everyone had ignored, the one from the retirement center. That door isn't locked at night. It would have been quite easy for Aimee or one of the others to ring for the nurse and draw him away from the nurses' station while someone else came through that door and down to Mary's or Emma's room.

"And as a nurse, you'd have known how to manage things—what drugs, the necessary dosage, maybe even how to get them."

She sat silently for a moment. Her usually animated face was mask-like and the color was gone from her cheeks. I felt like I'd just mugged my Sunday school teacher.

"I guess I am the logical one, and I'm willing to confess, but *not* to implicate my friends. I'm sorry for the trouble we've caused Juan and the other nurses. We can't let one of them be blamed."

I thought of Betty Katzen in prison. Or in a courtroom. And I thought of what I'd have done in her situation. I knew I'd have joined the pact, and having done that, I would have had to fulfill my promise to the others.

I took a deep breath. I was about to make myself an accessory to murder. "I don't really think that's necessary," I said. "The police don't have enough to charge anyone. Juan may have to flee immigration, but your confession wouldn't have any effect on that."

"You won't tell them?"

"Tell them what, that a group of consenting adults are taking care of each other's last wishes?"

She looked skeptical. "But you came here to solve the crime. Can you leave with it unsolved?"

"I came to assure my aunt that she would not be murdered in her bed. I can do that. I've done my job."

We've continued with the oral history class, and we even have a couple of new members. My mother is terribly proud of me for taking time to visit Janet and the other old ladies. She wouldn't understand if I told her that in this class, I'm the student.

Only recently has Larry Block been sufficiently praised for all the wonderful things he's done for the mystery novel.

Some prefer the Matt Scudder novels (dark) to the Bernie Rhodenbarrs (light), but most people are sensible enough to enjoy and admire them each in their way. He is the pro's pro, sleek, savvy, relentless, and always capable of startling you.

A serious look at Block's career, which began in the late fifties, also becomes a serious look at the crime field in general during that same amount of time. He has written spies, capers, private detectives, noirs, and espionage—changing with the times, but never being merely faddy. He has brought something new and engaging to every sub-genre he's worked in.

He also said the truest thing ever uttered about mystery novels, that there are two kinds—those with cats and those without.

A Blow for Freedom
LAWRENCE BLOCK

The gun was smaller than Elliot remembered. At Kennedy, waiting for his bag to come up on the carrousel, he'd been irritated with himself for buying the damned thing. For years now, ever since Pan Am had stranded him in Milan with the clothes he was wearing, he'd made an absolute point of never checking luggage. He'd flown to Miami with his favorite carry-on bag; returning, he'd checked the same bag, all because it now contained a Smith & Wesson revolver and a box of fifty .38-caliber shells.

At least he hadn't had to take a train. "Oh, for Christ's sake," he'd told Huebner, after they'd bought the gun together, "I'll have to take the train back, won't I? I can't get on the plane with a gun in my pocket."

"It's not recommended," Huebner had said. "But all you have to do is check your bag with the gun and shells in it."

"Isn't there a regulation against it?"

"Probably. There's rules against everything. All I know is, I do it all the time, and I never heard of anyone getting into any trouble over it. They scope the checked bags, or at least they're supposed to, but they're looking for bombs. There's nothing very dangerous about a gun locked away in the baggage compartment."

"Couldn't the shells explode?"

"In a fire, possibly. If the plane goes down in flames, the bullets may go off and put a hole in the side of your suitcase."

"I guess I'm being silly."

"Well, you're a New Yorker. You don't know a whole lot about guns."

"No." He'd hesitated. "Maybe I should have bought one of those plastic ones."

"The Glock?" Huebner smiled. "It's a nice weapon, and it's probably the one I'll buy next. But you couldn't carry it on a plane."

"But I thought—"

"You thought it would fool the scanners and metal detectors at airport security. It won't. That's hardly the point of it, a big gun like that. No, they replaced a lot of the metal with high-impact plastic to reduce the weight. It's supposed to lessen recoil slightly, too, but I don't know if it does. Personally, I like the looks of it. But it'll show up fine on a scanner if you put it in a carry-on bag, and it'll set off alarms if you walk it through a metal detector." He snorted. "Of course, that didn't keep some idiots from introducing bills banning it in the U.S. Nobody in politics likes to let a fact stand in the way of a grandstand play."

His bag was one of the last ones up. Waiting for it, he worried that there was going to be trouble about the gun. When it came, he had to resist the urge to open the bag immediately and make sure the gun was still there. The bag felt light, and he decided some baggage handler had detected it and appropriated it for his own use.

Nervous, he thought. Scared it's there, scared it's not.

He took a cab home to his Manhattan apartment and left the bag unopened while he made himself a drink. Then he unpacked, and the gun was smaller than he remembered it. He picked it up and felt its weight, and that was greater than he recalled. And it was empty. It would be even heavier fully loaded.

After Huebner had helped him pick out the gun, they'd driven way out on Route 27, where treeless swamps extended for miles in every direction. Huebner pulled off the road a few yards from a wrecked car, its tires missing and most of its window glass gone.

"There's our target," he said. "You find a lot of cars abandoned along this stretch, but you don't want to start shooting up the newer ones."

"Because someone might come back for them?"

Huebner shook his head. "Because there might be a body in the trunk. This is where the drug dealers tend to drop off the unsuccessful competition, but no self-respecting drug dealer would be caught dead in a wreck like this one. You figure it'll be a big enough target for you?"

Embarrassingly enough, he missed the car altogether with his first shot. "You pulled up on it," Huebner told him. "Probably anticipating the recoil. Don't waste time worrying where the bullets are going yet. Just get used to pointing and firing."

And he got used to it. The recoil was considerable and so was the weight of the gun, but he did get used to both and began to be able to make the shots go where he wanted them to go. After Elliott had used up a full box of shells, Huebner got a pistol of his own from the glove compartment and put a few rounds into the fender of the ruined automobile. Huebner's gun was a nine-millimeter automatic with a clip that held twelve cartridges. It was much larger, noisier and heavier than the .38, and it did far more damage to the target.

"Got a whole lot of stopping power," Huebner said. "Hit a man in the arm with this, you're likely to take him down. Here, try it. Strike a blow for freedom."

The recoil was greater than the .38's, but less so than he would have guessed. Elliott fired off several rounds, enjoying the sense of power. He returned the gun to Huebner, who emptied the clip into the old car.

Driving back, Elliott said, "A phrase you used: 'Strike a blow for freedom.' "

"Oh, you never heard that? I had an uncle used that expression every time he took a drink. They used to say that during Prohibition. You hoisted a few then in defiance of the law, you were striking a blow for freedom."

The gun, the first article Elliott unpacked, was the last he put away.

He couldn't think of what to do with it. Its purchase had seemed appropriate in Florida, where they seemed to have gun shops everywhere. You walked into one and walked out owning a weapon. There was even a town in central Georgia where they'd passed their own local version of gun control, an ordinance requiring the adult population to go about armed. There had never been any question of enforcing the law, he knew; it had been passed as a statement of local sentiment.

Here in New York, guns were less appropriate. They were illegal, to begin with. You could apply for a carry permit, but unless there was some genuine reason connected with your occupation, your application was virtually certain to be denied. Elliott worked in an office and never carried anything to it or from it but a briefcase filled with papers, nor did his work take him down streets any meaner than the one he lived on. As far as the law was concerned, he had no need for a gun.

Yet he owned one, legally or not. Its possession was at once unsettling and thrilling, like the occasional ounce or so of marijuana secreted in his various living quarters during his twenties. There was something exciting, something curiously estimable, about having that which was prohibited, and at the same time, there was a certain amount of danger connected with its possession.

There ought to be security as well, he thought. He'd bought the gun for his protection in a city that increasingly seemed incapable of protecting its own inhabitants. He turned the gun over, let the empty cylinder swing out, accustomed his fingers to the cool metal.

His apartment was on the twelfth floor of a prewar building. Three shifts of doormen guarded the lobby. No other building afforded access to any of his windows, and those near the fire escape were protected by locked window gates, the key to which hung out of reach on a nail. The door to the hallway had two dead-bolt locks, each with its cylinder secured by an escutcheon plate. The door had a steel core and was further reinforced by a Fox police lock.

Elliott had never felt insecure in his apartment, nor were its security measures the result of his own paranoia. They had all been in place when he moved in. And they were standard for the building and the neighborhood.

He passed the gun from hand to hand, at once glad to have it and, like an impulse shopper, wondering why he'd bought it.

Where should he keep it?

The drawer of the night stand suggested itself. He put the gun and the box of shells in it, closed the drawer, and went to take a shower.

It was almost a week before he looked at the gun again. He didn't mention it and rarely thought about it. News items would bring it to mind. A hardware-store owner in Rego Park killed his wife and small daughter with an unregistered handgun, then turned the weapon on himself; reading about it in the paper, Elliott thought of the revolver in his night-stand drawer. An honor student was slain in his bedroom by a stray shot from a high-powered assault rifle, and Elliott, watching TV, thought again of his gun.

On the Friday after his return, some item about the shooting of a drug dealer again directed his thoughts to the gun, and it occurred to him that he ought at least to load it. Suppose someone came crashing through his door or used some advance in criminal technology to cut the gates on his windows. If he were reaching hurriedly for a gun, it should be loaded.

He loaded all six chambers. He seemed to remember that you were supposed to leave one chamber empty as a safety measure. Otherwise, the gun might discharge if dropped. Cocking the weapon would presumably rotate the cylinder and ready it for shooting. Still, it wasn't going to fire itself just sitting in his night-stand drawer, was it, now? And if he reached for it, if he needed it in a hurry, he'd want it fully loaded.

If you had to shoot at someone, you didn't want to shoot once or twice and then stop. You wanted to empty the gun.

Had Huebner told him that? Or had someone said it in a movie or on television? It didn't matter, he decided. Either way, it was sound advice.

A few days later, he saw a movie in which the hero, a renegade cop up against an entrenched drug mob, slept with a gun under his pillow. It was a much larger gun than Elliott's, something like Huebner's big automatic.

"More gun than you really need in your situation," Huebner had told him. "And it's too big and too heavy. You want something you can slip into a pocket. A cannon like this, you'd need a whole shoulder rig or it'd pull at your suit coat something awful."

Not that he'd ever carry it.

That night, he got the gun out of the drawer and put it under his pillow. He thought of the princess who couldn't sleep with a pea under her mattress. He felt a little silly, and he felt, too, some of what he had felt playing with toy guns as a child.

He got the gun from under his pillow and put it back in the drawer, where it belonged. He lay for a long time, inhaling the smell of the gun, metal and machine oil, interesting and not unpleasant.

A masculine scent, he thought. Blend in a little leather and tobacco, maybe a little horse shit, and you've got something to slap on after a shave. Win the respect of your fellows and drive the women wild.

He never put the gun under his pillow again. But the linen held the scent of the gun, and even after he'd changed the sheets and pillow-cases, he could detect the smell on the pillow.

It was not until the incident with the panhandler that he ever carried the gun outside the apartment.

There were panhandlers all over the place, had been for several years now. It seemed to Elliott that there were more of them every year, but he wasn't sure if that was really the case. They were of either sex and of every age and color, some of them proclaiming well-rehearsed speeches on subway cars, some standing mute in doorways and extending paper cups, some asking generally for spare change or specifically for money for food or for shelter or for wine.

Some of them, he knew, were homeless people, ground down by the system. Some belonged in mental institutions. Some were addicted to crack. Some were lay-abouts, earning more this way than they could at a menial job. Elliott couldn't tell which was which and wasn't sure how he felt about them, his emotions ranging from sympathy to irritation, depending on circumstances. Sometimes he gave money, sometimes he didn't. He had given up trying to devise a consistent policy and simply followed his impulse of the moment.

One evening, walking home from the bus stop, he encountered a panhandler who demanded money. "Come on," the man said. "Gimme a dollar."

Elliott started to walk past him, but the man moved to block his path. He was taller and heavier than Elliott, wearing a dirty Army jacket, his face partly hidden behind a dense black beard. His eyes, slightly exophthalmic, were fierce.

"Didn't you hear me? Gimme a fuckin' dollar!"

Elliott reached into his pocket, came out with a handful of change. The man made a face at the coins Elliott placed in his hand, then evidently decided the donation was acceptable.

"Thank you kindly," he said. "Have a nice day."

Have a nice day, indeed. Elliott walked on home, nodded to the doorman, let himself into his apartment. It wasn't until he had engaged the locks that he realized his heart was pounding and his hands trembling.

He poured himself a drink. It helped, but it didn't change anything.

Had he been mugged? There was a thin line, he realized, and he wasn't sure if the man had crossed it. He had not been asking for money, he had been demanding it, and the absence of a specific threat did not mean there was no menace in the demand. Elliott, certainly, had given him money out of fear. He'd been intimidated. Unwilling to display his wallet, he'd fished out a batch of coins, including a couple of quarters and a subway token, currently valued at $1.15.

A small enough price, but that wasn't the point. The point was that he'd been made to pay it. *Stand and deliver*, the man might as well have said. Elliott had stood and delivered.

A block from his own door, for God's sake. A good street in a good neighborhood. Broad daylight.

And you couldn't even report it. Not that anyone reported anything anymore. A friend at work had reported a burglary only because you had to in order to collect on your insurance. The police, he'd said, had taken the report over the phone. "I'll send somebody if you want," the cop had said, "but I've got to tell you, it's a waste of your time and ours." Someone else had been robbed of his watch and wallet at gunpoint and had not bothered reporting the incident, "What's the point?" he'd said.

But even if there were a point, Elliott had nothing to report. A man had asked for money and he'd given it to him. They had a right to ask for money, some judge had ruled. They were exercising their First Amendment right of free speech. Never mind that there had been an unvoiced threat, that Elliott had paid the money out of intimidation. Never mind that it damn well felt like a mugging.

First Amendment rights. Maybe he ought to exercise his own rights under the Second Amendment—the right to bear arms.

That same evening he took the gun from the drawer and tried it in various pockets. Unloaded now, he tried tucking it into his belt, first in front, then behind, in the small of his back. He practiced reaching for it, drawing it. He felt foolish, and it was uncomfortable walking around with the gun in his belt like that.

It was comfortable in his right-hand jacket pocket, but the weight of it spoiled the line of the jacket. The pants pocket on the same side was better. He had reached into that pocket to produce the handful of change that had mollified the panhandler. Suppose he had come out with a gun instead?

"Thank you kindly. Have a nice day."

Later, after he'd eaten, he went to the video store on the next block to rent a movie for the evening. He was out the door before he realized he still had the gun in his pocket. It was still unloaded, the six shells lying where he had spilled them on his bed. He had reached for the keys to lock up and there was the gun.

He got the keys, locked up, and went out with the gun in his pocket. The sensation of being on the street with a gun in his pocket was an interesting one. He felt as though he were keeping a secret from everyone he met, and that the secret empowered him. He spent longer than usual in the video store. Two fantasies came and went. In one, he held up the clerk, brandishing his empty gun and walking out with all the money in the register. In the other, someone else attempted to rob the place and Elliott drew his weapon and foiled the holdup.

Back home, he watched the movie, but his mind insisted on replaying the second fantasy. In one version, the holdup man spun toward him, gun in hand, and Elliott had to face him with an unloaded revolver.

When the movie ended, he reloaded the gun and put it back in the drawer.

The following evening, he carried the gun, loaded this time. The night after that was a Friday, and when he got home from the office, he put the gun in his pocket almost without thinking about it. He went out for a bite of dinner, then played cards at a friend's apartment a dozen blocks away. They played, as always, for low stakes, but Elliott was the big winner. Another player joked that he had better take a cab home.

"No need," he said. "I'm armed and dangerous."

He walked home, and on the way, he stopped at a bar and had a couple of beers. Some people at a table near where he stood were talking about a recent outrage, a young advertising executive in Greenwich Village shot dead while using a pay phone around the corner from his apartment. "I'll tell you something," one of the party said. "I'm about ready to start carrying a gun."

"You can't, legally," someone said.

"Screw legally."

"So a guy tries something and you shoot him and you're the one winds up in trouble."

"I'll tell you something," the man said. "I'd rather be judged by twelve than carried by six."

He carried the gun the whole weekend. It never left his pocket. He was at home much of the time, watching a ball game on television, catching up with his bookkeeping, but he left the house several times each day and always had the gun on his person.

He never drew it, but sometimes he would put his hand in his pocket and let his fingers curl around the butt of it. He found its presence increasingly reassuring. If anything happened, he was ready.

And he didn't have to worry about an accidental discharge. The chamber under the hammer was unloaded. He had worked all that out. If he dropped the gun, it wouldn't go off. But if he cocked it and worked the trigger, it would fire.

When he took his hand from his pocket and held it to his face, he could smell the odor of the gun on his fingers. He liked that.

By Monday morning, he had grown used to the gun. It seemed perfectly natural to carry it to the office.

On the way home, not that night but the following night, the same aggressive panhandler accosted him. His routine had not changed. "Come on," he said. "Gimme a dollar."

Elliott's hand was in his pocket, his fingers touching the cold metal. "Not tonight," he said.

Maybe something showed in his eyes.

"Hey, that's cool," the panhandler said. "You have a good day just the same." And stepped out of his path.

A week or so after that, he was riding the subway, coming home late after dinner with married friends in Forest Hills. He had a paperback with him, but he couldn't concentrate on it, and he realized that the two young men across the car from him were looking him over, sizing him up. They were wearing untied basketball sneakers and warm-up jackets and looked street smart, and dangerous. He was wearing the suit he'd worn to the office and had a briefcase beside him; he looked prosperous and vulnerable.

The car was almost empty. There was a derelict sleeping a few yards away, a woman with a small child all the way down at the other end. One of the pair nudged the other, then turned his eyes toward Elliott again.

Elliott took the gun out of his pocket. He held it on his lap and let them see it, then put it back in his pocket.

The two of them got off at the next station, leaving Elliott to ride home alone.

When he got home, he took the gun from his pocket and set it on the night stand. (He no longer bothered tucking it in the drawer.) He went into the bathroom and looked at himself in the mirror.

"Fucking thing saved my life," he said.

One night, he took a woman friend to dinner. Afterward, they went back to her place and wound up in bed. At one point, she got up to use the bathroom, and while she was up, she hung up her own clothing and went to put his pants on a hanger.

"These weigh a ton," she said. "What have you got in here?"

"See for yourself," he said. "But be careful."

"My God. Is it loaded?"

"They're not much good if they're not."

"My God."

He told her how he'd bought it in Florida, how it had now become second nature for him to carry it. "I'd feel naked without it," he said.

"Aren't you afraid you'll get into trouble?"

"I look at it this way," he told her. "I'd rather be judged by twelve than carried by six."

One night, two men cut across the avenue toward him while he was walking home from his Friday card game. Without hesitation, he drew the gun.

"Whoa!" the nearer of the two sang out. "Hey, it's cool, man. Thought you were somebody else is all."

They veered off, gave him a wide berth.

Thought I was somebody else, he thought. Thought I was a victim, is what you thought.

There were stores around the city that sold police equipment. Books to study for the sergeant's exam. Copies of the latest revised penal code. A T-shirt that read, N.Y.P.D. HOMICIDE SQUAD. OUR DAY BEGINS WHEN YOUR DAY ENDS.

He stopped in and didn't buy anything, then returned for a kit to clean his gun. He hadn't fired it yet, except in Florida, but it seemed as though he ought to clean it from time to time, anyway. He took the kit home and unloaded the gun and cleaned it, working an oiled patch of cloth through the short barrel. When he was finished, he put everything away and reloaded the gun.

He liked the way it smelled, freshly cleaned with gun oil.

A week later, he returned and bought a bulletproof vest. They had two types, one significantly more expensive than the other. Both were made of Kevlar, whatever that was.

"Your more expensive one provides you with a little more protection," the proprietor explained. "Neither one's gonna stop a shot from an assault rifle. The real high-powered rounds, concrete don't stop 'em. This here, though, it provides protection against a knife thrust. Neither one's a sure thing to stop a knife, but this here's reinforced.''

He bought the better vest.

One night, lonely and sad, he unloaded the gun and put the barrel to his temple. His finger was inside the trigger guard, curled around the trigger.

You weren't supposed to dry-fire the gun. It was bad for the firing pin to squeeze off a shot when there was no cartridge in the chamber.

Quit fooling around, he told himself.

He cocked the gun, then took it away from his temple. He uncocked it, put the barrel in his mouth. That was how the cops did it when they couldn't take it anymore. Eating your gun, they called it.

He didn't like the taste, the metal, the gun oil. Liked the smell but not the taste.

He loaded the gun and quit fooling around.

A little later, he went out. It was late, but he didn't feel like sitting around the apartment, and he knew he wouldn't be able to sleep. He wore the Kevlar vest—he wore it all the time lately—and, of course, he had the gun in his pocket.

He walked around, with no destination in mind. He stopped for a beer but drank only a few sips of it, then headed out to the street again. The moon came into view, and he wasn't surprised to note that it was full.

He had his hand in his pocket, touching the gun. When he breathed deeply, he could feel the vest drawn around his chest. He liked the sensation.

When he reached the park, he hesitated. Years ago, back when the city was safe, you knew not to walk in the park at night. It was dangerous even then. It could hardly be otherwise now, when every neighborhood was a jungle.

So? If anything happened, if anybody tried anything, he was ready.

Wendy cherishes the details and grace notes of fiction.

She doesn't do the Big Truths (leaving those to louder and often lesser writers); instead she gives us the small truths, and the throwaway grace notes, that make up life for most of us.

For instance, she knows that a crabby grocery clerk can ruin your whole morning, and she can spin a beautifully wrought story off just such a minor incident.

Wendy is very much a voice of the nineties, without any of the dogma of the eighties or the disco frivolity of the seventies. She captures better than just about anybody the plight of the single woman and single mother in this hard and mostly hapless era when surviving in the middle-class often requires something akin to trench warfare.

Plus she's always one hell of a lot of fun to read.

Nine Sons
WENDY HORNSBY

I saw Janos Bonachek's name in the paper this morning. There was a nice article about his twenty-five years on the federal bench, his plans for retirement. The Boy Wonder, they called him, but the accompanying photograph showed him to be nearly bald, a wispy white fringe over his ears the only remains of his once remarkable head of yellow hair.

For just a moment, I was tempted to write him, or call him, to put to rest forever questions I had about the death that was both a link and a wedge between us. In the end I didn't. What was the point after all these years? Perhaps Janos's long and fine career in the law was sufficient atonement, for us all, for events that happened so long ago.

It occurred on an otherwise ordinary day. It was April, but Spring was still only a tease. If anything stood out among the endless acres of black mud and gray slush, it was two bright dabs of color: first the blue crocus pushing through a patch of dirty snow, then the bright yellow head of Janos Bonachek as he ran along the line of horizon toward his parent's farm after school. Small marvels maybe, the spring crocus and young Janos, but in that frozen place, and during those hard times, surely they were miracles.

The year was 1934, the depths of the Great Depression. Times were bad, but in the small farm town where I had been posted by the school board, hardship was an old acquaintance.

I had arrived the previous September, fresh from teacher college, with a new red scarf in my bag and the last piece of my birthday cake. At twenty, I wasn't much older than my high-school-age pupils.

Janos was ten when the term began, and exactly the height of ripe wheat. His hair was so nearly the same gold as the bearded grain that he could run through the uncut fields and be no more noticeable than the ripples made by a prairie breeze. The wheat had to be mown before Janos could be seen at all.

On the northern plains, the season for growing is short, a quick breath of summer between the spring thaw and the first frost of fall. Below the surface of the soil, and within the people who forced a living from it, there seemed to be a layer that never had time to warm all the way through. I believe to this day that if the winter hadn't been so long, the chilling of the soul so complete, we would not have been forced to bury Janos Bonachek's baby sister.

Janos came from a large family, nine sons. Only one of them, Janos, was released from chores to attend school. Even then, he brought work with him in the form of his younger brother, Boya. Little Boya was then four or five. He wasn't as brilliant as Janos, but he tried hard. Tutored and cajoled by Janos, Boya managed to skip to the second-grade reader that year.

Around Halloween, that first year, Janos was passed up to me by the elementary grades teacher. She said she had nothing more to teach him. I don't know that I was any better prepared than she was, except that the high school textbooks were on the shelves in my room. I did my best.

Janos was a challenge. He absorbed everything I had to offer and demanded more, pushing me in his quiet yet insistent way to explain or to find out. He was eager for everything. Except geography. There he was a doubter. Having lived his entire life on a flat expanse of prairie, Janos would not believe the earth was a sphere, or that there were bodies of water vaster than the wheat fields that stretched past his horizon. The existence of mountains, deserts, and oceans he had to take on faith, like the heavenly world the nuns taught me about in catechism.

Janos was an oddball to his classmates, certainly. I can still see that shiny head bent close to his books, the brow of his pinched little face furrowed as he took a new set of universal truths from the world beyond the Central Grain Exchange. The other students deferred to him, respected him, though they never played with him. He spent recesses and lunch periods sitting on the school's front stoop, waiting for me to ring the big brass bell and let him back inside. I wonder how that affected him as a judge, this boy who never learned how to play.

Janos shivered when he was cold, but he seemed otherwise oblivious to external discomfort or appearances. Both he and Boya came to school barefoot until there was snow on the ground. Then they showed up in mismatched boots sizes too big, yet no one called attention to them, which I found singular. Janos's coat, even in blizzards, was an old gray blanket that I'm sure he slept under at night. His straight yellow hair stuck out in chunks as if it had been scythed like the wheat. He never acknowledged that he was in any way different from his well-scrubbed classmates.

While his oblivion to discomfort gave Janos an air of stoic dignity, it did impose some hardship on me. When the blizzards came and I knew school should be closed, I went out anyway because I knew Janos would be there, with Boya. If I didn't come to unlock the classroom, I was sure they would freeze waiting.

Getting there was itself a challenge. I boarded in town with the doctor and his wife, my friend Martha. When the snow blew in blinding swirls and the road was impassable to any automobile, I would persuade the doctor to harness his team of plow horses to his cutter and drive me out. The doctor made only token protest after the first trip: the boys had been at the school for some time before we arrived, huddled together on the stoop like drifted snow.

Those were the best days, alone, the two boys and I. I would bring books from Martha's shelves, books not always on the school board approved list. We would read together, and talk about the world on the far side of the prairie and how one day we would see it for ourselves. We would, as the snow drifts piled up to the sills outside, try to imagine the sultry heat of the tropics, the pitch and roll of the oceans, men in pale suits in electric-lit parlors discussing being and nothingness while they sipped hundred-year-old sherry.

We had many days together. That year the first snow came on All Saints Day and continued regularly until Good Friday. I would have despaired during the ceaseless cold if it weren't for Janos and the lessons I received at home on the evenings of those blizzardy days.

Invariably, on winter nights when the road was impassable and sensible people were at home before the fire, someone would call for the doctor's services. He would harness the cutter, and go. Martha, of course, couldn't sleep until she heard the cutter return. We would keep each other entertained, sometimes until after the sun came up.

Martha had gone to Smith or Vassar. I'm not sure which because Eastern girl's schools were so far from my experience that the names meant nothing to me then. She was my guide to the world I had only seen in magazines and slick-paged catalogues, where people were polished to a smooth and shiny perfection, where long underwear, if indeed any was worn, never showed below their hems. These people were oddly whole, no scars, no body parts lost to farm machinery. In their faces I saw a peace of mind I was sure left them open to the world of ideas. I longed for them, and was sure Martha did as well.

Martha took life in our small community with grace, though I knew she missed the company of other educated women. I had to suffice.

Just as I spent my days preparing Janos, Martha spent her evenings teaching me the social graces I would need if I were ever to make my escape. Perhaps I was not as quick a pupil as Janos, but I was as eager.

Lessons began in the attic where Martha kept her trunks. Packed in white tissue was the elegant trousseau she had brought with her from the East, gowns of wine-colored taffeta moiré and green velvet and a pink silk so fine I feared touching it with my callused hands.

I had never actually seen a live woman in an evening gown, though I knew Martha's gowns surpassed the mail order gowns that a woman might order for an Eastern Star ritual, if she had money for ready-made.

Martha and I would put on the gowns and drink coffee with brandy and read to each other from Proust, or take turns at the piano. I might struggle through a Strauss waltz or the Fat Lady Polka. She played flawless Dvorak and Debussey. This was my finishing school, long nights in Martha's front parlor, waiting for the cutter to bring the doctor home, praying the cutter hadn't overturned, hoping the neighbor he had gone to tend was all right.

When he did return, his hands so cold he needed help out of his layers of clothes, Martha's standard getting was, "Delivering Mrs. Bonachek?" This was a big joke to us, because, of course, Mrs. Bonachek delivered herself. No one knew how many pregnancies she had had beyond her nine living sons. Poor people, they were rich in sons.

That's what I kept coming back to that early spring afternoon as I walked away from the Bonachek farm. I had seen Janos running across the fields after school. If he hadn't been hurrying home to help his mother, then where had he gone? And where were his brothers?

It lay on my mind.

As I said, the day in question had been perfectly ordinary. I had stayed after my students to sweep the classroom, so it was nearly four before I started for home. As always, I walked the single-lane road toward town, passing the Bonachek farm about half way. Though underfoot the black earth was frozen hard as tarmac, I was looking for signs of spring, counting the weeks until the end of the school term.

My feet were cold inside my new Sears and Roebuck boots and I was mentally drafting a blistering letter to the company. The catalogue copy had promised me boots that would withstand the coldest weather, so, as an act of faith in Sears, I had invested a good chunk of my slim savings for the luxury of warm feet. Perhaps the copywriter in a Chicago office could not imagine ground as cold as this road.

I watched for Janos's mother as I approached her farm. For three days running, I had seen Mrs. Bonachek working in the fields as I walked to school in the morning, and as I walked back to town in the dusky afternoon. There was no way to avoid her. The distance between the school and the Bonachek farm was uninterrupted by hill or wall or stand of trees.

Mrs. Bonachek would rarely glance up as I passed. Unlike the other parents, she never greeted me, never asked how her boys were doing in little English, but neither did many of the other parents, or my own.

She was an enigma. Formless, colorless, Mrs. Bonachek seemed no more than a piece of the landscape as she spread seed grain onto the plowed ground from a big pouch in her apron. Wearing felt boots, she walked slowly along the straight furrows, her thin arm moving in a sweep as regular as any motor-powered machine.

Hers was an odd display of initiative, I thought. No one else was out in the fields yet. It seemed to me she risked losing her seed to mildew or to a last spring freeze by planting so early. Something else bothered me more. While I was a dairyman's daughter and knew little about growing wheat, I knew what was expected of farm children. There were six in my family, my five brothers and myself. My mother never went to the barns alone when there was a child at hand. Mrs. Bonachek had nine sons. Why I wondered, was she working in the fields all alone?

On the afternoon of the fourth day, as had become my habit, I began looking for Mrs. Bonachek as soon as I locked the school house door.

When I couldn't find her, I felt a pang of guilty relief that I wouldn't have to see her that afternoon, call out a greeting that I knew she wouldn't return.

So I walked more boldly, dressing down Sears in language I could never put down on paper, enjoying the anarchy of my phrases even as I counted the blue crocus along the road.

Just as I came abreast of the row of stones that served to define the beginning of the Bonachek driveway, I saw her. She sat on the ground between the road and the small house, head bowed, arms folded across her chest. Her faded calico apron, its big seed pocket looking flat and empty, was spread on the ground beside her. She could have been sleeping, she was so still. I thought she might be sick, and would have gone to her, but she turned her head toward me, saw me, and shifted around until her back was toward me.

I didn't stop. The road curved and after a while I couldn't see her without turning right around. I did look back once and saw Mrs. Bonachek upright again. She had left her apron on the ground, a faded-red bundle at the end of a furrow. She gathered up the skirt of her dress, filled it with seed grain, and continued her work. So primitive, I thought. How was it possible she had spawned the bright light that was Janos?

I found Martha in an extravagant mood when I reached home. The weather was frigid, but she, too had seen the crocus. She announced that we would hold a tea to welcome spring. We would put on the tea frocks from her trunk and invite in some ladies from town. It would be a lark, she said, a coming out. I could invite anyone I wanted.

I still had Mrs. Bonachek on my mind. I couldn't help picturing her rising from her squat in the muddy fields to come sit on Martha's brocade sofa, so I said I would invite her first. The idea made us laugh until I had the hiccups. I said the woman had no daughters and probably needed some lively female company.

Martha went to the piano and banged out something suitable for a melodrama. I got a pan of hot water and soaked my cold feet while we talked about spring and the prospect of being warm again, truly warm, in all parts at once. I wondered what magazine ladies did at teas.

We were still planning little sandwiches and petit fours and onions cut into daisies when the doctor came in for supper. There were snow-flakes on his beard and I saw snow falling outside, a lacy white curtain over the evening sky. When Martha looked away from the door, I saw tears in her eyes.

"You're late," Martha said to the doctor, managing a smile. "Out delivering Mrs. Bonachek?"

"No such luck." The doctor seemed grim. "I wish that just once the woman would call me in time. She delivered herself again. The baby died, low body temperature I suspect. A little girl. A pretty, perfect little girl."

I was stunned but I managed to blurt, "But she was working in the fields just this afternoon."

Martha and the doctor exchanged a glance that reminded me how much I still had to learn. Then the doctor launched into a speech about some people not having sense enough to take to their beds and what sort of life could a baby born into such circumstances expect, anyway?

"The poor dear," Martha said when he had run down. "She finally has a little girl to keep her company and it dies." She grabbed me by the arm. "We must go offer our consolation."

We put on our boots and coats and waited for the doctor to get his ancient Ford back out of the shed. It made a terrible racket, about which Martha complained gently, but there wasn't enough snow for the cutter. We were both disappointed—the cutter gave an occasion a certain weight.

"Say your piece then leave," the doctor warned as we rattled over the rutted road. "These are private people. They may not understand your intentions."

He didn't understand that Martha and I were suffering a bit of guilt from the fun we had had at poor Mrs. Bonachek's expense. And we were bored. Barn sour, my mother would say. Tired of being cooped up all winter and in desperate need of some diversion.

We stormed the Bonachek's tiny clapboard house, our offers of consolation translated by a grim faced Janos. Martha was effusive. A baby girl should have a proper send-off, she said. There needed to be both a coffin and a dress. When was the funeral?

Mrs. Bonachek looked from me to Martha, a glaze over her mud-colored eyes. Janos shrugged his skinny shoulders. There was no money for funerals, he said. When a baby died, you called in the doctor for a death certificate, then the county came for the remains. That was all.

Martha patted Mrs. Bonachek's scaly hands. Not to worry. We would take care of everything. And we did. Put off from our Spring Tea by the sudden change in the weather, we diverted our considerable social energy to the memorial services.

I found a nice wooden box of adequate size in the doctor's storeroom and painted it white. Martha went up to the attic and brought down her beautiful pink silk gown and an old feather pillow. She didn't even wince as she ran her sewing shears up the delicate hand-turned seams.

I wept. She hugged me and talked about God's will being done and Mrs. Bonachek's peasant strength. I was thinking about the spoiled dress.

We worked half the night. We padded the inside of the box with feathers and lined it with pink silk. We made a tiny dress and bonnet to match. The doctor had talked the county into letting us have a plot in the cemetery. It was such a little bit of ground, they couldn't refuse.

We contacted the parish priest, but he didn't want to perform the services. The county cemetery wasn't consecrated and he didn't know the Bonacheks. We only hoped it wasn't a rabbi that was needed because there wasn't one for miles. Martha reasoned that heaven was heaven and the Methodist preacher would have to do, since he was willing.

By the following afternoon everything was ready. The snow had turned to slush but our spirits weren't dampened. We set off, wearing prim navy blue because Martha said it was more appropriate for a child's funeral than somber black.

When the doctor drove us up to the small house, the entire Bonachek family, scrubbed and brushed, turned out to greet us.

Janos smiled for the first time I could remember. He fingered a frayed necktie that hung below his twine belt. He looked awkward, but I knew he felt elegant. Everyone, even Boya, wore some sort of shoes. It was a gala, if solemn event.

Mr. Bonachek, a scrawny, pale-faced man, relieved us of the makeshift coffin and led us into the single bedroom. The baby, wrapped in a scrap of calico, lay on the dresser. I unfolded the little silk dress on the bed while Martha shooed Mr. Bonachek out of the room.

"We should wash her," Martha said. A catch in her voice showed that her courage was failing. She began to unwrap the tiny creature. It was then I recognized the calico—Mrs. Bonachek's faded apron.

I thought of the nine sons lined up in the next room and Mrs. Bonachek sitting in the field with her apron spread on the cold ground beside her. Mrs. Bonachek who was so rich in sons.

I needed to know how many babies, how many girls, had died before this one wrapped in the apron. Janos would tell me, Janos who had been so matter-of-fact about the routine business of death. I hadn't the courage at that moment to ask him.

Martha was working hard to maintain her composure. She had the baby dressed and gently laid her in the coffin. The baby was beautiful, her porcelain face framed in soft pink silk. I couldn't bear to see her in the box, like a shop-window doll.

I wanted to talk with Martha about the nagging suspicion that was taking shape in my mind. I hesitated too long.

Janos appeared at the door and I didn't want to hear what I had to say. Actually, his face was so thin and expectant that it suddenly occurred to me that we hadn't brought any food for a proper wake.

"Janos," Martha whispered. "Tell your mother she may come in now."

Janos led his mother only as far as the threshold when she stopped stubbornly. I went to her, put my arm around her and impelled her to come closer to the coffin. When she resisted, I pushed. I was desperate to see some normal emotion from her. If she had none, what hope was there for Janos?

Finally, she shuddered and reached out a hand to touch the baby's cheek. She said something in her native language. I could understand neither the words nor the tone. It could have been a prayer, it could have been a curse.

When I let her go, she turned and looked at me. For the barest instant there was a flicker in her eyes that showed neither fear nor guilt about what I might have seen the afternoon before. I was disquieted because for the length of that small glimmer, she was beautiful. I saw who she might have become at another time, in a different place. When the tears at last came to my eyes, they were for her and not the baby.

Janos and Boya carried the coffin out to the bare front room and set it on the table. The preacher arrived and he gave his best two-dollar service even though there would be no payment. He spoke to the little group, the Bonacheks, Martha, the doctor and I, as if we were a full congregation. I don't remember what he said. I wasn't listening. I traced the pattern of the cheap, worn linoleum floor with my eyes and silently damned the poverty of the place and the cold that seeped in under the door.

We were a small, depressed-looking procession, walking down the muddy road to the county cemetery at the edge of town, singing along to hymns only the preacher seemed to know. At the gravesite, the preacher prayed for the sinless and consigned her to the earth. It didn't seem to bother him that his principal mourners didn't understand a word he said.

Somehow, the doctor dissuaded Martha from inviting all of the Bonacheks home for supper—she, too, had belatedly thought about food.

As we walked back from the cemetery, I managed to separate the doctor from the group. I told him what was on my mind, what I had seen in the fields the day before. She had left her bundled apron at the end of a furrow and gone back to her work. I could not keep that guilty knowledge to myself.

The doctor wasn't as shocked as I expected him to be. But he was a man of worldly experience and I was merely a dairyman's daughter— the oldest child, the only girl in a family of five boys.

As the afternoon progressed, the air grew colder, threatening more snow. To this day, whenever I am very cold, I think of that afternoon. Janos, of course, fills that memory.

I think the little ceremony by strangers was sort of a coming out for him. He was suddenly not only a man of the community, but of the world beyond the road that ran between his farm and the school house, out where mountains and oceans were a possibility. It had been a revelation.

Janos called out to me and I stopped to wait for him, watching him run. He seemed incredibly, small, outlined against the flat horizon. He was golden, and oddly ebullient.

Pale sunlight glinted off his bright head as he struggled through the slush on the road. Mud flew off his big boots in thick gobs and I thought his skinny legs would break with the weight of it. He seemed not to notice—mud was simply a part of the season's change, a harbinger of warmer days.

When he caught up, Janos was panting and red in the face. He looked like a wise little old man for whom life held no secrets. As always, he held himself with a stiff dignity that I imagine suited him quite well when he was draped in his judge's robes.

Too breathless to speak, he placed in my hand a fresh blue crocus he had plucked from the slush.

"Very pretty," I said, moved by his gesture. I looked into his smiling face and found courage. "What was the prayer your mother said for the baby?"

He shrugged and struggled for breath. Then he reached out and touched the delicate flower that was already turning down from the warmth of my hand.

"No prayer," he said. "It's what she says. 'Know peace. Your sisters in heaven wait to embrace you.' "

I put my hand on his shoulder and looked up at the heavy, gathering clouds. "If it's snowing tomorrow," I said, "which books shall I bring?"

I have noted many times that Pronzini has accomplished what no other crime writer ever has—given us his autobiography measured out in the form of seventeen novels. I'm speaking of his Nameless series which, in the course of seventeen novels, tell us about this big, gruff, grouchy, moral, and sourly funny Italian guy whose only name is ... Nameless. All that said, the Nameless novels are also exciting, mysterious, beautifully rendered, and filled with a lot of humor about the vagaries of life in San Francisco.

F. Scott Fitzgerald once said that all first-rate writers are moralists. Pronzini, in the course of his detection, aims to tell us about himself and his times, and where both have failed. Nameless is a bit of secular priest.

When my generation of crime novelists has gone to dust, Pronzini's Nameless books will be on the keeper shelf for the next several generations to enjoy.

Incident in a Neighborhood Tavern
BILL PRONZINI

When the holdup went down I was sitting at the near end of the Foghorn Tavern's scarred mahogany bar talking to the owner, Matt Candiotti.

It was a little before seven of a midweek evening, lull-time in working-class neighborhood saloons like this one. Blue-collar locals would jam the place from four until about six-thirty, when the last of them headed home for dinner; the hard-core drinkers wouldn't begin filtering back in until about seven-thirty or eight. Right now there were only two customers, and the jukebox and computer hockey games were quiet. The TV over the back bar was on but with the sound turned down to a tolerable level. One of the customers, a porky guy in his fifties, drinking

144

Anchor Steam out of the bottle, was watching the last of the NBC national news. The other customer, an equally porky and middle-aged female barfly, half in the bag on red wine, was trying to convince him to pay attention to her instead of Tom Brokaw.

I had a draft beer in front of me, but that wasn't the reason I was there. I'd come to ask Candiotti, as I had asked two dozen other merchants here in the Outer Mission, if he could offer any leads on the rash of burglaries that were plaguing small businesses in the neighborhood. The police hadn't come up with anything positive after six weeks, so a couple of the victims had gotten up a fund and hired me to see what I could find out. They'd picked me because I had been born and raised in the Outer Mission, I still had friends and shirttail relatives living here, and I understood the neighborhood a good deal better than any other private detective in San Francisco.

But so far I wasn't having any more luck than the SFPD. None of the merchants I'd spoken with today had given me any new ideas, and Candiotti was proving to be no exception. He stood slicing limes into wedges as we talked. They might have been onions the way his long, mournful face was screwed up, like a man trying to hold back tears. His gray-stubbled jowls wobbled every time he shook his head. He reminded me of a tired old hound, friendly and sad, as if life had dealt him a few kicks but not quite enough to rob him of his good nature.

"Wish I could help," he said. "But hell, I don't hear nothing. Must be pros from Hunters Point or the Fillmore, hah?"

Hunters Point and the Fillmore were black sections of the city, which was a pretty good indicator of where his head was at. I said, "Some of the others figure it for local talent."

"Out of this neighborhood, you mean?"

I nodded, drank some of my draft.

"Nah, I doubt it," he said. "Guys that organized, they don't shit where they eat. Too smart, you know?"

"Maybe. Any break-ins or attempted break-ins here?"

"Not so far. I got bars on all the windows, double dead-bolt locks on the storeroom door off the alley. Besides, what's for them to steal besides a few cases of whiskey?"

"You don't keep cash on the premises overnight?"

"Fifty bucks in the till," Candiotti said, "that's all; that's my limit. Everything else goes out of here when I close up, down to the night deposit at the B of A on Mission. My mama didn't raise no airheads." He scraped the lime wedges off his board, into a plastic container, and racked the serrated knife he'd been using. "One thing I did hear," he said. "I heard some of the loot turned up down in San Jose. You know about that?"

"Not much of a lead there. Secondhand dealer named Pitman had a few pieces of stereo equipment stolen from the factory outlet store on Geneva. Said he bought it from a guy at the San Jose flea market, somebody he didn't know, never saw before."

"Yeah, sure," Candiotti said wryly. "What do the cops think?"

"That Pitman bought it off a fence."

"Makes sense. So maybe the boosters are from San Jose, hah?"

"Could be," I said, and that was when the kid walked in.

He brought bad air in with him; I sensed it right away and so did Candiotti. We both glanced at the door when it opened, the way you do, but we didn't look away again once we saw him. He was in his early twenties, dark-skinned, dressed in chinos, a cotton wind-breaker, sharp-toed shoes polished to a high gloss. But it was his eyes that put the chill on my neck, the sudden clutch of tension down low in my belly. They were bright, jumpy, on the wild side, and in the dim light of the Foghorn's interior, the pupils were so small they seemed nonexistent. He had one hand in his jacket pocket and I knew it was clamped around a gun even before he took it out and showed it to us.

He came up to the bar a few feet on my left, the gun jabbing the air in front of him. He couldn't hold it steady; it kept jerking up and down, from side to side, as if it had a kind of spasmodic life of its own. Behind me, at the other end of the bar, I heard Anchor Steam suck in his breath, the barfly make a sound like a stifled moan. I eased back a little on the stool, watching the gun and the kid's eyes flick from Candiotti to me to the two customers and back around again. Candiotti didn't move at all, just stood there staring with his hound's face screwed up in that holding-back-tears way.

"All right all right," the kid said. His voice was high pitched, excited, and there was drool at one corner of his mouth. You couldn't get much more stoned than he was and still function. Coke, crack, speed—maybe a combination. The gun that kept flicking this way and that was a goddamn Saturday Night Special. "Listen good, man, everybody listen good. I don't want to kill none of you, man, but I will if I got to, you believe it?"

None of us said anything. None of us moved.

The kid had a folded-up paper sack in one pocket; he dragged it out with his free hand, dropped it, broke quickly at the middle to pick it up without lowering his gaze. When he straightened again there was sweat on his forehead, more drool coming out of his mouth. He threw the sack on the bar.

"Put the money in there, Mr. Cyclone Man," he said to Candiotti. "All the money in the register but not the coins; I don't want the fuckin' coins, you hear me?"

Candiotti nodded; reached out slowly, caught up the sack, turned toward the back with his shoulders hunched up against his neck. When he punched No Sale on the register, the ringing thump of the cash drawer sliding open seemed overloud in the electric hush. For a few seconds the kid watched him scoop bills into the paper sack; then his eyes and the gun skittered my way again. I had looked into the muzzle of a handgun before and it was the same feeling each time: dull fear, helplessness, a kind of naked vulnerability.

"Your wallet on the bar, man, all your cash." The gun barrel and the wild eyes flicked away again, down the length of the plank, before I could move to comply. "You down there, dude, you and fat mama put your money on the bar. All of it, hurry up."

Each of us did as we were told. While I was getting my wallet out I managed to slide my right foot off the stool, onto the brass rail, and to get my right hand pressed tight against the beveled edge of the bar. If I had to make any sudden moves, I would need the leverage.

Candiotti finished loading the sack, turned from the register. There was a grayish cast to his face now—the wet gray color of fear. The kid said to him, "Pick up their money, put it in the sack with the rest. Come on come on come on!"

Candiotti went to the far end of the plank, scooped up the wallets belonging to Anchor Steam and the woman; then he came back my way, added my wallet to the contents of the paper sack, put the sack down carefully in front of the kid.

"Okay," the kid said, "okay all right." He glanced over his shoulder at the street door, as if he'd heard something there; but it stayed closed. He jerked his head around again. In his sweaty agitation the Saturday Night Special almost slipped free of his fingers; he fumbled a tighter grip on it, and when it didn't go off I let the breath I had been holding come out thin and slow between my teeth. The muscles in my shoulders and back were drawn so tight I was afraid they might cramp.

The kid reached out for the sack, dragged it in against his body. But he made no move to leave with it. Instead he said, "Now we go get the big pile, man."

Candiotti opened his mouth, closed it again. His eyes were almost as big and starey as the kid's.

"Come on, Mr. Cyclone Man, the safe, the safe in your office. We goin' back there *now*."

"No money in that safe," Candiotti said in a thin, scratchy voice. "Nothing valuable."

"Oh man I'll kill you man I'll blow your fuckin' head off! I ain't playin' no games I want that money!"

He took two steps forward, jabbing with the gun up close to Candiotti's gray face. Candiotti backed off a step, brought his hands up, took a tremulous breath.

"All right," he said, "but I got to get the key to the office. It's in the register."

"Hurry up hurry up!"

Candiotti turned back to the register, rang it open, rummaged inside with his left hand. But with his right hand, shielded from the kid by his body, he eased up to the top on a large wooden cigar box adjacent. The hand disappeared inside; came out again with metal in it, glinting in the back bar lights. I saw it and I wanted to yell at him, but it wouldn't have done any good, would only have warned the kid . . . and he was already turning with it, bringing it up with both hands now— the damn gun of his own he'd had hidden inside the cigar box. There was no time for me to do anything but shove away from the bar and sideways off the stool just as Candiotti opened fire.

The state he was in, the kid didn't realize what was happening until it was too late for him to react; he never even got a shot off. Candiotti's first slug knocked him halfway around, and one of the three others that followed it opened up his face like a piece of ripe fruit smacked by a hammer. He was dead before his body, driven backward, slammed into the cigarette machine near the door, slid down to the floor.

The half-drunk woman was yelling in broken shrieks, as if she couldn't get enough air for a sustained scream. When I came up out of my crouch I saw that Anchor Steam had hold of her, clinging to her as much for support as in an effort to calm her down. Candiotti stood flat-footed, his arms down at his sides, the gun out of sight below the bar, staring at the bloody remains of the kid as if he couldn't believe what he was seeing, couldn't believe what he'd done.

Some of the tension in me eased as I went to the door, found the lock on its security gate, fastened it before anybody could come in off the street. The Saturday Night Special was still clutched in the kid's hand; I bent, pulled it free with my thumb and forefinger, broke the cylinder. It was loaded, all right—five cartridges. I dropped it into my jacket pocket, thought about checking the kid's clothing for identification, didn't do it. It wasn't any of my business, now, who he'd been. And I did not want to touch him or any part of him. There was a queasiness in my stomach, a fluttery weakness behind my knees—the same delayed reaction I always had to violence and death—and touching him would only make it worse.

To keep from looking at the red ruin of the kid's face, I pivoted back to the bar. Candiotti hadn't moved. Anchor Steam had gotten the woman to stop screeching and had coaxed her over to one of the handful of tables near the jukebox; now she was sobbing, "I've got to go home, I'm gonna be sick if I don't go home." But she didn't make any move to get up and neither did Anchor Steam.

I walked over near Candiotti, pushed hard words at him in an undertone. "That was a damn fool thing to do. You could have got us all killed."

"I know," he said. "I know."

"Why'd you do it?"

"I thought . . . hell, you saw the way he was waving that piece of his . . ."

"Yeah," I said. "Call the police. Nine-eleven."

"Nine-eleven. Okay."

"Put that gun of yours down first. On the bar."

He did that. There was a phone on the back bar; he went away to it in shaky strides. While he was talking to the Emergency operator I picked up his weapon, saw that it was a .32 Charter Arms revolver. I held it in my hand until Candiotti finished with the call, set it down again as he came back to where I stood.

"They'll have somebody here in five minutes," he said.

I said, "You know that kid?"

"Christ, no."

"Ever see him before? Here or anywhere else?"

"No."

"So how did he know your safe?"

Candiotti blinked at me. "What?"

"The safe in your office. Street kid like that . . . how'd he know about it?"

"How should I know? What difference does it make?"

"He seemed to think you keep big money in that safe."

"Well, I don't. There's nothing in it."

"That's right, you told me you don't keep more than fifty bucks on the premises overnight. In the till."

"Yeah."

"Then why have you got a safe, if it's empty?"

Candiotti's eyes narrowed. "I used to keep my receipts in it, all right? Before all these burglaries started. Then I figured I'd be smarter to take the money to the bank every night."

"Sure, that explains it," I said. "Still, a kid like that, looking for a big score to feed his habit, he wasn't just after what was in the till and our wallets. No, it was as if he'd gotten wind of a heavy stash—a grand or more."

Nothing from Candiotti.

I watched him for a time. Then I said, "Big risk you took, using that .32 of yours. How come you didn't make your play the first time you went to the register? How come you waited until the kid mentioned your office safe?"

"I didn't like the way he was acting, like he might start shooting any second. I figured it was our only chance. Listen, what're you getting at, hah?"

"Another funny thing," I said, "is the way he called you 'Mr. Cyclone Man.' Now why would a hopped-up kid use a term like that to a bar owner he didn't know?"

"How the hell should I know?"

"Cyclone," I said. "What's a cyclone but a big destructive wind? Only one other thing I can think of."

"Yeah? What's that?"

"A fence. A cyclone fence."

Candiotti made a fidgety movement. Some of the wet gray pallor was beginning to spread across his cheeks again, like a fungus.

I said, "And a fence is somebody who receives and distributes stolen goods. A Mr. Fence Man. But then you know that, don't you. Candiotti? We were talking about that kind of fence before the kid came in . . . how Pitman, down in San Jose, bought some hot stereo equipment off of one. That fence could just as easily be operating here in San Francisco, though. Right here in this neighborhood, in fact. Hell, suppose the stuff taken in all those burglaries never left the neighborhood. Suppose it was brought to a place nearby and stored until it could be trucked out to other cities—a tavern storeroom, for instance. Might even be some of it is *still* in that storeroom. And the money he got for the rest he'd keep locked up in his safe, right? Who'd figure it? Except maybe a poor junkie who picked up a whisper on the street somewhere—"

Candiotti made a sudden grab for the .32, caught it up, backed up a step with it leveled at my chest. "You smart son of a bitch," he said. "I ought to kill you too."

"In front of witnesses? With the police due any minute?"

He glanced over at the two customers. The woman was still sobbing, lost in a bleak outpouring of self-pity; but Anchor Steam was staring our way, and from the expression on his face he'd heard every word of my exchange with Candiotti.

"There's still enough time for me to get clear," Candiotti said grimly. He was talking to himself, not to me. Sweat had plastered his lank hair to his forehead; the revolver was not quite steady in his hand. "Lock you up in my office, you and those two back there . . ."

"I don't think so," I said.

"Goddamn you, you think I won't use this gun again?"

"I *know* you won't use it. I emptied out the last two cartridges while you were on the phone."

I took the two shells out of my left-hand jacket pocket and held them up where he could see them. At the same time I got the kid's Saturday Night Special out of the other pocket, held it loosely pointed in his direction. "You want to put your piece down now, Candiotti? You're not going anywhere, not for a long time."

He put it down—dropped it clattering onto the bartop. And as he did his sad hound's face screwed up again, only this time he didn't even try to keep the wetness from leaking out of his eyes. He was leaning against the bar, crying like the woman, submerged in his own outpouring of self-pity, when the cops showed up a little while later.

Marcia Muller always had the makings of a first-rate storyteller but her recent books show just how much an author can grow in style and authority. Marica's books are no longer simply first-rate mysteries—they're first-rate novels. And the critical establishment is finally starting to understand this.

Few writers yield the pleausre that Marcia does. There's her hard but forgiving eye for the human condition; her quiet but occasionally lacerating humor; and her ability to fuse the rules of the mysery with the freedom of a very personal style.

Marcia Muller is not only one of the world's most successful mystery authors, she's also one of the very best.

The Broken Men
MARCIA MULLER

I

Dawn was breaking when I returned to the Diablo Valley Pavilion. The softly rounded hills that encircled the amphitheater were edged with pinkish gold, but their slopes were still dark and forbidding. They reminded me of a herd of humpbacked creatures huddling together while they waited for the warmth of the morning sun; I could imagine them stretching and sighing with relief when its rays finally touched them.

I would have given a lot to have daylight bring me that same sense of relief, but I doubted that would happen. It had been a long, anxious night since I'd arrived here the first time, over twelve hours before. Returning was a last-ditch measure, and a long shot at best.

152

I drove up the blacktop road to where it was blocked by a row of posts and got out of the car. The air was chill; I could see my breath. Somewhere in the distance a lone bird called, and there was a faint, monotonous whine that must have had something to do with the security lights that topped the chain-link fence at intervals, but the overall silence was heavy, oppressive. I stuffed my hands into the pockets of my too-light suede jacket and started toward the main entrance next to the box office.

As I reached the fence, a stocky, dark-haired man stepped out of the adjacent security shack and began unlocking the gate. Roy Canfield, night supervisor for the pavilion. He'd been dubious about what I'd suggested when I'd called him from San Francisco three quarters of an hour ago, but had said he'd be glad to cooperate if I came back out here. Canfield swung the gate open and motioned me through one of the turnstiles that had admitted thousands to the Diablo Valley Clown Festival the night before.

He said, "You made good time from the city."

"There's no traffic at five a.m. I could set my own speed limit."

The security man's eyes moved over me appraisingly, reminding me of how rumpled and tired I must look. Canfield himself seemed as fresh and alert as when I'd met him before last night's performance. But then, *he* hadn't been chasing over half the Bay Area all night, hunting for a missing client.

"Of course," I added, "I was anxious to get here and see if Gary Fitzgerald might still be somewhere on the premises. Shall we take a look around?"

Canfield looked as dubious as he'd sounded on the phone. He shrugged and said, "Sure we can, but I don't think you'll find him. We check every inch of the place after the crowd leaves. No way anybody could still be inside when we lock up."

There had been a note of reproach in his words, as if he thought I was questioning his ability to do his job. Quickly I said, "It's not that I don't believe you, Mr. Canfield. I just don't have any place else left to look."

He merely grunted and motioned for me to proceed up the wide concrete steps. They led uphill from the entrance to a promenade whose arms curved out in opposite directions around the edge of the amphitheater. As I recalled from the night before, from the promenade the lawn sloped gently down to the starkly modernistic concert shell. Its stage was wide—roughly ninety degrees of the circle—with wings and dressing rooms built back into the hill behind it. The concrete roof, held aloft by two giant pillars, was a curving slab shaped like a warped arrowhead, its tip pointing to the northeast, slightly off center. Formal seating was limited to a few dozen rows in a semi-circle in front of the stage; the pavilion had been designed mainly for the casual type of concert-goer who prefers to lounge on a blanket on the lawn.

I reached the top of the steps and crossed the promenade to the edge of the bowl, then stopped in surprise.

The formerly pristine lawn was now mounded with trash. Paper bags, cups and plates, beer cans and wine bottles, wrappers and crumpled programs and other indefinable debris were scattered in a crazy-quilt pattern. Trash receptacles placed at strategic intervals along the promenade had overflowed, their contents cascading to the ground. On the low wall between the formal seating and the lawn stood a monumental pyramid of Budweiser cans. In some places the debris was only thinly scattered, but in others it lay deep, like dirty drifted snow.

Canfield came up behind me, breathing heavily from the climb. "A mess, isn't it?" he said.

"Yes. Is it always like this after a performance?"

'Depends. Shows like last night, where you get a lot of young people, families, picnickers, it gets pretty bad. A symphony concert, that's different."

"And your maintenance crew doesn't come on until morning?" I tried not to sound disapproving, but allowing such debris to lie there all night was faintly scandalous to a person like me, who had been raised to believe that not washing the supper dishes before going to bed just might constitute a cardinal sin.

"Cheaper that way—we'd have to pay overtime otherwise. And the job's easier when it's light anyhow."

As if in response to Canfield's words, daylight—more gold than pink now—spilled over the hills in the distance, slightly to the left of the stage. It disturbed the shadows on the lawn below us, making them assume different, distorted forms. Black became gray, gray became white; short shapes elongated, others were truncated; fuzzy lines came into sharp focus. And with the light a cold wind came gusting across the promenade.

I pulled my jacket closer, shivering. The wind rattled the fall-dry leaves of the young poplar trees—little more than saplings—planted along the edge of the promenade. It stirred the trash heaped around the receptacles, then swept down the lawn, scattering debris in its wake. Plastic bags and wads of paper rose in an eerie dance, settled again as the breeze passed. I watched the undulation—a paper wave upon a paper sea—as it rolled toward the windbreak of cypress trees to the east.

Somewhere in the roiling refuse down by the barrier between the lawn and the formal seating I spotted a splash of yellow. I leaned forward, peering toward it. Again I saw the yellow, then a blur of blue and then a flicker of white. The colors were there, then gone as the trash settled.

Had my eyes been playing tricks on me in the half-light? I didn't think so, because while I couldn't be sure of the colors, I was distinctly aware of a shape that the wind's passage had uncovered—long, angular, solid-looking. The debris had fallen in a way that didn't completely obscure it.

The dread that I had held in check all night spread through me. After a frozen moment, I began to scramble down the slope toward the spot I'd been staring at. Behind me, Canfield called out, but I ignored him.

The trash was deep down by the barrier, almost to my knees. I waded through bottles, cans, and papers, pushing their insubstantial mass aside, shoveling with my hands to clear a path. Shoveled until my fingers encountered something more solid . . .

I dropped to my knees and scooped up the last few layers of debris, hurling it over my shoulder.

He lay on his back, wrapped in his bright yellow cape, his baggy blue plaid pants and black patent leather shoes sticking out from underneath it. His black beret was pulled halfway down over his white clown's face hiding his eyes. I couldn't see the red vest that made up the rest of the costume because the cape covered it, but there were faint red stains on the irridescent fabric that draped across his chest.

I yanked the cape aside and touched the vest. It felt sticky, and when I pulled my hand away it was red too. I stared at it, wiped it off on a scrap of newspaper. Then I felt for a pulse in his carotid artery, knowing all the time what a futile exercise it was.

"Oh, Jesus!" I said. For a moment my vision blurred and there was a faint buzzing in my ears.

Roy Canfield came thrashing up behind me, puffing with exertion. "What . . . Oh, my God!"

I continued staring down at the clown; he looked broken, an object that had been used up and tossed on a trash heap. After a moment, I touched my thumb to his cold cheek, brushed at the white makeup. I pushed the beret back, looked at the theatrically blackened eyes. Then I tugged off the flaxen wig. Finally I pulled the fake bulbous nose away.

"Gary Fitzgerald?" Canfield asked.

I looked up at him. His moonlike face creased in concern. Apparently the shock and bewilderment I was experiencing showed.

"Mr. Canfield," I said, "this man is wearing Gary's costume, but it's not him. I've never seen him before in my life."

II

The man I *was* looking for was half of an internationally famous clown act, Fitzgerald and Tilby. The world of clowning, like any other artistic realm, has its various levels—from the lowly rodeo clown whose chief function is to keep bull riders from being stomped on, to circus clowns such as Emmett Kelly and universally acclaimed mimes like Marcel Marceau. Fitzgerald and Tilby were not far below Kelly and Marceau in that hierarchy and gaining on them every day. Instead of merely employing the mute body language of the typical clown, the two Britishers combined it with a subtle and sophisticated verbal comedy routine. Their fame had spread beyond aficionados of clowning in the late seventies when they had made a series of artful and entertaining television commercials for one of the Japanese auto makers, and subsequent ads for, among others, a major U.S. airline, one of the big insurance companies, and a computer firm had assured them of a place in the hearts of humor-loving Americans.

My involvement with Fitzgerald and Tilby came about when they agreed to perform at the Diablo Valley Clown Festival, a charity benefit co-sponsored by the Contra Costa County Chamber of Commerce and KSUN, the radio station where my friend Don De Boccio works as a disc jockey. The team's manager, Wayne Kabalka, had stipulated only two conditions to their performing for free: that they be given star billing, and that they be provided with a bodyguard. Since Don was to be emcee of the show, he was in on all the planning, and when he heard of Kabalka's second stipulation, he suggested me for the job.

As had been the case ever since I'd bought a house near the Glen Park district of San Francisco the spring before, I was short of money at the time. And All Souls Legal Cooperative, where I am staff investigator, had no qualms about me moonlighting provided it didn't interfere with any of the co-op's cases. Since things had been slack at All Souls during September, I felt free to accept. Bodyguarding isn't my idea of challenging work, but I had always enjoyed Fitzgerald and Tilby, and the idea of meeting them intrigued me. Besides, I'd be part of the festival and get paid for my time, rather than attending on the free pass Don had promised me.

So on that hot Friday afternoon in late September, I met with Wayne

Kabalka in the lounge at KSUN's San Francisco studios. As radio stations go, KSUN is a casual operation, and the lounge gives full expression to this orientation. It is full of mismatched Salvation Army reject furniture, the posters on the walls are torn and tattered, and the big coffee table is always littered with rumpled newspapers, empty Coke cans and coffee cups, and overflowing ashtrays. On this particular occasion, it was also graced with someone's half-eaten Big Mac.

When Don and I came in, Wayne Kabalka was seated on the very edge of one of the lumpy chairs, looking as if he were afraid it might have fleas. He saw us and jumped as if one had just bitten him. *His* orientation was anything but casual: in spite of the heat, he wore a tan three-piece suit that almost matched his mane of tawny hair, and a brown striped tie peeked over the V of his vest. Kabalka and his clients might be based in L.A., but he sported none of the usual Hollywoodish accoutrements—gold chains, diamond rings, or Adidas running shoes. Perhaps his very correct appearance was designed to be in keeping with his clients, Englishmen with rumored connections to the aristocracy.

Don introduced us and we all sat down, Kabalka again doing his balancing act on the edge of his chair. Ignoring me, he said to Don, "I didn't realize the bodyguard you promised would be female."

Don shot me a look, his shaggy black eyebrows raised a fraction of an inch.

I said, "Please don't let my gender worry you, Mr. Kabalka. I've been a private investigator for nine years, and before that I worked for a security firm. I'm fully qualified for the job."

To Don he said, "But has she done this kind of work before?"

Again Don looked at me.

I said, "Bodyguarding is only one of any number of types of assignments I've carried out. And one of the most routine."

Kabalka continued looking at Don. "Is she licensed to carry firearms?"

Don ran his fingers over his thick black mustache, trying to hide the beginnings of a grin. "I think," he said, "that I'd better let the two of you talk alone."

Kabalka put out a hand as if to stay his departure, but Don stood. "I'll be in the editing room if you need me."

I watched him walk down the hall, his gait surprisingly graceful for such a tall, stocky man. Then I turned back to Kabalka. "To answer your question, sir, yes, I'm firearms qualified."

He made a sound halfway between clearing his throat and a grunt. "Uh . . . then you have no objection to carrying a gun on this assignment?"

"Not if it's necessary. But before I can agree to that, I'll have to know why you feel your clients require an armed bodyguard."

"I'm sorry?"

"Is there some threat to them that indicates the guard should be armed?"

"Threat. Oh . . . no."

"Extraordinary circumstances, then?"

"Extraordinary circumstances. Well, they're quite famous, you know. The TV commercials—you've seen them?"

I nodded.

"Then you know what a gold mine we have here. We're due to sign for three more within the month. Bank of America, no less. General Foods is getting into the act. Mobil Oil is hedging, but they'll sign. Fitzgerald and Tilby are important properties; they must be protected."

Properties, I thought, not people. "That still doesn't tell me what I need to know."

Kabalka laced his well-manicured fingers together, flexing them rhythmically. Beads of perspiration stood out on his high forehead; no wonder, wearing that suit in this heat. Finally he said, "In the past couple of years we've experienced difficulty with fans when the boys have been on tour. In a few instances, the crowds got a little too rough."

"Why haven't you hired a permanent bodyguard, then? Put one on staff?"

"The boys were opposed to that. In spite of their aristocratic connections, they're men of the people. They didn't want to put any more distance between them and their public than necessary."

The words rang false. I suspected the truth of the matter was that Kabalka was too cheap to hire a permanent guard. "In a place like the Diablo Valley Pavilion, the security is excellent, and I'm sure that's been explained to you. It hardly seems necessary to hire an armed guard when the pavilion personnel—"

He made a gesture of impatience. "Their security force will have dozens of performers to protect, including a number who will be wandering throughout the audience during the show. My clients need extra protection."

I was silent, watching him. He shifted his gaze from mine, looking around with disproportionate interest at the tattered wall posters. Finally I said, "Mr. Kabalka, I don't feel you're being quite frank with me. And I'm afraid I can't take on this assignment unless you are."

He looked back at me. His eyes were a pale blue, washed out—and worried. "The people here at the station speak highly of you," he said after a moment.

"I hope so. They—especially Mr. Del Boccio—know me well." Especially Don; we'd been lovers for more than six months now.

"When they told me they had a bodyguard lined up, all they said was that you were a first-rate investigator. If I was rude earlier because I was surprised by your being a woman, I apologize."

"Apology accepted."

"I assume by first-rate, one of the things they mean is that you are discreet."

"I don't talk about my cases, if that's what you want to know."

He nodded. "All right, I'm going to entrust you with some information. It's not common knowledge, and you're not to pass it on, gossip about it to your friends—"

Kabalka was beginning to annoy me. "Get on with it, Mr. Kabalka. Or find yourself another bodyguard." Not easy to do, when the performers needed to arrive at the pavilion in about three hours.

His face reddened, and he started to retort, but bit back the words. He looked down at his fingers, still laced together and pressing against one another in a feverish rhythm. "All right. Once again I apologize. In my profession you get used to dealing with such scumbags that you lose perspective—"

"You were about to tell me . . . ?"

He looked up, squared his shoulders as if he were about to deliver a state secret to an enemy agent. "All right. There *is* a reason why my clients require special security precautions at the Diablo Valley Pavilion. They—Gary Fitzgerald and John Tilby—are originally from Contra Costa County."

"What? I thought they were British."

"Yes, of course you did. And so does almost everyone else. It's part of the mystique, the selling power."

"I don't understand."

"When I discovered the young men in the early seventies, they were performing in a cheap club in San Bernardino, in the valley east of L.A. They were cousins, fresh off the farm—the ranch, in their case. Tilby's father was a dairy rancher in the Contra Costa hills, near Clayton; he raised both boys—Gary's parents had died. When old Tilby died, the ranch was sold and the boys ran off to seek fortune and fame. Old story. And they'd found the glitter doesn't come easy. Another old story. But when I spotted them in that club, I could see they were good. Damned good. So I took them on and made them stars."

"The oldest story of all."

"Perhaps. But now and then it does come true."

"Why the British background?"

"It was the early seventies. The mystique still surrounded such singing groups as the Rolling Stones and the Beatles. What could be better than a British clown act with aristocratic origins? Besides, they were already doing the British bit in their act when I discovered them, and it worked."

I nodded, amused by the machinations of show business. "So you're afraid someone who once knew them might get too close out at the pavilion tonight and recognize them?"

"Yes."

"Don't you think it's a long shot—after all these years?"

"They left there in sixty-nine. People don't change all that much in sixteen years."

That depended, but I wasn't about to debate the point with him. "But what about makeup? Won't that disguise them?" Fitzgerald and Tilby wore traditional clown white-face.

"They can't apply the makeup until they're about to go on—in other circumstances, it might be possible to put it on earlier, but not in this heat."

I nodded. It all made sense. But why did I feel there was something Kabalka wasn't telling me about his need for an armed guard? Perhaps it was the way his eyes had once again shifted from mine to the posters on the walls. Perhaps it was the nervous pressing of his laced fingers. Or maybe it was only that sixth sense that sometimes worked for me: what I called a detective's instinct and others—usually men—labeled woman's intuition.

"All right, Mr. Kabalka," I said, "I'll take the job."

III

I checked in with Don to find out when I should be back at the studios, then went home to change clothing. We would arrive at the pavilion around four; the show—an early one because of its appeal for children—would begin at six. And I was certain that the high temperature—sure to have topped 100 in the Diablo Valley—would not drop until long after dark. Chambray pants and an abbreviated tank top, with my suede jacket to put on in case of a late evening chill were all I would need. That, and my .38 special, tucked in the outer compartment of my leather shoulderbag.

By three o'clock I was back at the KSUN studios. Don met me in the lobby and ushered me to the lounge where Kabalka, Gary Fitzgerald, and John Tilby waited.

The two clowns were about my age—a little over thirty. Their British accents might once have been a put-on, but they sounded as natural now as if they'd been born and raised in London. Gary Fitzgerald was tall and lanky, with straight dark hair, angular features that stopped just short of being homely, and a direct way of meeting one's eye. John Tilby was shorter, sandy haired—the type we used to refer to in high school as "cute." His shy demeanor was in sharp contrast to his cousin's straightforward greeting and handshake. They didn't really seem like relatives, but then neither do I in comparison to my four siblings and numerous cousins. All of them resemble one another—typical Scotch-Irish towheads—but I have inherited all the characteristics of our one-eighth Shoshone Indian blood. And none of us are similar in personality or outlook, save for the fact we care a great deal about one another.

Wayne Kabalka hovered in the background while the introductions were made. The first thing he said to me was, "Did you bring your gun?"

"Yes, I did. Everything's under control."

Kabalka wrung his hands together as if he only wished it were true. Then he said, "Do you have a car, Ms. McCone?"

"Yes."

"Then I suggest we take both yours and mine. I have to swing by the hotel and pick up my wife and John's girlfriend."

"All right. I have room for one passenger in mine. Don, what about you? How are you getting out there?"

"I'm going in the Wonder Bus."

I rolled my eyes. The Wonder Bus was a KSUN publicity ploy—a former schoolbus painted in rainbow hues and emblazoned with the station call letters. It traveled to all KSUN-sponsored events, plus to anything else where management deemed its presence might be beneficial. As far as I was concerned, it was the most outrageous in a panoply of the station's brazen efforts at self-promotion, and I took every opportunity to expound this viewpoint to Don. Surprisingly, Don—a quiet classical musician who hated rock-and-roll and the notoriety that went with being a D.J.—never cringed at riding the Wonder Bus. If anything, he took an almost perverse pleasure in the motorized monstrosity.

Secretly, I had a shameful desire to hitch a ride on the Wonder Bus myself.

Wayne Kabalka looked somewhat puzzled at Don's statement. "Wonder Bus?" he said to himself. Then, "Well, if everyone's ready, let's go."

I turned to Don and smiled in a superior fashion. "Enjoy your ride."

We trooped out into the parking lot. Heat shimmered off the concrete paving. Kabalka pulled a handkerchief from his pocket and wiped his brow. "Is it always this hot here in September?"

"This is the month we have our true summer in the city, but no, this is unusual." I went over and placed my bag carefully behind the driver's seat of my MG convertible.

When John Tilby saw the car, his eyes brightened; he came over to it, running a hand along one of its battle-scarred flanks as if it were a brand new Porsche. "I used to have one of these."

"I'll bet it was in better shape than this one."

"Not really." A shadow passed over his face and he continued to caress the car in spite of the fact that the metal must be burning hot to the touch.

"Look," I said, "if you want to drive it out to the pavilion, I wouldn't mind being a passenger for a change."

He hesitated, then said wistfully, "That's nice of you, but I can't . . . I don't drive. But I'd like to ride along—"

"John!" Kabalka's voice was impatient behind us. "Come on, we're keeping Corinne and Nicole waiting."

Tilby gave the car a last longing glance, then shrugged. "I guess I'd better ride out with Wayne and the girls." He turned and walked off to Kabalka's new-looking Seville that was parked at the other side of the lot.

Gary Fitzgerald appeared next to me, a small canvas bag in one hand, garment bag in the other. "I guess you're stuck with me," he said, smiling easily.

"That's not such a bad deal."

He glanced back at Tilby and Kabalka, who were climbing into the Cadillac. "Wayne's right to make John go with him. Nicole would be jealous if she saw him drive up with another woman." His tone was slightly resentful. Of Nicole? I wondered. Perhaps the girlfriend had caused dissension between the cousins.

"Corinne is Wayne's wife?" I asked as we got into the MG.

"Yes. You'll meet both of them at the performance; they're never very far away." Again I heard the undertone of annoyance.

We got onto the freeway and crossed the Bay Bridge. Commute traffic out of the city was already getting heavy; people left their offices early on hot Fridays in September. I wheeled the little car in and out from lane to lane, bypassing trucks and A.C. Transit buses. Fitzgerald didn't speak. I glanced at him a couple of times to see if my maneuvering bothered him, but he sat slumped against the door, his almost-homely features shadowed with thought. Pre-performance nerves, possibly.

From the bridge, I took Highway 24 east toward Walnut Creek. We passed through the outskirts of Oakland, smog-hazed and sprawling— ugly duckling of the Bay Area. Sophisticates from San Francisco scorned Oakland, repeating Gertrude Stein's overused phrase, "There is no there there," but lately there had been a current of unease in their mockery. Oakland's thriving port had stolen much of the shipping business from her sister city across the Bay; her politics were alive and spirited; and on the site of former slums, sleek new buildings had been put up. Oakland was at last shedding her pinfeathers, and it made many of my fellow San Franciscans nervous.

From there we began the long ascent through the Berkeley Hills to the Caldecott Tunnel. The MG's aged engine strained as we passed lumbering trucks and slower cars, and when we reached the tunnel— three tunnels, actually, two of them now open to accommodate the eastbound commuter rush—I shot into the far lane. At the top of the grade midway through the tunnel, I shifted into neutral to give the engine a rest. Arid heat assailed us as we emerged; the temperature in San Francisco had been nothing compared to this.

The freeway continued to descend, past brown sunbaked hills covered with live oak and eucalyptus. Then houses began to appear, tucked back among the trees. The air was scented with dry leaves and grass and dust. Fire danger, I thought. One spark and those houses become tinderboxes.

The town of Orinda appeared on the right. On the left, in the center of the freeway, a BART train was pulling out of the station. I accelerated and tried to outrace it, giving up when my speedometer hit eighty and waving at some schoolkids who were watching from the train. Then I dropped back to sixty and glanced at Fitzgerald, suddenly embarrassed by my childish display. He was sitting up straighter and grinning.

I said, "The temptation was overwhelming."

"I know the feeling."

Feeling more comfortable now that he seemed willing to talk, I said, "Did Mr. Kabalka tell you that he let me in on where you're really from?"

For a moment he looked startled, then nodded.

"Is this the first time you've been back here in Contra Costa County?"

"Yes."

"You'll find it changed."

"I guess so."

"Mainly there are more people. Places like Walnut Creek and Concord have grown by leaps and bounds in the last ten years."

The county stretched east from the ridge of hills we'd just passed over, toward Mount Diablo, a nearly 4,000-foot peak which had been developed into a 15,000-acre state park. On the north side of the county was the Carquinez Strait, with its oil refineries, Suisun Bay, and the San Joaquin River which separated Contra Costa from Sacramento County and the Delta. The city of Richmond and environs, to the west, were also part of the county, and their inclusion had always struck me as odd. Besides being geographically separated by the expanse of Tilden Regional Park and San Pablo Reservoir, the mostly black industrial city was culturally light years away from the rest of the suburban, upwardly mobile county. With the exception of a few towns like Pittsburgh or Antioch, this was affluent, fast-developing land; I supposed one day even those north-county backwaters would fall victim to expensive residential tracts and shopping centers full of upscale boutiques.

When Fitzgerald didn't comment, I said, "Does it look different to you?"

"Not really."

"Wait till we get to Walnut Creek. The area around the BART station is all highrise buildings now. They're predicting it will become an urban center that will eventually rival San Francisco."

He grunted in disapproval.

"About the only thing they've managed to preserve out here is the area around Mount Diablo. I suppose you know it from when you were a kid."

"Yes."

"I went hiking in the park last spring, during wildflower season. It was really beautiful that time of year. They say if you climb high enough you can see thirty-five counties from the mountain."

"This pavilion," Fitzgerald said, "is it part of the state park?"

For a moment I was surprised, then realized the pavilion hadn't been in existence in 1969, when he'd left home. "No, but near it. The land around it is relatively unspoiled. Horse and cattle ranches, mostly. They built it about eight years ago, after the Concord Pavilion became such a success. I guess that's one index of how this part of the Bay Area has grown, that it can support two concert pavilions."

He nodded. "Do they ever have concerts going at the same time at both?"

"Sure."

"It must really echo off these hills."

"I imagine you can hear it all the way to Port Chicago." Port Chicago was where the Naval Weapons Station was located, on the edge of Suisun Bay.

"Well, maybe not all the way to Chicago."

I smiled at the feeble joke, thinking that for a clown, Fitzgerald really didn't have much of a sense of humor, then allowed him to lapse back into his moody silence.

IV

When we arrived at the pavilion, the parking lot was already crowded, the gates having opened early so people could picnic before the show started. An orange-jacketed attendant directed us to a far corner of the lot which had been cordoned off for official parking near the performers' gate. Fitzgerald and I waited in the car for about fifteen minutes, the late afternoon sun beating down on us, until Wayne Kabalka's Seville pulled up alongside. With the manager and John Tilby were two women: a chic, fortyish redhead, and a small, dark-haired woman in her twenties. Fitzgerald and I got out and went to greet them.

The redhead was Corinne Kabalka; her strong handshake and level gaze made me like her immediately. I was less sure about Nicole Leland; the younger woman was beautiful, with short black hair sculpted close to her head and exotic features, but her manner was very cold. She nodded curtly when introduced to me, then took Tilby's arm and led him off toward the performers' gate. The rest of us trailed behind.

Security was tight at the gate. We met Roy Canfield, who was personally superintending the check-in, and each of us was issued a pass. No one, Canfield told us, would be permitted backstage or through the gate without showing his pass. Security personnel would also be stationed in the audience to protect those clowns who, as part of the show, would be performing out on the lawn.

We were then shown to a large dressing room equipped with a couch, a folding card table and chairs. After everyone was settled there I took Kabalka aside and asked him if he would take charge of the group for about fifteen minutes while I checked the layout of the pavilion. He nodded distractedly and I went out front.

Stage personnel were scurrying around, setting up sound equipment and checking the lights. Don had already arrived, but he was conferring with one of the other KSUN jocks and didn't look as if he could be disturbed. The formal seating was empty, but the lawn was already crowded. People lounged on blankets, passing around food, drink and an occasional joint. Some of the picnics were elaborate—fine china, crystal wineglasses, ice buckets, and in one case, a set of lighted silver candelabra; others were of the paper-plate and plastic-cup variety. I spotted the familiar logos of Kentucky Fried Chicken and Jack-in-the-Box here and there. People called to friends, climbed up and down the hill to the restroom and refreshment facilities, dropped by other groups' blankets to see what goodies they had to trade. Children ran through the crowd, an occasional Frisbee sailed through the air. I noticed a wafting trail of iridescent soap bubbles, and my eyes followed it to a young woman in a red halter top who was blowing them, her face aglow with childlike pleasure.

For a moment I felt a stab of envy, realizing that if I hadn't taken on this job I could be out front, courtesy of the free pass Don had promised me. I could have packed a picnic, perhaps brought along a woman friend, and Don could have dropped by to join us when he had time. But instead, I was bodyguarding a pair of clowns who—given the pavilion's elaborate security measures—probably didn't need me. And in addition to Fitzgerald and Tilby, I seemed to be responsible for an entire group. I could see why Kabalka might want to stick close to his clients, but why did the wife and girlfriend have to crowd into what was already a stuffy, hot dressing room? Why couldn't they go out front and enjoy the performance? It complicated my assignment, having to contend with an entourage, and the thought of those complications made me grumpy.

The grumpiness was probably due to the heat, I decided. Shrugging it off, I familiarized myself with the layout of the stage and the points at which someone could gain access. Satisfied that pavilion security could deal with any problems that might arise there, I made my way through the crowd—turning down two beers, a glass of wine, and a pretzel—and climbed to the promenade. From there I studied the stage once more, then raised my eyes to the sun-scorched hills to the east.

The slopes were barren, save for an occasional outcropping of rock and live oak trees, and on them a number of horses with riders stood. They clustered together in groups of two, four, six and even at this distance, I sensed they shared the same camaraderie as the people on the lawn. They leaned toward one another, gestured, and occasionally passed objects—perhaps they were picnicking too—back and forth.

What a great way to enjoy a free concert, I thought. The sound, in this natural echo chamber, would easily carry to where the watchers were stationed. How much more peaceful it must be on the hill, free of crowds and security measures. Visibility, however, would not be very good. . . .

And then I saw a flare of reddish light and glanced over to where a lone horseman stood under the sheltering branches of a live oak. The light flashed again, and I realized he was holding binoculars which had caught the setting sun. Of course—with binoculars or opera glasses, visibility would not be bad at all. In fact, from such a high vantage point it might even be better than from many points on the lawn. My grumpiness returned; I'd have loved to be mounted on a horse on that hillside.

Reminding myself that I was here on business that would pay for part of the new bathroom tile, I turned back toward the stage, then started when I saw Gary Fitzgerald. He was standing on the lawn not more than six feet from me, looking around with one hand forming a visor over his eyes. When he saw me he started too, and then waved.

I rushed over to him and grabbed his arm. "What are you doing out here? You're supposed to stay backstage!"

"I just wanted to see what the place looks like."

"Are you out of your mind? Your manager is paying good money for me to see that people stay away from you. And here you are, wandering through the crowd—"

He looked away, at a family on a blanket next to us. The father was wiping catsup from the smallest child's hands. "No one's bothering me."

"That's not the point." Still gripping his arm, I began steering him toward the stage. "Someone might recognize you, and that's precisely what Kabalka hired me to prevent."

"Oh, Wayne's just being a worrywart about that. No one's going to recognize anybody after all this time. Besides, it's common knowledge in the trade that we're not what we're made out to be."

"In the trade, yes. But your manager's worried about the public." We got to the stage, showed our passes to the security guard, and went back to the dressing room.

At the door Fitzgerald stopped. "Sharon, would you mind not mentioning my going out there to Wayne?"

"Why shouldn't I?"

"Because it would only upset him, and he's nervous enough before a performance. Nothing happened—except that I was guilty of using bad judgment."

His smile was disarming, and I took the words as an apology. "All right. But you'd better go get into costume. There's only half an hour before the grand procession begins."

V

The next few hours were uneventful. The grand procession—a parade through the crowd in which all the performers participated—went off smoothly. After they returned to the dressing room, Fitzgerald and Tilby removed their makeup—which was already running in the intense heat—and the Kabalkas fetched supper from the car—deli food packed in hampers by their hotel. There was a great deal of grumbling about the quality of the meal, which was not what one would have expected of the St. Francis, and Fitzgerald teased the others because he was staying at a small bed-and-breakfast establishment in the Haight-Ashbury which had better food at half the price.

Nicole said, "Yes, but your hotel probably has bedbugs."

Fitzgerald glared at her, and I was reminded of the disapproving tone of voice in which he'd first spoken of her. "Don't be ignorant. Urban chic has come to the Haight-Ashbury."

"Making it difficult for you to recapture your misspent youth there, no doubt."

"Nicole," Kabalka said.

"That *was* your intention in separating from the rest of us, wasn't it, Gary?" Nicole added.

Fitzgerald was silent.

"Well, Gary?"

He glanced at me. "You'll have to excuse us for letting our hostilities show."

Nicole smiled nastily. "Yes, when a man gets to a certain age, he must try to recapture—"

"Shut up, Nicole," Kabalka said.

She looked at him in surprise, then picked up her sandwich and nibbled daintily at it. I could understand why she had backed off; there was something in Kabalka's tone that said he would put up with no more from her.

After the remains of supper were packed up, everyone settled down. None of them displayed the slightest inclination to go out front and watch the show. Kabalka read—one of those slim volumes that claim you can make a financial killing in spite of the world economic crisis. Corinne crocheted—granny squares. Fitzgerald brooded. Tilby played solitaire. Nicole fidgeted. And while they engaged in these activities, they also seemed to be watching one another. The covert vigilant atmosphere puzzled me; after a while I concluded that maybe the reason they all stuck together was that each was afraid to leave the others alone. But why?

Time crawled. Outside, the show was going on; I could hear music, laughter, and—occasionally—Don's enthusiastic voice as he introduced the acts. Once more I began to regret taking this job.

After a while Tilby reshuffled the cards and slapped them on the table. "Sharon, do you play gin rummy?"

"Yes."

"Good. Let's have a few hands."

Nicole frowned and made a small sound of protest.

Tilby said to her, "I offered to teach you. It's not my fault you refused."

I moved my chair over to the table and we played in silence for a while. Tilby was good, but I was better. After about half an hour, there was a roar from the crowd and Tilby raised his head. "Casey O'Connell must be going on."

"Who?" I said.

"One of our more famous circus clowns."

"There really is quite a variety among the performers in your profession, isn't there?"

"Yes, and quite a history: clowning is an old and honored art. They had clowns back in ancient Greece. Wandering entertainers, actually, who'd show up at a wealthy household and tell jokes, do acrobatics, or juggle for the price of a meal. Then in the Middle Ages, mimes appeared on the scene."

"That long ago?"

"Uh-huh. They were the cream of the crop back then. Most of the humor in the Middle Ages was kind of basic; they loved buffoons, jesters, simpletons, that sort of thing. But they served the purpose of making people see how silly we really are."

I took the deuce he'd just discarded, then lay down my hand to show I had gin. Tilby frowned and slapped down his cards; nothing matched. Then he grinned. "See what I mean—I'm silly to take this game so seriously."

I swept the cards together and began to shuffle. "You seem to know a good bit about the history of clowning."

"Well, I've done some reading along those lines. You've heard the term *commedia dell'arte*?"

"Yes."

"It appeared in the late 1500s, an Italian brand of the traveling comedy troupe. The comedians always played the same role—a Harlequin or a Pulcinella or a Pantalone. Easy for the audience to recognize.''

"I know what a Harlequin is, but what are the other two?''

"Pantalone is a personification of the overbearing father figure. A stubborn, temperamental old geezer. Pulcinella was costumed all in white, usually with a dunce's cap; he assumed various roles in the comedy—lawyer, doctor, servant, whatever—and was usually greedy, sometimes pretty coarse. One of his favorite tricks was urinating onstage.''

"Good Lord!''

"Fortunately we've become more refined since then. The British contributed a lot, further developing the Harlequin, creating the Punch and Judy shows. And of course, the French had their Figaro. The Indians created the *vidushaka*—a form of court jester. The entertainers at the Chinese court were known as *Chous*, after the dynasty in which they originated. And Japan has a huge range of comic figures appearing in their *Kyogen* plays—the humorous counterpart of the *Noh* play.''

"You really have done your homework.''

"Well, clowning's my profession. Don't you know about the history of yours?''

"What I know is mostly fictional; private investigation is more interesting in books than in real life, I'm afraid.''

"Gin.'' Tilby spread his cards on the table. "Your deal. But back to what I was saying, it's the more contemporary clowns that interest me. And I use the term 'clown' loosely.''

"How so?''

"Well, do you think of Will Rogers as a clown?''

"No.''

"I do. And Laurel and Hardy, Flip Wilson, Mae West, Woody Allen, Lucille Ball. As well as the more traditional figures like Emmett Kelly, Charlie Chaplin, and Marceau. There's a common denominator among all those people; they're funny and, more important, they all make the audience take a look at humanity's foibles. They're as much descended from those historical clowns as the whiteface circus performer.''

"The whiteface is the typical circus clown, right?''

"Well, there are three basic types; whiteface is your basic slaphappy fellow. The Auguste—who was created almost simultaneously in Germany and France—usually wears pink- or blackface and is the one you see falling all over himself in the ring, often sopping wet from having buckets of water thrown at him. The Grotesque is usually a midget or a dwarf, or has some other distorted feature. And there are performers whom you can't classify because they've created something unique, such as Kelly's Weary Willie, or Russia's Popov, who is such an artist that he doesn't even need to wear makeup.''

"It's fascinating. I never realized there was such variety. Or artistry.''

"Most people don't. They think clowning is easy, but a lot of the time it's just plain hard work. Especially when you have to go on when you aren't feeling particularly funny.'' Tilby's mouth drooped as he spoke, and I wondered if tonight was one of those occasions for him.

I picked up a trey and said, "Gin," then tossed my hand on the table and watched as he shuffled and dealt. We fell silent once more. The sounds of the show went on, but the only noise in the dressing room was the slap of the cards on the table. It was still uncomfortably hot. Moths fluttered around the glaring bare bulbs of the dressing tables. At about ten-thirty, Fitzgerald stood up.

"Where are you going?" Kabalka said.

"The men's room. Do you mind?"

I said, "I'll go with you.''

Fitzgerald smiled faintly. "Really, Sharon, that's above and beyond the call of duty.''

"I mean, just to the door.''

He started to protest, then shrugged and picked up his canvas bag. Kabalka said, "Why are you taking that?"

"There's something in it I need.''

"What?"

"For Christ's sake, Wayne!" He snatched up his yellow cape, flung it over one shoulder.

Kabalka hesitated. "All right, go. But Sharon goes with you.''

Fitzgerald went out into the hall and I followed. Behind me, Nicole said, "Probably Maalox or something like that for his queasy stomach. You can always count on Gary to puke at least once before a performance.''

Kabalka said, "Shut up, Nicole.''

Fitzgerald started off, muttering, "Yes, we're one big happy family.''

I followed him and took up a position next to the men's room door. It was ten mintues before I realized he was taking too long a time, and when I did I asked one of the security guards to go in after him. Fitzgerald had vanished, apparently through an open window high off the floor—a trash receptacle had been moved beneath it, which would have allowed him to climb up there. The window opened onto the pavilion grounds rather than outside of the fence, but from there he could have gone in any one of a number of directions—including out the performers' gate.

From then on, all was confusion. I told Kabalka what had happened and again left him in charge of the others. With the help of the security personnel, I combed the backstage area—questioning the performers, stage personnel, Don, and the other people from KSUN. No one had seen Fitzgerald. The guards in the audience were alerted, but no one in baggy plaid pants, a red vest, and a yellow cape was spotted. The security man on the performers' gate knew nothing; he'd only come on minutes ago, and the man he had relieved had left the grounds on a break.

Fitzgerald and Tilby were to be the last act to go on—at midnight, as the star attraction. As the hour approached, the others in their party grew frantic and Don and the KSUN people grew grim. I continued to search systematically. Finally I returned to the performers' gate; the guard had returned from his break and Kabalka had buttonholed him. I took over the questioning. Yes, he remembered Gary Fitzgerald. He'd left at about ten thirty, carrying his yellow cape and a small canvas bag. But wait—hadn't he returned just a few minutes ago, before Kabalka had come up and started asking questions? But maybe that wasn't the same man, there had been something different . . .

Kabalka was on the edge of hysterical collapse. He yelled at the guard and only confused him further. Maybe the man who had just come in had been wearing a red cape . . . maybe the pants were green rather than blue . . . no, it wasn't the same man after all . . .

Kabalka yelled louder, until one of the stage personnel told him to shut up, he could be heard out front. Corinne appeared and momentarily succeeded in quieting her husband. I left her to deal with him and went back to the dressing room. Tilby and Nicole were there. His face was pinched, white around the mouth. Nicole was pale and—oddly enough—had been crying. I told them what the security guard had said, cautioned them not to leave the dressing room.

As I turned to go, Tilby said, "Sharon, will you ask Wayne to come in here?"

"I don't think he's in any shape—"

"Please, it's important."

"All right. But why?"

Tilby looked at Nicole. She turned her tear-streaked face away toward the wall.

He said, "We have a decision to make about the act."

"I hardly think so. It's pretty clear cut. If Gary doesn't turn up, you simply can't go on."

He stared bleakly at me. "Just ask Wayne to come in here."

Of course the act didn't go on. The audience was disappointed, the KSUN people were irate, and the Fitzgerald and Tilby entourage were grim—a grimness that held a faint undercurrent of tightly-reined panic.

No one could shed any light on where Fitzgerald might have gone, or why—at least, if anyone had suspicions, he was keeping it to himself. The one thing everyone agreed on was that his disappearance wasn't my fault; I hadn't been hired to prevent treachery within the ranks. I myself wasn't so sure of my lack of culpability.

So I'd spent the night chasing around, trying to find a trace of him. I'd gone to San Francisco: to Fitzgerald's hotel in the Haight-Ashbury, to the St. Francis where the rest of the party were staying, even to the KSUN studios. Finally I went back to the Haight, to a number of the after-hours places I knew of, in the hopes Fitzgerald was there recapturing his youth, as Nicole had termed it earlier. And I still hadn't found a single clue to his whereabouts.

Until now. I hadn't located Gary Fitzgerald, but I'd found his clown costume. On another man. A dead man.

VI

After the county sheriff's men had finished questioning me and said I could go, I decided to return to the St. Francis and talk to my clients once more. I wasn't sure if Kabalka would want me to keep searching for Fitzgerald now, but he—and the others—deserved to hear from me about the dead man in Gary's costume, before the authorities contacted them. Besides, there were things bothering me about Fitzgerald's disappearance, some of them obvious, some vague. I hoped talking to Kabalka and company once more would help me bring the vague ones into more clear focus.

It was after seven by the time I had parked under Union Square and entered the hotel's elegant, dark-paneled lobby. The few early risers who clustered there seemed to be tourists, equipped with cameras and anxious to get on with the day's adventures. A dissipated-looking couple in evening clothes stood waiting for an elevator, and a few yards away in front of the first row of expensive shops, a maid in the hotel uniform was pushing a vacuum cleaner with desultory strokes. When the elevator came, the couple and I rode up in silence; they got off at the floor before I did.

Corinne Kabalka answered my knock on the door of the suite almost immediately. Her eyes were deeply shadowed, she wore the same white linen pantsuit—now severely rumpled—that she'd had on the night before,. and in her hand she clutched her crocheting. When she saw me, her face registered disappointment.

"Oh," she said, "I thought . . ."

"You hoped it would be Gary."

"Yes. Well, any of them, really."

"Them? Are you alone?"

She nodded and crossed the sitting room to a couch under the heavily-draped windows, dropping onto it with a sigh and setting down the crocheting.

"Where did they go?"

"Wayne's out looking for Gary. He refuses to believe he's just . . . vanished. I don't know where John is, but I suspect he's looking for Nicole."

"And Nicole?"

Anger flashed in her tired eyes. "Who knows?"

I was about to ask her more about Tilby's unpleasant girlfriend when a key rattled in the lock, and John and Nicole came in. His face was pulled into taut lines, reflecting a rage more sustained than Corinne's brief flare-up. Nicole looked haughty, tight-lipped, and a little defensive.

Corinne stood. "Where have you two been?"

Tilby said, "*I* was looking for Nicole. It occurred to me that we didn't want to lose another member of this happy party."

Corinne turned to Nicole. "And you?"

The younger woman sat on a spindly chair, studiously examining her plum-colored fingernails. "I was having breakfast."

"Breakfast?"

"I was hungry, after that disgusting supper last night. So I went around the corner to a coffee shop—"

"You could have ordered from room service. Or eaten downstairs where John could have found you more easily."

"I needed some air."

Now Corinne drew herself erect. "Always thinking of Nicole, aren't you?"

"Well, what of it? Someone around here has to act sensibly."

In their heated bickering, they all seemed to have forgotten I was there. I remained silent, taking advantage of the situation; one could learn very instructive things by listening to people's unguarded conversations.

Tilby said, "Nicole's right, Corinne. We can't all run around like Wayne, looking for Gary when we have no idea where to start."

"Yes, *you* would say that. You never did give a damn about him, or anyone. Look how you stole Nicole from your own cousin—"

"Good God, Corinne! You can't *steal* one person from another."

"You did. You stole her and then you wrecked—"

"Let's not go into this, Corinne. Especially in front of an outsider." Tilby motioned at me.

Corinne glanced my way and colored. "I'm sorry, Sharon. This must be embarrassing for you."

On the contrary, I wished they would go on. After all, if John had taken Nicole from his cousin, Gary would have had reason to resent him—perhaps even to want to destroy their act.

I said to Tilby, "Is that the reason Gary was staying at a different hotel—beacuse of you and Nicole?"

He looked startled.

"How long have you two been together?" I asked.

"Long enough." He turned to Corinne. "Wayne hasn't come back or called, I take it?"

"I've heard nothing. He was terribly worried about Gary when he left."

Nicole said, "He's terribly worried about the TV commercials and his cut of them."

"Nicole!" Corinne whirled on her.

Nicole looked up, her delicate little face all innocence. "You now it's true. All Wayne cares about is money. I don't know why he's worried, though. He can always get someone to replace Gary, Wayne's good at doing that sort of thing—"

Corinne stepped forward and her hand lashed out at Nicole's face, connecting with a loud smack. Nicole put a hand to the reddening stain on her cheekbone, eyes widening; then she got up and ran from the room. Corinne watched her go, satisfaction spreading over her handsome features. When I glanced at Tilby, I was surprised to see he was smiling.

"Round one to Corinne," he said.

"She had it coming." The older woman went back to the couch and sat, smoothing her rumpled pantsuit. "Well, Sharon, once more you must excuse us. I assume you came here for a reason?"

"Yes." I sat down in the chair Nicole had vacated and told them about the dead man at the pavilion. As I spoke, the two exchanged glances that were at first puzzled, then worried, and finally panicky.

When I had finished, Corinne said, "But who on earth can the man in Gary's costume be?" The words sounded theatrical, false.

"The sheriff's department is trying to make an identification. Probably his fingerprints will be on file somewhere. In the meantime, there are a few distinctive things about him which may mean something to you or John.''

John sat down next to Corinne. "Such as?"

"The man had been crippled, probably a number of years ago, according to the man from the medical examiner's office. One arm was bent badly, and he wore a lift to compensate for a shortened leg. He would have walked with a limp.''

The two of them looked at each other, and then Tilby said—too quickly—"I don't know anyone like that.''

Corinne also shook her head, but she didn't meet my eyes.

I said, "Are you sure?"

"Of course we're sure." There was an edge of annoyance in Tilby's voice.

I hesitated, then went on, "The sheriff's man who examined the body theorizes that the dead man may have been from the countryside around there, because he had fragments of madrone and chapparal leaves caught in his shoes, as well as foxtails in the weave of his pants. Perhaps he's someone you knew when you lived in the area?''

"No, I don't remember anyone like that.''

"He was about Gary's height and age, but with sandy hair. He must have been handsome once, in an elfin way, but his face was badly scarred.''

"I said, I don't know who he is.''

I was fairly certain he was lying, but accusing him would get me nowhere.

Corinne said, "Are you sure the costume was Gary's? Maybe this man was one of the other clowns and dressed similarly.''

"That's what I suggested to the sheriff's man, but the dead man had Gary's pass in his vest pocket. We all signed our passes, remember?''

There was a long silence. 'So what you're saying,'' Tilby finally said, "is that Gary *gave* his pass and costume to this man.''

"It seems so.''

"But why?''

"I don't know. I'd hoped you could provide me with some insight.''

They both stared at me. I noticed Corinne's face had gone quite blank. Tilby was as white-lipped as when I'd come upon him and Nicole in the dressing room shortly after Fitzgerald's disappearance.

I said to Tilby, "I assume you each have more than one change of costume.''

It was Corinne who answered. "We brought three on this tour. But I had the other two sent out to the cleaner when we arrived here in San Francisco . . . Oh!''

''What is it?''

''I just remembered. Gary asked me about the other costumes yesterday morning. He called from that hotel where he was staying. And he was very upset when I told him they would be at the cleaner until this afternoon.''

''So he planned it all along. Probably he hoped to give his extra costume to the man, and when he found he couldn't, he decided to make a switch.'' I remembered Fitzgerald's odd behavior immediately after we'd arrived at the pavilion—his sneaking off into the audience when he'd been told to stay backstage. Had he had a confederate out there? Someone to hand the things to? No. He couldn't have turned over either the costume or the pass to anyone, because the clothing was still backstage, and he'd needed his pass when we returned to the dressing room.

Tilby suddenly stood up. ''The son of a bitch! After all we've done—''

''John!'' Corinne touched his elbow with her hand.

''John,'' I said, ''why was your cousin staying at the hotel in the Haight?''

He looked at me blankly for a moment. ''What? Oh, I don't know. He claimed he wanted to see how it had changed since he'd lived there.''

''I thought you grew up together on your father's ranch near Clayton and then went to Los Angeles.''

''We did. Gary lived in the Haight before we left the Bay Area.''

''I see. Now, you say he 'claimed' that was the reason. Was there something else?''

Tilby was silent, then looked at Corinne. She shrugged.

''I guess,'' he said finally, ''he'd had about all he could take of us. As you may have noticed, we're not exactly a congenial group lately.''

''Why is that?''

''Why is what?''

''That you're all at odds? It hasn't always been this way, has it?''

This time Tilby shrugged. Corinne was silent, looking down at her clasped hands.

I sighed, silently empathizing with Fitzgerald's desire to get away from these people. I myself was sick of their bickering, lies, backbiting, and evasions. And I knew I would get nowhere with them—at least not now. Better to wait until I could talk with Kabalka, see if he were willing to keep on employing me. Then, if he was, I could start fresh.

I stood up, saying, ''The Contra Costa authorities will be contacting you. I'd advise you to be as frank as possible with them.''

To Corinne, I added, "Wayne will want a personal report from me when he comes back; ask him to call me at home." I took out a card with both my All Souls and home number, lay it on the coffee table, and started for the door.

As I let myself out, I glanced back at them. Tilby stood with his arms folded across his chest, looking down at Corinne. They were still as statues, their eyes locked, their expressions bleak and helpless.

VII

Of course, by the time I got home to my brown-shingled cottage the desire to sleep had left me. It was always that way when I harbored nagging unanswered questions. Instead of going to bed and forcing myself to rest, I made coffee and took a cup of it out on the back porch to think.

It was a sunny, clear morning and already getting hot. The neighborhood was Saturday noisy: to one side, my neighbors, the Halls, were doing something to their backyard shed that involved a lot of hammering; on the other side, the Curleys' dog was barking excitedly. Probably, I thought, my cat was deviling the dog by prancing along the top of the fence, just out of his reach. It was Watney's favorite game lately.

Sure enough, in a few minutes there was a thump as Wat dropped down from the fence onto an upturned half barrel I'd been meaning to make into a planter. His black-and-white spotted fur was full of foxtails; undoubtedly he'd been prowling around in the weeds at the back of the Curleys' lot.

"Come here, you," I said to him. He stared at me, tail swishing back and forth. "Come here!" He hesitated, then galloped up. I managed to pull one of the foxtails from the ruff of fur over his collar before he trotted off again, his belly swaying pendulously, a great big horse of a cat . . .

I sat staring at the foxtail, rolling it between my thumb and forefinger, not really seeing it. Instead, I pictured the hills surrounding the pavilion as I'd seen them the night before. The hills that were dotted with oak and madrone and chapparal . . . that were sprinkled with people on horses . . . where a lone horseman had stood under the sheltering branches of a tree, his binoculars like a signal flare in the setting sun. . . .

I got up and went inside to the phone. First I called the Contra Costa sheriff's deputy who had been in charge of the crime scene at the pavilion. No, he told me, the dead man hadn't been identified yet;

the only personal item he had been carrying was a bus ticket—issued yesterday—from San Francisco to Concord which had been tucked into his shoe. While this indicated he was not a resident of the area, it told them nothing else. They were still hoping to get an identification on his fingerprints, however.

Next I called the pavilion and got the home phone number of Jim Hayes, the guard who had been on the performers' gate when Fitzgerald had vanished. When Hayes answered my call, he sounded as if I'd woken him, but he was willing to answer a few questions.

"When Fitzgerald left he was wearing his costume, right?" I asked.

"Yes."

"What about makeup?"

"No. I'd have noticed that; it would have seemed strange, him leaving with his face all painted."

"Now, last night you said you thought he'd come back in a few minutes after you returned from your break. Did he show you his pass?"

"Yes, everyone had to show one. But—"

"Did you look at the name on it?"

"Not closely. I just checked to see if it was valid for that date. Now I wish I *had* looked, because I'm not sure it was Fitzgerald. The costume seemed the same, but I just don't know."

"Why?"

"Well, there was something different about the man who came in. He walked funny. The guy you found murdered, he was crippled."

So that observation might or might not be valid. The idea that the man walked "funny" could have been planted in Hayes' mind by his knowing the dead man was a cripple. "Anything else?"

He hesitated. "I think . . . yes. You asked if Gary Fitzgerald was wearing makeup when he left. And he wasn't. But the guy who came in, he *was* made up. That's why I don't think it was Fitzgerald."

"Thank you, Mr. Hayes. That's all I need to know."

I hung up the phone, grabbed my bag and car keys, and drove back out to the pavilion in record time.

The heat-hazed parking lots were empty today, save for a couple of trucks that I assumed belonged to the maintenance crew. The gates were locked, the box office windows shuttered, and I could see no one. That didn't matter, however. What I was interested in lay outside the chain-link fence. I parked the MG near the trucks and went around the perimeter of the amphitheater to the area near the performers' gate, then looked up at the hill to the east. There was a fire break cut through the high wheat-colored grass, and I started up it.

Halfway to the top, I stopped, wiping sweat from my forehead and looking down at the pavilion. Visibility was good from here. Pivoting, I surveyed the surrounding area. To the west lay a monotonous grid-like pattern of tracts and shopping centers, broken here and there by hills and the upthrusting skyline of Walnut Creek. To the north I could see smoke billowing from the stacks of the paper plant at Antioch, and the bridge spanning the river toward the Sacramento Delta. Further east, the majestic bulk of Mount Diablo rose; between it and this foothill were more hills and hollows—ranch country.

The hill on which I stood was only lightly wooded, but there was an outcropping of rock surrounded by madrone and live oak about a hundred yards to the south, on a direct line from the tree where the lone horseman with the signal-like binoculars had stood. I left the relatively easy footing of the fire break and waded through the dry grass toward it. It was cool and deeply shadowed under the branches of the trees, and the air smelled of vegetation gone dry and brittle. I stood still for a moment, wiping the sweat away once more, then began to look around. What I was searching for was wedged behind a low rock that formed a sort of table; a couple of tissues smeared with makeup. Black and red and white greasepaint—the theatrical makeup of a clown.

The dead man had probably used this rock as a dressing table, applying what Fitzgerald had brought him in the canvas bag. I remembered Gary's insistence on taking the bag with him to the men's room; of course he needed it; the makeup was a necessary prop to their plan. While Fitzgerald could leave the pavilion without his greasepaint, the other man couldn't enter un-madeup; there was too much of a risk that the guard might notice the face didn't match the costume or the name on the pass.

I looked down at the dry leaves beneath my feet. Oak, and madrone, and brittle needles of chapparal. And the foxtails would have been acquired while pushing through the high grass between here and the bottom of the hills. That told me the route the dead man had taken, but not what had happened to Fitzgerald. In order to find that out, I'd have to learn where one could rent a horse.

I stopped at a feed store in the little village of Hillside, nestled in a wooded hollow southeast of the pavilion. It was all you could expect of a country store, with wood floors and big sacks and bins of feed. The weatherbeaten old man in overalls who looked up from the saddle he was polishing completed the rustic picture.

He said, "Help you with something?"

I took a closer look at the saddle, then glanced around at the handtooled leather goods hanging from the hooks on the far wall. "That's beautiful work. Do you do it yourself?"

"Sure do."

"How much does a saddle like that go for these days?" My experience with horses had ended with the lessons I'd taken in junior high school.

"Custom job like this, five hundred, thereabouts."

"Five hundred! That's more than I could get for my car."

"Well . . ." He glanced through the door at the MG.

"I know. You don't have to say another word."

"It runs, don't it?"

"Usually." Rapport established, I got down to business. "What I need is some information. I'm looking for a stable that rents horses."

"You want to set up a party or something?"

"I might."

"Well, there's MacMillan's, on the south side of town. I wouldn't recommend them, though. They've got some mean horses. This would be for a bunch of city folks?"

"I wasn't aware it showed."

"Doesn't, all that much. But I'm good at figuring out about folks. You don't look like a suburban lady, and you don't look country either." He beamed at me, and I nodded and smiled to compliment his deductive ability. "No," he went on, "I wouldn't recommend MacMillan's if you'll have folks along who maybe don't ride so good. Some of those horses are mean enough to kick a person from here to San Jose. The place to go is Wheeler's; they got some fine mounts."

"Where is Wheeler's?"

"South too, a couple of miles beyond MacMillan's. You'll know it by the sign."

I thanked him and started out. "Hey!" he called after me. "When you have your party, bring your city friends by. I got a nice selection of handtooled belts and wallets."

I said I would, and waved at him as I drove off.

About a mile down the road on the south side of the little hamlet stood a tumble-down stable with a hand-lettered sign advertising horses for rent. The poorly recommended MacMillan's, no doubt. There wasn't an animal, mean or otherwise, in sight, but a large, jowly woman who resembled a bulldog greeted me, pitchfork in hand.

I told her the story that I'd hastily made up on the drive: a friend of mine had rented a horse the night before to ride up on the hill and watch the show at the Diablo Valley Pavilion. He had been impressed with the horse and the stable it had come from, but couldn't remember the name of the place. Had she, by any chance, rented to him? As I spoke, the woman began to frown, looking more and more like a pugnacious canine every minute.

"It's not honest," she said.

"I'm sorry?"

"It's not honest, people riding up there and watching for free. Stealing's stealing, no matter what name you put on it. Your Bible tells you that."

"Oh." I couldn't think of any reply to that, although she was probably right.

She eyed me severely, as if she suspected me of pagan practices. "In answer to your question, no, I didn't rent to your friend. I wouldn't let a person near one of my horses if he was going to ride up there and watch."

"Well, I don't suppose my friend admitted what he planned to do—"

"Any decent person would be too ashamed to admit to a thing like that." She motioned aggressively with the pitchfork.

I took a step backwards. "But maybe you rented to him not knowing—"

"You going to do the same thing?"

"What?"

"Are you going to ride up there for tonight's concert?"

"Me? No, ma'am. I don't even ride all that well. I just wanted to find out if my friend had rented his horse from—"

"Well, he didn't get the horse from here. We aren't open evenings, don't want our horses out in the dark with people like you who can't ride. Besides, even if people don't plan it, those concerts are an awful temptation. And I can't sanction that sort of thing. I'm a born-again Christian, and I won't help people go against the Lord's word."

"You know," I said hastily, "I agree with you. And I'm going to talk with my friend about his behavior. But I still want to know where he got that horse. Are there any other stables around here besides yours?"

The woman looked somewhat mollified. "There's only Wheeler's. They do a big business—trail trips on Mount Diablo, hayrides in the fall. And, of course, folks who want to sneak up to that pavilion. They'd rent to a person who was going to rob a bank on horseback if there was enough money in it."

Stifling a grin, I started for my car. "Thanks for the information."

"You're welcome to it. But you remember to talk to your friend, tell him to mend his ways."

I smiled and got out of there in a hurry.

Next to MacMillan's, Wheeler's Riding Stables looked prosperous and attractive. The red barn was freshly painted, and a couple of dozen healthy, sleek horses grazed within white rail fences. I rumbled down a dirt driveway and over a little bridge that spanned a gully, and parked in front of a door labeled OFFICE. Inside, a blond-haired man in faded Levi's and a T-shirt lounged in a canvas chair behind the counter, reading a copy of *Playboy*. He put it aside reluctantly when I came in.

I was tired of my manufactured story, and this man looked like someone I could be straightforward with. I showed him the photostat of my license and said, "I'm cooperating with the county sheriff's department on the death at the Diablo Valley Pavilion last night. You've heard about it?"

"Yes, it made the morning news."

"I've got reason to believe that the dead man may have rented a horse prior to the show last night."

The man raised a sun-bleached eyebrow and waited, as economical with his words as the woman at MacMillan's had been spendthrift.

"Did you rent any horses last night?"

"Five. Four to a party, another later on."

"Who rented the single horse?"

"Tall, thin guy. Wore jeans and a plaid shirt. At first I thought I knew him."

"Why?"

"He looked familiar, like someone who used to live near here. But then I realized it couldn't be. His face was disfigured, his arm crippled up, and he limped. Had trouble getting on the horse, but once he was mounted, I could tell he was a good rider."

I felt a flash of excitement, the kind you get when things start coming together the way you've hoped they would. "That's the man who was killed."

"Well, that explains it."

"Explains what?"

"Horse came back this morning, riderless."

"What time?"

"Oh, around five, five-thirty."

That didn't fit the way I wanted it to. "Do you keep a record of who you rent the horses to?"

"Name and address. And we take a deposit that's returned when they bring the horses back."

"Can you look up the man's name?"

He grinned and reached under the counter for a looseleaf notebook.

"I can, but I don't think it will help you identify him. I noted it at the time—Tom Smith. Sounded like a phony."

"But you still rented to him?"

"Sure. I just asked for double the deposit. He didn't look too prosperous, so I figured he'd be back. Besides, none of our horses are so terrific that anyone would trouble to steal one."

I stood there for a few seconds, tapping my fingers on the counter. "You said you thought he was someone you used to know."

"At first, but the guy I knew wasn't crippled. Must have been just a chance resemblance."

"Who was he?"

"Fellow who lived on a ranch near here back in the late sixties. Gary Fitzgerald."

I stared at him.

"But like I said, Gary Fitzgerald wasn't crippled."

"Did this Gary have a cousin?" I asked.

"Yeah, John Tilby. Tilby's dad owned a dairy ranch. Gary lived with them."

"When did Gary leave here?"

"After the old man died. The ranch was sold to pay the debts and both Gary and John took off. For southern California." He grinned again. "Probably had some cock-eyed idea about getting into show business."

"By any chance, do you know who was starring on the bill at the pavilion last night?"

"Don't recall, no. It was some kind of kid show, wasn't it?"

"A clown festival."

"Oh." He shrugged. "Clowns don't interest me. Why?"

"No reason." Things definitely weren't fitting together the way I'd wanted them to. "You say the cousins took off together after John Tilby's father died."

"Yes."

"And went to southern California."

"That's what I heard."

"Did Gary Fitzgerald ever live in the Haight-Ashbury?"

He hesitated. "Not unless they went there instead of L.A. But I can't see Gary in the Haight, especially back then. He was just a country boy, if you know what I mean. But what's all this about him and John? I thought—"

"How much to rent a horse?"

The man's curiosity was easily sidetracked by business. "Ten an hour. Twenty for the deposit."

"Do you have a gentle one?"

"You mean for you? Now?"

"Yes."

"Got all kinds, gentle or lively."

I took out my wallet and checked it. Luckily, I had a little under forty dollars. "I'll take the gentlest one."

The man pushed the looseleaf notebook at me, looking faintly surprised. "You sign the book, and then I'll go saddle up Whitefoot."

VIII

Once our transaction was completed, the stable man pointed out the bridle trail that led toward the pavilion, wished me a good ride, and left me atop one of the gentlest horses I'd ever encountered. Whitefoot—a roan who did indeed have one white fetlock—was so placid I was afraid he'd go to sleep. Recalling my few riding lessons, which had taken place sometime in my early teens, I made some encouraging clicking sounds and tapped his flanks with my heels. Whitefoot put his head down and began munching a clump of dry grass.

"Come on, big fellow," I said. Whitefoot continued to munch.

I shook the reins—gently, but with authority.

No response. I stared disgustedly down the incline of his neck, which made me feel I was sitting at the top of a long slide. Then I repeated the clicking and tapping process. The horse ignored me.

"Look, you lazy bastard," I said in a low, menacing tone, "get a move on!"

The horse raised his head and shook it, glancing back at me with one sullen eye. Then he started down the bridle trail in a swaying, lumbering walk. I sat up straighter in correct horsewoman's posture, feeling smug.

The trail wound through a grove of eucalyptus, then began climbing uphill through grassland. The terrain was rough, full of rocky outcroppings and eroded gullies, and I was thankful for both the well-traveled path and Whitefoot's slovenly gait. After a few minutes I began to feel secure enough in the saddle to take stock of my surroundings, and when we reached the top of a rise, I stopped the horse and looked around.

To one side lay grazing land dotted with brown-and-white cattle. In the distance, I spotted a barn and a corral with horses. To the other side, the vegetation was thicker, giving onto a canyon choked with

·manzanita, scrub oak, and bay laurel. This was the type of terrain I was looking for—the kind where a man can easily become disoriented and lost. Still, there must be dozens of such canyons in the surrounding hills; to explore all of them would take days.

I had decided to ride a little further before plunging into rougher territory, when I noticed a movement under the leafy overhang at the edge of the canyon. Peering intently at the spot, I made out a tall figure in light-colored clothing. Before I could identify it as male or female, it slipped back into the shadows and disappeared from view.

Afraid that the person would see me, I reined the horse to one side, behind a large sandstone boulder a few yards away. Then I slipped from the saddle and peered around the rock toward the canyon. Nothing moved there. I glanced at Whitefoot and decided he would stay where he was without being tethered; true to form, he had lowered his head and was munching contentedly. After patting him once for reassurance, I crept through the tall grass to the underbrush. The air there was chill and pungent with the scent of bay laurel—more reminiscent of curry powder than of the bay leaf I kept in a jar in my kitchen. I crouched behind the billowy bright green mat of a chapparal bush while my eyes became accustomed to the gloom. Still nothing stirred; it was as if the figure had been a creature of my imagination.

Ahead of me, the canyon narrowed between high rock walls. Moss coated them, and stunted trees grew out of their cracks. I came out of my shelter and started that way, over ground that was sloping and uneven. From my right came a trickling sound; I peered through the underbrush and saw a tiny stream of water falling over the outcropping. A mere dribble now, it would be a full cascade in the wet season.

The ground became even rougher, and at times I had difficulty finding a foothold. At a point where the mossy walls almost converged, I stopped, leaning against one of them, and listened. A sound, as if someone were thrashing through thick vegetation, came from the other side of the narrow space. I squeezed between the rocks and saw a heavily forested area. A tree branch a few feet from me looked as if it had recently been broken.

I started through the vegetation, following the sounds ahead of me. Pine boughs brushed at my face, and chapparal needles scratched my bare arms. After a few minutes, the thrashing sounds stopped. I stood still, wondering if the person I was following had heard me.

Everything was silent. Not even a bird stirred in the trees above me. I had no idea where I was in relation to either the pavilion or the stables. I wasn't even sure if I could find my way back to where I'd left the horse.

Foolishly I realized the magnitude of the task I'd undertaken; such a search would better be accomplished with a helicopter than on horseback.

And then I heard the voices.

They came from the right, past a heavy screen of scrub oak. They were male, and from their rhythm I could tell they were angry. But I couldn't identify them or make out what they were saying. I edged around a clump of manzanita and started through the trees, trying to make as little sound as possible.

On the other side of the trees was an outcropping that formed a flat rock shelf that appeared to drop off sharply after about twenty feet. I clambered up on it and flattened onto my stomach, then crept forward. The voices were louder now, coming from straight ahead and below. I identified one as belonging to the man I knew as Gary Fitzgerald.

"... didn't know he intended to blackmail anyone. I thought he just wanted to see John, make it up with him." The words were labored, twisted with pain.

"If that were the case, he could have come to the hotel." The second man was Wayne Kabalka. "He didn't have to go through all those elaborate machinations of sneaking into the pavilion."

"He told me he wanted to reconcile. After all, he was John's own cousin—"

"Come on, Elliott. You knew he had threatened us. You knew all about the pressure he'd put on us the past few weeks, ever since he found out the act would be coming to San Francisco."

I started at the strange name, even though I had known the missing man wasn't really Gary Fitzgerald. Elliott. Elliott who?

Elliott was silent.

I continued creeping forward, the mossy rock cold through my clothing. When I reached the edge of the shelf, I kept my head down until Kabalka spoke again. "You knew we were all afraid of Gary. That's why I hired the McCone woman; in case he tried anything, I wanted an armed guard there. I never counted on you playing the Judas."

Again Elliott was silent. I risked a look over the ledge.

There was a sheer drop of some fifteen or twenty feet to a gully full of jagged rocks. The man I'd known as Gary Fitzgerald lay at its bottom, propped into a sitting position, his right leg twisted at an unnatural angle. He was wearing a plaid shirt and jeans—the same clothing the man at the stables had described the dead man as having on. Kabalka stood in front of him, perhaps two yards from where I lay, his back to me. For a minute, I was afraid Elliott would see my head, but then I realized his eyes were glazed half blind with pain.

"What happened between John and Gary?" he asked.

Kabalka shifted his weight and put one arm behind his back, sliding his hand into his belt.

"Wayne, what happened?"

"Gary was found dead at the pavilion this morning. Stabbed. None of this would have happened if you hadn't connived to switch clothing so he could sneak backstage and threaten John."

Elliott's hand twitched, as if he wanted to cover his eyes but was too weak to lift it. "Dead." He paused. "I was afraid something awful had happened when he didn't come back to where I was waiting with the horse."

"Of course you were afraid. You knew what would happen."

"No . . ."

"You planned this for weeks, didn't you? The thing about staying at the fleabag in the Haight was a ploy, so you could turn over one of your costumes to Gary. But it didn't work, because Corinne had sent all but one to the cleaner. When did you come up with the scheme of sneaking out and trading places?"

Elliott didn't answer.

"I suppose it doesn't matter when. But why, Elliott? For God's sake, *why*?"

When he finally answered, Elliott's voice was weary. "Maybe I was sick of what you'd done to him. What we'd *all* done. He was so pathetic when he called me in L.A. And when I saw him . . . I thought maybe that if John saw him too, he might persuade you to help Gary."

"And instead he killed him."

"No. I can't believe that."

"And why not?"

"John loved Gary."

"John loved Gary so much he took Nicole away from him. And then he got into a drunken quarrel with him and crashed the car they were riding in and crippled him for life."

"Yes, but John's genuinely guilty over the accident. And he hates you for sending Gary away and replacing him with me. What a fraud we've all perpetrated—"

Kabalka's body tensed and he began balancing aggressively on the balls of his feet. "That fraud has made us a lot of money. Would have made us more until you pulled this stunt. Sooner or later they'll identify Gary's body and then it will all come out. John will be tried for the murder—"

"I still don't believe he killed him. I want to ask him about it."

Slowly Kabalka slipped his hand from his belt—and I saw the

knife. He held it behind his back in his clenched fingers and took a step toward Elliott.

I pushed up with my palms against the rock. The motion caught Elliott's eye and he looked around in alarm. Kabalka must have taken the look to be aimed at him because he brought the knife up.

I didn't hesitate. I jumped off the ledge. For what seemed like an eternity I was falling toward the jagged rocks below. Then I landed heavily—directly on top of Kabalka.

As he hit the ground, I heard the distinctive sound of cracking bone. He went limp, and I rolled off of him—unhurt, because his body had cushioned my fall. Kabalka lay unconscious, his head against a rock. When I looked at Elliott, I saw he had passed out from pain and shock.

IX

The room at John Muir Hospital in Walnut Creek was antiseptic white, with bright touches of red and blue in the curtains and a colorful spray of fall flowers on the bureau. Elliott Larson—I'd found out that was his full name—lay on the bed with his right leg in traction. John Tilby stood by the door, his hands clasped formally behind his back, looking shy and afraid to come any further into the room. I sat on a chair by the bed, sharing a split of smuggled-in wine with Elliott.

I'd arrived at the same time as Tilby, who had brought the flowers. He'd seemed unsure of a welcome, and even though Elliott had acted glad to see him, he was still keeping his distance. But after a few awkward minutes, he had agreed to answer some questions and had told me about the drunken auto accident five years ago in which he had been thrown clear of his MG and the real Gary Fitzgerald had been crippled. And about how Wayne Kabalka had sent Gary away with what the manager had termed an "ample settlement"—and which would have been except for Gary's mounting medical expenses, which eventually ate up all his funds and forced him to live on welfare in a cheap San Francisco hotel. Determined not to lose the bright financial future the comedy team had promised him, Kabalka had looked around for a replacement for Gary and found Elliott performing in a seedy Haight-Ashbury club. He'd put him into the act, never telling the advertisers who were clamoring for Fitzgerald and Tilby's services that one of the men in the whiteface was not the clown they had contracted with. And he'd insisted Elliott totally assume Gary's identity.

"At first," Elliott said, "it wasn't so bad. When Wayne found me, I was on a downslide. I was heavy into drugs, and I'd been kicked out of my place in the Haight and was crashing with whatever friends would let me. At first it was great making all that money, but after a while I began to realize I'd never be anything more than the shadow of a broken man."

"And then," I said, "Gary reappeared."

"Yes. He needed some sort of operation and he contacted Wayne in L.A. Over the years Wayne had been sending him money—hush money, I guess you could call it—but it was barely enough to cover his minimum expenses. Gary had been seeing all the ads on TV, reading about how well we were doing, and he was angry and demanding a cut."

"And rightly so," Tilby added. "I'd always thought Gary was well provided for, because Wayne took part of my earnings and said he was sending it to him. Now I know most of it was going into Wayne's pocket."

"Did Wayne refuse to give Gary the money for the operation?" I asked.

Tilby nodded. "There was a time when Gary would merely have crept back into the woodwork when Wayne refused him. But by then his anger and hurt had festered, and he wasn't taking no for an answer. He threatened Wayne, and continued to make daily threats by phone. We were all on edge, afraid of what he might do. Corinne kept urging Wayne to give him the money, especially because we had contracted to come to San Francisco, where Gary was, for the clown festival. But Wayne was too stubborn to give in."

Thinking of Corinne, I said, "How's she taking it, anyway?"

"Badly," Tilby said. "But she's a tough lady. She'll pull through."

"And Nicole?"

"Nicole has vanished. Was packed and gone by the time I went back to the hotel after Wayne's arrest." He seemed unconcerned; five years with Nicole had probably been enough.

I said, "I talked to the sheriff's department. Wayne hasn't confessed." After I'd revived Elliott out there in the canyon, I'd given him my gun and made my way back to where I'd left the horse. Then I'd ridden—the most energetic ride of old Whitefoot's life—back to the stables and summoned the sheriff's men. When we'd arrived at the gully, Wayne had regained consciousness and was attempting to buy Elliott off. Elliott seemed to be enjoying bargaining and then refusing.

Remembering the conversation I'd overhead between the two men, I said to Elliott, "Did Wayne have it right about you intending to loan Gary one of your spare costumes?"

"Yes. When I found I didn't have an extra costume to give him, Gary came up with the plan of signaling me from a horse on the hill. He knew the area from when he lived there and had seen a piece in the paper about how people would ride up on the hill to watch the concerts. You guessed about the signal?"

"I saw it happen. I just didn't put it together until later, when I thought about the fragments of leaves and needles they found in Gary's clothing." No need to explain about the catalyst to my thought process—the horse of a cat named Watney.

"Well," Elliott said, "that was how it worked. The signal with the field glasses was to tell me Gary had been able to get a horse and show me where he'd be waiting. At the prearranged time, I made the excuse about going to the men's room, climbed out the window, and left the pavilion. Gary changed and got himself into white face in a clump of trees with the aid of a flashlight. I put on his clothes and took the horse and waited, but he never came back. Finally the crowd was streaming out of the pavilion, and then the lights went out; I tried to ride down there, but I'm not a very good horseman, and I got turned around in the dark. Then something scared the horse and it threw me into that ravine and bolted. As soon as I hit the rocks I knew my leg was broken."

"And you lay there all night."

"Yes, half frozen. And in the morning I heard Wayne thrashing through the underbrush. I don't know if he intended to kill me at first, or if he planned to try to convince me that John had killed Gary and we should cover it up."

"Probably the latter, at least initially." I turned to Tilby. "What happened at the pavilion with Gary?"

"He came into the dressing room. Right off I knew it was him, by the limp. He was angry, wanted money. I told him I was willing to give him whatever he needed, but that Wayne would have to arrange for it. Gary hid in the dressing room closet and when you came in there, I asked you to get Wayne. He took Gary away, out into the audience, and when he came back, he said he'd fixed everything." He paused, lips twisting bitterly. "And he certainly had."

We were silent for a moment. Then Elliott said to me, "Were you surprised to find out I wasn't really Gary Fitzgerald?"

"Yes and no. I had a funny feeling about you all along."

"Why?"

"Well, first there was the fact you and John just didn't look like you were related. And then when we were driving through Contra Costa County, you didn't display much interest in it—not the kind of curiosity a man would have when returning home after so many years. And there was one other thing."

"What?"

"I said something about sound from the two pavilions being audible all the way to Port Chicago. That's the place where the Naval Weapons Station is, up on the Strait. And you said, 'Not all the way to Chicago.' You didn't know what Port Chicago was, but I took it to mean you were making a joke. I remember thinking that for a clown, you didn't have much of a sense of humor."

"Thanks a lot." But he grinned, unoffended.

I stood up. "So now what? Even if Wayne never confesses, they've got a solid case against him. You're out a manager, so you'll have to handle your own future plans."

They shrugged almost simultaneously.

"You've got a terrific act," I said. "There'll be some adverse publicity, but you can probably weather it."

Tilby said, "A couple of advertisers have already called to withdraw their offers."

"Others will be calling with new ones."

He moved hesitantly toward the chair I'd vacated. "Maybe."

"You can count on it. A squeaky clean reputation isn't always an asset in show business; your notoriety will hurt you in some ways, but help you in others." I picked up my bag and squeezed Elliott's arm, went toward the door, touching Tilby briefly on the shoulder. "At least think about keeping the act going."

As I went out, I looked back at them. Tilby had sat down in the chair. His posture was rigid, tentative, as if he might flee at any moment. Elliott looked uncertain, but hopeful.

What was it, I thought, that John had said to me about clowns when we were playing gin in the dressing room at the pavilion? Something to the effect that they were all funny but, more important, that they all made people take a look at their own foibles. John Tilby and Elliott Larson—in a sense both broken men like Gray Fitzgerald had been—knew more about those foibles than most people. Maybe there was a way they could continue to turn that sad knowledge into laughter.

Carolyn Wheat's quiet realism recalls, at least for me, the literary fiction of the fifties and sixties. Intelligent, controlled, ironic, and always just a wee bit melancholy, Wheat's stories and novels see justice of any kind as a goal only rarely attained, at least in the nightmare of today's American legal machinery.

Of late, lawyers and legal thrillers have infested our field. It is difficult to imagine that most of these writers will have careers once the fad has faded.

Wheat is one of the few lawyer-writers who has her own point of view, and who actually has something to say. She is one of even fewer lawyer-writers who can also write well.

That others are richer, better known, and pose more winsomely for their dust jackets (female and male alike) is no reflection on Carolyn who will, one hopes, soon find the major audience she deserves.

Ghost Station
CAROLYN WHEAT

If there's one thing I can't stand, it's a woman drunk. The words burned my memory the way Irish whiskey used to burn my throat, only there was no pleasant haze of alcohol to follow. Just bitter heartburn pain.

It was my first night back on the job, back to being Sergeant Maureen Gallagher instead of "the patient." Wasn't it hard enough being a transit cop, hurtling beneath the streets of Manhattan on a subway train that should have been in the Transit Museum? Wasn't it enough that after four weeks of detox I felt empty instead of clean and sober? Did I *have* to have some rookie's casually cruel words ricocheting in my brain like a wild-card bullet?

Why couldn't I remember the good stuff? Why couldn't I think about O'Hara's beefy handshake, Greenspan's "Glad to see ya, Mo," Ianuzzo's smiling welcome? Why did I have to run the tape in my head of Manny Delgado asking Captain Lomax for a different partner?

"Hey, I got nothing against a lady sarge, Cap," he'd said. "Don't get me wrong. It's just that if there's one thing I can't stand . . ." Et cetera.

Lomax had done what any standup captain would—kicked Delgado's ass and told him the assignment stood. What he hadn't known was that I'd heard the words and couldn't erase them from my mind.

Even without Delgado, the night hadn't gotten off to a great start. Swinging in at midnight for a twelve-to-eight, I'd been greeted with the news that I was on Graffiti Patrol, the dirtiest, most mind-numbing assignment in the whole transit police duty roster. I was a sergeant, damn it, on my way to a gold shield, and I wasn't going to earn it dodging rats in tunnels or going after twelve-year-olds armed with spray paint.

Especially when the rest of the cop world, both under- and aboveground, was working overtime on the torch murders of homeless people. There'd been four human bonfires in the past six weeks, and the cops were determined there wouldn't be a fifth.

Was Lomax punishing me, or was this assignment his subtle way of easing my entry back into the world? Either way, I resented it. I wanted to be a real cop again, back with Sal Minucci, my old partner. He was assigned to the big one, in the thick of the action, where both of us belonged. I should have been with him. I was Anti-Crime, for God's sake, I should have been assigned—

Or should I? Did I really want to spend my work nights prowling New York's underground skid row, trying to get information from men and women too zonked out to take care of legs gone gangrenous, whose lives stretched from one bottle of Cool Breeze to another?

Hell, yes. If it would bring me one step closer to that gold shield, I'd interview all the devils in hell. On my day off.

If there's one thing I can't stand, it's a woman drunk.

What did Lomax think—that mingling with winos would topple me off the wagon? That I'd ask for a hit from some guy's short dog and pass out in the Bleecker Street station? Was that why he'd kept me off the big one and had me walking a rookie through routine Graffiti Patrol?

Was I getting paranoid, or was lack of alcohol rotting my brain?

Manny and I had gone to our respective locker rooms to suit up. Plain clothes—and I do mean plain. Long johns first; damp winter had a way of seeping down into the tunnels and into your very blood. Then a pair of denims the Goodwill would have turned down. Thick wool socks, fisherman's duck boots, a black turtleneck, and a photographer's vest with lots of pockets. A black knit hat pulled tight over my red hair.

Then the gear: flashlight, more important than a gun on this assignment, handcuffs, ticket book, radio, gun, knife. A slapper, an oversize blackjack, hidden in the rear pouch of the vest. They were against regulations; I'd get at least a command discipline if caught with it, but experience told me I'd rather have it than a gun going against a pack of kids.

I'd forgotten how heavy the stuff was; I felt like a telephone lineman. I looked like a cat burglar.

Delgado and I met at the door. It was obvious he'd never done vandal duty before. His tan chinos were immaculate, and his hiking boots didn't look waterproof. His red plaid flannel shirt was neither warm enough nor the right dark color. With his Latin good looks, he would have been stunning in an L. L. Bean catalog, but after ten minutes in a subway tunnel, he'd pass for a chimney sweep.

"Where are we going?" he asked, his tone a shade short of sullen. And there was no respectful "Sergeant" at the end of the question, either. This boy needed a lesson in manners.

I took a malicious delight in describing our destination. "The Black Hole of Calcutta," I replied cheerfully, explaining that I meant the unused lower platform of the City Hall station downtown. The oldest, darkest, dankest spot in all Manhattan. If there were any subway alligators, they definitely lurked in the Black Hole.

The expression on Probationary Transit Police Officer Manuel Delgado's face was all I could have hoped for. I almost—but not quite—took pity on the kid when I added, "And after that, we'll try one or two of the ghost stations."

"Ghost stations?" Now he looked really worried. "What are those?"

This kid wasn't just a rookie; he was a suburbanite. Every New Yorker knew about ghost stations, abandoned platforms where trains no longer stopped. They were still lit, though, and showed up in the windows of passing trains like ghost towns on the prairie. They were ideal canvases for the aspiring artists of the underground city.

I explained on the subway, heading downtown. The car, which rattled under the city streets like a tin lizzie, was nearly riderless at 1:00 A.M. A typical Monday late tour.

The passengers were one Orthodox Jewish man falling asleep over his Hebrew Bible, two black women, both reading thick paperback romances, the obligatory pair of teenagers making out in the last seat, and an old Chinese woman.

I didn't want to look at Delgado. More than once I'd seen a fleeting smirk on his face when I glanced his way. It wasn't enough for insubordination; the best policy was to ignore it.

I let the rhythm of the subway car lull me into a litany of the AA slogans I was trying to work into my life: EASY DOES IT. KEEP IT SIMPLE, SWEETHEART. ONE DAY AT A TIME. I saw them in my mind the way they appeared on the walls at meetings, illuminated, like old Celtic manuscripts.

This night I had to take one hour at a time. Maybe even one minute at a time. My legs felt wobbly. I was a sailor too long from the sea. I'd lost my subway legs. I felt white and thin, as though I'd had several major organs removed.

Then the drunk got on. One of the black women got off, the other one looked up at the station sign and went back to her book, and the drunk got on.

If there's one thing I can't stand, it's a woman drunk.

ONE DAY AT A TIME. EASY DOES IT.

I stiffened. The last thing I wanted was to react in front of Delgado, but I couldn't help it. The sight of an obviously intoxicated man stumbling into our subway car brought the knowing smirk back to his face.

There was one at every AA meeting. No matter how nice the neighborhood, how well dressed most people attending the meeting were, there was always a drunk. A real drunk, still reeling, still reeking of cheap booze. My sponsor, Margie, said they were there for a reason, to let us middle-class, recovery-oriented types remember that "there but for the grace of God . . ."

I cringed whenever I saw them, especially if the object lesson for the day was a woman.

"Hey, kid," the drunk called out to Delgado, in a voice as inappropriately loud as a deaf man's, "how old are you?" The doors closed and the car lurched forward; the drunk all but fell into his seat.

"Old enough," Manny replied, flashing the polite smile a well-brought-up kid saves for his maiden aunt.

The undertone wasn't so pretty. Little sidelong glances at me that said, *See how nice I am to this old fart. See what a good boy I am. I like drunks, Sergeant Gallagher.*

To avoid my partner's face, I concentrated on the subway ads as though they contained all the wisdom of the Big Book. "Heres's to birth defects," proclaimed a pregnant woman about to down a glass of beer. Two monks looked to heaven, thanking God in Spanish for the fine quality of their brandy.

Weren't there any signs on this damn train that didn't involve booze? Finally an ad I could smile at: the moon in black space; on it, someone had scrawled, "Alice Kramden was here, 1959."

My smile faded as I remembered Sal Minucci's raised fist, his Jackie Gleason growl. "One a these days, Gallagher, you're goin' to the moon. To the *moon!*"

It wasn't just the murder case I missed. It was Sal. The easy partnership of the man who'd put up with my hangovers, my depressions, my wild nights out with the boys.

"Y'know how old I am?" the drunk shouted, almost falling over in his seat. He righted himself. "Fifty-four in September," he announced, an expectant look on his face.

After a quick smirk in my direction, Manny gave the guy what he wanted. "You don't look it," he said. No trace of irony appeared on his Spanish altar boy's face. It was as though he'd never said the words that were eating into me like battery-acid AA coffee.

The sudden jab of anger that stabbed through me took me by surprise, especially since it wasn't directed at Delgado. *No, you don't look it,* I thought. *You look more like seventy.* White wisps of hair over a bright pink scalp. The face more than pink; a slab of raw calves' liver. Road maps of broken blood vessels on his nose and cheeks. Thin white arms and matchstick legs under too-big trousers. When he lifted his hand, ropy with bulging blue veins, it fluttered like a pennant in the breeze. *Like Uncle Paul's hands.*

I turned away sharply. I couldn't look at the old guy anymore. The constant visual digs Delgado kept throwing in my direction were nothing compared to the pain of looking at a man dying before my eyes. I didn't want to see blue eyes in that near-dead face. *As blue as the lakes of Killarney,* Uncle Paul used to say in his mock-Irish brogue.

I focused on the teenagers making out in the rear of the car. A couple of Spanish kids, wearing identical pink T-shirts and black leather jackets. If I stared at them long enough, would they stop groping and kissing, or would an audience spur their passion?

Uncle Paul. After Daddy left us, he was my special friend, and I was his best girl.

I squeezed my eyes shut, but the memories came anyway. The red bike Uncle Paul gave me for my tenth birthday. The first really big new thing, bought just for me, that I'd ever had. The best part was showing it off to cousin Tommy. For once I didn't need his hand-me-downs, or Aunt Bridget's clucking over me for being poor. *God bless the child who's got her own.*

I opened my eyes just as the Lex passed through the ghost station at Worth Street. Closed off to the public for maybe fifteen years, it seemed a mirage, dimly seen though the dirty windows of the subway car. Bright color on the white tile walls told me graffiti bombers had been there. A good place to check, but not until after City Hall. I owed Manny Delgado a trip to the Black Hole.

"Uh, Sergeant?"

I turned; a patronizing smile played on Delgado's lips. He'd apparently been trying to get my attention. "Sorry," I said, feigning a yawn. "Just a little tired."

Yeah, sure, his look remarked. "We're coming to Brooklyn Bridge. Shouldn't we get off the train?"

"Right." *Leave Uncle Paul where he belongs.*

At the Brooklyn Bridge stop, we climbed up the steps to the upper platform, showed our ID to the woman token clerk, and told her we were going into the tunnel toward City Hall. Then we went back downstairs, heading for the south end of the downtown platform.

As we were about to go past the gate marked NO UNAUTHORIZED PERSONNEL BEYOND THIS POINT, I looked back at the lighted platform, which made a crescent-shaped curve behind us. Almost in a mirror image, the old drunk was about to pass the forbidden gate and descend into the tunnel heading uptown.

He stepped carefully, holding on to the white, bathroom-tile walls, edging himself around the waist-high gate. He lowered himself down the stone steps the exact replica of the ones Manny and I were about to descend then disappeared into the blackness.

I couldn't let him go. There were too many dangers in the subway, dangers beyond the torch killer everyone was on the hunt for. How many frozen bodies had I stumbled over on the catwalks between tunnels? How many huddled victims had been hit by trains as they lay in sodden sleep? And yet, I had to be careful. My friend Kathy Denzer had gone after a bum sleeping on the catwalk, only to have the man stab her in the arm for trying to save his life.

I couldn't let him go. Turning to Delgado, I said, "Let's save City Hall for later. I saw some graffiti at Worth Street on the way here. Let's check that out first."

He shrugged. At least he was being spared the Black Hole, his expression said.

Entering the tunnel's blackness, leaving behind the brightly lit world of sleepy riders, a tiny rush of adrenaline, like MSG after a Chinese dinner, coursed through my bloodstream. Part of it was pure reversion to childhood's fears. Hansel and Gretel. Snow White. Lost in dark woods, with enemies all around. In this case, rats. Their scuffling sent shivers up my spine as we balanced our way along the catwalk above the tracks.

The other part was elation. This was my job. I was good at it. I could put aside my fears and step boldly down into murky depths where few New Yorkers ever went.

Our flashlights shone dim as fireflies. I surveyed the gloomy underground world I'd spent my professional life in.

My imagination often took over in the tunnels. They became caves of doom. Or an evil wood, out of *Lord of the Rings*. The square columns holding up the tunnel roof were leafless trees, the constant trickle of foul water between the tracks a poisonous stream from which no one drank and lived.

Jones Beach. Uncle Paul's huge hand cradling my foot, then lifting me high in the air and flinging me backward, laughing with delight, into the cool water. Droplets clinging to his red beard, and Uncle Paul shaking them off into the sunlight like a wet Irish setter.

Me and Mo, we're the only true Gallaghers. The only redheads. I got straight A's in English; nobody's grammar was safe from me— except Uncle Paul's.

I thought all men smelled like him: whiskey and tobacco.

As Manny and I plodded along the four-block tunnel between the live station and the dead one, we exchanged no words. The acrid stench of an old track fire filled my nostrils the way memories flooded my mind. Trying to push Uncle Paul away, I bent all my concentration on stepping carefully around the foul-smelling water, the burned debris I didn't want to identify.

I suspected Delgado's silence was due to fear; he wouldn't want a shaking voice to betray his tension. I knew how he felt. The first night-time tunnel trek was a landmark in a young transit cop's life.

When the downtown express thundered past, we ducked into the coffin-sized alcoves set aside for transit workers. My heart pounded as the wind wake of the train pulled at my clothes; the fear of falling forward, landing under those relentless steel wheels, never left me, no matter how many times I stood in the well. I always thought of Anna Karenina; once in a while, in my drinking days, I'd wondered how it would feel to edge forward, to let the train's undertow pull me toward death.

I could never do it. I'd seen too much blood on the tracks.

Light at the end of the tunnel. The Worth Street station sent rays of hope into the spidery blackness. My step quickened; Delgado's pace matched mine. Soon we were almost running toward the light, like cavemen coming from the hunt to sit by the fire of safety.

We were almost at the edge of the platform when I motioned Delgado to stop. My hunger to bathe in the light was as great as his, but our post was in the shadows, watching.

A moment of panic. I'd lost the drunk. Had he fallen on the tracks, the electrified third rail roasting him like a pig at a barbecue? Not possible; we'd have heard, and smelled.

I had to admit, the graffiti painting wasn't a mindless scrawl. It was a picture, full of color and life. Humanlike figures in bright primary shades, grass green, royal blue, orange, sun yellow, and carnation pink—colors unknown in the black-and-gray tunnels—stood in a line, waiting to go through a subway turnstile. Sexless, they were cookie-cutter replicas of one another, the only difference among them the color inside the black edges.

A rhythmic clicking sound made Delgado jump. "What the hell—?"

"Relax, Manny," I whispered. "It's the ball bearing in the spray-paint can. The vandals are here. As soon as the paint hits the tiles, we jump out and bust them."

Four rowdy teenagers, ranging in color from light brown to ebony, laughed raucously and punched one another with a theatrical style that said *We bad. We* real *bad.* They bounded up the steps from the other side of the platform and surveyed their artwork, playful as puppies, pointing out choice bits they had added to their mural.

It should have been simple. Two armed cops, with the advantage of surprise, against four kids armed with Day-Glo spray paint. Two things kept it from being simple: the drunk, wherever the hell he was, and the fact that one of the kids said, "Hey, bro, when Cool and Jo-Jo gettin' here?"

A very black kid with a nylon stocking on his head answered, "Jo-Jo be comin' with Pinto. Cool say he might be bringin' Slasher and T. P."

Great. Instead of two against four, it sounded like all the graffiti artists in New York City were planning a convention in the Worth Street ghost station.

"Sarge?" Delgado's voice was urgent. "We've gotta—"

"I know," I whispered back. "Get on the radio and call for backup."

Then I remembered. Worth Street was a dead spot. Lead in the ceiling above our heads turned our radios into worthless toys.

"Stop," I said wearily as Manny pulled the antenna up on his hand-held radio. "It won't work. You'll have to go back to Brooklyn Bridge. Alert Booth Robert two-twenty-one. Have them call Operations. Just ask for backup, don't make it a ten thirteen." A 10-13 meant "officer in trouble," and I didn't want to be the sergeant who cried wolf.

"Try the radio along the way," I went on. "You never know when it will come to life. I'm not sure where the lead ends."

Watching Delgado trudge back along the catwalk, I felt lonely, helpless, and stupid. No one knew we'd gone to Worth Street instead of the Black Hole, and that was my fault.

"Hey," one of the kids called, pointing to a pile of old clothes in the corner of the platform, "what this dude be doin' in our crib?"

Dude? What dude? Then the old clothes began to rise; it was the drunk from the train. He was huddled into a fetal ball, hoping not to be noticed by the graffiti gang.

Nylon Stocking boogied over to the old drunk, sticking a finger in his ribs. "What you be doin' here, ol' man? Huh? Answer me."

A fat kid with a flat top walked over, sat down next to the drunk, reached into the old man's jacket pocket, and pulled out a half-empty pint bottle.

A lighter-skinned, thinner boy slapped the drunk around, first lifting him by the scruff of the neck, then laughing as he flopped back to the floor. The old guy tried to rise, only to be kicked in the ribs by Nylon Stocking.

The old guy was bleeding at the mouth. Fat Boy held the pint of booze aloft, teasing the drunk the way you tease a dog with a bone. The worst part was that the drunk was reaching for it, hands flapping wildly, begging. He'd have barked if they'd asked him to.

I was shaking, my stomach starting to heave. God, where was Manny? Where was my backup? I had to stop the kids before their friends got there, but I felt too sick to move. *If there's one thing I can't stand, it's a woman drunk.* It was as though every taunt, every kick, was aimed at me, not just at the old man.

I reached into my belt for my gun, then opened my vest's back pouch and pulled out the slapper. Ready to charge, I stopped cold when Nylon Stocking said, "Yo, y'all want to do him like we done the others?"

Fat Boy's face lit up. "Yeah," he agreed. "Feel like a cold night. We needs a little fire."

"You right, bro," the light-skinned kid chimed in. "I got the kerosene. Done took it from my momma heater."

"What he deserve, man," the fourth member of the gang said, his voice a low growl. "Comin' into our crib, pissin' on the art, smellin' up the place. This here *our* turf, dig?'' He prodded the old man in the chest.

''I—I didn't mean nothing,'' the old man whimpered. ''I just wanted a place to sleep.''

Uncle Paul, sleeping on our couch when he was too drunk for Aunt Rose to put up with him. He was never too drunk for Mom to take him in. Never too drunk to give me one of his sweet Irish smiles and call me his best girl.

The light-skinned kid opened the bottle—ironically, it looked as if it once contained whiskey—and sprinkled the old man the way my mother sprinkled clothes before ironing them. Nylon Stocking pulled out a book of matches.

By the time Delgado came back, with or without backup, there'd be one more bonfire if I didn't do something. Fast.

Surprise was my only hope. Four of them, young and strong. One of me, out of shape and shaky.

I shot out a light. I cracked the bulb on the first shot. Target shooting was my best asset as a cop, and I used it to give the kids the impression they were surrounded.

The kids jumped away from the drunk, moving in all directions. ''Shit,'' one said, ''who shootin'?''

I shot out the second and last bulb. In the dark, I had the advantage. They wouldn't know, at least at first, that only one cop was coming after them.

''Let's book,'' another cried. ''Ain't worth stayin' here to get shot.''

I ran up the steps, onto the platform lit only by the moonlike rays from the other side of the tracks. Yelling ''Stop, police,'' I waded into the kids, swinging my illegal slapper.

Thump into the ribs of the kid holding the kerosene bottle. He dropped it, clutching his chest and howling. I felt the breath whoosh out of him, heard the snap of rib cracking. I wheeled and slapped Nylon Stocking across the knee, earning another satisfying howl.

My breath came in gasps, curses pouring out of me. Blood pounded in my temples, a thumping noise that sounded louder than the express train.

The advantage of surprise was over. The other two kids jumped me, one riding my back, the other going for my stomach with hard little fists. All I could see was a maddened teenage tornado circling me with blows. My arm felt light as I thrust my gun deep into the kid's stomach. He doubled, groaning.

It was like chugging beer at a cop racket. Every hit, every satisfying *whack* of blackjack against flesh made me hungry for the next. I whirled and socked. The kids kept coming, and I kept knocking them down like bowling pins.

The adrenaline rush was stupendous, filling me with elation. I was a real cop again. There was life after detox.

At last they stopped. Panting, I stood among the fallen, exhausted. My hair had escaped from my knit hat and hung in matted tangles over a face red-hot as a griddle.

I pulled out my cuffs and chained the kids together, wrist to wrist, wishing I had enough sets to do each individually. Together, even cuffed, they could overpower me. Especially since they were beginning to realize I was alone.

I felt weak, spent. As though I'd just made love.

I sat down on the platform, panting, my gun pointed at Nylon Stocking. "You have the right to remain silent," I began.

As I finished the last Miranda warning on the last kid, I heard the cavalry coming over the hill. Manny Delgado, with four reinforcements.

As the new officers took the collars, I motioned Manny aside, taking him to where the drunk lay sprawled in the corner, still shaking and whimpering.

"Do you smell anything?" I asked.

Manny wrinkled his nose. I looked down at the drunk.

A trickle of water seeped from underneath him; his crotch was soaked.

Uncle Paul, weaving his way home, singing off-key, stopping to take a piss under the lamppost. Nothing unusual in that, except that this time Julie Ann Mackinnon, my eighth-grade rival, watched from across the street. My cheeks burned as I recalled how she'd told the other kids what she'd seen, her hand cupped over her giggling mouth.

"Not that," I said, my tone sharp, my face reddening. "The kerosene. These kids are the torch killers. They were going to roast this guy. That's why I had to take them on alone."

Delgado's face registered the skepticism I'd seen lurking in his eyes all night. Could he trust me? He'd been suitably impressed at my chain gang of prisoners, but now I was talking about solving the crime that had every cop in the city on overtime.

"Look, just go back to Brooklyn Bridge and radio"—I was going to say Captain Lomax, when I thought better—"Sal Minucci in Anti-Crime. He'll want to have the guy's coat analyzed. And make sure somebody takes good care of that bottle." I pointed to the now-empty whiskey bottle the light-skinned boy had poured kerosene from.

"Isn't that his?" Manny indicated the drunk.

"No, his is a short dog," I said, then turned away as I realized the term was not widely known in nondrunk circles.

Just go, kid, I prayed. *Get the hell out of here before—*

He turned, following the backup officers with their chain gang. "And send for Emergency Medical for this guy," I added. "I'll stay here till they come."

I looked down at the drunk. His eyes were blue, a watery, no-color blue with all the life washed out of them. Uncle Paul's eyes.

Uncle Paul, blurry-faced and maudlin, too blitzed to care that I'd come home from school with a medal for the best English composition. I'd put my masterpiece by his chair, so he could read it after dinner. He spilled whiskey on it; the blue-black ink ran like tears and blotted out my carefully chosen words.

Uncle Paul, old, sick, and dying, just like this one. Living by that time more on the street than at home, though there were people who would take him in. His eyes more red than blue, his big frame wasted. I felt a sob rising, like death squeezing my lungs. I heaved, grabbing for air. My face was wet with tears I didn't recall shedding.

I hate you, Uncle Paul. I'll never be like you. Never.

I walked over to the drunk, still sprawled on the platform. I was a sleepwalker; my arm lifted itself. I jabbed the butt of my gun into old, thin ribs, feeling it bump against bone. It would be a baseball-size bruise. First a raw red-purple, then blue-violent, finally a sickly yellow-gray.

I lifted my foot, just high enough to land with a thud near the kidneys. The old drunk grunted, his mouth falling open. A drizzle of saliva fell to the ground. He put shaking hands to his face and squeezed his eyes shut. I lifted my foot again. I wanted to kick and kick and kick.

Uncle Paul, a frozen lump of meat found by some transit cop on the aboveground platform at 161st Street. The Yankee Stadium stop, where he took me when the Yanks played home games. We'd eat at the Yankee Tavern, me wolfing down a corned beef on rye and cream soda, Uncle Paul putting away draft beer after draft beer.

Before he died, Uncle Paul had taken all the coins out of his pocket, stacking them in neat little piles beside him. Quarters, dimes, nickels, pennies. An inventory of his worldly goods.

I took a deep, shuddering breath, looked down at the sad old man I'd brutalized. A hot rush of shame washed over me.

I knelt down, gently moving the frail, blue-white hands away from the near-transparent face. The fear I saw in the liquid blue eyes sent a piercing ray of self-hatred through me.

If there's anything I can't stand, it's a woman drunk. Me too, Manny, I can't stand women drunks either.

The old man's lips trembled; tears filled his eyes and rolled down his thin cheeks. He shook his head from side to side, as though trying to wake himself from a bad dream.

"Why?" he asked, his voice a raven's croak.

"Because I loved you so much." The words weren't in my head anymore, they were slipping out into the silent, empty world of the ghost station. As though Uncle Paul weren't buried in Calvary Cemetery but could hear me with the ears of this old man who looked too damn much like him. "Because I wanted to be just like you. And I am." My voice broke. "I'm just like you, Uncle Paul. I'm a drunk." I put my head on my knee and sobbed like a child. All the shame of my drinking days welled up in my chest. The stupid things I'd said and done, the times I'd had to be taken home and put to bed, the times I'd thrown up in the street outside the bar. *If there's one thing I can't stand . . .*

"Oh, God, I wish I were dead."

The bony hand on mine felt like a talon. I started, then looked into the old man's watery eyes. I sat in the ghost station and saw in this stranger the ghost that had been my dying uncle.

"Why should you wish a thing like that?" the old man asked. His voice was clear, no booze-blurred slurring, no groping for words burned out of the brain by alcohol. "You're a young girl. You've got your whole life ahead of you."

My whole life. To be continued . . .

One day at a time. One night at a time.

When I got back to the District, changed out of my work clothes, showered, would there be a meeting waiting for me? Damn right; in the city that never sleeps, AA never sleeps either.

I reached over to the old man. My fingers brushed his silver stubble.

"I'm sorry, Uncle Paul," I said. "I'm sorry."

P. G. Wodehouse did not merely create a world of his own. He created a universe of his own.

Much the same might be said of Charlotte MacLeod.

Charlotte is every bit as enamored of good prose, strange characters, charm, and oddball plot turns as Wodehouse ever was—plus she writes great traditional mysteries.

MacLeod, along with a few other writers, spent the seventies completely overhauling the contemporary traditional mystery.

She believed then, and believes even more strongly now, that just because something is amusing doesn't mean it's fluff or piffle.

It can be smart, sub-textual as all hell, and even have a certain weary world view. As does each and every one of Charlotte's fine novels.

All that said, Charlotte occasionally indulges a darker side. Not Mickey Spillane-dark, or James Ellroy-dark—but Charlotte MacLeod-dark.

"More Like Martine" is indeed dark in its way, and will stay with you just as long as it's stayed with me—for many, many years.

More Like Martíne
CHARLOTTE MACLEOD

"You've got to feed the whole child." Martine spoke decisively, as always.

"It's about all I can do to feed the end that hollers." Betsy spoke wearily, as usual.

"I know, dear. If you'd only planned—"

"How can you plan to have twins?"

"But did you have to have them so soon after Peggy?"

"Jim and I wanted our kids to grow up in a bunch. It's more fun for them."

"But, darling, fun isn't everything. You must develop their aesthetic awareness, too."

"I don't think mine have any."

"Oh, but all children do, dear. I saw the most charming exhibition of Guatemalan hand-weaving yesterday, done by six- to ten-year-olds. So fresh and spontaneous."

"Peg does hand-weaving. She made me this potholder at the playground."

"Sweet." Martine barely glanced at her niece's clumsy effort.

"Don't you think it's sort of fresh and spontaneous?" Betsy hung the red-and-green-and-yellow mess back on its hook. Martine was right, she supposed.

Martine was always right. Martine had been graduated from high school with all possible honors while Betsy was squeaking through third grade by the skin of her brace-laden teeth. Martine had been May Queen and Phi Beta Kappa at college and would soon be vice-president of her firm. Martine wore designer models and gave perfect little dinners to amusing people. Betsy handed out peanut-butter sandwiches.

"You mustn't vegetate in the suburbs," Martine was saying for the fifty-seventh time since Jim and Betsy had bought the house. "You have to keep broadening your horizons."

"Sorry." Betsy shoved another load into the washer. "I don't have the time right now."

"But you could do it in little ways, dear. Put some glamour into your meals, for instance. Dine by candlelight. Serve exotic foods."

"Jim likes steak and potatoes."

Her sister left, wearing that what-can-you-do-with-her expression Betsy had been seeing all her life. Somewhere, right now, some aunt or other must be wondering, "Why couldn't Betsy have turned out more like Martine?"

She slammed the empty coffee cups into the dishwasher. Betsy hated these unexpected flying visits. They always meant Martine had something to tell her for her own good. The awful part was, Martine always did. Maybe, deep down, Jim found his marriage boring. Maybe some day the kids would resent not having had a more well-rounded childhood.

The twins whooped in demanding lunch. "How about some nice cream of mushroom soup for a change?" she asked them timidly. The *yecch* was deafening.

Betsy tried again at dinner. She knew better than to tamper with the menu because if she served anything fancy, Jim would say in a sorrowful tone, "I thought we were having steak and potatoes." But she went all-out on gracious touches. She set the table with flowers and hand-embroidered place mats. She shut her eyes to the probable consequences and gave everybody, even the twins, crystal goblets instead of peanut-butter tumblers. She put on the green velvet hostess gown Martine had given her for Christmas a year ago, that she never wore because it was much too beautiful to fry an egg or scrub a twin in. She still hadn't got around to taking up the hem. Even with her highest heels, the skirt brushed the floor.

Her family reacted much as she'd expected. Jim grinned and rumpled the hairdo she'd fussed over. "Hi, Gorgeous. When do we eat?" Peggy demanded, "Is it a party, Mummy? Why, Mummy?" The twins yelled, "Who gets the presents?"

It was Mike who knocked over his goblet. Jim got most of the milk in his lap. "Why did you give it to him?" he roared, sopping frantically with his napkin.

"I'll get a sponge." Betsy jumped up, caught a spike heel in her too-long skirt, and went sprawling.

Jim was beside her, his big hands under her shoulders. "Can't you watch where you're going? Come on, kid."

"Jim, don't!" She hadn't meant to scream. "My leg."

"Let's see." He clawed away at the slippery velvet, cursing its endless folds. The angle of the bones sickened him. "Oh my God!"

He ran for the telephone. The children were all around her, trying to help by crying and patting her face with sticky fingers and offering to kiss it and make it better. Then Jim was back, shooing them off. "They say don't try to move. The ambulance is on its way. It's okay, kids, Mum's going to be fine. Oh Christ, who's going to stay with them?"

"Get Martine." She was talking from inside a tunnel. "Call Martine."

"That's it. Martine will know what to do."

From then on it was all bits and pieces: Jim's hand holding hers too tight, voices saying things like dislocation and compound fracture, then a needle in her arm, then nothing. When she woke up, she was in traction.

"They'll have to get me out of this. I have to get home to the kids."

She must have said it aloud. Somebody said, "Relax and enjoy it, honey. You won't be going anywhere for a while." Red hair and a red satin bathrobe with *I'm the Greatest* embroidered in white on it. Kind hands, raising her head, holding a glass with a straw in it. Something cool and wet going down her throat. Then more sleep, then a terrible business with a bedpan that started the hip and leg throbbing, then it was night and Jim was with her. She held his hand against her cheek and drifted into a pleasant nothingness where the pain was something happening a long way off. She could hear Jim talking. Sometimes it made sense.

"Martine was teaching the kids to finger paint. Peg did a mural for the playroom."

"That's nice." She supposed it was her own voice answering. "Did you eat?"

"Oh sure. Martine had a real gourmet meal waiting when I got home." After a while, he kissed her and left.

The next day Betsy was less groggy, which meant she felt the pain more. She was in a room with three other women. She hadn't quite grasped that fact before. One was very old and groaned a lot. One had a tube up her nose and lay watching the little television set over her bed. The redhead in the red satin bathrobe prowled around wearing a pair of white gym socks for slippers. She had friends all up and down the corridor. When they took their shuffling walks, they'd stick their heads into the room looking for her. "Hi," they'd say to Betsy when they saw her eyes open. "How's it going?"

It was a comfort having people around. Even the old lady who groaned was nice, the redhead said. It was just the medication that made her like that. The redhead herself was feeling great and didn't see why they wouldn't let her out. Those goddamn doctors thought they knew everything. Betsy said she hoped they did. The redhead laughed.

"Hey, you're going to be fine. How about if I get you some juice?"

That night, Jim brought her ice cream. She ate a little, but the plastic spoon was too heavy to keep lifting. "Here, you finish it."

"Thanks, I couldn't. Martine put on a Spanish meal. We had gazpacho."

"What's that?"

"Cold soup with a lot of stuff floating around in it."

"Did the twins eat any?"

"Sure, they thought it was great."

"What else did you have?"

"Don't ask me. Some kind of chicken and rice thing. She served Spanish wine with it. Only half a bottle," he added rather embarrassedly. "She used those glasses Aunt Florrie gave us. She says it's a shame not to enjoy them."

"You yelled at me when I did that." Betsy just barely kept herself from saying it. Did Martine always have to make such a howling success of what she herself fell flat on her face trying to do? Jim misunderstood her silence, of course.

"Don't worry, she'll take good care of them. She's got the place shined up so you wouldn't know it." On the whole, his visit was less of a comfort than Betsy had expected it to be.

She'd just finished her lunch the following day when Martine blew in with a big box from the most expensive florist in town and a book on Guatemalan folk art. Martine stopped in the doorway and stared around the crowded four-bed ward, at the woman with the tube up her nose and her television blaring, at the old lady groaning in the corner, at the redhead's white gym socks and *I'm the Greatest* bathrobe. Before Betsy had a chance to ask her, "Who's staying with the kids?" she was gone. Maybe ten minutes later Martine was back leading a troop of doctors, nurses, attendants, technicians, and an orderly wheeling a gurney.

"It's all fixed, Betsy," she caroled. "You're moving."

"To where?"

"A private room, of course. You can't stay in this rat trap. Now don't worry about the extra charges, darling. I know Jim's insurance won't cover them, but Big Sister's will. I carry a special rider just for you. Just lie perfectly still. You're going to be joggled around a bit, so they have to give you something for the pain first."

That was that. When Betsy woke again, she was in a tastefully decorated room with a handsome floral arrangement on the dresser, a book on Guatemalan folk art ready to hand on the bedside table, and no ministering angel in a red satin bathrobe and white gym socks to offer her a drink of juice. And who was staying with the kids?

She was still groggy from the shot, she supposed. She'd missed supper, but they brought her soup and some whitish stuff in a little plastic bowl. She picked at it, then turned her head away and shut her eyes. Jim didn't come. She wondered if he'd stopped by on his way home from the office and couldn't find her in the new room. She asked the nurse who came to fix her up for the night. The nurse said she wouldn't know; she wasn't on duty then. Maybe Jim had stayed home to take care of the kids. Betsy took her medication like a good girl. There was nothing to stay awake for, not in this lonesome place.

The next day lasted forever. When she couldn't endure lying there staring at her flower arrangement any longer, she got the attendant to turn on the television, and lay there watching soap operas, like the woman with the tube up her nose. They were all about people falling in love with people they weren't supposed to be in love with.

Jim came at last. He said he was sorry to be late. Martine had rearranged the living room furniture, taken the children to the art museum, and served coquilles St. Jacques with an amusing little sauterne. Betsy said how nice.

After that, one day was as bad as another. Betsy lay there watching men make love to other men's wives and women chase after other women's husbands. They started getting her up for physical therapy. It hurt, so they gave her something for the pain. She asked the nurse what would happen if she took two of the little red pills together instead of one at a time. The nurse put on her professional smile and said. "Oh, you wouldn't want to do that."

She got cards and flowers, but not visitors. The aunts were too far away. The neighbors were either working or taking care of their kids. Martine didn't come again, either. She must be too busy repapering the walls and feeding the whole child. The children couldn't have come even if anybody had tried to bring them. Nobody under eight was allowed in the rooms. Betsy asked for a telephone so she could at least hear their voices, but the floor nurse said she couldn't have one. Orders. The nurse didn't say whose.

Jim came every night but he never stayed long. He always told her what Martine had served for dinner, but he never told her what they talked about over the candlelight and wine after Peggy and the twins had been tucked in their beds with visions of Guatemalan hand-weaving dancing in their heads. He was beginning to look drawn and anguished, like all the Joshuas and Jeremies in the soap operas who dreaded having to hurt the Jessicas and Jennifers they'd married on a boyish whim and had to stick with on account of the children.

How could it have happened? Martine was years older than Jim. She'd always gone for suave, sophisticated middle-aged types who held important positions and got divorced a lot. But the current fashion was for glamorous older women in important positions to form attachments with less glamorous younger men in relatively insignificant positions, some of whom had never been divorced at all. Betsy could see it happening every day, right there on the television screen.

Jim wouldn't walk out on Peg and the twins. He'd hang around looking anguished and noble, Jim who seldom looked anything but glad or mad or quietly content except when he did his barnyard imitations for the kids to laugh at. He wouldn't give up Martine, either. Martine wouldn't let him. Sooner or later, Martine would decide it was best for all of them that Betsy give Jim a nice, quiet, uncontested divorce.

Then what? Jim didn't earn enough to support two households. Even

Martine wouldn't be able to make him live on her money. Betsy would have to get some scroungy, ill-paid job as a clerk or waitress and try to scrimp by. What sort of life would that be for Peg and the twins? And who'd look after them while she was at work? Inevitably, they'd wind up with Jim and Martine.

Martine would broaden their horizons. She'd break Peg of needing to run in out of the sandbox for a quick cuddle now and then, sand and all. She'd send her to boarding school, turn her into a slick young sophisticate. At least Peg wouldn't grow up listening to her great-aunts moaning, "What a shame she's not more like Martine."

Martines didn't mess up their lives. They took what they wanted and. hung on to it while the Betsys floundered around breaking their bones and wrecking their marriages. When the nurse brought her the little red pill, Betsy asked for two. The nurse said sorry, she couldn't have two.

Her leg was progressing nicely. The therapist was proud of her. The doctor said she could go home Saturday. She told Jim that night and he said, "Great!" But he looked awfully anguished when he said it.

After that, when they brought her the little red pills, she pretended to swallow them and didn't. When she couldn't sleep, she lay there dredging up, one after another, all her memories of Martine acting for the best. Always Martine's kind of best, never Betsy's. Always having to knuckle under and be grateful. How she hated being grateful! Or was it Martine she hated?

How could she? Sisters didn't hate sisters. Except in soap operas. Would those millions of viewers stand for so much sororal venom if at least some of them didn't hate their sisters, too? By Saturday morning she had half a dozen red pills hidden inside her toothbrush holder. Six should be enough. Only she still hadn't made up her mind who was going to take them.

As far as herself was concerned, there was no problem. If she had to give up Jim and the kids she'd have nothing left to live for, so why bother trying? But why must she give them up? Martine didn't really love the kids, she'd barely glanced at Peggy's potholder. She'd do her duty by them the same way she'd always done it by Betsy, snatching them away from the dirty old sandbox, packing them tidily inside an impeccably tasteful cage.

Nor did she love Jim, not the way Betsy did, not the Jim who let his whiskers grow on the weekends and took the kids wading in the swamp to see the bullfrogs. Once the trend to not-so-handsome younger men had spent itself, she'd stack him away on the shelf with the rest of the back numbers and find somebody who'd do more to enhance her corporate image. It was appalling to think of murdering one's own flesh and blood, but if it was a matter of keeping Jim and the kids from being smothered in Guatemalan folk art, there was no choice Martine could make for her.

After Betsy was dressed and the nurse's aide had left her to pack her few things, she wrapped the six red pills in a tissue and stuck them in the pocket of her blouse. She'd know what to do when the time came.

And the time was at hand. When Jim came to get her, he was so wired up she wanted to scream at him, "Go on, say it. Get it over." But they were almost to the house before he pulled off the road.

"Betsy, before we get home, there's something I have to tell you." When she spoke, the voice didn't sound like hers. "It's about Martine."

Jim took a deep, deep breath. "Betsy, I know how close you are to your sister. I fought it, Betsy. You've got to believe me."

She could only wait.

"But goddamn it to hell, Betsy, I couldn't stand her! Japanese flower arrangements in my fishing creel. The kids whining for peanut butter and getting gazpacho. When I got home that third night and she threw it in my face how she'd gone to the hospital and got you switched to a private room because she could take proper care of her baby sister even if I couldn't support my wife, I went straight off the deep end. I told her it was her own goddamn fault you got hurt in the first place, her and her goddamn crap about gracious living. I told her to butt out and let us run our own lives. I told her to take her goddamn gazpacho and ... all right, get sore. But honest to God, Betsy, if I'd had her around for one more day, I actually think I'd have killed her."

His arms were trembling as he pulled her against him. "The doctor said you needed absolute rest and no worries, so what could I do? I had to keep telling everybody you weren't allowed phone calls or visitors so they wouldn't spill the beans and get you all upset. But oh God, it's been tough! If you only knew the strain I've been under."

She got one hand free after a while and ran it over his face, making sure he was really there. "Jim, it's okay. Believe me it is. But who kept the kids?"

"I did, mostly. I called the office and told them I was on vacation as of then. We've been giving the hamburger stand a lot of business."

Incredibly, she could still laugh. "No candlelight dinners?"

He snorted. "I used to memorize a fancy menu out of your cookbooks every day so I'd have something to talk about. That wasn't what I wanted to say, kid."

His hands were exploring, confidently now that he knew she was still his. "What the hell? You're lumpy."

"Oh." Betsy shoved his hand away and grabbed at her breast pocket. "It's just some stupid pills from the hospital." She rolled down the car window and scattered them into the woods. "I won't need them now. Who's keeping the kids?"

Jim grinned all the way to his jawbones. "Our new maid. I stuck an ad in the paper for somebody to help out till you get your act back together. Damned if I didn't get an answer from that woman who'd been in the ward with you. She showed up in a T-shirt that had *I'm the Greatest* stamped on it. She was the one Martine really went up in flames over, so I figured she'd just about do for us. She's teaching the twins to box and Peg to referee. You know, broadening their horizons."

"Poor Martine. She really does mean well, Jim. At least she thinks she does."

"If you say so, baby. Just so she means it to somebody else. You know, I'd never realized how totally different you two are. Isn't it a shame Martine couldn't try to be more like you."

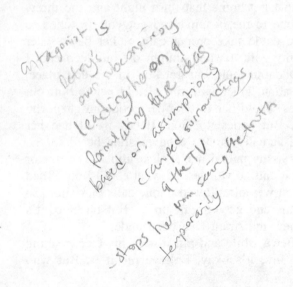

antagonist is Betsy's own subconscious

leading her on & formulating false ideas based on assumptions

cramped surroundings @ the TV set

seeing the truth

—stops her from temporarily

The first female private-eye to "break out" was one with the unlikely name of V. I. Warshawski.

She was everything the male private eye rarely was—book-smart, serious but not sanctimonious, and sensitive to things other than whiskey and remorse.

She was a private-eye, and a woman, perfectly suited to her era of the eighties, and on into the nineties.

Sara Paretsky's popularity continues to grow. As this is being written, her latest New York book has just appeared on the *Times* bestseller list.

I was in a bookstore recently where I saw a woman buy four Paretsky reissues. I asked her if she was reading her for the first time. "Oh, no, but I loan them out and never get them back." I asked her why she found V. I. so engaging. "It's like sitting down with your best friend for a good, long talk. Any time I pick up a Sara Paretsky book, it's like going home."

Skin Deep
SARA PARETSKY

1

The warning bell clangs angrily and the submarine dives sharply. Everyone to battle stations. The Nazis pursuing closely, the bell keeps up its insistent clamor, loud, urgent, filling my head. My hands are wet: I can't remember what my job is in this cramped, tiny boat. If only someone would turn off the alarm bell. I fumble with some switches, pick up an intercom. The noise mercifully stops.

"Vic! Vic, is that you?"

"What?"

"I know it's late. I'm sorry to call so late, but I just got home from work. It's Sal, Sal Barthele."

"Oh, Sal. Sure." I looked at the orange clock readout. It was four-thirty. Sal owns the Golden Glow, a bar in the south Loop I patronize.

"It's my sister, Vic. They've arrested her. She didn't do it. I know she didn't do it."

"Of course not, Sal—Didn't do what?"

"They're trying to frame her. Maybe the manager . . . I don't know."

I swung my legs over the side of the bed. "Where are you?"

She was at her mother's house, 95th and Vincennes. Her sister had been arrested three hours earlier. They needed a lawyer, a good lawyer. And they needed a detective, a good detective. Whatever my fee was, she wanted me to know they could pay my fee.

"I'm sure you can pay the fee, but I don't know what you want me to do," I said as patiently as I could.

"She—they think she murdered that man. She didn't even know him. She was just giving him a facial. And he dies on her."

"Sal, give me your mother's address. I'll be there in forty minutes."

The little house on Vincennes was filled with neighbors and relatives murmuring encouragement to Mrs. Barthele. Sal is very black, and statuesque. Close to six feet tall, with a majestic carriage, she can break up a crowd in her bar with a look and a gesture. Mrs. Barthele was slight, frail, and light-skinned. It was hard to picture her as Sal's mother.

Sal dispersed the gathering with characteristic firmness, telling the group that I was here to save Evangeline and that I needed to see her mother alone.

Mrs. Barthele sniffed over every sentence. "Why did they do that to my baby?" she demanded of me. "You know the police, you know their ways. Why did they come and take my baby, who never did a wrong thing in her life?"

As a white woman, I could be expected to understand the machinations of the white man's law. And to share responsibility for it. After more of this meandering, Sal took the narrative firmly in hand.

Evangeline worked at La Cygnette, a high-prestige beauty salon on North Michigan. In addition to providing facials and their own brand-name cosmetics at an exorbitant cost, they massaged the bodies and feet of their wealthy clients, stuffed them into steam cabinets, ran them through a Bataan-inspired exercise routine, and fed them herbal teas. Signor Giuseppe would style their hair for an additional charge.

Evangeline gave facials. The previous day she had one client booked after lunch, a Mr. Darnell.

"Men go there a lot?" I interrupted.

Sal made a face. "That's what I asked Evangeline. I guess it's part of being a Yuppie—go spend a lot of money getting cream rubbed into your face."

Anyway, Darnell was to have had his hair styled before his facial, but the hairdresser fell behind schedule and asked Evangeline to do the guy's face first.

Sal struggled to describe how a La Cygnette facial worked—neither of us had ever checked out her sister's job. You sit in something like a dentist's chair, lean back, relax—you're naked from the waist up, lying under a big down comforter. The facial expert—cosmetician was Evangeline's official title—puts cream on your hands and sticks them into little electrically-heated mitts, so your hands are out of commission if you need to protect yourself. Then she puts stuff on your face, covers your eyes with heavy pads, and goes away for twenty minutes while the face goo sinks into your hidden pores.

Apparently while this Darnell lay back deeply relaxed, someone had rubbed some kind of poison into his skin. "When Evangeline came back in to clean his face, he was sick—heaving, throwing up, it was awful. She screamed for help and started trying to clean his face—it was terrible, he kept vomiting on her. They took him to the hospital, but he died around ten tonight.

"They came to get Baby at midnight—you've got to help her, V. I.—even if the guy tried something on her, she never did a thing like that—she'd haul off and slug him, maybe, but rubbing poison into his face? You go help her."

2

Evangeline Barthele was a younger, darker edition of her mother. At most times, she probably had Sal's energy—sparks of it flared now and then during our talk—but a night in the holding cells had worn her down.

I brought a clean suit and makeup for her; justice may be blind but her administrators aren't. We talked while she changed.

"This Darnell—you sure of the name?—had he ever been to the salon before?"

She shook her head. "I never saw him. And I don't think the other girls knew him either. You know, if a client's a good tipper or a bad one they'll comment on it, be glad or whatever that he's come in. Nobody said anything about this man."

"Where did he live?"

She shook her head. "I never talked to the guy, V. I."

"What about the PestFree?" I'd read the arrest report and talked briefly to an old friend in the M.E.'s office. To keep roaches and other vermin out of their posh Michigan Avenue offices, La Cygnette used a potent product containing a wonder chemical called chorpyrifos. My informant had been awe-struck—"Only an operation that didn't know shit about chemicals would leave chorpyrifos lying around. It's got a toxicity rating of five—it gets you through the skin—you only need a couple of tablespoons to kill a big man if you know where to put it."

Whoever killed Darnell had either known a lot of chemistry or been lucky—into his nostrils and mouth, with some rubbed into the face for measure, the pesticide had made him convulsive so quickly that even if he knew who killed him he'd have been unable to talk, or even reason.

Evangeline said she knew where the poison was kept—everyone who worked there knew, knew it was lethal and not to touch it, but it was easy to get at. Just in a little supply room that wasn't kept locked.

"So why you? They have to have more of a reason than just that you were there."

She shrugged bitterly. "I'm the only black professional at La Cygnette—the other blacks working there sweep rooms and haul trash. I'm trying hard not to be paranoid, but I gotta wonder."

She insisted Darnell hadn't made a pass at her, or done anything to provoke an attack—she hadn't hurt the guy. As for anyone else who might have had opportunity, salon employees were always passing through the halls, going in and out of the little cubicles where they treated clients—she'd seen any number of people, all with legitimate business in the halls, but she hadn't seen anyone emerging from the room where Darnell was sitting.

When we finally got to bond court later that morning, I tried to argue circumstantial evidence—any of La Cygnette's fifty or so employees could have committed the crime, since all had access and no one had motive. The prosecutor hit me with a very unpleasant surprise: the police had uncovered evidence linking my client to the dead man. He was a furniture buyer from Kansas City who came to Chicago six times a year, and the doorman and the maids at his hotel had identified Evangeline without any trouble as the woman who accompanied him on his visits.

Bail was denied. I had a furious talk with Evangeline in one of the interrogation rooms before she went back to the holding cells.

"Why the hell didn't you tell me? I walked into the courtroom and got blindsided."

"They're lying," she insisted.

"Three people identified you. If you don't start with the truth right now, you're going to have to find a new lawyer and a new detective. Your mother may not understand, but for sure Sal will."

"You can't tell my mother. You can't tell Sal!"

"I'm going to have to give them some reason for dropping your case, and knowing Sal it's going to have to be the truth."

For the first time she looked really upset. "You're my lawyer. You should believe my story before you believe a bunch of strangers you never saw before."

"I'm telling you, Evangeline, I'm going to drop your case. I can't represent you when I know you're lying. If you killed Darnell we can work out a defense. Or if you didn't kill him and knew him we can work something out, and I can try to find the real killer. But when I know you've been seen with the guy any number of times, I can't go into court telling people you never met him before."

Tears appeared on the ends of her lashes. "The whole reason I didn't say anything was so Mama wouldn't know. If I tell you the truth, you've got to promise me you aren't running back to Vincennes Avenue talking to her."

I agreed. Whatever the story was, I couldn't believe Mrs. Barthele hadn't heard hundreds like it before. But we each make our own separate peace with our mothers.

Evangeline met Darnell at a party two years earlier. She liked him, he liked her—not the romance of the century, but they enjoyed spending time together. She'd gone on a two-week trip to Europe with him last year, telling her mother she was going with a girlfriend.

"First of all, she has very strict morals. No sex outside marriage. I'm thirty, mind you, but that doesn't count with her. Second, he's white, and she'd murder me. She really would. I think that's why I never fell in love with him—if we wanted to get married I'd never be able to explain it to Mama."

This latest trip to Chicago, Darnell thought it would be fun to see what Evangeline did for a living, so he booked an appointment at La Cygnette. She hadn't told anyone there she knew him. And when she found him sick and dying, she'd panicked and lied.

"And if you tell my mother of this, V. I.—I'll put a curse on you. My father was from Haiti and he knew a lot of good ones."

"I won't tell your mother. But unless they nuked Lebanon this morning or murdered the mayor, you're going to get a lot of lines in the paper. It's bound to be in print."

She wept at that, wringing her hands. So after watching her go off with the sheriff's deputies, I called Murray Ryerson at the *Herald-Star* to plead with him not to put Evangeline's liaison in the paper. "If you do she'll wither your testicles. Honest."

"I don't know, Vic. You know the *Sun-Times* is bound to have some kind of screamer headline like DEAD MAN FOUND IN FACE-LICKING SEX ORGY. I can't sit on a story like this when all the other papers are running it."

I knew he was right, so I didn't push my case very hard.

He surprised me by saying, "Tell you what: you find the real killer before my deadline for tomorrow's morning edition and I'll keep your client's personal life out of it. The sex scoop came in too late for today's paper. The *Trib* prints on our schedule and they don't have it, and the *Sun-Times* runs older, slower presses, so they have to print earlier."

I reckoned I had about eighteen hours. Sherlock Holmes had solved tougher problems in less time.

3

Roland Darnell had been the chief buyer of living-room furnishings for Alexander Dumas, a high-class Kansas City department store. He used to own his own furniture store in the nearby town of Lawrence, but lost both it and his wife when he was arrested for drug smuggling ten years earlier. Because of some confusion about his guilt—he claimed his partner, who disappeared the night he was arrested, was really responsible—he'd only served two years. When he got out, he moved to Kansas City to start a new life.

I learned this much from my friends at the Chicago police. At least, my acquaintances. I wondered how much of the story Evangeline had known. Or her mother. If her mother didn't want her child having a white lover, how about a white ex-con, ex-(presumably) drug-smuggling lover?

I sat biting my knuckles for a minute. It was eleven now. Say they started printing the morning edition at two the next morning, I'd have to have my story by one at the latest. I could follow one line, and one line only—I couldn't afford to speculate about Mrs. Barthele—and anyway, doing so would only get me killed. By Sal. So I looked up the area code for Lawrence, Kansas, and found their daily newspaper.

The *Lawrence Daily Journal-World* had set up a special number for handling press inquiries. A friendly woman with a strong drawl told me Darnell's age (forty-four); place of birth (Eudora, Kansas); ex-wife's name (Ronna Perkins); and ex-partner's name (John Crenshaw). Ronna Perkins was living elsewhere in the country and the *Journal-World* was protecting her privacy. John Crenshaw had disappeared when the police arrested Darnell.

Crenshaw had done an army stint in Southeast Asia in the late sixties. Since much of the bamboo furniture the store specialized in came from the Far East, some people speculated that Crenshaw had set up the smuggling route when he was out there in the service. Especially since Kansas City immigration officials discovered heroin in the hollow tubes making up chair backs. If Darnell knew anything about the smuggling, he had never revealed it.

"That's all we know here, honey. Of course, you could come on down and try to talk to some people. And we can wire you photos if you want."

I thanked her politely—my paper didn't run too many photographs. Or even have wire equipment to accept them. A pity—I could have used a look at Crenshaw and Ronna Perkins.

La Cygnette was on an upper floor of one of the new marble skyscrapers at the top end of the Magnificent Mile. Tall, white doors opened onto a hushed waiting room reminiscent of a high-class funeral parlor. The undertaker, a middle-aged, highly made-up woman seated at a table that was supposed to be French provincial, smiled at me condescendingly.

"What can we do for you?"

"I'd like to see Angela Carlson. I'm a detective."

She looked nervously at two clients seated in a far corner. I lowered my voice. "I've come about the murder."

"But—but they made an arrest."

I smiled enigmatically. At least I hoped it looked enigmatic. "The police never close the door on all options until after the trial." If she knew anything about the police she'd know that was a lie—once they've made an arrest you have to get a presidential order to get them to look at new evidence.

The undertaker nodded nervously and called Angela Carlson in a whisper on the house phone. Evangeline had given me the names of the key players at La Cygnette; Carlson was the manager.

She met me in the doorway leading from the reception area into the main body of the salon. We walked on thick, silver pile through a white maze with little doors opening onto it. Every now and then we'd pass a white-coated attendant who gave the manager a subdued hello. When we went by a door with a police order slapped to it, Carlson winced nervously.

"When can we take that off? Everybody's on edge and that sealed door doesn't help. Our bookings are down as it is."

"I'm not on the evidence team, Ms. Carlson. You'll have to ask the lieutenant in charge when they've got what they need."

I poked into a neighboring cubicle. It contained a large white dentist's chair and a tray covered with crimson pots and bottles, all with the cutaway swans that were the salon's trademark. While the manager fidgeted angrily I looked into a tiny closet where clients changed—it held a tiny sink and a few coat hangers.

Finally she burst out, "Didn't your people get enough of this yesterday? Don't you read your own reports?"

"I like to form my own impressions, Ms. Carlson. Sorry to have to take your time, but the sooner we get everything cleared up, the faster your customers will forget this ugly episode."

She sighed audibly and led me on angry heels to her office, although the thick carpeting took the intended ferocity out of her stride. The office was another of the small treatment rooms with a desk and a menacing phone console. Photographs of a youthful Mme, de Leon. founder of La Cygnette, covered the walls.

Ms. Carlson looked through a stack of pink phone messages. "I have an incredibly busy schedule, Officer. So if you could get to the point. . . ."

"I want to talk to everyone with whom Darnell had an appointment yesterday. Also the receptionist on duty. And before I do that I want to see their personnel files."

"Really! All these people were interviewed yesterday." Her eyes narrowed suddenly. "Are you really with the police? You're not, are you. You're a reporter. I want you out of here now. Or I'll call the real police."

I took my license photostat from my wallet. "I'm a detective. That's what I told your receptionist. I've been retained by the Barthele family. Ms. Barthele is not the murderer and I want to find out who the real culprit is as fast as possible."

She didn't bother to look at the license. "I can barely tolerate answering police questions. I'm certainly not letting some snoop for hire take up my time. The police have made an arrest on extremely good evidence. I suppose you think you can drum up a few by getting Evangeline's family excited about her innocence, but you'll have to look elsewhere for your money."

I tried an appeal to her compassionate side, using half-forgotten arguments from my court appearances as a public defender. (Outstanding employee, widowed mother, sole support, intense family pride, no prior arrests, no motive.) No sale.

"Ms. Carlson, you the owner or the manager here?"

"Why do you want to know?"

"Just curious about your stake in the success of the place and your responsibility for decisions. It's like this: you've got a lot of foreigners working here. The immigration people will want to come by and check out their papers.

"You've got lots and lots of tiny little rooms. Are they sprinklered? Do you have emergency exits? The fire department can make a decision on that.

"And how come your only black professional employee was just arrested and you're not moving an inch to help her out? There are lots of lawyers around who'd be glad to look at a discrimination suit against La Cygnette.

"Now if we could clear up Evangeline's involvement fast, we could avoid having all these regulatory people trampling around upsetting your staff and your customers. How about it?"

She sat in indecisive rage for several minutes: how much authority did I have, really? Could I offset the munificent fees the salon and the building owners paid to various public officials just to avoid such investigations? Should she call headquarters for instruction? Or her lawyer? She finally decided that even if I didn't have a lot of power I could be enough of a nuisance to affect business. Her expression compounded of rage and defeat, she gave me the files I wanted.

Darnell had been scheduled with a masseuse, the hair expert Signor Giuseppe, and with Evangeline. I read their personnel files, along with that of the receptionist who had welcomed him to La Cygnette, to see if any of them might have hailed from Kansas City or had any unusual traits, such as an arrest record for heroin smuggling. The files were very sparce. Signor Giuseppe Fruttero hailed from Milan. He had no next-of-kin to be notified in the event of an accident. Not even a good friend. Bruna, the masseuse, was Lithuanian, unmarried, living with her mother. Other than the fact that the receptionist had been born as Jean Evans in Hammond but referred to herself as Monique from New Orleans, I saw no evidence of any kind of cover-up.

Angela Carlson denied knowing either Ronna Perkins or John Crenshaw or having any employees by either of those names. She had never been near Lawrence herself. She grew up in Evansville, Indiana, came to Chicago to be a model in 1978, couldn't cut it, and got into the beauty business. Angrily she gave me the names of her parents in Evansville and summoned the receptionist.

Monique was clearly close to sixty, much too old to be Roland Darnell's ex-wife. Nor had she heard of Ronna or Crenshaw.

"How many people knew that Darnell was going to be in the salon yesterday?"

"Nobody knew." She laughed nervously. "I mean, of course, *I* knew—I made the appointment with him. And Signor Giuseppe knew when I gave him his schedule yesterday. And Bruna, the masseuse, of course, and Evangeline."

"Well, who else could have seen their schedules?"

She thought frantically, her heavily mascaraed eyes rolling in agitation. With another nervous giggle she finally said, "I suppose anyone could have known. I mean, the other cosmeticians and the makeup artists all come out for their appointments at the same time. I mean, if anyone was curious they could have looked at the other people's lists."

Carlson was frowning. So was I. "I'm trying to find a woman who'd be forty now, who doesn't talk much about her past. She's been divorced and she won't have been in the business long. Any candidates?"

Carlson did another mental search, then went to the file cabinets. Her mood was shifting from anger to curiosity and she flipped through the files quickly, pulling five in the end.

"How long has Signor Giuseppe been here?"

"When we opened our Chicago branch in 1980 he came to us from Miranda's—I guess he'd been there for two years. He says he came to the States from Milan in 1970."

"He a citizen? Has he got a green card?"

"Oh, yes. His papers are in good shape. We are very careful about that at La Cygnette." My earlier remark about the immigration department had clearly stung. "And now I really need to get back to my own business. You can look at those files in one of the consulting rooms— Monique, find one that won't be used today."

It didn't take me long to scan the five files, all uninformative. Before returning them to Monique I wandered on through the back of the salon. In the rear a small staircase led to an upper story. At the top was another narrow hall lined with small offices and storerooms. A large mirrored room at the back filled with hanging plants and bright lights housed Signor Giuseppe. A dark-haired man with a pointed beard and a bright smile, he was ministering gaily to a thin, middle-aged woman, talking and laughing while he deftly teased her hair into loose curls.

He looked at me in the mirror when I entered. "You are here for the hair, Signora? You have the appointment?"

"No, Signor Giuseppe. Sono qui perchè la sua fama se è sparsa di fronte a lei. Milano è una bella città, non è vero?"

He stopped his work for a moment and held up a deprecating hand. "Signora, it is my policy to speak only English in my adopted country."

"Una vera stupida e ignorante usanza io direi." I beamed sympathetically and sat down on a high stool next to an empty customer chair. There were seats for two clients. Since Signor Giuseppe reigned alone, I pictured him spinning at high speed between customers, snipping here, pinning there.

"Signora, if you do not have the appointment, will you please leave? Signora Dotson here, she does not prefer the audience."

"Sorry, Mrs. Dotson," I said to the lady's chin. "I'm a detective. I need to talk to Signor Giuseppe, but I'll wait."

I strolled back down the hall and entertained myself by going into one of the storerooms and opening little pots of La Cygnette creams and rubbing them into my skin. I looked in a mirror and could already see an improvement. If I got Evangeline sprung maybe she'd treat me to a facial.

Signor Giuseppe appeared with a plastically groomed Mrs. Dotson. He had shed his barber's costume and was dressed for the street. I followed them down the stairs. When we got to the bottom I said, "In case you're thinking of going back to Milan—or even to Kansas—I have a few questions."

Mrs. Dotson clung to the hairdresser, ready to protect him.

"I need to speak to him alone, Mrs. Dotson. I have to talk to him about bamboo."

"I'll get Miss Carlson, Signor Giuseppe," his guardian offered.

"No, no, Signora. I will deal with this crazed woman myself. A million thanks. *Grazie, grazie.*"

"Remember, no Italian in your adopted America," I reminded him nastily.

Mrs. Dotson looked at us uncertainly.

"I think you should get Ms. Carlson," I said. "Also a police escort. Fast."

She made up her mind to do something, whether to get help or flee I wasn't sure, but she scurried down the corridor. As soon as she had disappeared, he took me by the arm and led me into one of the consulting rooms.

"Now, who are you and what is this?" His accent had improved substantially.

"I'm V. I. Warshawski. Roland Darnell told me you were quite an expert on fitting drugs into bamboo furniture."

I wasn't quite prepared for the speed of his attack. His hands were around my throat. He was squeezing and spots began dancing in front of me. I didn't try to fight his arms, just kicked sharply at his shin, following with my knee to his stomach. The pressure at my neck eased. I turned in a half circle and jammed my left elbow into his rib cage. He let go.

I backed to the door, keeping my arms up in front of my face and backed into Angelo Carlson.

"What on earth are you doing with Signor Giuseppe?" she asked.

"Talking to him about furniture." I was out of breath. "Get the police and don't let him leave the salon."

A small crowd of white-coated cosmeticians had come to the door of the tiny treatment room. I said to them, "This isn't Giuseppe Fruttero. It's John Crenshaw. If you don't believe me, try speaking Italian to him—he doesn't understand it. He's probably never been to Milan. But he's certainly been to Thailand, and he knows an awful lot about heroin."

4

Sal handed me the bottle of Black Label. "It's yours, Vic. Kill it tonight or save it for some other time. How did you know he was Roland Darnell's ex-partner?"

"I didn't. At least not when I went to La Cygnette. I just knew it had to be someone in the salon who killed him, and it was most likely someone who knew him in Kansas. And that meant either Darnell's ex-wife or his partner. And Giuseppe was the only man on the professional staff. And then I saw he didn't know Italian—after praising Milan and telling him he was stupid in the same tone of voice and getting no response it made me wonder."

"We owe you a lot, Vic. The police would never have dug down to find that. You gotta thank the lady, Mama."

Mrs. Barthele grudgingly gave me her thin hand. "But how come those police said Evangeline knew that Darnell man? My baby wouldn't know some convict, some drug smuggler."

"He wasn't a drug smuggler, Mama. It was his partner. The police have proved all that now. Roland Darnell never did anything wrong." Evangeline, chic in red with long earrings that bounced as she spoke, made the point hotly.

Sal gave her sister a measuring look. "All I can say, Evangeline, is it's a good thing you never had to put your hand on a Bible in court about Mr. Darnell."

I hastily poured a drink and changed the subject.

The eighties saw several new traditional writers come to prominence, among them Joan Hess. Joan's books are not quite like anyone else's—Agatha Christie meets Andy of Mayberry, at least on occasion, with the kind of social comedy Margaret Millar favored in her later years.

Hess brought realistic underpinnings to the comic mystery, her heroines dealing with divorce, children, and loneliness. We've come a long ways from the drawing-room puzzles of the twenties and thirties.

Dead On Arrival
JOAN HESS

The girl's body lay in the middle of my living room floor. Long, black hair partially veiled her face and wound around her neck like a silky scarf. Her hands were contorted, her eyes flat and unfocused. The hilt of a knife protruded from her chest, an unadorned wooden marker in an irregular blotch of blood.

For a long, paralytic minute, all I did was stare, trying to convince myself that I was in the throes of some obscure jet lag syndrome that involved a particularly insidious form of hallucination. I finally dropped my suitcase, purse, nylon carry-on bag and sack of groceries I'd bought on the way from the airport, stuck my knuckles in my mouth, and edged around the sofa for a closer look.

It was not a good idea. I stumbled back, doing my best not to scream or swoon or something equally unproductive, and made it to the telephone in the kitchen. I thought I'd manage to avoid hysterics, but by the time Peter came on the line, my voice was an octave too high and I was slumped on the floor with my back against a cabinet door.

"There's a body in the living room," I said.

"Claire? Are you all right?"

"No, I am not all right, but I'm a damn sight better than that poor girl in the living room, because she's dead and I'm going to scream any minute and you'd—"

"I thought you were in Atlanta at that booksellers' convention until Thursday?"

"Well, I'm not," I said unsteadily and perhaps a shade acerbically. "I got home about three minutes ago, and there's this body in the living room and I'd appreciate it if you'll stop behaving like a nosy travel agent and do something because I really, truly am going to lose control—"

"Get out of there," Peter cut in harshly. "No! Go downstairs and wait until we get there."

I dropped the receiver and gazed down the hall at my bedroom door, Caron's bedroom and the bathroom door. All three were closed. I looked up at the back door, which was bolted from the inside. I listened intently for a sound, a faint intake of breath or the merest scuffle of a nervous foot. Or a bellow from a maniacal monster with a bad attitude and another knife.

It took several seconds of mental lecturing to get myself up, out of the kitchen and back through the living room, where I kept my eyes on the front door with the determination of a dieter passing a bakery or a mild-mannered bookseller passing a corpse. I then ran down the steps to the ground floor apartment and pounded on the door in a most undignified fashion. I was prepared to beat it down with my fists if need be when the lock clicked and the door opened a few inches, saving me countless splinters and an unpleasant conversation with the miserly landlord.

"Mrs. Malloy?" said a startled voice. "I thought you were in Atlanta for another couple of days."

The apartment had been rented a few weeks earlier to two college boys with the unremarkable names of Jonathon and Sean. I hadn't bothered to figure out which was which, and at the moment I still wasn't interested.

"I am not in Atlanta. Let me in, please. There's been an—an accident upstairs. There may be someone hiding up there. The police are coming. I need to stay here."

"The police?" he said as he opened the door and gestured for me to come in. Jonathon (I thought) was a tall boy with blue eyes and stylish blond hair. At the moment his hair was dripping on the floor like melting icicles and he was clutching a towel around his waist. "I was taking a shower," he explained in case I was unable to make the leap unassisted. "Police, huh? I guess I'd better put some clothes on."

"Good idea." I sank down on a nubby Salvation Army sofa and rubbed my face, fighting not to visualize the body ten feet above my head. In my living room. Partly on the area rug.

"I'll tell Sean to get you something to drink," Jonathon continued, still attempting to play the gracious host in his towel.

He went into one of the bedrooms, and after a minute the other boy appeared. Sean moved slowly, his dark hair ruffled and his expression groggy. "Hi, Mrs. Malloy," he said through a yawn. "I was taking a nap. I stayed up all night because of a damn calculus exam this morning. Jon said the police are coming. That's weird, real weird. You want a glass of wine? I think we got some left from a party last weekend."

Before I could decline, sirens whined in the distance, becoming louder as they neared the usually quiet street across from the campus lawn. Blue lights flashed, doors slammed, feet thudded on the porch, and voices barked like angry mastiffs. The Farberville cavalry, it seemed, had arrived.

Several hours later I was allowed to sit on my own sofa. The chalk outline on the other side of the coffee table looked like a crude paper-doll, and I tried to keep my eyes away from it. Peter Rosen of the Farberville CID, a man of great charm upon occasion, alternated between scribbling in his notebook and rubbing my neck.

"You're sure you didn't recognize her?" he said for not the first time.

"I'm very, very sure. Who was she? How did she get into my apartment, Peter?"

"We checked, and the deadbolt hasn't been tampered with. You've said several times now that you've got the only key and the door was locked when you came upstairs."

I leaned back and stared at the network of cracks in the ceiling. "When I got to the porch, I had to put everything down to unlock that door. I then put the key between my lips, picked everything up and trudged upstairs to my landing, where I had to put everything down again to unlock this door. It was locked; I'm sure of it."

"Caron doesn't have a key?"

"No one else has a key—not even the landlord. He had someone put on the deadbolts about five years ago and told me that I'd have to pay for a replacement if I lost my key. I considered having a copy made for Caron, but never got around to it. The only key is right there on the coffee table."

We both glared at the slightly discolored offender. When it failed to offer any hints, Peter opted to nuzzle my ear and murmur about the stupidity of citizens dallying in their scene-of-the-crime apartments when crazed murderers might be lurking in closets or behind closed doors.

The telephone rang, ending that nonsense. To someone's consternation, Peter took the call in the kitchen. Luckily, someone could overhear his side despite his efforts to mutter, and I was frowning when he rejoined me.

"Her name was Wendy, right?" I said. "I can't think of anyone I've ever known named Wendy. Well, one, but I doubt she and a boy in green tights flew through an upstairs window."

"Wendy Billingsberg, a business major at the college. She was twenty-two and lived alone on the top floor of that cheap brick apartment house beside the copy shop. She was from some little town about forty miles from here called Hasty. Her family's being notified now, and I suppose I'll question them tomorrow when they've had a chance to assimilate this. It's even harder when the victim is young." He looked away for a moment. "Wendy Billingsberg. Perhaps she came into the Book Depot. Try to remember if you've seen the name on a check or a credit card."

I did as directed, then shook my head. "I make the students produce a battery of identification, and I think I'd remember the name. I did look at her face when they—took her out. She was a pretty girl and that long black hair was striking. I can't swear she's never been in the bookstore or walked past me on the sidewalk, but I'm almost certain I never spoke to her, Peter. Why was she in my apartment and how did she get inside?"

Peter flipped through his notebook and sighed. "The medical examiner said the angle of the weapon was such that the wound could not have been self-inflicted, so she wasn't the only one here."

"What about the two boys downstairs? Have they ever seen her before, or noticed her hanging around the neighborhood?"

"Jorgeson had them look at the victim and then interviewed them briefly. Neither one recognized her or offered any theory concerning what she was doing in your apartment. Could she have been a friend of Caron's?"

"I don't think so," I said, then went to the telephone, dialed Inez's number, and asked to speak to Caron.

She responded with the customary grace of a fifteen-year-old controlled solely by hormonal tides. "What, Mother? Inez and I were just about to go over to Rhonda's house to watch a movie. Aren't you supposed to be in Atlanta?''

"Yes, I am supposed to be in Atlanta," I said evenly, "but I am not. I am home and this is important. Do you know a twenty-two-year-old girl named Wendy Billingsberg?''

"No. Is that all? Inez and I really, really need to go now. Rhonda's such a bitch that she won't bother to wait for us. Some people have no consideration.'' Her tone made it clear there was more than one inconsiderate person in her life.

I reported the gist to Peter, who sighed again and said he'd better return to the police station to see if Jorgeson had dug up anything further. He promised to send by a uniformed officer to install a chain until I could have the lock rekeyed, and then spent several minutes asking my earlobes if I would be all right.

We all assured him I would, but after he'd gone, I caught myself tiptoeing around the apartment as I unpacked groceries and put away my suitcase. The front door had been locked; the back door had been bolted from the inside. The locks on the windows were unsullied except for a patina of black dust from being examined for fingerprints. They were not the only things to have been dusted, of course. Most of the surfaces in the apartment had been treated in a similar fashion, and had produced Caron's prints all over everything (including the bottle of perfume Peter'd given me for my birthday), mine, and one on a glass on the bedside table that had resulted in a moment of great excitement, until Peter suggested they compare it to his. The success of this resulted in a silence and several smirky glances.

Wendy and her companion had not searched the apartment. There was no indication they'd gone further than the living room. Why had they chosen my apartment—and how had they gotten inside?

An idea struck, and I hurried into the kitchen and hunted through junky drawers until I found the telephone number of my landlord. I crossed my fingers as I dialed the number, and was rewarded with a grouchy hello. "Mr. Fleechum," I said excitedly, "this is Claire Malloy. I need to ask you something.''

"Look, I told you when you moved in that I didn't want any damn excuses about the rent. I ain't your father, and I don't care about your financial problems. I got to pay the bank every month, so there's no point in—''

"That's not why I called," I interrupted before he worked himself into an impressive fettle. "I was hoping you might remember the name of the locksmith who installed the deadbolts several years ago . . .''

"Yeah, I know his name. You lose the key, Mizz Malloy? I told you then that I wasn't going to waste money on a spare."

I wasn't inclined to explain the situation at the moment. "No, I didn't lose the key. I was thinking about having a deadbolt installed on the back door—at my expense, naturally. My daughter and I would feel more secure."

Fleechum grumbled under his breath, then said, "That's all right with me, as long as I don't have to pay for it. But you'll have to find your own locksmith. My deadbeat brother-in-law put in the deadbolts, due in part to owing me money. He cleared out three, four years ago, taking his tools. My sister had everything else hauled off to the dump. I'm just sorry that sorry husband of hers couldn't have been in the bottom of the load."

"And no one knows where he is now?"

"No one cares where he is now, Mizz Malloy, including me. Last I heard he was in Arizona or some place like that, living in a trailer with a bimbo. Probably beating her like he did my sister. You want to have locks installed, do it."

He replaced the receiver with an unnecessary vigor. I put mine down more gently and regretfully allowed my brilliant idea to deflate like a cooling souffle. Mr. Fleechum's brother-in-law had been gone for three or four years. It seemed unlikely that he had made an extra key, kept it all that time, and then waited until my apartment was empty for a few days so that he could invite a college girl over to murder her.

I was still tiptoeing, but I couldn't seem to shake a sense of someone or something hovering in the apartment, possessing it in the tradition of a proper British ghost in the tower. I went so far as to stand in the dining room doorway, trying to pick up some psychic insight into an earlier scene when two people had entered the room and one had departed.

I tried to envision them as burglars. They'd have been seriously disappointed burglars when they saw the decrepit stereo system and small television set. But why choose my apartment to begin with? The duplex fit in well with the neighborhood ambiance of run-down rental property and transient tenants. There were people downstairs, single boys who were likely to come and go at unpredictable hours and have a stream of visitors.

Okay, Wendy and her companion weren't burglars and they hadn't come in hopes of filching the Hope Diamond and other fancy stuff. The girl had come to see me, and her murderer had followed her, bringing his knife with him. She hadn't known I was out of town—and why would she, since she didn't know me from Mary Magdalen?

A knock on the door interrupted my admittedly pointless mental exercise. It also knotted my stomach and threatened my knees, and my voice was shaky as I said, "Who is it?"

"Jorgeson and Corporal Katz, Mrs. Malloy. Katz is going to put up the chain so you'll feel safe tonight."

I let them in. Katz immediately busied himself with screwdrivers and such, while Jorgeson watched with the impassiveness of a road-crew supervisor. I subtly sidled over and said. "Have you turned up anything more about the victim?"

"The lieutenant said not to discuss it with you, ma'am," Jorgeson said, his bulldog face turning pink. "He said that you're not supposed to meddle in an official police investigation—this time."

"Oh, Jorgeson," I said with a charmingly wry chuckle, "we both know the lieutenant didn't mean that I wasn't supposed to know anything whatsoever about the victim. I might be able to remember something if I knew more about her. What if she'd been a contestant in that ghastly beauty pageant I helped direct, or been a waitress at the beer garden across from the Book Depot? You know how awkward it is to run into someone you've seen a thousand times, but you can't place him because he's out of context. When I saw this Wendy Billingsberg, she was decidedly out of context."

Jorgeson's jaw crept out further and his ears gradually matched the hue of his face. "The lieutenant said you'd try something like that, ma'am. As far as we know, the victim didn't have any connections with any of the locals. She attended classes sporadically and pretty much hung out with the more unsavory elements of the campus community."

"Ah," I said wisely, "drugs." When Jorgeson twitched, I bit back a smile and continued. "Peter's right; none of the druggies buy books at the store or hold down jobs along Thurber Street. Was she dealing?"

"I'm not supposed to discuss it, ma'am. Hurry up, Katz. I told those boys downstairs to wait for me."

Katz hurried up, and within a few minutes, Jorgeson wished me a nice day (and hadn't it been dandy thus far?) and led his cohort out of my apartment. I waited until I heard them reach the ground floor, then eased open my door and crept as close to the middle landing as I dared.

Jorgeson, bless his heart, had opted to conduct his interview from the foyer. "Wendy Billingsberg," he said in a low voice. "You both sure that doesn't ring a bell? She was a business major. Either of you have any classes in the department?'' There was a pause during which I assumed they'd made suitable nonverbal responses. ''She lived in the Bellaire Apartments. You been there?'' Another pause. ''And she used to be seen on the street with a coke dealer nicknamed Hambone. Tall guy, dirty blond ponytail, brown beard, disappeared at the end of the last semester, probably when he caught wind of a pending warrant. Ever heard of this Hambone?''

''Hambone?'' Jonathon echoed. ''The description doesn't sound like anyone I know, but we're not exactly in that social circle. What's his real name?''

''We're still working on that,'' Jorgeson said. ''What about you? You ever heard of someone named Hambone?''

''Nope,'' Sean said firmly. ''Look, Officer, I was up all night studying. I've already told you that I didn't see anyone and I didn't hear anything.''

''Neither did I,'' Jonathon said with equal conviction. ''I went out for a hamburger and a brew at the beer garden, then came back and watched some old war movie. Fell asleep on the couch.''

''What time did you leave and subsequently return?'' Jorgeson asked, still speaking softly but with an edge of intensity.

''Jesus, I don't know. I went out at maybe ten and got back at maybe midnight. You can ask the chubby blond waitress; she's seen me enough times to remember me.''

''The medical examiner's initial estimate is that the girl was killed around midnight, with an hour margin of error on either side. It looks like the girl and her friend managed to sneak upstairs while you were out and your roommate was studying in his bedroom. You didn't notice anyone on the sidewalk when you came back?''

After a pause, Jonathon said, ''Well, there was a couple, but they were heading away from the duplex and having a heated discussion about him forgetting her birthday or something. I didn't pay much attention, and it was too dark to get a good look at them. Other than them, I don't think I saw anyone during the last couple of blocks. There was a guy going around the corner the other way, but all I saw was the back of his head.''

''Did he have a ponytail?'' Jorgeson said quickly.

''I just caught a glimpse of him. Sorry.''

I heard the sound of Jorgeson's pencil scratching a brief note. ''And you didn't hear anything?'' he added, now speaking to the other boy.

''No,'' Sean said, ''I've already told you that. Nothing.''

''That's enough for the moment,'' Jorgeson said. ''Both of you need to come to the station tomorrow morning so we can take formal statements. In the meantime, if you think of anything at all that might help, call Lieutenant Rosen or myself.''

The front door closed. The downstairs door closed. Shortly thereafter, two car doors closed. I closed my door and tested the chain Katz had installed. It allowed the door to open two or three inches and seemed solid enough until I could get the lock rekeyed, which was pretty darn close to the top of my priorities list. Breathing, number one. Deadbolt rekeyed, number two.

I went into the kitchen, made sure the bolt on the back door was still in place, and started to make myself a cup of tea while I assimilated the latest information so graciously shared with me.

Wendy was known to have consorted with a dealer. He'd vanished, and no doubt preferred to remain thus. She'd run into him, recognized him, and threatened to expose him. She found a way into my apartment and ended up on the living room floor. I again checked the bolt, then turned off the burner beneath the tea kettle and made myself a nice, stiff drink. I went back into the living room, checked that the chain was in place and the deadbolt secured, and sat down on the sofa, wondering if the emergent compulsion to maintain security would be with me for weeks, months, or decades.

I put down my drink, checked that the chain and deadbolt had not slipped loose, and went into the kitchen to call a locksmith and pay for an after-hours emergency visit. And after a moment of revelation, found myself calling someone else.

Half an hour later I went downstairs and knocked on the boys' door. Jonathon opened the door. His expression tightened as he saw me, as though he expected another bizarre outburst from the crazy lady who cohabited with bats in the upstairs belfry.

"Hi," I said in a thoroughly civilized voice. "I realize it's been an awful day for all of us, but I'm not going to be able to relax, much less sleep, if I don't have the locksmith in to rekey the deadbolt. He said he'd be here in an hour. I just thought I'd warn you and Sean so you wouldn't come storming out the door."

"Sean's sacked out under the air conditioner, so he couldn't hear a freight train drive across the porch. I'll see if I can get through to him, though. We're both pretty rattled by all this. Thanks for telling me, but I think I'll wander down to the beer garden and soothe myself with a pitcher. Two pitchers. Whatever it takes."

I went back upstairs, secured the chain and the deadbolt, and sat down to wait. Ten minutes later I heard the front door downstairs close and footsteps on the porch. So far, so good. I turned on the television to give a sense of security to my visitor as he came creeping up the squeaky stairs, the key to my door in what surely was a very sweaty hand.

To my chagrin, it was all for naught, because he walked up the stairs like he owned them (or rented them, anyway) and knocked on my door.

"Who is it?" I said with the breathlessness of a gothic heroine.

"It's Sean, Mrs. Malloy. I wanted to talk to you for a minute. There's something that occurred to me, and I don't know if it's important enough to call the police now."

"Sorry," I said through the door, "but I'm too terrified to open the door to anyone except the locksmith. Go ahead and call Lieutenant Rosen; I'm sure he'll want to hear whatever you have."

I listened with increasing disappointment as he went downstairs and into his apartment. A window unit began to hum somewhere below.

"Phooey," I said as I switched off the television and did a quick round to ascertain all my locks were locked. I was brooding on the sofa several minutes later when I heard a tell-tale series of squeaks. A key rustled into the keyhole. As I stared, fascinated and rather pleased with myself, the knob of the lock clicked to one side, the doorknob twisted silently, and the door edged open. I went so far as to assume the standard gothic heroine stance: hands clasped beside my chest, eyelids frozen in mid-flutter, lips pursed.

Then the chain reached its limit, of course, and the door came to a halt. A male voice let out a muted grunt of frustration, but became much louder as the police came thundering upstairs. Once the arguing and protesting abated, I removed the chain and opened the door.

Jonathon had been handcuffed and was in the process of being escorted downstairs by Jorgeson and Katz, among others. Peter gave me a pained look and said, "I was about to remove the evidence from your lock when you did that, Claire. Why don't you wait inside like a good little girl?"

"Because I'm not," I said, now opting for the role of gothic dowager dealing with inferiors. "I happen to be the one who figured out the key problem, you know."

"You happen to be the one who swore there was only one key for the deadbolt. That's what threw me off in the first place."

"Don't pull that nonsense. You heard me say that I used the same key downstairs as upstairs. It was perfectly obvious that my door, the boys' door and the front door are all keyed the same. Fleechum, the prince of penury, saved himself big bucks. Once I told the boys that a locksmith was coming, both of them realized they'd have to have their deadbolt rekeyed, too. Sean was puzzled, but I'm afraid Jonathon was panicked enough to try something unpleasant.''

"It would have come to me at two in the morning," Peter said. "I would have sat up in bed, slapped my forehead, and called Jorgeson to rush over here and test the theory.''

"Then I'm delighted that your sleep will be uninterrupted.''

"When I get some, which won't be anytime soon. Now we've got to see if anyone at the beer garden noticed Wendy recognize her old boyfriend and follow him back to his apartment. Sean wouldn't have heard any discussion, but he might have had problems with a corpse in his living room the next morning. Did you tell the boys you'd be in Atlanta until Thursday?''

"I asked them to collect my mail.''

"So Jonathon, a.k.a. Hambone, figured he had a couple of days to do something with the body. Unfortunately, you returned.''

"Unfortunately, my fanny! If I hadn't come home early, he might have had a chance to take Wendy's body out in the woods where she wouldn't have been discovered for weeks. Months. Decades. And don't you find it a bit ironic that you sent me downstairs—to the murderer's apartment—when I discovered the body?'' I was warming up for another onslaught of righteous indignation when Peter put his arms around me.

"And why did you come home early?'' he murmured.

"Because every now and then I like being told that I'm a meddlesome busybody who interferes in official police investigations,'' I retorted, now warming up for entirely different reasons. "No one in Atlanta had anything but nice things to say about me.''

"Are you saying you missed me?''

"Jorgeson, you fool,'' I said. "I missed Jorgeson.''

I wondered if his soft laugh meant he didn't believe me.

Faye Kellerman's books have found a large audience because they are written for intelligent, inquisitive readers who don't want any of the easy answers that mystery novels too frequently settle for.

Kellerman's world is shaped by our times, yet is remarkably free of cant and doctrine. She is too good a novelistic-reporter to let a political agenda get in the way of the truths she sees.

There is no one quite like her in contemporary mystery fiction, and that's all to the good. She constantly surprises, and who could possibly object to that?

Malibu Dog
FAYE KELLERMAN

Stubborn and mean are a lethal combination, a perfect case in point being Conroy Bittune—an old coot of sixty, as skinny and dried-up as a stick of jerky. He was a wiry man with small brown eyes, thin lips, and a mouth full of brown stained teeth. His cheeks were never without wads of chewing tobacco, giving him a stale smell and his scrawny face a pouchy appearance. I've always wondered how he managed to talk and chew without choking. Conroy was retired, having earned modest money doing something for the IRS. He was and always had been short of friends, so no one in the Estates was surprised when Conroy bought himself a companion—a pitbull terrier named Maneater.

I was as close as you could call a friend to Conroy, which meant we were on speaking terms. He and I were next-door neighbors in a condominium complex called The Sand and Sea Estates. The development consisted of one- and two-bedroom boxes built above one-car garages. The units were framed with the cheapest grade lumber, drywalled with the thinnest plasterboard and roofed with layers of tar paper. The interiors were equally as chintzy. The ceilings were finished with cottage cheese stucco and the floors were nothing more than low-pile carpet over cement slab. Who would buy such junk? Fact was the condos were snapped up faster than flies around frogs.

Why?

Not only did the condos grace the golden sands of Malibu Beach, but they were also granted *private* beach rights. That meant residents of the Estates could romp in the blue Pacific without mixing with the *public* riffraff. The units sold for three hundred grand and upward, depending on location and size. Of course, Conroy Bittune's little bit of paradise sat on the choicest parcel of land—a corner spot that allowed a view of the famous Malibu sunsets.

Me? I'm a lowly tenant, paying my out-of-town landlord four hundred a month for the privilege of residing there. I came out to the Estates during one of my college term breaks to visit a friend. I was instantly entranced by the endless horizon, the splashy sunsets, the nighttime sky, sometimes as black as tar winking with millions of stars. Five years later the ocean still has me under her spell. I earn my living as a handywoman, keeping my rent down by doing free repairs on my unit and a couple of others that my landlord owns.

My connection with Conroy was tenuous. One Saturday morning, his sink pipe burst, spewing water in his face and all over his ultramodern compact kitchen. He came banging on my door at seven in the morning, waking me up, demanding that I do something.

Conroy never asks, he demands.

Being an easygoing gal, I took his harsh tone of voice in stride and went next door. The pipe repair took all of five minutes—a loose joint—and just to show what kind of sport I was, I didn't even charge him. He never did thank me, but from that day on, I was the only one in the complex whom he never threatened to sue. We never became friendly enough to carry on a true conversation—the kind with give-and-take. But I would condo-watch his place when he went away on vacation, which was about four times a year.

One Friday afternoon, Conroy showed up at my door, beaming like a new father as he presented me to the pitbull. The dog was white and black, seemed to be molded from pounds of muscle and had teeth like razors.

Conroy spat a wad of tobacco into my geranium box. Still chomping his Skoal, he said, "Don't need you no more, Lydia." He spat again. "Meet my new watchdog, Maneater."

The dog was on a leash and, by way of introduction, bared his fangs.

"Lookie at this, Liddy."

Conroy smacked the dog soundly across the mouth with a rolled-up newspaper. The pitbull let out a menacing growl but didn't budge. Conroy hit him again and again. The dog never moved an inch. Then Conroy pried open Maneater's mouth and stuck his nose inside the gaping maws. The dog endured the ordeal but wasn't pleased. And Conroy? He just stood there, smiling wickedly.

"Now you try to pet him, girl," he told me.

Slowly, I raised my hand toward Maneater's scruff. The dog snapped so hard, you could hear an echo from his jaws banging shut. Only quick reflexes prevented me from becoming an amputee. Conroy broke into gales of laughter that turned into a hacking cough, sending bits of tobacco over my threshold.

"Cute, Conroy," I said. "You're going to win loads of friends with this one."

"Don't need no friends," Conroy answered. "I need a good guard dog. One that'll attack anyone *I* say to attack. One that'll protect me with his life no matter how I whop the shit out of 'im."

"That's why you bought a dog?" I said. "To whop the shit out of him?"

"For protection, Liddy," Conroy said. "Now, look at this." He looked down at the dog. "Nice, Maneater, let her make nice."

He turned to me and said, "Go ahead and pet him now."

"Once burned, twice shy, Conroy."

"Go ahead, Liddy." His smile bordered on a smirk.

Call me irresponsible, but I reached out for the dog again. This time, he was as passive as a baby, moaning under my touch.

"Amazing," I said.

"Now if *you* tell him to be nice," Conroy said, "it won't mean a thing. He only responds to *my* voice, *my* words. That's what I call a well-trained dog."

"You trained him?" I asked.

"Of course not, girlie!" More laughter mixed with coughing. "I spent six months looking for the choicest breeders, another six sorting through litters to find the perfect pup. *Look* at 'im, girl. Broad chest, strong shoulder, massive forequarters, a jaw as powerful as a vice. Look, *look*!"

I looked.

Conroy spat, then continued. "Before he was even weaned from his mama's tit, I hired the best trainer money could afford. And now he's all mine. Perfect dog for the perfect man."

I gazed down upon Maneater's mug. The pleasure of my company had worn off and he was growling again.

"I don't know, Conroy," I said. "A dog that mean. He could get you into lots of trouble."

"Bull piss," Conroy spat. "You know how them thieves are. They see Malibu, they think money, money, money. Well, let them burgle the other condos! No one's gonna touch *my* property unless they wanna be hamburger."

"I don't know, Conroy," I said again. "You'd better keep him locked up during the day or else there's going to be trouble."

Conroy's mouth turned into one of his evil grins. "Liddy, where does a two-ton elephant sleep?"

"Where?" I said.

"Anywhere he wants," Conroy said. "Get what I'm saying?"

I got what he was saying. But before I closed the door, I reiterated my warning. He'd better keep an eye on the dog.

And of course Conroy, being the cooperative fellow that he was, let the dog go wherever he pleased. The dog tore up Mrs. Nelson's geranium boxes, turned over Mrs. Bermuda's trash cans, and peed on Dr. Haberson's BMW car cover. He chased after the resident dogs and cats—terrified them so badly, they refused to go out for walks even when carried by their owners. Maneater should have been called Bird Eater. He ingested with gusto the avian life that roosted in the banana bushes, chased sea gulls, spraying feathers along the walkways. Whenever he ran along the shore, he kicked sand and grit in everyone's faces.

Since his purchase of Maneater, Conroy had taken many more day trips. When he went away, the dog posted guard in front of the corner condo, not letting anyone get within ten feet of it. Postal carriers stopped delivering mail to neighboring units, leaving letters in a clump at the guardhouse. The gardeners refused to maintain the nearby lawns and planter boxes. Soon the greenery gave way to invading weeds, the grass dried up until it was a patch of straw.

But the biggest problem had to do with the walkway. One of the two main beach access paths curved by Conroy's condo. Technically, you could pass without getting lunged at if you hugged the extreme right side of the walkway. But pity the poor soul who wasn't aware of this and walked in the middle. Maneater would leap up and scare him to a near faint. Most of us learned to avoid the path whenever Conroy was away. But that wasn't the point at all.

Conroy thought it was hysterically funny. The rest of the tenants were livid. They tried the individual approach, knocking on Conroy's door, only to get frightened away by a low-pitched growl and a flash of white teeth. Every time they were turned away, they heard the old man laugh and hack. One of the tenants finally took the step and called in Animal Control. Problem was that Maneater hadn't actually succeeded with any of his attempted attacks. Unless they caught him in the act, there wasn't anything they could do.

So the people of the Estates did what they usually do when at wit's end. They called a condo meeting: *Sans* Conroy, of course.

The complaints came fast and furious.

"This used to be a peaceful co-op until Conroy and his dog came along. We didn't pay all this money to have to be scared stiff by a wild beast or have sand thrown on our backs. This is Malibu, for God's sake. People just don't behave like that here. Something has to be done. And it has to be done immediately. Call the City Council. Call the movie-star mayor and ask him to declare Malibu a pitbull free zone. Call the Chamber of Commerce."

After living in Malibu all these years, we all knew that the local political bodies didn't wield any real power. It was the moneyed ones with their connections downtown who sat on the throne. And since none of us in this development had enough California gold to buy us the ordinance we needed, we were left to deal with the problem on our own.

That left just one recourse. Someone would have to convince Conroy to keep his dog tied up or on a leash. Someone would have to square off with him face-to-face. Someone would be appointed to speak for the group.

That someone was me.

I knocked on his door, identified myself, and Conroy told me to come in.

He was on the floor wrestling with Maneater, baiting the dog with a raw steak. The match was hot and heavy, Conroy all red-faced and panting, saliva and bits of tobacco leaking out of his mouth. Every time the dog would try to get the meat, Conroy would whip him across the back with a blackjack. I hated the dog, but I winced whenever the leather made contact with the rippling canine muscles. Maneater's pelt was striped with oozing red lines, his legs and paws inflamed. The pitbull was *furious*, snapping, growling, digging in with his hind legs as if ready to charge. But he never so much as laid a paw on Conroy. I wondered how long *that* was going to last.

"He's going to maul you one of these days," I said.

"Not a chance."

"I wouldn't be so sure of that," I said.

Conroy stopped wrestling, spat into a bowl and told the pitbull to be nice to me. I went over and petted the poor thing. At last, Conroy threw the steak to the ceiling and gave Maneater verbal permission to fetch it. The dog leaped into the air and caught it on the rebound.

"I'm telling you," I said. "He's going to get you."

"You don't know a thing, Liddy, so quit wastin' your breath. This dog was well trained. I spent two years finding the right breeders ..."

He launched into his Maneater pedigree speech. When it was over, I shook my head. "I don't know, Conroy. Seems to me the dog is angry because he's mistreated."

"They need a strong hand, girl."

"But not a cruel one."

"What are you, Liddy? Some kind of dog headshrinker?"

"I know an angry dog when I see one."

"He's supposed to be angry, girlie," Conroy said. "That's what he was trained to do."

"But it goes beyond that," I said. "He's a menace, Conroy. He doesn't just protect, he destroys."

Conroy spat again. "The condo board must be pretty pissed 'bout him guarding the accessway."

And there it was. The famous Conroy smirk!

"That," I said, "but much more. Maneater charges after the local cats and dogs—"

"If the local cats and dogs come too close, he's gonna chase them," Conroy said. "If *they'd* stay away, Maneater wouldn't do nothin'."

"When he runs on the beach, he kicks sand in everyone's faces, Conroy."

"Well, ain't that too bad." Conroy smirked. "How 'bout if I teach him to say 'Scuse me'?" Then he laughed and hacked, laughed and hacked and finally spat. "They don't like sand, tell them to get off the beach."

"They like the sand, just not in their faces."

"That's their problem, Liddy."

"Conroy, the beach belongs to the whole group."

"They got a complaint with Maneater," Conroy said, "take it up with him. Otherwise, tell them to mind their own damn business."

"You're not going to do anything about curbing the dog's behavior?" I said.

"Girlie, I spent hard-earned money on training him to do what he's doing," Conroy said. "Don't particularly feel like undoing it right now."

I was disgusted. I turned to leave, but before I did, I repeated that the dog was going to get him.

And Conroy? He just laughed and coughed.

No doubt about it. We were stuck with the two of them.

I remember the Sunday because it was such a perfect beach day. The sky was cloudless, smogless, a rich iridescent blue and full of gulls and pelicans. The sun was strong, shining on the water like a ribbon of gold. The ocean was just right for swimming—seventy degrees with mild waves breaking against the shore in tufts of soft white foam. A saline breeze wafted through the air. Everyone was outdoors building sand castles, reading or just working on their tans.

We were a funny sight. All of us bunched up on the left side of the beach, tobacco-cheeked Conroy and Maneater owning the right. It didn't seem the least bit fair, but what could we do about it? The inequity had become a fact of life.

Conroy was in perfect form, laughing and coughing, goading us with kissy noises and rude names. We tried to ignore him, but it was getting more intolerable by the minute.

"You guys are lily-livered pussies. Afraid of Maneater. Lookie here."

He took a towel and whacked Maneater on the back. A gasp rose from our group.

"Here he goes again," I said.

"Why does he do that?" Mrs. Bermuda said.

"Because he's a sociopath," said Dr. Haberson. "And that's a professional diagnosis."

"Lookie here," Conroy teased. "You pussies *couldn't* be afraid of a dog like this."

Conroy kicked the pitbull in the stomach. The dog let out a high-pitched squeal, followed by an angry bark.

"Can't we call the ASPCA?" Mrs. Nelson said.

"He'd just deny it," Mrs. Bermuda said.

"Not if we could show marks on the animal," Dr. Haberson said.

"And who could prove Bittune made the marks?" Mrs. Bermuda said.

"Do something, Liddy," Mrs. Nelson said.

"I tried," I said. "He won't listen." I yelled to Conroy. "He's going to get you one day!"

"In a pig's eye, Liddy."

"Yes, he will."

"Yes, he will," Conroy imitated me, "Just lookie at this, girl."

He punched the dog in the snout. Did it again. The dog started circling him like a hawk around its prey.

I eyed Dr. Haberson. Dr. Haberson eyed Mrs. Bermuda. Conroy was making nervous wrecks out of all of us. The dog was getting more and more agitated—barking louder, baring his teeth.

"You're a bleeping sadist, Bittune!" Mrs. Nelson shouted. "Any second now that dog's going to chew you up!"

With that, Conroy doubled over with big, deep guffaws, followed by his spasmodic cough. His face was flushed, beaded with sweat. "You pussies!" he screamed. "Lookie here!"

He grabbed the dog by the neck and yanked him down onto the sand. Then he picked him up by the front paws and swung him around, huffing and puffing from the effort. The dog was all snarls and barks during the ride.

"Watch it, Conroy," I shouted. "Maneater's starting to foam at the mouth."

"Wimps!" Conroy shouted back, spraying bits of saliva and tobacco out of his mouth. "You weak, itty bitty pussies!"

He put the dog down and doubled over. We expected to hear more derisive laughter but none came.

We waited a couple of seconds, a half minute, a minute. The dog was still snarling. Suddenly everyone became aware that no one was talking.

Finally, Mrs. Bermuda said, "What's with Bittune?"

Good question. Even the dog looked puzzled. Conroy's face had turned deep red and he was jumping up and down.

"A rare Indian rain dance?" Mrs. Bermuda said.

"Figures," Mrs. Nelson said. "Conroy *would* rain on our parade."

"I don't think that's what he's doing," I said.

Conroy was still jumping, his face getting redder and redder. One hand went to his chest, the other to his neck. He seemed to be gasping for air.

I jumped and shouted, "He's having a heart attack!"

Applause broke out.

"We've got to help him," I yelled.

No one said a word.

"Dr. Haberson," I scolded, "we both know CPR. We've got to—"

"All right, all right," Dr. Haberson said. He got up slowly, brushed the sand from his legs. Meanwhile, Conroy's lips had turned blue.

I ran toward the old man, but was immediately halted by Maneater's growl.

"Nice dog," I tried. "Make nice, nice dog."

I took a step forward and so did he. I took a step backward and so did he.

"For God's sake, Conroy," I shouted in desperation. "Call Maneater off!"

Conroy pointed to his throat.

"You're *choking*?" I said.

Conroy gave a vigorous nod.

His right cheek was empty.

"The tobacco! He's chokin on his *tobacco*," I yelled out. "Give Maneater a hand signal."

Conroy flailed his hands in the air. Maneater sat, acting as though the signals meant something. Yet when I tried to approach Conroy, the dog lunged at me.

We were hamstrung. The dog wouldn't let us near Conroy, and Conroy couldn't call Maneater off.

"Hit your chest, old man." Dr. Haberson said. "Try to do a Heimlich maneuver on yourself. Hit your sternum hard! Right here!" Dr. Haberson demonstrated the procedure.

Conroy tried and tried again. Meanwhile, he was turning bluer and bluer.

"Give it another try, Conroy!" I said. "Or just hold the dog off physically."

By then, Conroy was the color of the sky. He fell onto the sand and blacked out, his body shaking as if he were having a seizure. It was awful. Maneater circled his master, licking his quivering arms and legs, nudging his face. But he snarled at anyone who attempted to come within helping range.

Mrs. Bermuda said, "First time I've ever seen a dog protect his master to death."

We tried to tempt Maneater away with meat. We tried to poke him away. We even tried a decoy method, using me as bait. Nothing would lure him away from his master. By the time Animal Control came with the tranquilizing gun, it was too late.

The dog was well trained.

Some writers shock, some scream, some beat and pound their readers about the head. Margaret Maron's books are quiet, even dignified in certain respects, and yet they are all the more powerful for the restraint they show, and stay with you long after some of the noisier novels have faded from memory.

One senses that her first decade or so was mere prelude, that even better books, and more acclaim, are just ahead.

Lieutenant Harald
and the Impossible Gun
MARGARET MARON

The calendar said late September, but summer hung on in the city like a visiting uncle who'd overstayed his welcome and sat out on the front stoop in a smelly sweatshirt, scratching his belly and smoking a cheap cigar all day. The unseasonable heat had blanketed New York for so long that the air felt stale and grimy, as if every wino in the city had breathed it before, replacing oxygen with cheap muscatel and sewer fumes. Even the trees along the street and scattered through dozens of vest pocket parks drooped beneath a sun that held in check the cleansing autumn storms that should strip away wilted, half-turned leaves and leave the clean grace of bare limbs.

In the air-conditioned coolness of her office, Lieutenant Sigrid Harald looked up from a report she was typing to see Detective Tildon standing in the open doorway.

"Could we talk to you a minute, Lieutenant?" His normally cheerful round face wore a look of serious worry. Behind him, equally solemn, stood a younger uniformed patrolman of similar height and the same sandy-colored hair.

Sigrid pushed the typing stand aside, swung her chair back around to face them and motioned to the chairs in front of her neatly ordered desk. Tildon hesitated a moment before electing to close the door. "Lieutenant, this is my cousin. Officer James Boyle."

As he named his cousin's current Brooklyn posting, the woman acknowledged the introduction with a formal nod.

"Glad to meet you, ma'am," said Boyle, but his heart had sunk at first glance. Tillie had made the lieutenant sound like Wonder Woman and here she was, thin, mid-thirties probably, taller than average, with a long neck and a wide unsmiling mouth. Her thick dark hair was skinned back into a utilitarian knot without even a stray wisp to soften the strong lines of her face.

Boyle was irresistibly reminded of Sister Paula Immaculata, his third grade teacher. Where Sister Paula had worn a long dark habit, Lieutenant Harald wore an equally concealing pantsuit of a shapeless cut which did nothing to flatter. Similar, too, was the way she sat motionless, her slender ringless fingers lightly laced on the desk before her as her wide gray eyes studied him dispassionately. Thus had Sister Paula Immaculata sat and weighed his tales of why he hadn't handed in his arithmetic homework or who had thrown the first punch in that kickball fracas at recess.

"What can I do for you?" asked Lieutenant Harald in her low cool voice; and for the first time since Tillie had proposed coming, Boyle felt hopeful. He remembered now that Sister Paula Immaculata had always known when he was telling the truth.

"A man named Ray Macken was shot last night," said Tildon, "and Jimmy—I mean, Officer Boyle thinks he's going to be charged with it."

"Not think, Tillie. *Know*!" said Boyle. "My sergeant gave me the name of a lawyer to get in touch with. A guy who specializes in cases of police shootings."

"And did you shoot this Ray Macken?" she asked mildly.

"Ma'am, I've never fired a gun at all except on the pistol range; but they've got the .38 that killed Ray and it has my fingerprints on it."

"Your own piece?"

"No, ma'am, but it was locked up tight in a property cabinet at the station house and everybody says I had the only key."

Sigrid Harald lifted an eyebrow. "Explain," she said, leaning back in her chair.

The uniformed Boyle looked helplessly at his plainclothes older cousin. His professional training faltered before such intensely personal involvement, as if he simply didn't know where to begin. Sigrid almost smiled as Detective Charles Tildon—Tillie the Toiler to his cowork-ers—took over with one of his inevitable thick yellow legal pads.

To compensate for his lack of imagination, a lack he was humbly aware of, Tillie followed the book to the letter and was scrupulous about detail. His reports could be a superior's despair, but Sigrid knew that if any vital clues were present at the scene of any crime or had been elicited in a witness's interview, they would appear somewhere in his meticulous notes; and she preferred his thorough plodding to the breezier hotshots in the department who were sloppy about detail and who bordered on insubordination when required to take her orders.

Now she listened quietly as Tillie described Ray Macken, a swag-gering native of Boyle's Brooklyn precinct, who'd married the neigh-borhood beauty and moved to Texas to cash in on the sunbelt boom. His glib and easy manner had started him up half a dozen ladders, but alcohol and an aversion to hard work kept knocking him off.

Three months ago his mother had died and left him the two-family house of his childhood. Since he'd exhausted all the unemployment benefits Texas had to offer, the rental from the top floor and his moth-er's small insurance benefits were enough to bring him back north to Flatbush with his wife and son.

"He promised her a mansion," growled Boyle, "then he brought her back to an old house that hasn't had a new stick of furniture in thirty years. No air conditioner, no dishwasher in the kitchen, just a beat-up stove and refrigerator from the fifties!"

He lapsed into moody silence.

Sigrid fished four linked silver circles from a small glass bowl on her desk and toyed with them as Tillie resumed his narrative. It was a new Turkish puzzle ring which someone, knowing her fondness for them, had sent to her disassembled. She hadn't quite found the trick of fitting these particular sinuous circlets back into a single band, but it was something to occupy her eyes as she waited for what she suspected was coming.

Emotion always embarrassed her and this was the old familiar tale of high school sweethearts reunited, of a still-beautiful wife who realizes she picked the wrong man, of a young police officer who suddenly falls in love all over again: the secret meetings, the husband's suspicion and jealousy, the bruises where he's hit her in drunken rages.

Then, last night, the tenants upstairs had overheard a loud abusive argument, followed by the banging of the back door as Liz Macken fled to a friend's house. Afterwards, only silence until Ray Macken's body was found early this morning with a .38 bullet lodged just under his heart.

As a woman, Sigrid had remained curiously untouched by love or hate, but as a police officer she knew its motivating force. "Involuntary manslaughter?" she asked.

Tillie shrugged.

"Hey, no way!" cried Boyle. "Liz isn't a killer and anyhow, she couldn't have used that particular gun."

He slumped back down in his chair dispiritedly. "Nobody could have used it except me and I swear I didn't."

"Tell me about that gun," Sigrid said.

"It was four days ago," Boyle began. "Friday, and St. Simon's kindergarten class."

Even though Labor Day had marked the official end of summer vacation, everyone at Boyle's precinct house kept finagling for extra leave time while the heat wave continued and beach weather held. Sergeant Fitzpatrick, the duty officer, had juggled rosters until his temper frayed and he'd made it profanely clear when he tacked up the month's final version that no officer would be excused from duty unless he could produce a death certificate signed by three doctors and an undertaker.

Unfortunately, he'd forgotten about Sister Theresa, which is how Boyle got yanked from patrol duty that hot September morning.

"You'll take over for Sergeant Hanley until further notice," Fitzpatrick had informed him at morning shape-up.

"Hanley?" Boyle was puzzled. Hanley was a real old-timer who was trying to finish out thirty years on the force. He was nearly crippled with arthritis and, as far as Boyle knew, only puttered around the station house and kept the coffee urns full. He'd been on sick leave all week and, except for grousing about coffee, no one seemed to miss him. Boyle was incautious enough to voice that thought to the sergeant.

This earned him a blistering lecture about macho motor jockeys who thought riding around in an air-conditioned patrol car was all there was to being a policeman.

An hour later, a sweaty Jimmy Boyle stood before a blackboard in the briefing room, clutching Hanley's keys, and faced the true reason Fitzpatrick needed a sacrificial goat: Sister Theresa, nineteen wide-eyed five-year-olds, and two of their mothers.

One of those mothers was Liz Macken, cool and lovely in a simple cotton sundress that he'd slipped from her tanned shoulders only a few days earlier in one of their stolen mornings together in his bachelor apartment. As his lover, she made his blood course wildly; today, however, was the first time that he'd seen her in her maternal role and it'd taken him several minutes before he could meet her mischievous smile with a casual smile of his own.

Luckily a fight broke out over a lecture pointer just then and Sister Theresa clucked in dismay as she tried to separate the combatants. Mrs. DiLucca, a six-time grade mother, confiscated the pointer and promised the two kids she'd rap it over their heads if they didn't settle down.

Every September, Sister Theresa taught a unit called "Our Community Helpers" to her kindergarten class at St. Simon's.

Already they had trooped over to the clinic on Arrow Street where a nice nurse had taken their blood pressure and given them tongue depressors, to the local firehouse where they'd slid down the pole and clambered over a pumper truck, and to the branch post office where they'd seen mail sorted and had their hands postmarked with a rubber stamp.

"And today," chirped Sister Theresa, "this nice Officer Boyle is going to show us exactly what policemen do to help our community."

Nineteen pairs of skeptical eyes swung to him and Jimmy Boyle scrapped any thought of giving them a comprehensive view of the department. No way were these kids going to sit still for a lecture on hack licensing, housing violations and the other unexciting details policemen have to keep tabs on. Besides, with Liz sitting there he couldn't concentrate, so he yielded to the kids' appetite for sensationalism and passed out handcuffs for them to examine before herding them upstairs.

The drunk tank was empty for once and a deceptively fragile-looking child got herself wedged between the bars while another shinnied up to the ceiling and swung from the wire-caged light fixture.

He heard Liz say firmly, "Tommy Macken, you get down from there this minute!" and he looked closely at the little acrobat who could have been his son if things had gone differently.

If Liz hadn't thought him dull and square seven years ago.

If Ray hadn't dazzled her with a silky line and visions of the rich life in Texas.

The rest of the hour was just as hectic. In the basement, Boyle showed the children the small outdated lab that no longer got much use since all the complex needs were handled by a central forensic lab elsewhere. They compared hairs under a microscope—Tommy yanked a few from the small blond girl beside him and Liz gave him a quick swat on the bottom. He demonstrated how litmus paper works, then fired several shots from an old .38 into a cotton mattress and retrieved the slugs to show how the markings matched up for positive identification.

"Did that gun ever kill somebody?" they asked eagerly.

Boyle knew they'd be bored with the true story of two derelicts arguing over a bottle of cherry brandy, so he improvised on a television program he'd seen the week before and they ate up the blood and gore. Several grubby little hands had clutched at the pistol, but he put it back in the property cabinet and locked it securely. Of that he was positive.

He had capped the tour by taking every child's fingerprints and warning them mock-ferociously that if any crimes were committed, the department would know whom to pick up. There was a moment of sheepish shuffling and a sudden emptying of pockets.

"Oh dear!" said Sister Theresa as ink pads, handcuffs, a set of picklocks and Sergeant Hanley's keys were returned to him. Liz laughed outright, but Mrs. DiLucca pursed her lips in disapproval.

Upstairs, he had passed out some lollipops from Hanley's desk and managed to wave back as the children filed down the front steps onto a sidewalk shimmering with heat. Sister Theresa had chirped again, "Now aren't policemen *nice*?"

Liz had smiled back at him then, the memory of their last meeting in her eyes, but Boyle didn't think Lieutenant Harald would be interested in that particular detail.

"So you're positive the key to the gun cabinet was still on the ring when the kids gave it back?" asked Tillie.

"It had to be, Tillie, because it was sure there when Sergeant Fitzpatrick asked for the keys this morning. Ballistics got a make on the gun right away and they knew where to go for it. Ever since the kids left, those keys've been locked in my own locker at the station. I stuck them there Friday afternoon and forgot to return them when the sarge said I could go back to my own beat. Nobody needed them. Hanley's still out." Boyle twisted his blue hat in his hands and shook his head. "I just don't see how the gun was taken and then put back."

"No sign of the cabinet's lock or hinges being tampered with?" asked Sigrid.

"No, ma'am," he said unhappily.

"Do you have the M.E.'s report?" she asked Tildon.

Tillie shook his head. "Too soon. But I talked to Dr. Abramson, who did the autopsy. He said the bullet entered about here"—he demonstrated an area just under his left midriff—"and traveled up at an angle to nick the heart and lodge in the pleural cavity. The actual cause of death was internal hemorrhaging. Macken might have lived if he'd been rushed to a hospital in time; instead, he drowned in his own blood, so to speak."

Sigrid looked up from her puzzle ring. "The bullet traveled upward? That means he was standing while the killer sat or—"

"Or the killer stood over him and fired down?" asked Boyle eagerly. "Liz said they had a fight in the kitchen while she was trying to fix herself a glass of iced tea. That old icebox ought to be in a museum the way the frost builds up around the freezer so fast. Ray'd been drinking and he grabbed her. She twisted away and he slipped on a piece of ice and was lying on the floor half-zonked as she ran out the door. What if he never got up? Just lay there till someone who hated him came along and shot him. Liz certainly didn't stop to lock the door. Anybody could've—"

He saw the lieutenant's imperceptible frown. "Yeah," he said, slumping again. "That damn gun."

"Did the tenants or neighbors hear the shot?" asked Sigrid.

Young Boyle shook his head. "No. The neighbors on either side had their windows closed with air conditioners running and the tenants said they slept with a fan that was so noisy it could drown out fire engines."

"Abramson said Macken wasn't shot from close range," said Tillie, reading from his notes. "No powder burns and the fact that the bullet only penetrated four or five inches show that; but there's a bruise around the wound that puzzles him. Maybe he fought with his killer first and got punched there? And all Abramson can give us is an approximation of when the shooting occurred since, like I said, Macken didn't die as soon as he was shot."

Sigrid nodded and resumed her manipulation of the four silver circles. Young Boyle looked at his cousin and started to speak, but Tillie signalled for silence. After a moment, she lifted those penetrating gray eyes and said to Boyle, "What did Tommy Macken give back?"

Boyle looked blank. "Give back?"

Her tone was coldly patient. "In describing the tour you gave those unruly children, you said that several of them had pocketed different items which your remark about fingerprints caused them to give back. What did Tommy Macken take?"

Boyle thought hard, visualizing the scene in his mind. "Nothing," he said finally. "He never touched the keys, if that's what you're thinking. It was the other kids who took things, not Tommy."

"I rather doubt that a child as agile and inquisitive as you've described would have gone home empty-handed," she said dryly.

Three of the silver circles lay perfectly stacked between her slender fingers. Delicately, she inserted a knob of the fourth circlet between the first two and gently rotated it until all four locked into place and formed one ring. She examined it for a moment, then returned it to the glass bowl on her desk with a small sigh of regret at how easy it had been to solve.

Equally regretful was the look she gave Tillie's young cousin. "I'm sorry, Boyle, but my first opinion stands. I really don't see how anyone else could have killed him except Mrs. Macken."

"You're nuts!" cried Boyle. He pushed up from his chair so hard that it scraped loudly against the tiled floor. He glared at Detective Tildon angrily. "You said she could help, Tillie. Is this how? By pinning it on Liz?"

"Sit down, Boyle." There was icy authority in Sigrid Harald's voice. She pushed her telephone toward him. "Someone must still be posted at the Macken house. Call."

Resentfully he dialed and when one of his fellow officers from the precinct answered, he identified first himself and then Lieutenant Harald, who gave crisp suggestions as to where he should search and what he should search for. She held on to the receiver and only a few minutes had elapsed before the unseen officer returned to his end and admiringly reported, "Right where you thought, Lieutenant—stuck down in one of the garbage pails in the alley. It's already on its way to the lab."

"An ice pick?" whispered Jimmy Boyle. "He was *stabbed* first?"

"First and only, I'm afraid," said Sigrid. "It was hot last night. You said she was trying to make iced tea when the fight began. A lot of those old refrigerators only make chunks of ice, not cubes, so it's logical to assume she had an ice pick in her hand. Afterwards, she must have remembered your lecture on rifling marks and pushed that slug into the wound to make it look as if an impossible gun had shot her husband."

"And the blow when she stabbed him with the pick must have made the bruise that bothered Abramson," Tillie mused.

She nodded. "Of course, someone will have to question the boy— make him admit he palmed one of those demonstration slugs and that his mother had confiscated it. He may have bragged about it to some of the other children."

"Sorry, Jimmy," Tildon said, awkwardly patting the stunned young patrolman's shoulder.

Boyle stood up and he still wore a dazed expression. "Not your fault, Tillie." Purpose returned to his face. "I'm still going to call that lawyer the sarge told me about. If Liz did stab Ray, it's got to be self-defense, right?"

"Right," Tillie answered sturdily; but after his cousin had departed, he turned back to Sigrid. "What do you think, Lieutenant?"

She shrugged. "The stabbing might not have been premeditated, but driving the slug into him definitely was. And didn't Abramson say Macken didn't die immediately? The prosecution's bound to bring that up."

Sigrid pulled the typing stand back in place and scanned the half-completed report Tillie had interrupted.

He started to leave, then paused in the doorway. "I didn't think you knew much about kids. What made you guess Tommy took that slug?"

"I have cousins, too," Sigrid said grimly. "They all have children. And all the children have sticky little fingers."

Her own slender fingers attacked the keyboard in slashing precision and Tillie was careful not to grin until he'd pulled the door closed behind him.

After all these years, it's difficult to say anything new about Ed McBain/Evan Hunter. Yes, for all practical purposes, he remains the most important procedural writer of all time—even more important, one thinks, than those who take credit for founding the genre. And yes, his books are quintessentially American; and state-of-the-art entertaining; and yes, he sure does seem to write his fair share of books; and yes—

Yes, he gets taken for granted, too much so. Like Marcia Muller, you can chart the American dream by his McBains—nice cozy sit-com 87th books of the fifties; much darker and angrier in the sixties; downright cynical by the seventies; sort of stunned and in shock by the eighties, their city (like most cities) starting to seriously come apart; and then, in the nineties, seeming to circle back toward the fifties again, their spiritual values a little more certain now, even though their city is still disintegrating around them.

For the most part, the 87th books get better each time out, McBain trying to give them the richer textures of the novel rather than the simpler acrobatics of the thriller. It's difficult to imagine a more important—or purely entertaining—body of work of crime fiction in this half of the century.

Long live McBain.

Death Flight
ED MCBAIN

Squak Mountain was cold at this time of the year. The wind groaned around Davis, and the trees trembled bare limbs, and even at this distance he could hear the low rumble of planes letting down at Boeing and Renton. He found the tree about a half-mile east of the summit. The DC-4 had struck the tree and then continued flying. He looked at the jagged, splintered wood and then his eyes covered the surrounding terrain. Parts of the DC-4 were scattered all over the ridge in a fifteen-

256

hundred-foot radius. He saw the upper portion of the plane's vertical fin, the number-two propeller, and a major portion of the rudder. He examined these very briefly, and then he began walking toward the canyon into which the plane had finally dropped.

Davis turned his head sharply once, thinking he had heard a sound. He stood stock-still, listening, but the only sounds that came to him were the sullen moan of the wind and the muted hum of aircraft in the distant sky.

He continued walking.

When he found the plane, it made him a little sick. The Civil Aeronautics Board report had told him that the plane was demolished by fire. The crash was what had obviously caused the real demolition. But the report had only been typed words. He saw *impact* now, and *causing fire*, and even though the plane had been moved by the investigating board, he could imagine something of what had happened.

It had been in nearly vertical position when it struck the ground, and the engines and cockpit had bedded deep in soft, muddy loam. Wreckage had been scattered like shrapnel from a hand grenade burst, and fire had consumed most of the plane, leaving a ghostlike skeleton that confronted him mutely. He stood watching it for a time, then made his way down to the charred ruins.

The landing gear was fully retracted, as the report had said. The wings flaps were in the twenty-five-degree down position.

He studied these briefly and then climbed up to the cockpit. The plane still stank of scorched skin and blistered paint. When he entered the cockpit, he was faced with complete havoc. It was impossible to obtain a control setting or an instrument reading from the demolished instrument panel. The seats were twisted and tangled. Metal jutted into the cockpit and cabin at grotesque angles. The windshield had shattered into a million jagged shards.

He shook his head and continued looking through the plane, the stench becoming more overpowering. He was silently grateful that he had not been here when the bodies were still in the plane, and he still wondered what he was doing here anyway, even now.

He knew that the report had proved indication of an explosion prior to the crash. There had been no structural failure or malfunctioning of the aircraft itself. The explosion had occurred in the cabin, and the remnants of the bomb had shown it to be a home-made job. He'd learned all this in the past few days, with the co-operation of the CAB. He also knew that the Federal Bureau of Investigation and the Military

Police were investigating the accident, and the knowledge had convinced him that this was not a job for him. Yet here he was.

Five people had been killed. Three pilots, the stewardess, and Janet Carruthers, the married daughter of his client, George Ellison. It could not have been a pleasant death.

Davis climbed out of the plane and started toward the ridge. The sun was high on the mountain, and it cast a feeble, pale yellow tint on the white pine and spruce. There was a hard grey winter sky overhead. He walked swiftly, with his head bent against the wind.

When the shots came, they were hard and brittle, shattering the stillness as effectively as twin-mortar explosions.

He dropped to the ground, wriggling sideways toward a high outcropping of quartz. The echo of the shots hung on the air and then the wind carried it toward the canyon and he waited and listened, with his own breathing the loudest sound on the mountain.

I'm out of my league, he thought. *I'm way out of my league. I'm just a small-time detective, and this is something big . . .*

The third shot came abruptly. It came from some highpowered rifle, and he heard the sharp *twang* of the bullet when it struck the quartz and ricocheted into the trees.

He pressed his cheek to the ground, and he kept very still, and he could feel the hammering of his heart against the hard earth. His hands trembled and he waited for the next shot.

The next shot never came. He waited for a half-hour, and then he bundled his coat and thrust it up over the rock, hoping to draw fire if the sniper was still with him. He waited for several minutes after that, and then he backed away from the rock on his belly, not venturing to get to his feet until he was well into the trees.

Slowly, he made his way down the mountain.

"You say you want to know more about the accident?" Arthur Porchek said. "I thought it was all covered in the CAB report."

"It was," Davis said. "I'm checking further. I'm trying to find out who set that bomb."

Porchek drew in on his cigarette. He leaned against the wall and the busy hum of radios in Seattle Approach Control was loud around them. "I've only told this story a dozen times already."

"I'd appreciate it if you could tell it once more," Davis said.

"Well," Porchek said heavily, "it was about twenty-thirty-six or so." He paused. "All our time is based on a twenty-four-hour clock, like the Army."

"Go ahead."

"The flight had been cleared to maintain seven thousand feet. When they contacted us, we told them to make a standard range approach to Boeing Field and requested that they report leaving each one-thousand-foot level during the descent. That's standard, you know."

"Were you doing all the talking to the plane?" Davis asked.

"Yes."

"All right, what happened?"

"First I gave them the weather."

"And what was that?"

Porchek shrugged, a man weary of repeating information over and over again. "Boeing Field," he said by rote. "Eighteen hundred scattered, twenty-two hundred overcast, eight-miles, wind south-southeast, gusts to thirty, altimeter twenty-nine, twenty-five; Seattle-Tacoma, measured nineteen hundred broken with thirty-one hundred overcast."

"Did the flight acknowledge?"

"Yes, it did. And it reported leaving seven thousand feet at twenty-forty. About two minutes later, it reported being over the outer marker and leaving the six-thousand-foot level."

"Go on." Davis said.

"Well, it didn't report leaving five thousand and then at twenty-forty-five, it reported leaving four thousand feet. I acknowledged that and told them what to do. I said, 'If you're not VFR by the time you reach the range you can shuttle on the northwest course at two thousand feet. It's possible you'll break out in the vicinity of Boeing Field for a south landing.' "

"What's VFR?" Davis asked, once again feeling his inadequacy to cope with the job.

"Visual Flight Rules. You see, it was overcast at twenty-two hundred feet. The flight was on instruments above that. They've got to report to us whether they're on IFR or VFR."

"I see. What happened next?"

"The aircraft reported at twenty-fifty that it was leaving three thousand feet, and I told them they were to contact Boeing Tower on one eighteen, point three for landing instructions. They acknowledged with 'Roger,' and that's the last I heard of them."

"Did you hear the explosion?"

"I heard something, but I figured it for static. Ground witnesses heard it, though."

"But everything was normal and routine before the explosion, is that right?"

Porchek nodded his head emphatically. "Yes, sir. A routine letdown."

"Almost," Davis said. He thanked Porchek for his time, and then left.

He called George Ellison from a pay phone. When the old man came on the line, Davis said, "This is Milt Davis, Mr. Ellison."

Ellison's voice sounded gruff and heavy, even over the phone. "Hello, Davis," he said. "How are you doing?"

"I'll be honest with you, Mr. Ellison. I'd like out."

"Why?" He could feel the old man's hackles rising.

"Because the FBI and the MPs are already onto this one. They'll crack it for you, and it'll probably turn out to be some nut with a grudge against the government. Either that, or a plain case of sabotage. This really doesn't call for a private investigation."

"Look, Davis," Ellison said. "I'll decide whether this calls for . . ."

"All right, you'll decide. I'm just trying to be frank with you. This kind of stuff is way out of my line. I'm used to trailing wayward husbands, or skip tracing, or an occasional bodyguard stint. When you drag in bombed planes, I'm in over my head."

"I heard you were a good man," Ellison said. "You stick with it. I'm satisfied you'll do a good job."

Davis sighed. "Whatever you say," he said. "Incidentally, did you tell anyone you'd hired me?"

"Yes, I did. As a matter of fact . . ."

"Who'd you tell?"

"Several of my employees. The word got to a local reporter somehow, though, and he came to my home yesterday. I gave him the story. I didn't think it would do any harm."

"Has it reached print yet?"

"Yes," Ellison said. "It was in this morning's paper. A small item. Why?"

"I was shot at today, Mr. Ellison. At the scene of the crash. Three times."

There was a dead silence on the line. Then Ellison said, "I'm sorry, Davis, I should have realized." It was a hard thing for a man like Ellison to say.

"That's all right," Davis assured him. "They missed."

"Do you think—do you think whoever set the bomb shot at you?"

"Possibly. I'm not going to start worrying about it now."

Ellison digested this and then said, "Where are you going now, Davis?"

"To visit your son-in-law, Nicholas Carruthers. I'll call in again."

"Fine, Davis."

Davis hung up, jotting down the cost of the call, and then made reservations on the next plane to Burbank. Nicholas Carruthers was chief pilot of Intercoastal Airways' Burbank Division. The fatal flight had been made in two segments; the first from Burbank to San Francisco, and the second from Frisco to Seattle. The DC-4 was to let down at Boeing, with Seattle-Tacoma designated as an alternate field. It was a simple ferry flight, and the plane was to pick up military personnel in Seattle, in accordance with the company's contract with the Department of National Defense.

Quite curiously, Carruthers had been along on the Burbank-to-Frisco segment of the hop, as company observer. He'd disembarked at Frisco, and his wife, Janet, had boarded the plane there as a non-revenue passenger. She was bound for a cabin up in Washington, or so old man Ellison had told Davis. He'd also said that Janet had been looking forward to the trip for a long time.

When Davis found Captain Nicholas Carruthers in the airport restaurant, he was sitting with a blonde in a black cocktail dress, and he had his arm around her waist. They lifted their martini glasses and clinked them together, the girl laughing. Davis studied the pair from the doorway and reflected that the case was turning into something he knew a little more about.

He hesitated inside the doorway for just a moment and then walked directly to the bar, taking the stool on Carruthers' left. He waited until Carruthers had drained his glass and then he said, "Captain Carruthers?"

Carruthers turned abruptly, a frown distorting his features. He was a man of thirty-eight or so, with prematurely graying temples and sharp gray eyes. He had thin lips and a thin straight nose that divided his face like an immaculate stone wall. He wore civilian clothing.

"Yes," he said curtly.

"Milton Davis. Your father-in-law has hired me to look into the DC-4 accident." Davis showed his identification. "I wonder if I might ask you a few questions?"

Carruthers hesitated, and then glanced at the blonde, apparently realizing the situation was slightly compromising. The blonde leaned over, pressing her breasts against the bar top, looking past Carruthers to Davis.

"Take a walk, Beth," Carruthers said.

The blonde drained her martini glass, pouted, lifted her purse from the bar, and slid off the stool. Davis watched the exaggerated swing of her hips across the room and then said, "I'm sorry if . . ."

"Ask your questions," Carruthers said.

Davis studied him for a moment. "All right, Captain," he said mildly. "I understand you were aboard the crashed DC-4 on the flight segment from Burbank to San Francisco. Is that right?"

"That's right," Carruthers said. "I was aboard as observer."

"Did you notice anything out of the ordinary on the trip?"

"If you mean did I see anyone with a goddamn bomb, no."

"I didn't—"

"And if you're referring to the false alarm, Mister Whatever-the-Hell-Your-Name-Is, you can just start asking your questions straight. You know all about the false alarm."

Davis felt his fists tighten on the bar top. "You tell me about it again."

"Sure," Carruthers said testily. "Shortly after take-off from Burbank, we observed a fire-warning signal in the cockpit. From number three engine."

"I'm listening," Davis said.

"As it turned out, it was a false warning. When we got to Frisco, the mechanics there checked and found no evidence of a fire having occurred. Mason told the mechanics—"

"Was Mason pilot in command?"

"Yes." A little of Carruthers' anger seemed to be wearing off. "Mason told the mechanics he was satisfied from the inspection that no danger of fire was present. He did not delay the flight."

"Were *you* satisfied with the inspection?" Davis asked.

"It was Mason's command."

"Yes, but your wife boarded the plane in Frisco. Were you satisfied there was no danger of fire?"

"Yes, I was."

"Did your wife seem worried about it?" Davis asked.

"I didn't get a chance to talk to Janet in Frisco," Carruthers said.

Davis was silent for a moment. Then he asked, "How come?"

"I had to take another pilot up almost the moment I arrived."

"I don't understand."

"For a hood test. I had to check him out. I'm chief pilot, you know. That's one of my jobs."

"And there wasn't even enough time to stop and say hello to your wife?"

"No. We were a little ahead of schedule. Janet wasn't there when we landed."

"I see."

"I hung around while the mechanics checked the firewarning system, and Janet still hadn't arrived. This other pilot was waiting to go up, so I left."

"Then you didn't see your wife at all," Davis said.

"Well, that's not what I meant. I meant I hadn't spoken to her. As we were taxiing for take-off, I saw her come onto the field."

"Alone?"

"No," Carruthers said. "She was with a man." The announcement did not seem to disturb him.

"Do you know who he was?"

"No. They were rather far from me, and I was in a moving ship. I recognized Janet's red hair immediately, of course, but I couldn't make out the man with her. I waved, but I guess she didn't see me."

"She didn't wave back?"

"No. She went directly to the DC-4. The man helped her aboard, and then the plane was behind us and I couldn't see any more."

"What do you mean, helped her aboard?"

"Took her elbow, you know. Helped her up the ladder."

"I see. Was she carrying luggage?"

"A suitcase, yes. She was bound for our cabin, you know."

"Yes," Davis said. "I understand she was on a company pass. What does that mean exactly, Captain?"

"We ride for a buck and a half," Carruthers said. "Normally, any pilot applies to his chief pilot for written permission for his wife to ride and then presents the permission at the ticket window. He then pays one-fifty for the ticket. Since I'm chief pilot, I simply got the ticket for Janet when she told me she was going up to the cabin."

"Mmm," Davis said. "Did you know all the pilots on the ship?"

"I knew one of them. Mason. The other two were new on the route. That's why I was along as observer."

"Did you know Mason socially?"

"No. Just business."

"And the stewardess??"

"Yes, I knew her. Business, of course."

"Of course," Davis said, remembering the blonde in the cocktail dress. He stood up and moved his jacket cuff off his wristwatch. "Well, I've got to catch a plane, Captain. Thanks for your help."

"Not at all," Carruthers said."When you report in to Dad, give him my regards, won't you?"

"I'll do that," Davis said. He thanked Carruthers again, and then went out to catch his return plane.

He bought twenty-five thousand dollars' worth of insurance for fifty cents from one of the machines in the waiting room, and then got aboard the plane at about five minutes before take-off. He browsed through the magazine he'd picked up at the newsstand, and when the fat fellow plopped down into the seat beside him, he just glanced up and then turned back to his magazine again. The plane left the ground and began climbing, and Davis looked back through the window and saw the field drop away below him.

"First time flying?" the fellow asked.

Davis looked up from the magazine into a pair of smiling green eyes. The eyes were embedded deep in soft, ruddy flesh. The man owned a nose like the handle of a machete, and a mouth with thick, blubbery lips. He wore an orange sports shirt against which the color of his complexion seemed even more fiery.

"No," Davis said. "I've been off the ground before."

"Always gives me a thrill," the man said. "No matter how many times I do it." He chuckled and added, "An airplane ride is just like a woman. Lots of ups and downs, and not always too smooth—but guaranteed to keep a man up in the air."

Davis smiled politely, and the fat man chuckled a bit more and then thrust a beefy hand at him. "MacGregor," he said. "Charlie or Chuck or just plain Mac, if you like."

Davis took his hand and said, "Milt Davis."

"Glad to know you, Milt," MacGregor said. "You down here on business?"

"Yes," he said briefly.

"Me, too," MacGregor said. "Business mostly." He grinned slyly. " 'Course, what the wife don't know won't hurt her, eh?"

"I'm not married," Davis told him.

"A wonderful institution," MacGregor said. He laughed aloud, and then added, "But who likes being in an institution?"

Davis hoped he hadn't winced. He wondered if he was to be treated to MacGregor's full repertoire of wornout gags before the trip was over. To discourage any further attempts at misdirected wit, he turned back to the magazine as politely as he could, smiling once to let MacGregor know he wasn't being purposely rude.

"Go right ahead," MacGregor said genially. "Don't mind me."

That was easy, Davis thought. *If it lasts.*

He was surprised that it did last. MacGregor stretched out in the seat beside him, closing his eyes. He did not speak again until the plane was ten minutes out of San Francisco.

"Let's walk to the john, eh, Milt?" he said.

Davis lifted his head and smiled. "Thanks, but—"

"This is a .38 here under my overcoat, Milt," MacGregor said softly.

For a second, Davis thought it was another of the fat man's tired jokes. He turned to look at MacGregor's lap. The overcoat was folded over his chunky left arm, and Davis could barely see the blunt muzzle of a pistol poking from beneath the folds.

He lifted his eyebrows a little. "What are you going to do after you shoot me, MacGregor? Vanish into thin air?"

MacGregor smiled. "Now who mentioned anything about shooting, Milt? Eh? Let's go back, shall we, boy?"

Davis rose and moved past MacGregor into the aisle. MacGregor stood up behind him, the coat over his arm, the gun completely hidden now. Together, they began walking toward the rear of the plane, past the food buffet on their right, and past the twin facing seats behind the buffet. An emergency window was set in the cabin wall there, and Davis sighed in relief when he saw that the seats were occupied.

When they reached the men's room, MacGregor flipped open the door and nudged Davis inside. Then he crowded in behind him, putting his wide back to the door. He reached up with one heavy fist, rammed Davis against the sink, and then ran his free hand over Davis' body.

"Well," he said pleasantly. "No gun."

"My name is Davis, not Spade," Davis told him.

MacGregor lifted the .38, pointing it at Davis' throat. "All right, Miltie, now give a listen. I want you to forget all about that crashed DC-4, I want you to forget there are even such things as airplanes, Miltie. Now, I know you're a smart boy, and so I'm not even going to mark you up, Miltie. I could mark you up nice with the sight and butt of this thing." He gestured with the .38 in his hand. "I'm not going to do that. Not now. I'm just telling you, nice-like, to lay off. Just lay off and go back to skip-tracing, Miltie boy, or you're going to get hurt. Next time, I'm not going to be so considerate."

"Look . . ." Davis started.

"So let's not have a next time, Miltie. Let's call it off now. You give your client a ring and tell him you're dropping it, Miltie boy. Have you got that?''

Davis didn't answer.

"Fine," MacGregor said. He reached up suddenly with his left hand, almost as if he were reaching up for a light cord. At the same time he grasped Davis' shoulder with his right hand and spun him around, bringing the hand with the gun down in a fast motion, flipping it butt-end up.

The walnut stock caught Davis at the base of his skull. He stumbled forward, his hands grasping the sink in front of him. He felt the second blow at the back of his head, and then his hands dropped from the sink, and the aluminum deck of the plane came up to meet him suddenly, all too fast . . .

Someone said, "He's coming around now," and he idly thought, *Coming around where?*

"How do you feel, Mr. Davis?" a second voice asked.

He looked up at the ring of faces. He did not recognize any of them. "Where am I?" he asked.

"San Francisco," the second voice said. The voice belonged to a tall man with a salt-and-pepper mustache and friendly blue eyes. Mac-Gregor had owned friendly green eyes, Davis remembered.

"We found you in the men's room after all the passengers had disembarked," the voice went on. "You've had a nasty fall, Mr. Davis. Nothing serious, however. I've dressed the cut, and I'm sure there'll be no complications."

"Thank you," Davis said. "I wonder . . . did you say all the passengers have already gone?"

"Why, yes."

"I wonder if I might see the passenger list? There was a fellow aboard I promised to look up, and I'm darned if I haven't forgotten his name."

"I'll ask the stewardess," the man said. "By the way, I'm Doctor Burke."

"How do you do?" Davis said. He reached for a cigarette and lighted it. When the stewardess brought the passenger list, he scanned it hurriedly.

There was no MacGregor listed, Charles or otherwise. This fact did not surprise him greatly. He looked down the list to see if there were any names with the initials C.M., knowing that when a person assumes an alias, he will usually choose a name with the same initials as his real name. There were no C. M.s on the list, either.

"Does that help?" the stewardess asked.

"Oh, yes. Thank you. I'll find him now."

The doctor shook Davis' hand, and then asked if he'd sign a release stating he had received medical treatment and absolving the airline. Davis felt the back of his head, and then signed the paper.

He walked outside and leaned against the building, puffing idly on his cigarette. The night was a nest of lights. He watched the lights and listened to the hum of aircraft all around him. It wasn't until he had finished his cigarette that he remembered he was in San Francisco.

He dropped the cigarette to the concrete and ground it out beneath his heel. Quite curiously, he found himself ignoring MacGregor's warning. He was a little surprised at himself, but he was also pleased. And more curious, he found himself wishing that he and MacGregor would meet again.

He walked briskly to the cyclone fence that hemmed in the runway area. Quickly, he showed the uniformed guard at the gate his credentials and then asked where he could find the hangars belonging to Intercoastal Airways. The guard pointed them out.

Davis walked through the gate and towards the hangars the guard had indicated, stopping at the first one. Two mechanics in greasy coveralls were leaning against a work bench, chatting idly. One was smoking, and the other tilted a Coke bottle to his lips, draining half of it in one pull. Davis walked over to them.

"I'm looking for the mechanics who serviced the DC-4 that crashed up in Seattle," he said.

They looked at him blankly for a few seconds, and then the one with the Coke bottle asked, "You from the CAB?"

"No," Davis said. "I'm investigating privately."

The mechanic with the bottle was short, with black hair curling over his forehead, and quick brown eyes that silently appraised Davis now. "If you're thinking about that fire warning," he said, "it had nothing to do with the crash. There was a bomb aboard."

"I know," Davis said. "Were you one of the mechanics?"

"I was one of them," he said.

"Good." Davis smiled and said, "I didn't catch your name."

"Jerry," the man said. "Mangione." His black brows pulled together suspiciously. "Who you investigating for?"

"A private client. The father of the girl who was a passenger."

"Oh. Carruthers' wife, huh?"

"Yes. Did you know her?"

"No. I just heard it was his wife. He's chief pilot down Burbank, ain't he?"

"Yes," Davis said.

Mangione paused and studied Davis intently. "What'd you want to know?"

"First, was the fire-warning system okay?"

"Yeah. We checked it out. Just one of those things, you know. False alarm."

"Did you go into the plane?"

"Yeah, sure. I had to check the signal in the cockpit. Why?"

"I'm just asking."

"You don't think *I* put that damn bomb on the plane, do you?"

"Somebody did," Davis said.

"That's for sure. But not me. There were a lot of people on that plane, mister. Any one of 'em could've done it."

"Be a little silly to bring a bomb onto a plane you were going to fly."

"I guess so. But don't drag me into this. I just checked the fire-warning system, that's all."

"Were you around when Mrs. Carruthers boarded the plane?"

"The redhead? Yeah, I was there."

"What'd she look like?"

Mangione shrugged. "A broad, just like any other broad. Red hair."

"Was she pretty?"

"The red hair was the only thing gave her any flash. In fact, I was a little surprised."

"Surprised? What about?"

"That Tony would bother, you know."

"Who? Who would bother?"

"Tony. Tony Radner. He brought her out to the plane."

"What?" Davis said.

"Yeah, Tony. He used to sell tickets inside. He brought her out to the plane and helped her get aboard."

"Are you sure about that? Sure you know who the man with her was?"

Mangione made an exasperated gesture with his hairy hands. "Hell, ain't I been working here for three years? Don't I know Tony when I see him? It was him, all right. He took the broad right to her seat.

Listen, it was him, all right. I guess maybe . . . well, I was surprised, anyway.''

"Why?"

"Tony's a good-looking guy. And this Mrs. Carruthers, well, she wasn't much. I'm surprised he went out of his way. But I guess maybe she wasn't feeling so hot. Tony's a gent that way.''

"Wasn't feeling so hot?''

"Well, I don't like to talk about anybody's dead, but she looked like she had a snootful to me. Either that, or she was pretty damn sick.''

"What makes you say that?''

"Hell, Tony had to help her up the ladder, and he practically carried her to her seat. Yeah, she musta been looped.''

"You said Radner used to work here. Has he quit?''

"Yeah, he quit.''

"Do you know where I can find him?''

Mangione shrugged. "Maybe you can get his address from the office in the morning. But, mister, I wouldn't bother him right now, if I was you.''

"Why not?''

Mangione smiled. "Because he's on his honeymoon,'' he said.

He slept the night through and when he awoke in the morning, the back of his head hardly hurt at all. He shaved and washed quickly, downed a breakfast of orange juice and coffee, and then went to the San Francisco office of Intercoastal Airways.

Radner, they told him, was no longer with them. But they did have his last address, and they parted with it willingly. He grabbed a cab, and then sat back while the driver fought with the California traffic. When he reached Radner's address, he paid and tipped the cabbie, and listed the expenditure in his book.

The rooming house was not in a good section of the city. It was red brick, with a brown front stoop. There was an old-fashioned bell pull set in the wide, wooden door jamb. He pulled this and heard the sound inside, and then he waited for footsteps. They came sooner than he expected.

The woman who opened the door couldn't have been more than fifty. Her face was still greasy with cold cream, and her hair was tied up in rags. "Yes?''

"I'm looking for Tony Radner,'' Davis said. "I'm an old friend of his, knew him in the Army. I went out to Intercoastal, but they told me he doesn't work for them any more. I wonder if you know where I can reach him."

The landlady regarded him suspiciously for a moment. "He doesn't live here anymore," she said.

"Darn," Davis said. He shook his head and assumed a false smile. "Isn't that always the way? I came all the way from New York, and now I can't locate him."

"That's too bad," the landlady agreed.

"Did he leave any forwarding address?" Davis asked.

"No. He left because he was getting married."

"Married!" Davis said. "Well, I'll be darned! Old Tony getting married!"

The landlady continued to watch Davis, her small eyes staring fixedly.

"You wouldn't know who he married, would you?"

"Yes," she said guardedly. "I guess I would."

"Who?" he asked.

"Trimble," the landlady said. "A girl named Alice Trimble."

"Alice Trimble," Davis said reflectively. "You wouldn't have her phone number, would you?"

"Come on in," the landlady said, finally accepting Davis at face value. She led him into the foyer of the house, and Davis followed her to the pay phone on the wall.

"They all scribble numbers here," she said. "I keep washing them off, but they keep putting them back again."

"Shame," Davis said sympathetically.

"Hers is up there, too. You just wait a second, and I'll tell you which one." She stepped close to the phone and examined the scribbled numbers on the wall. She stood very close to the wall, moving her head whenever she wanted to move her eyes. She stepped back at last and placed a long white finger on one of the numbers. "This one. This is the one he always called."

Davis jotted down the number hastily, and then said, "Well, gee, thanks a million. You don't know how much I appreciate this."

"I hope you find him," the landlady said. "Nice fellow, Mr. Radner."

"One of the best," Davis said.

He called the number from the first pay phone he found. He listened to the phone ring four times on the other end, and then a voice said, "Hello?"

"Hello," he said, "May I speak to Miss Trimble, please?"

"This is Miss Trimble," the voice said.

"My name is Davis," he said. "I'm an old friend of Tony Radner's. He asked me to look him up if ever I was in town ..." He paused and forced himself to laugh in embarrassment. "Trouble is, I can't seem to find him. His landlady said you and Tony ..."

"Oh," the girl said. "You must want my sister. This is *Anne* Trimble."

"Oh," he said. "I'm sorry. I didn't realize ..." He paused. "Is your sister there?"

"No, she doesn't live with me any more. She and Tony got married."

"Well, now, that's wonderful," Davis said. "Know where I can find them?"

"They're still on their honeymoon."

"Oh, that's too bad." He thought for a few seconds, and then said, "I've got to catch a plane back tonight. I wonder ... I wonder if I might come over and ... well, you could fill me in on what Tony's been doing and all. Hate like the devil to go back without knowing *something* about him."

The girl hesitated, and he could sense her reluctance.

"I promise I'll make it a very short visit. I've still got some business to attend to here. Besides ... well, Tony loaned me a little money once, and I thought ... well, if you don't mind, I'd like to leave it with you."

"I ... I suppose it would be all right," she said.

"Fine. May I have the address?"

She gave it to him, and he told her he'd be up in about an hour, if that was all right with her. He went to the coffee counter, ordered coffee and a toasted English, and browsed over them until it was time to go. He bought a plain white envelope on the way out, slipped twenty dollars into it, and sealed it. Then he hailed a cab.

He found the mailbox marked *A. Trimble*, and he realized the initial sufficed for both Alice and Anne. He walked up two flights, stopped outside apartment 22, and thumbed the ivory stud in the door jamb. A series of chimes floated from beyond the door, and then the peephole flap was thrown back.

"I'm Mr. Davis," he said to the flap. "I called about—"

"Oh, yes," Anne Trimble said. The flap descended, and the door swung wide.

She was a tall brunette, and her costume emphasized her height. She was wearing tightly tailored toreador slacks. A starched white blouse with a wide collar and long sleeves was tucked firmly into the band of the slacks. A bird in flight, captured in sterling, rested on the blouse just below the left breast pocket.

"Come in," she said, "won't you?" She had green eyes and black eyebrows, and she smiled pleasantly now.

Davis stepped into the cool apartment, and she closed the door behind him.

"I'm sorry if I seemed rude when you called me," she said. "I'm afraid you woke me."

"Then I should be the one to apologize," Davis said.

He followed her into a sunken living room furnished in Swedish modern. She walked to a long, low coffee table and took a cigarette from a box there, offering the box to him first. Davis shook his head and watched her as she lighted the cigarette. Her hair was cut close to her head, ringing her face with ebony wisps. She wore only lipstick, and Davis reflected that this was the first truly beautiful woman he had ever met. Two large, silver hoop earrings hung from her ears. She lifted her head, and the earrings caught the rays of the sun streaming through the blinds.

"Now," she said. "You're a friend of Tony's, are you?"

"Yes," he answered. He reached into his jacket pocket and took out the sealed envelope. "First, let me get this off my mind. Please tell Tony I sincerely appreciate the loan, won't you?"

She took the envelope without comment, dropping it on the coffee table.

This is a very cool one, Davis thought.

"I was really surprised to learn that Tony was married," he said.

"It was a little sudden, yes," she said.

"Oh? Hadn't he known your sister long?"

"Three months, four months."

Davis shook his head. "I still can't get over it. How'd he happen to meet your sister?"

"Like that," Anne said. "How do people meet? A concert, a club, a soda fountain." She shrugged. "You know, people meet."

"Don't you like Tony?" he asked suddenly.

She seemed surprised. "Me? Yes, as a matter of fact, I do. I think he'll be very good for Alice. He has a strong personality, and she needs someone like him. Yes, I like Tony."

"Well, that's good," Davis said.

"When we came to Frisco, you see, Alice was sort of at loose ends. We'd lived in L.A. all our lives, and Alice depended on Mom a good deal, I suppose. When Mom passed away, and this job opening came for me ... well, the change affected her. Moving and all. It was a good thing Tony came along.''

"You live here alone then, just the two of you?''

Anne Trimble smiled and sucked in a deep cloud of smoke. "Just two little gals from Little Rock,'' she said.

Davis smiled with her. "L.A., you mean.''

"The same thing. We're all alone in the world. Just Alice and me. Dad died when we were both little girls. Now, of course, Alice is married. Don't misunderstand me. I'm very happy for her.''

"When were they married?''

"January 6th,'' she answered. "It's been a long honeymoon.''

January 6th, Davis thought. *The day the DC-4 crashed.*

"Where are they now?'' he asked.

"Las Vegas.''

"Where in Las Vegas?''

Anne Trimble smiled again. "You're not planning on visiting a pair of honeymooners, are you, Mr. Davis?''

"God, no,'' he said. "I'm just curious.''

"Fact is,'' Anne said, "I don't know where they're staying. I've only had a wire from them since they were married. I don't imagine they're thinking much about me. Not on their honeymoon.''

"No, I guess not,'' Davis said. "I understand Tony left his job. Is that right?''

"Yes. It didn't pay much, and Tony is really a brilliant person. He and Alice said they'd look around after the honeymoon and settle wherever he could get located.''

"When did he quit?''

"A few days before they were married, I think. No, wait, it was on New Year's Eve, that's right. He quit then.''

"Then he wasn't selling tickets on the day of ...''

Anne looked at him strangely. "The day of what?''

"The day he was married,'' Davis said quickly.

"No, he wasn't.'' She continued looking at him, and then asked, "How do you happen to know Tony, Mr. Davis?''

"Oh, the Army,'' Davis said. "The last war, you know.''

"That's quite a feat,'' Anne said.

"Huh?'' Davis looked up.

"Tony was in the Navy.''

Once again, he felt like a damn fool. He cursed the crashed plane, and he cursed George Ellison, and he cursed the stupidity that had led him to take the job in the first place. He sighed deeply.

"Well," he said. "I guess I pulled a bloomer."

Anne Trimble stared at him coldly. "Maybe you'd better get out, Mr. Davis. If that's your name."

"It's my name. Look," he said, "I'm a private eye. I'm investigating the crash for my client. I thought . . ."

"*What* crash?"

"A DC-4 took a dive in Seattle. My client's daughter was aboard her when she went down. There was also a bomb aboard."

"Is this another one of your stories?"

Davis lifted his right hand. "God's truth, s'help me. I'm trying to find whoever put the bomb aboard.

"And you think Tony did?"

"No, I didn't say that. But I've got to investigate all the possibilities."

Anne suddenly smiled. "Are you new at this business?"

"No, I've been at it a long time now. This case is a little out of my usual line."

"You called yourself a private eye. Do private eyes really call themselves that? I thought that was just for the paperback trade."

"I'm afraid we really do," Davis said. "Private Investigator, shortened to Private I, and then naturally to private eye."

"It must be exciting."

"Well, I'm afraid it's usually deadly dull." He rose and said, "Thanks very much for your time, Miss Trimble. I'm sorry I got to see you on a ruse, but . . ."

"You should have just asked. I'm always willing to help the cause of justice." She smiled. "And I think you'd better take this money back."

"Well, thanks again," he said, taking the envelope.

"Not at all," she said. She led him to the door, and shook his hand, and her grip was firm and warm. "Good luck."

The door whispered shut behind him. He stood in the hallway for a few moments, sighed, and then made his way down to the courtyard and the street.

The time has come, he thought, *to replenish the bank account. If Ellison expects me to chase hither and yon, then Ellison should also realize that I'm a poor boy, raised by the side of a railroad car. And if a trip to Vegas is in the offing . . . the time has come to replenish the bank account.*

He thought no more about it. He hailed a cab for which Ellison would pay, and headed for the old man's estate.

*   *   *

The butler opened the door and announced, "Mr. Davis, sir,"

Davis smiled at the butler and entered the room. It was full of plates and pitchers and cups and saucers and mugs and jugs and platters. For a moment Davis thought he'd wandered into the pantry by error, but then he saw Ellison seated behind a large desk.

Ellison did not look old, even though Davis knew he was somewhere in his seventies. He had led an easy life, and the rich are expert at conserving their youth. The only signs of age on Ellison were in his face. It was perhaps a bit too ruddy for good health, and it reminded him of MacGregor's complexion—but Ellison was not a fat man. He had steel-gray hair cropped close to his head. His brows were black, in direct contrast to the hair on his head, and his eyes were a penetrating pale blue. Davis wondered from whom Janet had inherited her red hair, then let the thought drop when Ellison rose and extended his hand.

"Ah, Davis, come in, come in."

Davis walked to the desk, and Ellison took his hand in a tight grip.

"Hope you don't mind talking in here," he said. "I've got a new piece of porcelain, and I wanted to mount it."

"Not at all," Davis said.

"Know anything about porcelain?" Ellison asked.

"Not a thing, sir."

"Pity. Volkstedt wouldn't mean anything to you then, would it?"

"No, sir."

"Or Rudolstadt? It's more generally known as that."

"I'm afraid not, sir," Davis said.

"Here now," Ellison said. "Look at this sauce boat."

Davis looked.

"This dates back to 1783, Davis. Here, look." He turned over the sauce boat, but he did not let it out of his hands. "See the crossed hayforks? That's the mark, you know, shows it's genuine stuff. Funny thing about this. The mark so resembles the Meissen crossed swords . . ." He seemed suddenly to remember that he was not talking to a fellow connoisseur. He put the sauce boat down swiftly but gently. "Have you learned anything yet, Davis?"

"A little, Mr. Ellison. I'm here mainly for money."

Ellison looked up sharply and then began chuckling. "You're a frank man, aren't you?"

"I try to be," Davis said. "When it concerns money."

"How much will you need?"

"A thousand will do it. I'll probably be flying to Vegas and back, and I may have to spread a little money for information while I'm there."

Ellison nodded briefly. "I'll give you a check before you leave. What progress have you made, Davis?"

"Not very much. Do you know a Tony Radner?"

Ellison looked up swiftly. "Why?"

"He put your daughter on the DC-4, sir. Do you know him?"

Ellison's mouth lengthened, and he tightened his fists on the desk top. "Has that son of a bitch got something to do with this?" he asked.

"Do you know him, sir?"

"Of course I do! How do you know he put Janet on that plane?"

"An eyewitness, sir."

"I'll kill that bastard!" Ellison shouted. "If he had anything to do with . . ."

"How do you know him, Mr. Ellison?"

Ellison's rage subsided for a moment. "Janet was seeing him," he said.

"What do you mean, seeing him?"

"She fancied herself to be in love with him," Ellison said. "He's a no-good, Davis, a plain . . ."

"You mean she wanted to marry him, rather than Carruthers?"

"No, that's not what I mean. I mean she was seeing Radner *after* she and Nick were married. She . . . she had the supreme gall to tell me she wanted a divorce from Nick." Ellison clenched his hands and then relaxed them again. "You don't know Nick, Davis. He's a fine boy, one of the best. I feel toward him the way I'd feel toward my own son. I never had any boys, Davis, and Janet wasn't much of a daughter." He paused. "I'm grateful I've still got Nick," he said.

"Your daughter wanted to divorce Carruthers?"

"Yes," Ellison said.

"Did she tell Carruthers?"

"Yes, she did. But I told *her* I'd cut her off without a penny if she did any such damn-fool thing. She changed her mind mighty fast after that. Janet was used to money, Davis. The idea of marrying a ticket seller didn't appeal to her when she knew she'd have to do without it."

"So she broke it off with him?"

"On the spot."

"When was this?"

"About six months ago," Ellison said.

"And she hadn't seen him since?"

"Not that I knew of. Now you tell me he put her on that plane. I don't know what to think."

Davis nodded. "It *is* a little confusing."

"Do you suppose she was going to keep a rendezvous in Washington with Radner?" Ellison shook his head. "Dammit. I wouldn't put it past her."

"I don't think so. At least . . . well, I should think they'd have left together if that were the case."

"Not if she didn't want to be seen. She was travelling on a company pass, you know."

"That seems odd," Davis said. "I mean—"

"You mean, with all my money, why should she travel on a pass?" Ellison smiled. "I like to help Nick out, Davis. I keep him living well; did it when Janet was alive, and still do it. But he's a proud boy, and I've got to be careful with my methods of seeing to his welfare. Getting Janet her ticket was one of the things that kept his pride going."

"I see." Davis washed his hand over his face. "Well, I'll talk to Radner. Did you know he was married now?"

"No, I didn't."

"Yes. On the day of the crash."

"On the day . . . then what on earth was he doing with Janet?"

"That's a good question," Davis said. He paused, and then added, "Can I have that check now?"

It was not until after supper that evening that Nicholas Carruthers showed up. Davis had eaten lightly, and after a hasty cigarette he had begun packing a small bag for the Vegas trip. When the knock sounded on the door to his apartment, he dropped a pair of shorts into the suitcase and called, "Who is it?"

"Me. Carruthers."

"Second," Davis said. He went to the door rapidly, wondering what had occasioned this visit from the pilot. He threw back the night latch, and then unlocked the door.

Carruthers was in uniform this time. He wore a white shirt and black tie, together with the pale blue trousers and jacket of the airline, and a peaked cap.

"Surprised to see you, Carruthers," Davis said. "Come on in."

"Thanks," Carruthers said. He glanced around the simply furnished apartment noncommittally, then stepped inside and took off his cap, keeping it in his hands.

"Something to drink?" Davis asked. "Scotch okay?"

"Please," Carruthers replied.

Davis poured, and when Carruthers had downed the drink, he refilled the glass. "What's on your mind, Carruthers?"

Carruthers looked into the depths of his glass, sipped a bit of the scotch, and then looked up. "Janet," he said.

"What about her?"

"Let it lie. Tell the old man you're dropping it. Let it lie."

"Why?"

"How much is the old man paying you?" Carruthers asked, avoiding Davis' question.

"That's between the old man and myself."

"I'll match it," Carruthers said. "And then some. Just let's drop the whole damn thing."

Davis thought back to the genial Mr. MacGregor. "You remind me of someone else I know," he said.

Carruthers did not seem interested. "Look, Davis, what does this mean to you, anyway? Nothing. You're getting paid for a job. All right, I'm willing to pay you what you would have made. So why are you being difficult?"

"Am I being difficult? I didn't say I *wouldn't* drop it, did I?"

"Will you?"

"It depends. I'd like to know why you want it dropped."

"Let's just say I'd like it better if the whole thing were forgotten."

"A lot of people would like it better that way. Including the person who put that bomb on the plane."

Carruthers opened his eyes wide. "You don't think I did that, do you?"

"You were aboard the plane. You could have."

"Why would I do a thing like that?"

"I can think of several reasons," Davis said.

"Like what?" Carruthers sipped at the bourbon again.

"Maybe you didn't like the idea of Janet playing around with Tony Radner."

Carruthers laughed a short, brittle laugh. "You think that bothered me? That two-bit punk? Don't be ridiculous." He drank some more scotch and then said, "I was used to Janet's excursions. Radner didn't bother me at all."

"You mean there were others?"

"Others? Janet collected them the way the old man collects porcelain. A hobby, you know."

"Did the old man know this?"

"I doubt it. He knew his daughter was a bitch, but I think Radner was the first time it came into the open. He squelched that pretty damn fast, you can bet."

"But you knew about it? And it didn't bother you?"

"Not in the least. I'm no angel myself, Davis. If Janet wanted to roam, fine. If she thought of leaving me, that was another thing."

"That you didn't like," Davis said.

"That I didn't like at all." Carruthers paused. "Look, Davis. I like money. The old man has a lot of it. Janet was my wife, and the old man saw to it that we lived in style. I could have left the airline any time I wanted to, and he'd have set me up for life. Fact is, I like flying, so I stayed on. But I sure as hell wasn't going to let my meal ticket walk out."

"That's not the way I heard it," Davis said.

"What do you mean?"

"Janet's gone, and the old man is still feeding the kitty."

"Sure, but I didn't know it would work that way."

"Didn't you?"

Carruthers swallowed the remainder of his scotch. "I don't get you, Davis."

"Look at it this way, Carruthers. Janet's a handy thing to have around. She comes and goes, and you come and go, and the old man sees to it that you come and go in Cadillacs. A smart man may begin wondering why he needs Janet at all. If he can be subsidized even after she's gone, why not get rid of her? Why not give her a bomb to play with?"

"Why not?" Carruthers asked. "But I didn't."

"That's what they all say," Davis told him. "Right up to the gas chamber."

"You're forgetting that I didn't know what the old man's reactions would be. Still don't know. It's early in the game yet, and he's still crossing my palm, but that may change. Look, Davis, when a man takes out accident insurance, it's not because he hopes he'll get into an accident. The same thing with Janet. I needed her. She was my insurance. As long as she was around, my father-in-law saw to it that I wasn't needing." Carruthers shook his head. "No, Davis, I couldn't take a chance on my insurance lapsing."

"Perhaps not. Why do you want me to drop the case?"

"Because I want a status quo. The memory of Janet is fresh in the old man's mind. I'm coupled with the memory. That means he keeps my Cadillac full of gas. Suppose you crack this damned thing? Suppose you find out who set that bomb? It becomes something that's resolved. There's a conclusion, and the old man can file it away like a piece of rare porcelain. He loses interest—and maybe my Cadillac stops running."

"You know something, Carruthers? I don't think I like you very much."

Carruthers smiled. "Why? Because I'm trying to protect an investment? Because I don't give a damn that Janet is gone? Look, Davis, let's get this thing straight. We hated each other's guts. I stayed with her because I like the old man's money. And she stayed with me because she knew she'd be cut off penniless if she didn't. A very simple arrangement." He paused. "What do you say, Davis?"

"I say get the hell out of here."

"Be sensible, Davis. Look at it . . ."

"Take a walk, Carruthers. Take a long walk and don't come back."

Carruthers stared at Davis for a long time. He said nothing, and there was no enmity in his eyes. At last he rose and settled his cap on his head.

At the door, he turned and said, "You're not being smart, Davis."

Davis didn't answer him.

Maybe he *wasn't* being smart. Maybe Carruthers was right.

It would have been so much easier to have said no, right from the start. No, Mr. Ellison, I'm sorry. I won't take the case. Sorry.

That would have been the easy way. He had not taken the easy way. The money had appealed to him, yes, and so he'd stepped into something that was really far too big for him, something that still made very little sense to him. A bomb seemed an awfully elaborate way of killing someone, assuming the death of Janet Carruthers was, in fact, the reason for the bomb. It would have been so much easier to have used a knife, or a gun, or a rope, or even poison.

Unless the destruction of the plane was an important factor in the killing.

Did the killer have a grudge against the airline as well?

Carruthers worked for the airline, but he was apparently well satisfied with his job. Liked flying, he'd said. Besides, to hear him tell it, he'd never even considered killing his wife. Sort of killing the goose, you know. She was too valuable to him. She was—what had he alluded to?—insurance, yes, insurance.

Which, in a way, was true. Carruthers had no way of knowing how Ellison would react to his daughter's death. He could just as easily have washed his hands of Carruthers, and a man couldn't take a chance on . . .

"I'll be goddamned!" Davis said aloud.

He glanced at his watch quickly. It was too late now. He would have to wait until morning.

"I'll be goddamned," he said again.

It would be a long night.

Mr. Schlemmer was a balding man in his early fifties. A pair of rimless glasses perched on his nose, and his blue eyes were genial behind them.

"I can only speak for Aircraft Insurance Association of America, you understand," he said. "Other companies may operate on a different basis, though I think it unlikely."

"I understand," Davis said.

"First, you wanted to know how much insurance can be obtained from our machines at the San Francisco airport." Schlemmer paused. "We sell it at fifty cents for twenty-five thousand dollars' worth. Costs you two quarters in the machine."

"And what's the maximum insurance for any one person?"

"Two hundred thousand," Schlemmer said. "The premium is four dollars."

"Is there anything in your policy that excludes a woman travelling on a company pass?" Davis asked.

"No," Schlemmer said. "Our airline trip policy states 'travelling on ticket or pass.' No, this woman would not be excluded."

"Suppose the plane's accident occurred because of a bomb explosion aboard the plane while it was in flight? Would that invalidate a beneficiary's claim?"

"I should hardly think so. Just a moment, I'll read you the exclusions." He dug into his desk drawer and came out with a policy which he placed on the desk top, leafing through it rapidly. "No," he said. "The exclusions are disease, suicide, war, and of course, we will not insure the pilot or any active member of the crew."

"I see," Davis said. "Can I get down to brass tacks now?"

"By all means, do," Schlemmer said.

"How long does it take to pay?"

"Well, the claim must be filed within twenty days after the occurrence. Upon receipt of the claim, and within fifteen days, we must supply proof-of-loss forms to the claimant. As soon as these are completed and presented to us, we pay. We've paid within hours on some occasions. Sometimes it takes days, and sometimes weeks. It depends on how rapidly the claim is made, the proof of loss submitted—and all that. You understand?''

"Yes," Davis said. He took a deep breath. "A DC-4 crashed near Seattle on January 6th. Was anyone on that plane insured with your company?''

Schlemmer smiled, and a knowing look crossed his face. "I had a suspicion you were driving at that, Mr. Davis. That was the reason for your 'bomb' question, wasn't it?''

"Yes. Was anyone insured?''

"There was only one passenger," Schlemmer said. "We would not, of course, insure the crew.''

"The passenger was Janet Carruthers," Davis said. "Was she insured?''

"Yes.''

"For how much?''

Schlemmer paused. "Two hundred thousand dollars, Mr. Davis." He wiped his lips and said, "You know how it works, of course. You purchase your insurance from a machine at the airport. An envelope is supplied for the policy, and you mail this directly to your beneficiary or beneficiaries as the case may be, before you board the flight.''

"Yes, I've taken insurance," Davis said.

"A simple matter," Schlemmer assured him, "and well worth the investment. In this case, the beneficiaries have already received a check for two hundred thousand dollars.''

"They have?''

"Yes. The claim was made almost instantly, proof of loss filed, the entire works. We paid at once.''

"I see," Davis said. "I wonder . . . could you tell me . . . you mentioned suicide in your excluding clause. Was there any thought about Mrs. Carruthers' death being suicide?''

"We considered it," Schlemmer said. "But quite frankly, it seemed a bit absurd. An accident like this one is hardly conceivable as suicide. I mean, a person would have to be seriously unbalanced to take a plane and its crew with her when she chose to kill herself. Mrs. Carruthers' medical history showed no signs of mental instability. In fact, she was in amazingly good health all through her life. No, suicide was out. We paid.''

Davis nodded. "Can you tell me who the beneficiaries were?" he asked.

"Certainly," Schlemmer said. "Mr. and Mrs. Anthony Radner.''

*   *   *

He asked her to meet him in front of DiAngelo's and they lingered on the wharf a while, watching the small boats before entering the restaurant. When they were seated, Anne Trimble asked, "Have you ever been here before?"

"I followed a delinquent husband as far as the door once," he answered.

"Then it's your first time."

"Yes."

"Mine, too." She rounded her mouth in mock surprise. "Goodness, we're sharing a first."

"That calls for a drink," he said.

She ordered a daiquiri, and he settled for scotch on the rocks, and he sipped his drink slowly, thinking, *I wish I didn't suspect her sister of complicity in murder.*

They made small talk while they ate, and Davis felt he'd known her for a long time, and that made his job even harder. When they were on their coffee, she said, "I'm a silly girl, I know. But not silly enough to believe this is strictly social."

"I'm an honest man," he said. "It isn't."

She laughed. "Well, what is it then?"

"I want to know more about your sister."

"Alice? For heaven's sake, why?" Her brow furrowed, and she said, "I really should be offended, you know. You take me out and then want to know more about my sister."

"You've no cause for worry," he said very softly. He was not even sure she heard him. She lifted here coffee cup, and her eyes were wide over the brim.

"Will you tell me about her?" he asked.

"Do you think she put the bomb on the plane?"

He was not prepared for the question. He blinked his eyes in confusion.

"Do you?" she repeated. "Remember, you're an honest man."

"Maybe she did," he said.

Anne considered this, and then took another sip of coffee. "What do you want to know?" she asked.

"I want to . . ."

"Understand, Mr. Davis . . ."

"Milt," he corrected.

"All right. Understand that I don't go along with you, not at all. Not knowing my sister. But I'll answer any of your questions because that's the only way you'll see she had nothing to do with it.''

"That's fair enough," he said.

"All right, Milt. Fire away.''

"First, what kind of a girl is she?''

"A simple girl. Shy, often awkward. Honest, Milt, very honest. Innocent. I think Tony Radner is the first man she ever kissed.

"Do you come from a wealthy family, Anne?''

"No.''

"How does your sister feel about—''

"About not having a tremendous amount of money?'' Anne shrugged. "All right, I suppose. We weren't destitute, even after Dad died. We always got along very nicely, and I don't think she ever yearned for anything. What are you driving at, Milt?''

"Would two hundred thousand dollars seem like a lot of money to Alice?''

"Yes,'' Anne answered without hesitation. "Two hundred thousand would seem like a lot of money to anyone.''

"Is she easily persuaded? Can she be talked into doing things?''

"Perhaps. I know damn well she couldn't be talked into putting a bomb on a plane, though.''

"No. But could she be talked into sharing two hundred thousand that was come by through devious means?''

"Why all this concentration on two hundred thousand dollars? Is that an arbitrary sum, or has a bank been robbed in addition to the plane crash?''

"Could she be talked,'' Davis persisted, "into drugging another woman?''

"No,'' Anne said firmly.

"Could she be talked into forging another woman's signature on an insurance policy?''

"Alice wouldn't do anything like that. Not in a million years.''

"But she married Radner. A man without money, a man without a job. Doesn't that seem like a shaky foundation upon which to build a marriage?''

"Not if the two people are in love.''

"Or unless the two people were going to come into a lot of money shortly.''

Anne said, "You're making me angry. And just when I was beginning to like you.''

"Then please don't be angry. I'm just digging, believe me.''

"Well, dig a little more gently, please."

"What does your sister look like?"

"Fairly pretty, I suppose. Well, not really. I suppose she isn't pretty, in fact. I never appraised her looks."

"Do you have a picture of her?"

"Yes, I do."

She put her purse on the table and unclasped it. She pulled out a red leather wallet, unsnapped it, and then removed one of the pictures from the gatefold. "It's not a good shot," she apologized.

The girl was not what Davis would have termed pretty. He was surprised, in fact, that she could be Anne's sister. He studied the black-and-white photograph of a fair-haired girl with a wide forehead, her nose a bit too long, her lips thin. He studied the eyes, but they held the vacuous smile common to all posed snapshots.

"She doesn't look like your sister," he said.

"Don't you think so?"

"No, not at all. You're much prettier."

Anne screwed up her eyebrows and studied Davis seriously. "You have blundered upon my secret, Mr. Davis," she said with mock exaggeration.

"You wear a mask, Miss Trimble," he said, pointing his finger at her like a prosecuting attorney.

"Almost, but not quite. I visit a remarkable magician known as Antoine. He operates a beauty salon and fender-repair shop. He is responsible for the midnight of my hair and the ripe apple of my lips. He made me what I am today, and now you won't love me any more." She brushed away an imaginary tear.

"I'd love you if you were bald and had green lips," he said, hoping his voice sounded light enough.

"Goodness!" she said, and then she laughed suddenly, a rich, full laugh he enjoyed hearing. "I may very well be bald after a few more tinting sessions with Antoine."

"May I keep the picture?" he asked.

"Certainly," she said. "Why?"

"I'm going up to Vegas. I want to find your sister and Radner."

"Then you're serious about all this," she said softly.

"Yes, I am. At least, until I'm convinced otherwise. Anne . . ."

"Yes?"

"It's just a job. I . . ."

"I'm not really worried, you understand. I know you're wrong about Alice, and Tony, too. So I won't worry."

"Good," he said. "I hope I *am* wrong."

She lifted one raven brow, and there was no coyness or archness in the motion. "Will you call me when you get back?"

"Yes," he said. "Definitely."

"If I'm out when you call, you can call my next-door neighbor, Freida. She'll take the message." She scribbled the number on a sheet of paper. "You will call, won't you, Milt?"

He covered her hand with his and said, "Try and stop me."

He went to City Hall right after he left her. He checked on marriage certificates issued on January 6th, and he was not surprised to find that one had been issued to Anthony Louis Radner and Alice May Trimble. He left there and went directly to the airport, making a reservation on the next plane for Las Vegas. Then he headed back for his apartment to pick up his bag.

The door was locked, just as he had left it. He put his key into the lock, twisted it, and then swung the door wide.

"Close it," MacGregor said.

MacGregor was sitting in the armchair to the left of the door. One hand rested across his wide middle and the other held the familiar .38, and this time it was pointed at Davis' head. Davis closed the door, and MacGregor said, "Better lock it, Miltie."

"You're a bad penny, MacGregor," Davis said, locking the door.

MacGregor chuckled. "Ain't it the truth, Miltie?"

"Why are you back, MacGregor? Three strikes and I'm out, is that it?"

"Three . . ." MacGregor cut himself short, and then grinned broadly. "So you figured the mountain, huh, Miltie."

"I figured it."

"I wasn't aiming at you, you know. I just wanted to scare you off. You don't scare too easy, Miltie."

"Who's paying you, MacGregor?"

"Now, now," MacGregor said chidingly, waving the gun like an extended forefinger. "That's a secret now, ain't it?" Davis watched the way MacGregor moved the gun, and he wondered if he'd repeat the gesture again. It might be worth remembering, for later.

"So what do we do?" he asked.

"We take a little ride, Miltie."

"Like in the movies, huh? Real melodrama."

MacGregor scratched his head. "Is a pleasant little ride melodrama?"

"Come on, MacGregor, who hired you?" He poised himself on the balls of his feet, ready to jump the moment MacGregor started wagging the gun again. MacGregor's hand did not move.

"Don't let's be silly, Miltie boy," he said.

"Do you know *why* you were hired?"

"I was told to see that you dropped the case. That's enough instructions for me."

"Do you know that two hundred grand is involved? How much are you getting for handling the sloppy end of the stick?"

MacGregor lifted his eyebrows and then nodded his head. "Two hundred grand, huh?"

"Sure. Do you know there's a murder involved, MacGregor? Five murders, if you want to get technical. Do you know what it means to be accessory after?"

"Can it, Davis. I've been in the game longer than you're walking."

"Then you know the score. And you know I can go down to R and I, and identify you from a mug shot. Think about that, MacGregor. It adds up to rock-chopping."

"Maybe you'll never get to see a mug shot."

"Maybe not. But that adds another murder to it. Are they paying you enough for a homicide rap, MacGregor?"

"Little Miltie, we've talked enough."

"Maybe we haven't talked enough yet. Maybe you don't know that the Feds are in on this thing, and that the Army . . ."

"Oh, come on, Miltie. Come on now, boy. You're reaching."

"Am I? Check around, MacGregor. Find out what happens when sabotage is suspected, especially on a plane headed to pick up military personnel. Find out if the Feds aren't on the scene. And find out what happens when a big-time fools with the government."

"I never done a state pen," MacGregor said, seemingly hurt. "Don't call me a big-time."

"Then why are you juggling a potato as hot as this one? Do you yearn for Quentin, MacGregor? Wise up, friend. You've been conned. The gravy is all on the other end of the line. You're getting all the cold beans, and when it comes time to hang a frame, guess who'll be it? Give a good guess, MacGregor."

MacGregor said seriously, "You're a fast talker."

"What do you say, MacGregor? How do you feel, playing the boob in a big ante deal? How much are you getting?"

"Four G's," MacGregor said. "Plus."

"Plus what?"

MacGregor smiled the age-old smile of a man who has known a woman and is reluctant to admit it. "Just plus," he said.

"All right, keep the dough and forget you were hired. You've already had the 'plus,' and you can keep that as a memory."

"I've only been paid half the dough," MacGregor said.

"When's the rest due?"

"When you drop the case."

"I can't match it, MacGregor, but I'll give you a thou for your trouble. You're getting off easy, believe me. If I don't crack this, the Feds will, and then you'll really be in hot water."

"Yeah," MacGregor said, nodding.

"You'll forget it then?"

"Where's the G-note?"

Davis reached for his wallet on the dresser. "Who hired you, Mac-Gregor?" He looked up, and MacGregor's smile had widened now.

"I'll take it all, Miltie."

"Huh?"

"All of it." MacGregor waved the gun. "Everything in the wallet. Come on."

"You *are* a jackass, aren't you?" Davis said. He fanned out the money in the wallet, and then held it out to MacGregor. MacGregor reached for it, and Davis loosened his grip, and the bills began fluttering towards the floor.

MacGregor grabbed for them with his free hand, turning sideways at the same time, taking the gun off Davis.

It had to be then, and it had to be right, because the talking game was over and MacGregor wasn't buying anything.

Davis leaped, ramming his shoulder against the fat man's chest. Mac-Gregor staggered back, and then swung his arm around just as Davis' fingers clamped on his wrist. He did not fire, and Davis knew he probably didn't want to bring the apartment house down around his ears.

They staggered across the room in a clumsy embrace, like partners at a dance school for beginners. Davis had both hands on MacGregor's gun wrist now, and the fat man swung his arm violently, trying to shake the grip. They didn't speak or curse. MacGregor grunted loudly each time he swung his arm, and Davis' breath was audible as it rushed through his parted lips. He did not loosen his grip. He forced Mac-Gregor across the room, and when the fat man's back was against the wall Davis began methodically smashing the gun hand against the plaster.

"Drop it," he said through clenched teeth. "Drop it."

He hit the wall with MacGregor's hand again, and this time the fingers opened and the gun clattered to the floor. Davis stepped back for just an instant, kicking the gun across the room, and then rushed forward with his fist clenched.

He felt his fist sink into the flesh around MacGregor's middle. The fat man's face went white, and then he buckled over, his arms embracing his stomach. Davis dropped his fist and then brought it up from his shoe-laces, catching MacGregor on the point of his jaw. MacGregor lurched backward, slamming into the wall, knocking a picture to the floor. Davis hit him once more, and MacGregor pitched forward onto his face. He wriggled once, and was still.

Davis stood over him, breathing hard. He waited until he caught his breath, and then he glanced at his watch.

Quickly, he picked up the .38 from where it lay on the floor. He broke it open, checked the load, and then brought it to his suitcase, laying it on top of his shirts.

He snapped the suitcase shut, called the police to tell them he'd just subdued a burglar in his apartment, and then left to catch his Las Vegas plane.

He started with the hotels. He started with the biggest ones.

"Mr. and Mrs. Anthony Radner," he said. "Are they registered here?"

The clerks all looked the same.

"Radner, Radner. The name doesn't sound familiar, but I'll check, sir."

Then the shifting of the ledger, the turning of pages, the signatures, largely scrawled, and usually illegible.

"No, sir, I'm sorry. No Radner."

"Perhaps you'd recognize the woman, if I showed you her picture?"

"Well ...." The apologetic cough. "Well, we get an awful lot of guests, sir."

And the fair-haired girl emerging from the wallet. The black and white, stereotyped photograph of Alice Trimble, and the explanation, "She's a newlywed—with her husband."

"We get a lot of newlyweds, sir."

The careful scrutiny of the head shot, the tilting of one eyebrow, the picture held at arm's length, then closer.

"No, I'm sorry. I don't recognize her. Why don't you try ...?"

He tried them all, all the hotels, and then all the rooming houses, and then all the motor courts. They were all very sorry. They had no Radners registered, and couldn't identify the photograph.

So he started making the rounds then. He lingered at the machines, feeding quarters into the slots, watching the orange and lemons and cherries whirl before his eyes, but never watching them too closely, always watching the place instead, looking for the elusive woman named Alice Trimble Radner.

Or he sat at the bars, nursing along endless scotches, his eyes fastened to the mirrors that commanded the entrance doorways. He was bored, and he was tired, but he kept watching, and he began making the rounds again as dusk tinted the sky, and the lights of the city flicked their siren song on the air.

He picked up the newspaper by chance. He flipped through it idly, and he almost turned the page, even after he'd read the small head: FATAL ACCIDENT.

The item was a very small one. It told of a Pontiac convertible with defective brakes which had crashed through the guard rail on the highway, killing its occupant instantly. The occupant's name was Anthony Radner. There was no mention of Alice in the article.

Little Alice Trimble, Davis thought. *A simple girl. Shy, often awkward. Honest.*

Murder is a simple thing. All it involves is killing another person or persons. You can be shy and awkward, and even honest—but that doesn't mean you can't be a murderer besides. So what is it that takes a simple girl like Alice Trimble and transforms her into a murderess?

Figure it this way. Figure a louse named Tony Radner who sees a way of striking back at the girl who jilted him and coming in to a goodly chunk of dough besides. Figure a lot of secret conversation, a pile of carefully planned moves. Figure a wedding, planned to coincide with the day of the plotted murder, so the murderers can be far away when the bomb they planted explodes.

Radner gets to see Janet Carruthers on some pretext, perhaps a farewell drink to show there are no hard feelings. This is his wedding day, and he introduces her to his bride, Alice Trimble. They share a drink, perhaps, but the drink is loaded and Janet suddenly feels very woozy. They help her to the airport, and they stow the bomb in her valise. None of the pilots know Radner. The only bad piece of luck is the fact that the fire-warning system is acting up, and a mechanic named Mangione recognizes him. But that's part of the game.

He helps her aboard and then goes back to his loving wife, Alice. They hop the next plane for Vegas, and when the bomb explodes they're far, far away. They get the news from the papers, file claim, and come into two hundred thousand bucks.

Just like falling off Pier 8.

Except that it begins to get sour about there. Except that maybe Alice Trimble likes the big time now. Two hundred G's is a nice little pile. Why share it?

So Tony Radner meets with an accident. If he's not insured, the two hundred grand is still Alice's. If he is insured, there's more for her.

The little girl has made her debut. The shy, awkward thing has emerged.

Portrait of a killer.

Davis went back to the newsstand, bought copies of all the local newspapers and then went back to the hotel.

When he was in his room, he called room service and asked for a tall scotch, easy on the ice. He took off his shoes and threw himself on the bed.

The drink came, and he went back to the bed again.

The easy part was over, of course. The hard part was still ahead. He still had to tell Anne about it, and he'd give his right arm not to have that task ahead of him. Alice Trimble? The police would find her. She'd probably left Vegas the moment Radner piled up the Pontiac. She was an amateur, and it wouldn't be too hard to find her. But telling Anne, that was the difficult thing.

Davis sat upright, took a long swallow of the scotch, and then swung his stockinged feet to the floor. He walked to the pile of newspapers on the dresser, picked them up, and carried them back to the bed.

He thumbed through the first one until he found the item about Radner's accident. It was a small notice, and it was basically the same as the one he'd read. It did add that Alice Trimble was on her honeymoon, and that she had come from San Francisco where she lived with her sister.

He leafed through the second newspaper, scanning the story quickly. Again, basically the same facts. Radner had taken the car for a spin. Alice hadn't gone along because of a headache. The accident had been attributed to faulty brakes, and there was speculation that Alice might have grounds for suit, if she cared to press charges, against the dealer who'd sold them the car.

The third newspaper really did a bang-up job. They treated the accident as a human-interest piece, playing up the newly-wed angle. They gave it the tearful head, "FATE CHEATS BRIDE," and then went on to wring the incident dry. There was also a picture of Alice Trimble leaving the coroner's office. She was raising her hand to cover her face when the picture had been taken. It was a good shot, close up, clear. The caption read: *Tearful Alice Radner, leaving the coroner's office after identifying the body of her husband Anthony Radner.*

Davis did not notice any tears on Alice Trimble's face.

He looked at the photograph again.

He sat erect and took a long gulp of his scotch, and then he brought the newspaper closer to his face and stared at the picture for a long time.

And he suddenly remembered something important he'd forgotten to ask Anne about her sister. Something damned important. So important he nearly broke his neck getting to the phone.

He asked long distance for Anne's number, and then let the phone ring for fifteen minutes before he gave up. He remembered the alternate number she'd given him then, the one belonging to Freida, the girl next door. He fished the scrap of paper out of his wallet, studying the number in Anne's handwriting, recalling their conversation in the restaurant. He got long distance to work again, and the phone was picked up on the fourth ring.

"Hello?"

"Hello, Freida?"

"Yes?"

"My name is Milt Davis. You don't know me, but Anne said I could leave a message here if . . ."

"Oh, yes. Anne's told me all about you, Mr. Davis."

"Well, good, good. I just tried to phone her, and there was no answer. I wonder if you know where I can reach her?"

"Why, yes," Freida said. "She's in Las Vegas."

"What!"

"Yes. Her brother-in-law was killed in a car crash there. She . . ."

"You mean she's here? Now?"

"Well, I suppose so. She caught a plane early this evening. Yes, I'm sure she's there by now. Her sister called, you see. Alice. She called and asked Anne to come right away. Terrible thing, her husband getting killed like . . ."

"Oh, Christ!" Davis said. He thought for a moment and then asked, "Did she say where I could reach her?"

"Yes. Just a moment."

Freida put the phone down with a clatter, and Davis waited impatiently. By the time she returned, he was ready to start chewing the mouthpiece.

"What's the address?" he asked.

"It's outside of Las Vegas. A rooming house. Alice and Tony were lucky to get such a nice . . ."

"Please, the address!"

"Well, all right," Freida said, a little miffed. She read off the address and Davis scribbled it quickly. He said goodbye, and hung up immediately. There was no time for checking plane schedules now. No time for finding out which plane Anne had caught out of Frisco, nor for finding out what time it had arrived in Vegas.

There was only time to tuck MacGregor's .38 into the waistband of his trousers and then run like hell down to the street. He caught a cab and reeled off the address, and then sat on the edge of his seat while the lights of Vegas dimmed behind him.

When the cabbie pulled up in front of the clapboard structure, he gave him a fiver and then leaped out of the car. He ran up the front steps and pulled the door pull, listening to steps approaching inside. A white-haired woman opened the door, and Davis said, "Alice Radner. Where?"

"Upstairs, but who . . .?"

Davis shoved the woman aside and started up the flight of steps, not looking back. There was a door at the top of the stairwell, and he rapped on it loudly. When he received no answer, he shouted, "I know you're in there! Open the goddamn door!"

The door opened instantly, and Davis found himself looking into the bore of a .22.

"Come in," a woman's voice said softly.

"Where is she?" she asked.

"I'm afraid I had to tie her and gag her. She raised a bit of a fuss when she got here."

He stepped into the room, and she closed the door behind him. Anne was lying on the bed, her hands tied behind her, a scarf stuffed in her mouth. He made a move toward her and the voice came from the doorway, cool and crisp.

"Leave her alone."

"Why?" Davis said. "It's all over now, anyway."

She smiled, but there was no mirth in her eyes. "You should have stayed out of it. From the very beginning."

"Everybody's been telling me that," Davis said. "Right from go."

"You should have paid more attention to them, Mr. Davis. All this might have been avoided then."

"All what?"

She did not answer. She opened the door again, and called, "It's all right, Mrs. Mulready. He's a friend of mine." Then she slammed the door and bolted it.

"That takes care of her," she said, the .22 steady in her hand. She was a beautiful woman with a pale complexion and blue eyes set against the ivory of her skin. She stared at Davis solemnly.

"It all seemed out of whack," Davis said, "but I didn't know just where. It all pointed to Tony Radner and Alice Trimble, but I couldn't conceive of her as a murderess. Sure, I figured Tony led her into it. A woman in love can be talked into anything. But when I learned about Tony's accident here, a new Alice Trimble took shape. Not the gal who was talked into anything, and not the gal who'd do anything for love. This new Alice Trimble was a cold-blooded killer, a murderess who . . ."

Davis saw Anne's eyes widen. She struggled to speak.

"Anne," he said, "tell me something. Was your sister a redhead?"

Anne nodded dumbly, and he saw the confused look that stabbed her eyes. It was then that he realized he'd unconsciously used the past tense in talking about her sister.

"I'm sorry," he said. "I'm sorry as hell, Anne." He paused and drew a deep breath. "Alice is dead."

It was almost as if he'd struck her. She flinched, and then a strangled cry tried to shove its way past the gag.

"Believe me," he said, "I'm sorry. I . . ." He wiped his hand across his lips and then said, "I never thought to ask. About her hair, I mean. Hell, I had her picture and that was all I needed to identify her. I'm . . . I'm sorry, Anne."

He saw the tears spring into her eyes, and he went to her in spite of the .22 that was still pointed at him. He ripped the gag from her mouth, and she said, "I don't understand. I . . . what . . . what do you mean?"

"Alice left you on the sixth," he said, "to meet Tony Radner, allegedly to marry him. She didn't know about the trap that had been planned by Tony and Janet Carruthers."

Anne took her eyes from Davis and looked at the .22 in the woman's hand. "Is . . . is that who . . ."

"Janet Carruthers," Davis said, "who wanted to be free of her husband more than anything else in the world. But not at the expense of cutting herself off without a cent. So she and Tony figured it all out, and they started looking for a redhead who would take the hook. Your sister came along, starry-eyed and innocent, and Radner led her to the chopping block."

Davis paused and turned to the redhead with the gun. "I can fill it in, if you like. A lot of guessing, but I think I'm right."

"Go ahead," Janet said. "Fill it in."

"Sure. Alice met Tony as scheduled on the day they were to be married. He probably suggested a drink in celebration, drugged her, and then took her some place to get her into some of your clothes. He drove her to the airport because your signature was necessary on the insurance policy. You insured Alice, who was now in Janet Carruthers' clothing, with Janet Carruthers' identification in case anything was left of her after the crash, for two hundred thousand dollars. And Janet Carruthers' beneficiaries were Mr. and Mrs. Anthony Radner. You knew that Nick would be on the DC-4, but outside of him, no one else on the plane knew what you looked like. It would be simple to substitute Alice for you. You left the airport, probably to go directly to City Hall to wait for Tony. Tony waited until Nick took a pilot up on a test, and then he brought Alice to the plane, dumped her into her seat, with the bomb in her suitcase, and left to meet you. You got married shortly after the DC-4 took off. You used Alice Trimble's name, and most likely the identification—if it was needed—that Tony had taken from her. The switch had been completed, and you were now Mrs. Radner. You flew together to Las Vegas, and as soon as the DC-4 crashed, you made your claim for the two hundred G's."

"You're right except for the drug, Mr. Davis. That would have been overdoing it a bit."

"All right, granted. What'd Tony do, just get her too damned drunk to walk or know what was going on?"

"Exactly. Her wedding day, you know. It wasn't difficult."

Davis heard a sob catch in Anne's throat. He glanced at her briefly and then said to Janet, "Did Tony know he was going to be driving into a pile of rocks?"

Janet smiled. "Poor Tony. No, I'm afraid he didn't know. That part was all my idea. Even down to stripping the brakes. Tony never knew what hit him."

"Neither did all the people on that DC-4. It was a long way to go for a lousy hunk of cash," Davis said. "Was Tony insured, too?"

"Yes," Janet said, "but not for much." She smiled. "Enough, though."

Davis nodded. "One after the other, right down the line. And then you sent for Anne because she was the only living person who could know you were *not* Alice Trimble. And it had to be fast, especially after that picture appeared in the Las Vegas paper."

"Was that how you found out?" she asked.

"Exactly how. The picture was captioned *Alice Radner* but the girl didn't match the one in the photo I had. Then I began thinking about the color of Alice's hair, which I knew was light, and it got clear as a bell." He shook his head sadly. "I still don't know how you hoped to swing it. You obviously sent for Anne because you were afraid someone would recognize you in Frisco. Hell, someone would have recognized you sooner or later, anyway."

"In Mexico?" Janet asked. "Or South America? I doubt it. Two hundred thousand can do a lot outside of this country, Mr. Davis. Plus what I'll get on Tony's death. I'll manage nicely, don't you worry." She smiled pleasantly.

Davis smiled back. "Go ahead," he said. "Shoot. And then try to explain the shots to your landlady."

Janet Carruthers walked to the dresser, keeping the gun on Davis. "I hadn't wanted to do it here," she said, shrugging. "I was going to take Miss Trimble away after everyone was asleep. You're forcing my hand, though." She opened a drawer and came out with a long, narrow cylinder. The cylinder had holes punched into its sides, and Davis knew a silencer when he saw one. He saw Janet fitting the silencer to the end of the .22 and he saw the dull gleam in her eyes and knew it was time to move. He threw back his coat and reached for the .38 in his waistband. The .22 went off with a sharp *pouff* and he felt the small bullet rip into his shoulder. But he'd squeezed the trigger of the .38 and he saw her arm jerk as his larger bullet tore flesh and bone. Her fingers opened, and the silenced gun fell to the floor.

Her face twisted in pain. She closed her eyes, and he kicked the gun away, and then she began swearing. She kept swearing when he took her good arm and twisted it behind her back.

He heard footsteps rushing up the stairs, and then the landlady shouted. "What is it? *What is it?*"

"Get the police!" he yelled through the closed door. "Get them fast."

"You don't know what you're doing," Janet said. "This will kill my father."

Davis looked over to where Anne sat sobbing on the bed. He wanted to go to her and clasp her into his arms, but there would be time for that later.

"My father . . ." Janet started.

"Your father still has Nick," Davis said, "and his porcelain." His shoulder ached, and the trickle of blood down his jacket front was not pleasant to watch. He paused and lifted his eyes to Janet's. "That's all your father ever had."

Though this story was originally published in the sixties, you can hear the eighties and nineties in it—hear Joseph Wambaugh and James Ellroy and Sandra Scoppettone and Sara Paretsky and Marcia Muller in it. Hear race riots and angry cops and sad blown-out urban ghosts skittering on the very edges of existence. And hear hotshot TV reporters who would much rather tell us lies than truths.

And, of course, you can hear in it the kind of writer Joe Gores himself would go on to be—inventive, restless, eager, and, most especially, unafraid of new approaches to old writing problems.

Gores spent a long time in Hollywood working on movies and TV shows. Fortunately, he's done his penance by producing four new and wonderful novels in a reasonably short span of time.

Even in his comedies, and he's written some good ones, there's always an abiding melancholy in the protagonist, a man desperately trying to make sense of a world that makes no sense at all.

The Second Coming
JOE GORES

"But fix thy eyes upon the valley: for the river of blood draws nigh, in which boils every one who by violence injuries other."
Canto XII, 46–48
THE INFERNO OF DANTE ALIGHIERI

I've thought about it a lot, man; like why Victor and I made that terrible scene out there at San Quentin, putting ourselves on that it was just for kicks; they were a thing with him. He was a sharp dark-haired cat with bright eyes, built lean and hard like a French skin-diver. His old man dug only money, so he'd always had plenty of bread. We got this idea out at his pad on Potrero Hill—a penthouse, of course—one afternoon when we were lying around on the sun-porch in swim trunks and drinking gin.

297

"You know, man," he said, "I have made about every scene in the world. I have balled all the chicks, red and yellow and black and white, and I have gotten high on muggles, bluejays, redbirds, and mescaline. I have even tried the white stuff a time or two. But—"

"You're a goddamned tiger, dad."

"—but there is one kick I've never had, man."

When he didn't go on I rolled my head off the quart gin bottle I was using for a pillow and looked at him. He was giving me a shot with those hot, wild eyes of his.

"So like what is it?"

"I've never watched an execution."

I thought about it a minute, drowsily. The sun was so hot it was like nailing me right to the air mattress. Watching an execution. Seeing a man go through the wall. A groovy idea for an artist.

"Too much," I murmured. "I'm with you, dad."

The next day, of course, I was back at work on some abstracts for my first one-man show and had forgotten all about it; but that night Victor called me up.

"Did you write to the warden up at San Quentin today, man? He has to contact the San Francisco police chief and make sure you don't have a record and aren't a psycho and are useful to the community."

So I went ahead and wrote the letter because even sober it still seemed a cool idea for some kicks; I knew they always need twelve witnesses to make sure that the accused isn't sneaked out the back door or something at the last minute like an old Jimmy Cagney movie. Even so, I lay dead for two months before the letter came. The star of our show would be a stud who'd broken into a house trailer near Fort Ord to rape this Army lieutenant's wife, only right in the middle of it she'd started screaming so he'd put a pillow over her face to keep her quiet until he could finish. But she'd quit breathing. There were eight chicks on the jury and I think like three of them got broken ankles in the rush to send him to the gas chamber. Not that I cared. Kicks, man.

Victor picked me up at seven-thirty in the morning, an hour before we were supposed to report to San Quentin. He was wearing this really hip Italian import, and fifty-dollar shoes, and a narrow-brim hat with a little feather in it, so all he needed was a briefcase to be Chairman of the Board. The top was down on the Mercedes, cold as it was, and when he saw my black suit and hand-knit tie he flashed this crazy white-toothed grin you'd never see in any Director's meeting.

"*Too much*, killer! If you'd like comb your hair you could pass for an undertaker coming after the body."

Since I am a very long, thin cat with black hair always hanging in my eyes, who fully dressed weighs as much as a medium-sized collie, I guess he wasn't too far off. I put a pint of José Cuervo in the side pocket of the car and we split. We were both really turned on: I mean this senseless, breathless hilarity as if we'd just heard the world's funniest joke. Or were just going to.

It was one of those chilly California brights with blue sky and cold sunshine and here and there a cloud like Mr. Big was popping Himself a cap down beyond the horizon. I dug it all: the sail of a lone early yacht out in the Bay like a tossed-away paper cup; the whitecaps flipping around out by Angel Island like they were stoned out of their minds; the top down on the 300-SL so we could smell salt and feel the icy bite of the wind. But beyond the tunnel on U.S. 101, coming down towards Marin City, I felt a sudden sharp chill as if a cloud had passed between me and the sun, but none had; and then I dug for the first time what I was actually doing.

Victor felt it, too, for he turned to me and said, "Must maintain cool, dad."

"I'm with it."

San Quentin Prison, out on the end of its peninsula, looked like a sprawled ugly dragon sunning itself on a rock; we pulled up near the East Gate and there were not even any birds singing. Just a bunch of quiet cats in black, Quakers or Mennonites or something, protesting capital punishment by their silent presence as they'd done ever since Chessman had gotten his out there. I felt dark frightened things move around inside me when I saw them.

"Let's fall out right here, dad," I said in a momentary sort of panic, "and catch the matinee next week."

But Victor was in kicksville, like desperate to put on all those squares in the black suits. When they looked over at us he jumped up on the back of the bucket seat and spread his arms wide like the Sermon on the Mount. With his tortoise-shell shades and his flashing teeth and that suit which had cost three yards, he looked like Christ on his way to Hollywood.

"Whatsoever ye do unto the least of these, my brethren, ye do unto me," he cried in this ringing apocalyptic voice.

I grabbed his arm and dragged him back down off the seat. "For Christ sake, man, cool it!"

But he went into high laughter and punched my arm with feverish exuberance, and then jerked a tiny American flag from his inside jacket pocket and began waving it around above the windshield. I could see the sweat on his forehead.

"It's worth it to live in this country!" he yelled at them.

He put the car in gear and we went on. I looked back and saw one of those cats crossing himself. It put things back in perspective: they were from nowhere. The Middle Ages. Not that I judged them: that was their scene, man. Unto every cat what he digs the most.

The guard on the gate directed us to a small wooden building set against the outside wall, where we found five other witnesses. Three of them were reporters, one was a fat cat smoking a .45 caliber stogy like a politician from Sacramento, and the last was an Army type in lieutenant's bars, his belt buckle and insignia looking as if he'd been up all night with a can of Brasso.

A guard came in and told us to surrender everything in our pockets and get a receipt for it. We had to remove our shoes, too; they were too heavy for the fluoroscope. Then they put us through this groovy little room one-by-one to x-ray us for cameras and so on; they don't want anyone making the Kodak scene while they're busy dropping the pellets. We ended up inside the prison with our shoes back on and with our noses full of that old prison detergent-disinfectant stink.

The politician type, who had those cold slitted eyes like a Sherman tank, started coming on with rank jokes: but everyone put him down, hard, even the reporters. I guess nobody but fuzz ever gets used to executions. The Army stud was at parade rest with a face so pale his freckles looked like a charge of shot. He had reddish hair.

After a while five guards came in to make up the twelve required witnesses. They looked rank, as fuzz always do, and got off in a corner in a little huddle, laughing and gassing together like a bunch of kids kicking a dog. Victor and I sidled over to hear what they were saying.

"Who's sniffing the eggs this morning?" asked one.

"I don't know, I haven't been reading the papers." He yawned when he answered.

"Don't you remember?" urged another, "it's the guy who smothered the woman in the house trailer. Down in the Valley by Salinas."

"Yeah. Soldier's wife; and he was raping her and . . ."

Like dogs hearing the plate rattle, they turned in unison toward the Army lieutenant; but just then more fuzz came in to march us to the observation room. We went in a column of twos with a guard beside each one, everyone unconsciously in step as if following a cadence call. I caught myself listening for measured mournful drum rolls.

The observation room was built right around the gas chamber, with rising tiers of benches for extras in case business was brisk. The chamber itself was hexagonal; the three walls in our room were of plate glass with a waist-high brass rail around the outside like the railing in an old-time saloon. The three other walls were steel plate, with a heavy door, rivet-studded, in the center one, and a small observation window in each of the others.

Inside the chamber were just these two massive chairs, probably oak, facing the rear walls side-by-side; their backs were high enough to come to the nape of the neck of anyone sitting in them. Under each was like a bucket that I knew contained hydrochloric acid. At a signal the executioner would drop sodium cyanide pellets into a chute; the pellets would roll down into the bucket; hydrocyanic acid gas would form; and the cat in the chair would be wasted.

The politician type, who had this rich fruity baritone like Burl Ives, asked why they had two chairs.

"That's in case there's a double-header, dad," I said.

"You're kidding." But by his voice the idea pleased him. Then he wheezed plaintively: "I don't see why they turn the chairs away—we can't even watch his face while it's happening to him."

He was a true rank genuine creep, right out from under a rock with the slime barely dry on his scales; but I wouldn't have wanted his dreams. I think he was one of those guys who tastes the big draught many times before he swallows it.

We milled around like cattle around the chute when they smell the blood from inside and know they're somehow involved; then we heard sounds and saw the door in the back of the chamber swing open. A uniformed guard appeared to stand at attention, followed by a priest dressed all in black like Zorro, with his face hanging down to his belly button. He must have been a new man, because he had trouble maintaining his cool: just standing there beside the guard he dropped his little black book on the floor like three times in a row.

The Army cat said to me, as if he'd wig out unless he broke the silence: "They . . . have it arranged like a stage play, don't they?"

"But no encores," said Victor hollowly.

Another guard showed up in the doorway and they walked in the condemned man. He was like sort of a shock. You expect a stud to *act* like a murderer: I mean, cringe at the sight of the chair because he knows this is it, there's finally no place to go, no appeal to make, or else bound in there full of cheap bravado and go-to-hell. But he just seemed mildly interested, nothing more.

He wore a white suit with the sleeves rolled up, suntan that looked Army issue, and no tie. Under thirty, brown crewcut hair—the terrible thing is that I cannot even remember the features on his face, man. The

A MODERN TREASURY OF GREAT DETECTIVES

closest I could come to a description would be that he resembled the Army cat right there beside me with his nose to the glass.

The one thing I'll never forget is that stud's hands. He'd been on Death Row all these months, and here his hands were still red and chapped and knobby, as if he'd still been out picking turnips in the San Joaquin Valley. Then I realized: I was thinking of him in the past tense.

Two fuzz began strapping him down in the chair. A broad leather strap across the chest, narrower belts on the arms and legs. God they were careful about strapping him in. I mean they wanted to make sure he was comfortable. And all the time he was talking with them. Not that we could hear it, but I suppose it went *that's fine, fellows, no, that strap isn't too tight, gee, I hope I'm not making you late for lunch.*

That's what bugged me, he was so damned *apologetic*! While they were fastening him down over that little bucket of oblivion, that poor dead lonely son of a bitch twisted around to look over his shoulder at us, and he *smiled*. I mean if he'd had an arm free he might have *waved*! One of the fuzz, who had white hair and these sad gentle eyes like he was wearing a hair shirt, patted him on the head on the way out. No personal animosity, son, just doing my job.

After that the tempo increased, like your heartbeat when you're on a black street at three a.m. and the echo of your own footsteps begins to sound like someone following you. The warden was at one observation window, the priest and the doctor at the other. The blackrobe made the sign of the cross, having a last go at the condemned, but he was digging only Ben Casey. Here was this M.D. cat who'd taken the Hippocratic Oath to preserve life, waving his arms around like a TV director to show that stud the easiest way to *die*.

Hold your breath, then breathe deeply: you won't feel a thing. Of course hydrocyanic acid gas melts your guts into a red-hot soup and burns out every fiber in the lining of your lungs, but you won't be really feeling it as you jerk around: that'll just be raw nerve endings.

Like they should have called *his* the Hypocritical Oath.

So there we were, three yards and half an inch of plate glass apart, with us staring at him and him by just turning his head able to stare right back: but there were a million light years between the two sides of the glass. He didn't turn. He was shrived and strapped in and briefed on how to die, and he was ready for the fumes. I found out afterwards that he had even willed his body to medical research.

I did a quick take around.

Victor was sweating profusely, his eyes glued to the window.

The politician was pop-eyed, nose pressed flat and belly indented by the brass rail, pudgy fingers like plump garlic sausages smearing the glass on either side of his head. A look on his face, already, like that of a stud making it with a chick.

The reporters seemed ashamed, as if someone had caught them peeking over the transom into the ladies' john.

The Army cat just looked sick.

Only the fuzz were unchanged, expending no more emotion on this than on their targets after rapid-fire exercises at the range.

On no face was there hatred.

Suddenly, for the first time in my life, I was part of it. I wanted to yell out *STOP*! We were about to gas this stud and *none of us wanted him to die!* We've created this society and we're all responsible for what it does, but none of us as individuals is willing to take that responsibility. We're like that Nazi cat at Nuremberg who said that everything would have been all right if they'd only given him more ovens.

The warden signaled. I heard gas whoosh up around the chair.

The condemned man didn't move. He was following doctor's orders. Then he took the huge gulping breath the M.D. had pantomimed. All of a sudden he threw this tremendous convulsion, his body straining up against the straps, his head slewed around so I could see his eyes were shut tight and his lips were pulled back from his teeth. Then he started panting like a baby in an oxygen tent, swiftly and shallowly. Only it wasn't oxygen his lungs were trying to work on.

The lieutenant stepped back smartly from the window, blinked, and puked on the glass. His vomit hung there for an instant like a phosphorus bomb burst in a bunker; then two fuzz were supporting him from the room and we were all jerking back from the mess. All except the politician. He hadn't even noticed: he was in Henry Millersville, getting his sex kicks the easy way.

I guess the stud in there had never dug that he was supposed to be gone in two seconds without pain, because his body was still arched up in that terrible bow, and his hands were still claws. I could see the muscles standing out along the sides of his jaws like marbles. Finally he flopped back and just hung there in his straps like a machine-gunned paratrooper.

But that wasn't the end. He took another huge gasp, so I could see his ribs pressing out against his white shirt. After that one, twenty seconds. We decided that he had cut out.

Then another gasp. Then nothing. Half a minute nothing.

Another of those final terrible shuddering racking gasps. At last: all through. All used up. Making it with the angels.

But then he did it *again*. Every fiber of that dead wasted comic thrown-away body strained for air on this one. No air: only hydrocyanic acid gas. Just nerves, like the fish twitching after you whack it on the skull with the back edge of the skinning knife. Except that it wasn't a fish we were seeing die.

His head flopped sideways and his tongue came out slyly like the tongue of a dead deer. Then this gunk ran out of his mouth. It was just saliva—they said it couldn't be anything else—but it reminded me of the residue after light-line resistors have been melted in an electrical fire. That kind of black. That kind of scorched.

Very softly, almost to himself, Victor murmured: "Later, dad."

That was it. Dig you in the hereafter, dad. Ten little minutes and you're through the wall. Mistah Kurtz, he dead. Mistah Kurtz, he very very goddamn dead.

I believed it. Looking at what was left of that cat was like looking at a chick who's gotten herself bombed on the heavy, so when you hold a match in front of her eyes the pupils don't react and there's no one home, man. No one. Nowhere. End of the lineville.

We split.

But on the way out I kept thinking of that Army stud, and wondering what had made him sick. Was it because the cat in the chair had been the last to enter, no matter how violently, the body of his beloved, and now even that feeble connection had been severed? Whatever the reason, his body had known what perhaps his mind had refused to accept: this ending was no new beginning, this death would not restore his dead chick to him. This death, no matter how just in his eyes, had generated only nausea.

Victor and I sat in the Mercedes for a long time with the top down, looking out over that bright beautiful empty peninsula, not named, as you might think, after a saint, but after some poor dumb Indian they had hanged there a hundred years or so before. Trees and clouds and blue water, and still no birds making the scene. Even the cats in the black suits had vanished, but now I understood why they'd been there. In their silent censure, they had been sounding the right gong, man. *We* were the ones from the Middle Ages.

Victor took a deep shuddering breath as if he could never get enough air. Then he said in a barely audible voice: "How did you dig that action, man?"

I gave a little shrug and, being myself, said the only thing I could say. "It was a gas, dad."

"I dig, man. I'm hip. A gas."

Something was wrong with the way he said it, but I broke the seal on the tequila and we killed it in fifteen minutes, without even a lime to suck in between. Then he started the car and we cut out, and I realized what was wrong. Watching that cat in the gas chamber, Victor had realized for the very first time that life is far, far more than just kicks. We were both partially responsible for what had happened in there, and we had been ineluctably diminished by it.

On U.S. 101 he coked the Mercedes up to 104 m.p.h. through the traffic, and held it there. It was wild: it was the end: but I didn't sound. I was alone without my Guide by the boiling river of blood. When the Highway Patrol finally stopped us, Victor was coming on so strong and I was coming on so mild that they surrounded us with their holster flaps unbuckled, and checked our veins for needle marks.

I didn't say a word to them, man, not one. Not even my name. Like they had to look in my wallet to see who I was. And while they were doing that, Victor blew his cool entirely. You know, biting, foaming at the mouth, the whole bit—he gave a very good show until they hit him on the back of the head with a gun butt. I just watched.

They lifted his license for a year, nothing else, because his old man spent a lot of bread on a shrinker who testified that Victor had temporarily wigged out, and who had him put away in the zoo for a time. He's back now, but he still sees that wig picker, three times a week at forty clams a shot.

He needs it. A few days ago I saw him on Upper Grant, stalking lithely through a gray raw February day with the fog in, wearing just a T-shirt and jeans—and no shoes. He seemed agitated, pressed, confined within his own concerns, but I stopped him for a minute.

"Ah . . . How you making it, man? Like, ah, what's the gig?"

He shook his head cautiously. "They will not let us get away with it, you know. Like to them, man, just living is a crime."

"Why no strollers, dad?"

"I cannot wear shoes." He moved closer and glanced up and down the street, and said with tragic earnestness: "I can hear only with the soles of my feet, man."

Then he nodded and padded away through the crowds on silent naked soles like a puzzled panther, drifting through the fruiters and drunken teenagers and fuzz trying to bust some cat for possession who have inherited North Beach from the true swingers. I guess all Victor wants to listen to now is Mother Earth: all he wants to hear is the comforting sound of the worms, chewing away.

Chewing away, and waiting for Victor; and maybe for the Second Coming.

Ed Bryant started out as a science fiction writer of great note, and then gradually developed a consuming interest in the modern form of dark fantasy. Good as his sf was, his horror stories are even better. And his few forays into suspense fiction are better yet.

This story is one of the classics of our time, the first believably feminist crime story written by a man. And it is also, maybe best of all, funny as hell in its sly and knowing way.

Whenever I teach a writing class, I hand out Xerox copies of this story and say, "This is what modern suspense fiction should be all about."

Fresh, sassy, troubling, sad, and ultimately triumphant, it is a ringing denunciation of the wrong kind of guy—and the right kind of woman.

While She Was Out
EDWARD BRYANT

It was what her husband said then that was the last straw.

"Christ," muttered Kenneth disgustedly from the family room. He grasped a Bud longneck in one red-knuckled hand, the cable remote tight in the other. This was the time of night when he generally fell into the largest number of stereotypes. "I swear to God you're on the rag three weeks out of every month. PMS, my ass."

Della Myers deliberately bit down on what she wanted to answer. P*X*MS, she thought. That's what the twins' teacher had called it last week over coffee after the parent-teacher conference Kenneth had skipped. Pre-holiday syndrome. It took a genuine effort not to pick up the cordless Northwestern Bell phone and brain Kenneth with one savage, cathartic swipe. "I'm going out."

"So?" said her husband. "This is Thursday. Can't be the auto mechanics made simple for wusses. Self defense?" He shook his head.

"That's every other Tuesday. Something new, honey? Maybe a therapy group?"

"I'm going to Southeast Plaza. I need to pick up some things."

"Get the extra-absorbent ones," said her husband. He grinned and thumbed up the volume. ESPN was bringing in wide shots of something that looked vaguely like group tennis from some sweaty-looking third-world country.

"Wrapping paper," she said. "I'm getting some gift-wrap and ribbon." Were there fourth-world countries? she wondered. Would they accept political refugees from America? "Will you put the twins to bed by nine?"

"Stallone's on HBO at nine," Kenneth said. "I'll bag 'em out by half-past eight."

"Fine." She didn't argue.

"I'll give them a good bedtime story." He paused. "The Princess and the Pea."

"Fine." Della shrugged on her long down-filled coat. Any more, she did her best not to swallow the bait. "I told them they could each have a chocolate chip cookie with their milk."

"Christ, Della. Why the hell don't we just adopt the dentist? Maybe give him an automatic monthly debit from the checking account?"

"One cookie apiece," she said, implacable.

Kenneth shrugged, apparently resigned.

She picked up the keys to the Subaru. "I won't be long."

"Just be back by breakfast."

Della stared at him. What if I don't come back at all? She had actually said that once. Kenneth had smiled and asked whether she was going to run away with the gypsies, or maybe go off to join some pirates. It had been a temptation to say yes, dammit, yes, I'm going. But there were the twins. Della suspected pirates didn't take along their children. "Don't worry," she said. I've got nowhere else to go. But she didn't say that aloud.

Della turned and went upstairs to the twins' room to tell them good night. Naturally they both wanted to go with her to the mall. Each was afraid she wasn't going to get the hottest item in the Christmas doll department—the Little BeeDee Birth Defect Baby. There had been a run on the BeeDees, but Della had shopped for the twins early. "Daddy's going to tell you a story," she promised. The pair wasn't impressed.

"I want to see Santa," Terri said, with dogged, five-year-old insistence.

"You both saw Santa. Remember?"

"I forgot some things. An' I want to tell him again about BeeDee."

"Me, too," said Tammi. With Tammi, it was always "me too."

"Maybe this weekend," said Della.

"Will Daddy remember our cookies?" said Terri.

Before she exited the front door, Della took the chocolate chip cookies from the kitchen closet and set the sack on the stairstep where Kenneth could not fail to stumble over it.

"So long," she called.

"Bring me back something great from the mall," he said. His only other response was to heighten the crowd noise from Upper Zambo-somewhere-or-other.

Sleety snow was falling, the accumulation beginning to freeze on the streets. Della was glad she had the Subaru. So far this winter, she hadn't needed to use the four-wheel drive, but tonight the reality of having it reassured her.

Southeast Plaza was a mess. This close to Christmas, the normally spacious parking lots were jammed. Della took a chance and circled the row of spaces nearest to the mall entrances. If she were lucky, she'd be able to react instantly to someone's backup lights and snaffle a parking place within five seconds of its being vacated. That didn't happen. She cruised the second row, the third. Then—There! She reacted without thinking, seeing the vacant spot just beyond a metallic blue van. She swung the Subaru to the left.

And stamped down hard on the brake.

Some moron had parked an enormous barge of an ancient Plymouth so that it overlapped two diagonal spaces.

The Subaru slid to a stop with its nose about half an inch from the Plymouth's dinosaurian bumper. In the midst of her shock and sudden anger, Della saw the chrome was pocked with rust. The Subaru's headlights reflected back at her.

She said something unpleasant, the kind of language she usually only thought in dark silence. Then she backed her car out of the truncated space and resumed the search for parking. What Della eventually found was a free space on the extreme perimeter of the lot. She resigned herself to trudging a quarter mile through the slush. She hadn't worn boots. The icy water crept into her flats, soaked her toes.

"Shit," she said. "Shit shit shit."

Her shortest-distance-between-two points course took her past the Plymouth hogging the two parking spots. Della stopped a moment, contemplating the darkened behemoth. It was a dirty gold with the remnants of a vinyl roof peeling away like the flaking of a scabrous scalp. In the glare of the mercury vapor lamp, she could see that the rocker panels were riddled with rust holes. Odd. So much corrosion didn't happen in the dry Colorado air. She glanced curiously at the rear license plate. It was obscured with dirty snow.

She stared at the huge old car and realized she was getting angry. Not just irritated. Real, honest-to-god, hardcore pissed off. What kind of imbeciles would take up two parking spaces on a rotten night just two weeks before Christmas?

Ones that drove a vintage, not-terribly-kept-up Plymouth, obviously.

Without even thinking about what she was doing, Della took out the spiral notebook from her handbag. She flipped to the blank page past tomorrow's grocery list and uncapped the fine-tip marker (it was supposed to write across anything—in this snow, it had *better*) and scrawled a message:

DEAR JERK, IT'S GREAT YOU COULD USE UP TWO PARKING SPACES ON A NIGHT LIKE THIS. EVER HEAR OF THE JOY OF SHARING?

She paused, considering; then appended:

—A CONCERNED FRIEND

Della folded the paper as many times as she could, to protect it from the wet, then slipped it under the driver's-side wiper blade.

It wouldn't do any good—she was sure this was the sort of driver who ordinarily would have parked illegally in the handicapped zone—but it made her feel better. Della walked on to the mall entrance and realized she was smiling.

She bought some rolls of foil wrapping paper for the adult gifts—assuming she actually gave Kenneth anything she'd bought for him—and an ample supply of Strawberry Shortcake pattern for the twins' presents. Della decided to splurge—she realized she was getting tired—and selected a package of pre-tied ribbon bows rather than simply taking a roll. She also bought a package of tampons.

Della wandered the mall for a little while, checking out the shoe stores, looking for something on sale in deep blue, a pair she could wear after Kenneth's office party for staff and spouses. What she *really* wanted were some new boots. Time enough for those after the holiday when the prices went down. Nothing appealed to her. Della knew she should be shopping for Kenneth's family in Nebraska. She couldn't wait forever to mail off their packages.

The hell with it. Della realized she was simply delaying returning home. Maybe she *did* need a therapy group, she thought. There was no relish to the thought of spending another night sleeping beside Kenneth, listening to the snoring that was interrupted only by the grinding of teeth. She thought that the sound of Kenneth's jaws moving against one another must be like hearing a speeded-up recording of continental drift.

She looked at her watch. A little after nine. No use waiting any longer. She did up the front of her coat and joined the flow of shoppers out into the snow.

Della realized, as she passed the rusted old Plymouth, that something wasn't the same. *What's wrong with this picture?* It was the note. It wasn't there. Probably it had slipped out from under the wiper blade with the wind and the water. Maybe the flimsy notebook paper had simply dissolved.

She no longer felt like writing another note. She dismissed the irritating lumber barge from her reality and walked on to her car.

Della let the Subaru warm up for thirty seconds (the consumer auto mechanics class had told her not to let the engine idle for the long minutes she had once believed necessary) and then slipped the shift into reverse.

The passenger compartment flooded with light.

She glanced into the rearview mirror and looked quickly away. A bright, glaring eye had stared back. Another quivered in the side mirror.

"Jesus Christ," she said under her breath. "The crazies are out tonight." She hit the clutch with one foot, the brake with the other, and waited for the car behind her to remove itself. Nothing happened. The headlights in the mirror flicked to bright. "Dammit." Della left the Subaru in neutral and got out of the car.

She shaded her eyes and squinted. The front of the car behind hers looked familiar. It was the gold Plymouth.

Two unseen car-doors clicked open and chunked shut again.

The lights abruptly went out and Della blinked, her eyes trying to adjust to the dim mercury vapor illumination from the pole a few car-lengths away.

She felt a cold thrill of unease in her belly and turned back toward the car.

"I've got a gun," said a voice. "Really." It sounded male and young. "I'll aim at your snatch first."

Someone else giggled, high and shrill.

Della froze in place. This couldn't be happening. It absolutely could not.

Her eyes were adjusting, the glare-phantoms drifting out to the limit of her peripheral vision and vanishing. She saw three figures in front of her, then a fourth. She didn't see a gun.

"Just what do you think you're doing?" she said.

"Not doing *nothin',* yet." That, she saw, was the black one. He stood to the left of the white kid who had claimed to have a gun. The pair was bracketed by a boy who looked Chinese or Vietnamese and a young man with dark, Hispanic good looks. All four looked to be in their late teens or very early twenties. Four young men. Four ethnic groups represented. Della repressed a giggle she thought might be the first step toward hysteria.

"So what are you guys? Working on your merit badge in tolerance? Maybe selling magazine subscriptions?" Della immediately regretted saying that. Her husband was always riding her for smarting off.

"Funny lady," said the Hispanic. "We just happen to get along." He glanced to his left. "You laughing, Huey?"

The black shook his head. "Too cold. I'm shiverin' out here. I didn't bring no clothes for this."

"Easy way to fix that, man," said the white boy. To Della, he said, "Vinh, Tomas, Huey, me, we all got similar interests, you know?"

"Listen—" Della started to say.

"Chuckie," said the black Della now assumed was Huey, "Let's us just shag out of here, okay?"

"*Chuckie?*" said Della.

"Shut up!" said Chuckie. To Huey, he said, "Look, we came up here for a vacation, right? The word is fun." He said to Della, "Listen, we were having a good time until we saw you stick the note under the wiper." His eyes glistened in the vapor-lamp glow. "I don't like getting any static from some 'burb-bitch just 'cause she's on the rag."

"For God's sake," said Della disgustedly. She decided he didn't really have a gun. "Screw off!" The exhaust vapor from the Subaru spiraled up around her. "I'm leaving, boys."

"Any trouble here, Miss?" said a new voice. Everyone looked. It was one of the mall rent-a-cops, bulky in his fur trimmed jacket and Russian-styled cap. His hand lay casually across the unsnapped holster flap at his hip.

"Not if these underage creeps move their barge so I can back out," said Della.

"How about it, guys?" said the rent-a-cop.

Now there *was* a gun, a dark pistol, in Chuckie's hand, and he pointed it at the rent-a-cop's face. "Naw," Chuckie said. "This was gonna be a vacation, but what the heck. No witnesses, I reckon."

"For God's sake," said the rent-a-cop, starting to back away.

Chuckie grinned and glanced aside at his friends. "Remember the security guy at the mall in Tucson?" To Della, he said, "Most of these rent-a-pig companies don't give their guys any ammo. Liability laws and all that shit. Too bad." He lifted the gun purposefully.

The rent-a-cop went for his pistol anyway. Chuckie shot him in the face. Red pulp sprayed out the back of his skull and stained the slush as the man's body flopped back and forth, spasming.

"For chrissake," said Chuckie in exasperation. "Enough already. Relax, man." He leaned over his victim and deliberately aimed and fired, aimed and fired. The second shot entered the rent-a-cop's left eye. The third shattered his teeth.

Della's eyes recorded everything as though she were a movie camera. Everything was moving in slow motion and she was numb. She tried to make things speed up. Without thinking about the decision, she spun and made for her car door. She knew it was hopeless.

"Chuckie!"

"So? Where's she gonna go? We got her blocked. I'll just put one through her windshield and we can go out and pick up a couple of sixpacks, maybe hit the late show at some other mall."

Della heard him fire one more time. Nothing tore through the back of her skull. He was still blowing apart the rent-a-cop's head.

She slammed into the Subaru's driver seat and punched the door-lock switch, for all the good that would do. Della hit the four-wheel-drive switch. *That* was what Chuckie hadn't thought about. She jammed the gearshift into first, gunned the engine, and popped the clutch. The Subaru barely protested as the front tires clawed and bounced over the six-inch concrete row barrier. The barrier screeched along the underside of the frame. Then the rear wheels were over and the Subaru fish-tailed momentarily.

Don't over-correct, she thought. It was a prayer.

The Subaru straightened out and Della was accelerating down the mall's outer perimeter service road, slush spraying to either side. Now what? she thought. People must have heard the shots. The lot would be crawling with cops.

But in the meantime—

The lights, bright and blinding, blasted against her mirrors.

Della stamped the accelerator to the floor.

This was crazy! This didn't happen to people—not to *real* people. The mall security man's blood in the snow had been real enough.

In the rearview, there was a sudden flash just above the left-side headlight, then another. It was a muzzle-blast, Della realized. They were shooting at her. It was just like on TV. The scalp on the back of her head itched. Would she feel it when the bullet crashed through?

The twins! Kenneth. She wanted to see them all, to be safely with them. Just be anywhere but here!

Della spun the wheel, ignoring the stop sign and realizing that the access road dead-ended. She could go right or left, so went right. She thought it was the direction of home. Not a good choice. The lights were all behind her now; she could see nothing but darkness ahead. Della tried to remember what lay beyond the mall on this side. There were housing developments, both completed and under construction.

There had to be a 7-Eleven, a filling station, *something*. Anything. But there wasn't, and then the pavement ended. At first the road was suddenly rougher, the potholes yawning deeper. Then the slush-marked asphalt stopped. The Subaru bounced across the gravel; within thirty yards, the gravel deteriorated to roughly graded dirt. The dirt surface more properly could be called mud.

A wooden barrier loomed ahead, the reflective stripes and lightly falling snow glittering in the headlights.

It *was* like on TV, Della thought. She gunned the engine and ducked sideways, even with the dash, as the Subaru plowed into the barrier. She heard a sickening *crack* and shattered windshield glass sprayed down around her. Della felt the car veer. She tried to sit upright again, but the auto was spinning too fast.

The Subaru swung a final time and smacked firm against a low grove of young pine. The engine coughed and stalled. Della hit the light switch. She smelled the overwhelming tang of crushed pine needles flooding with the snow through the space where the windshield had been. The engine groaned when she twisted the key, didn't start.

Della risked a quick look around. The Plymouth's lights were visible, but the car was farther back than she had dared hope. The size of the lights wasn't increasing and the beams pointed up at a steep angle. Probably the heavy Plymouth had slid in the slush, gone off the road, was stuck for good.

She tried the key, and again the engine didn't catch. She heard something else—voices getting closer. Della took the key out of the ignition and glanced around the dark passenger compartment. Was there anything she could use? Anything at all? Not in the glovebox. She knew there was nothing there but the owner's manual and a large pack of sugarless spearmint gum.

The voices neared.

Della reached under the dash and tugged the trunk release. Then she rolled down the window and slipped out into the darkness. She wasn't too stunned to forget that the overhead light would go on if she opened the door.

At least one of the boys had a flashlight. The beam flickered and danced along the snow.

Della stumbled to the rear of the Subaru. By feel, she found the toolbox. With her other hand, she sought out the lug wrench. Then she moved away from the car.

She wished she had a gun. She wished she had learned to *use* a gun. That had been something tagged for a vague future when she'd finished her consumer mechanics course and the self defense workshop, and had some time again to take another night course. It wasn't, she had reminded herself, that she was paranoid. Della simply wanted to be better prepared for the exigencies of living in the city. The suburbs weren't *the city* to Kenneth, but if you were a girl from rural Montana, they were.

She hadn't expected *this*.

She hunched down. Her nose told her the shelter she had found was a hefty clump of sagebrush. She was perhaps twenty yards from the Subaru now. The boys were making no attempt at stealth. She heard them talking to each other as the flashlight beam bobbed around her stalled car.

"So, she in there chilled with her brains all over the wheel?" said Tomas, the Hispanic kid.

"You an optimist?" said Chuckie. He laughed, a high-pitched giggle. "No, she ain't here, you dumb shit. This one's a tough lady." Then he said, "Hey, lookie there!"

"What you doin'?" said Huey. "We ain't got time for that."

"Don't be too sure. Maybe we can use this."

What had he found? Della wondered.

"Now we do what?" said Vinh. He had a slight accent.

"This be the West," said Huey. "I guess now we're mountain men, just like in the movies."

"Right," said Chuckie. "Track her. There's mud. There's snow. How far can she get?"

"There's the trail," said Tomas. "Shine the light over there. She must be pretty close."

Della turned. Hugging the toolbox, trying not to let it clink or clatter, she fled into the night.

They cornered her a few minutes later.

Or it could have been an hour. There was no way she could read her watch. All Della knew was that she had run; she had run and she had attempted circling around to where she might have a shot at making it to the distant lights of the shopping mall. Along the way, she'd felt the brush clawing at her denim jeans and the mud and slush attempting to suck down her shoes. She tried to make out shapes in the clouded-over dark, evaluating every murky form as a potential hiding place.

"Hey, baby," said Huey from right in front of her.

Della recoiled, feinted to the side, collided painfully with a wooden fence. The boards gave only slightly. She felt a long splinter drive through the down coat and spear into her shoulder. When Della jerked away, she felt the splinter tear away from its board and then break off.

The flashlight snapped on, the beam at first blinding her, then lowering to focus on her upper body. From their voices, she knew all four were there. Della wanted to free a hand to pull the splinter loose from her shoulder. Instead she continued cradling the blue plastic toolbox.

"Hey," said Chuckie, "what's in that thing? Family treasure, maybe?"

Della remained mute. She'd already gotten into trouble enough, wising off.

"Let's see," said Chuckie. "Show us, Della-honey."

She stared at his invisible face.

Chuckie giggled. "Your driver's license, babe. In your purse. In the car."

Shit, she thought.

"Lousy picture," said Chuckie. "I think maybe we're gonna make your face match it." Again, that ghastly laugh. "Meantime, let's see what's in the box, okay?"

"Jewels, you think?" said Vinh.

"Naw, I don't think," said his leader. "But maybe she was makin' the bank deposit or something." He addressed Della, "You got enough goodies for us, maybe we can be bought off."

No chance, she thought. They want everything. My money, my rings, my watch. She tried to swallow, but her throat was too dry. My life.

"Open the box," said Chuckie, voice mean now.

"Open the box," said Tomas. Huey echoed him. The four started chanting, "Open the box, open the box, open the box."

"All right," she almost screamed. "I'll do it." They stopped their chorus. Someone snickered. Her hands moving slowly, Della's brain raced. Do it, she thought. But be careful. So careful. She let the lug wrench rest across her palm below the toolbox. With her other hand, she unsnapped the catch and slid up the lid toward the four. She didn't think any of them could see in, though the flashlight beam was focused now on the toolbox lid.

Della reached inside, as deliberately as she could, trying to betray nothing of what she hoped to do. It all depended upon what lay on top. Her bare fingertips touched the cold steel of the crescent wrench. Her fingers curled around the handle.

"This is pretty dull," said Tomas. "Let's just rape her."

Now!

She withdrew the wrench, cocked her wrist back and hurled the tool about two feet above the flashlight's glare. Della snapped it just like her daddy had taught her to throw a hardball. She hadn't liked baseball all that much. But now—

The wrench crunched something and Chuckie screamed. The flashlight dropped to the snow.

Snapping shut the toolbox, Della sprinted between Chuckie and the one she guessed was Huey.

The black kid lunged for her and slipped in the muck, toppling face-first into the slush. Della had a peripheral glimpse of Tomas leaping toward her, but his leading foot came down on the back of Huey's head, grinding the boy's face into the mud. Huey's scream bubbled; Tomas cursed and tumbled forward, trying to stop himself with out-thrust arms.

All Della could think as she gained the darkness was, I should have grabbed the light.

She heard the one she thought was Vinh, laughing. "Cripes, guys, neat. Just like Moe and Curley and that other one."

"Shut up," said Chuckie's voice. It sounded pinched and in pain. "Shut the fuck up." The timbre squeaked and broke. "Get up, you dorks. Get the bitch."

Sticks and stones—Della thought. Was she getting hysterical? There was no good reason not to.

As she ran—and stumbled—across the nightscape, Della could feel the long splinter moving with the movement of the muscles in her shoulder. The feeling of it, not just the pain, but the sheer, physical sensation of intrusion, nauseated her.

I've got to stop, she thought. I've got to rest. I've got to think.

Della stumbled down the side of a shallow gulch and found she was splashing across a shallow, frigid stream. Water. It triggered something. Disregarding the cold soaking her flats and numbing her feet, she turned and started upstream, attempting to splash as little as possible. This had worked, she seemed to recall, in *Uncle Tom's Cabin,* as well as a lot of bad prison escape movies.

The boys were hardly experienced mountain men. They weren't Indian trackers. This ought to take care of her trail.

After what she estimated to be at least a hundred yards, when her feet felt like blocks of wood and she felt she was losing her balance, Della clambered out of the stream and struggled up the side of the gulch. She found herself in groves of pine, much like the trees where her Subaru had ended its skid. At least the pungent evergreens supplied some shelter against the prairie wind that had started to rise.

She heard noise from down in the gulch. It was music. It made her think of the twins.

"What the *fuck* are you doing?" Chuckie's voice.

"It's a tribute, man. A gesture." Vinh. "It's his blaster."

Della recognized the tape. Rap music. Run DMC, the Beastie Boys, one of those groups.

"Christ, I didn't mean it." Tomas. "It's her fault."

"Well, he's dead," said Chuckie, "and that's it for him. Now turn that shit off. Somebody might hear."

"Who's going to hear?" said Vinh. "Nobody can hear out here. Just us, and her."

"That's the point. She can."

"So what?" said Tomas. "We got the gun, we got the light. She's got nothin' but that stupid box."

"We *had* Huey," said Chuckie. "Now we don't. Shut off the blaster, dammit."

"Okay." Vinh's voice sounded sullen. There was a loud click and the rap echo died.

Della huddled against the rough bark of a pine trunk, hugging the box and herself. The boy's dead, she thought. So? said her common sense. He would have killed you, maybe raped you, tortured you before pulling the trigger. The rest are going to have to die too.

No.

Yes, said her practical side. You have no choice. They started this.

I put the note under the wiper blade.

Get serious. That was harmless. These three are going to kill you. They will hurt you first, then they'll put the gun inside your mouth and—

Della wanted to cry, to scream. She knew she could not. It was absolutely necessary that she not break now.

Terri, she thought, Tammi. I love you. After a while, she remembered Kenneth. Even you. I love you too. Not much, but some.

"Let's look up above," came the voice from the gully. Chuckie. Della heard the wet scrabbling sounds as the trio scratched and pulled their way up from the stream-bed. As it caught the falling snow, the flashlight looked like the beam from a searchlight at a movie premiere.

Della edged back behind the pine and slowly moved to where the trees were closer together. Boughs laced together, screening her.

"Now what?" said Tomas.

"We split up." Chuckie gestured; the flashlight beam swung wide. "You go through the middle. Vinh and me'll take the sides."

"Then why don't you give me the light?" said Tomas.

"I stole the sucker. It's mine."

"Shit, I could just walk past her."

Chuckie laughed. "Get real, dude. You'll smell her, hear her, somethin'. Trust me."

Tomas said something Della couldn't make out, but the tone was unconvinced.

"Now *do* it," said Chuckie. The light moved off to Della's left. She heard the squelching of wet shoes moving toward her. Evidently Tomas had done some wading in the gully. Either that or the slush was taking its toll.

Tomas couldn't have done better with radar. He came straight for her.

Della guessed the boy was ten feet away from her, five feet, just the other side of the pine. The lug wrench was the spider type, in the shape of a cross. She clutched the black steel of the longest arm and brought her hand back. When she detected movement around the edge of the trunk, she swung with hysterical strength, aiming at his head.

Tomas staggered back. The sharp arm of the lug wrench had caught him under the nose, driving the cartilage back up into his face. About a third of the steel was hidden in flesh. "Unh!" He tried to cry out, but all he could utter was, "Unh, unh!"

"Tomas?" Chuckie was yelling. "What the hell are you doing?"

The flashlight flickered across the grove. Della caught a momentary glimpse of Tomas lurching backward with the lug wrench impaled in his face as though he were wearing some hideous Halloween accessory.

"Unh!" said Tomas once more. He backed into a tree, then slid down the trunk until he was seated in the snow. The flashlight beam jerked across that part of the grove again and Della saw Tomas' eyes stare wide open, dark and blank. Blood was running off the ends of the perpendicular lug wrench arms.

"I see her!" someone yelled. "I think she got Tomas. She's a devil!" Vinh.

"So chill her!"

Della heard branches and brush crashing off to her side. She jerked open the plastic toolbox, but her fingers were frozen and the container crashed to the ground. She tried to catch the contents as they cascaded into the slush and the darkness. Her fingers closed on something, one thing.

The handle felt good. It was the wooden-hafted screwdriver, the sharp one with the slot head. Her auto mechanics teacher had approved. Insulated handle, he'd said. Good forged steel shaft. You could use this hummer to pry a tire off its rim.

She didn't even have time to lift it as Vinh crashed into her. His arms and legs wound around her like eels.

"Got her!" he screamed. "Chuckie, come here and shoot her."

They rolled in the viscid, muddy slush. Della worked an arm free. Her good arm. The one with the screwdriver.

There was no question of asking him nicely to let go, of giving warning, of simply aiming to disable. Her self defense teacher had drilled into all the students the basic dictum of do what you can, do what you have to do. No rules, no apologies.

With all her strength, Della drove the screwdriver up into the base of his skull. She thrust and twisted the tool until she felt her knuckles dig into his stiff hair. Vinh screamed, a high keening wail that cracked and shattered as blood spurted out of his nose and mouth, splattering against Della's neck. The Vietnamese boy's arms and legs tensed and then let go as his body vibrated spastically in some sort of fit.

Della pushed him away from her and staggered to her feet. Her nose was full of the odor she remembered from the twins' diaper pail.

She knew she should retrieve the screwdriver, grasp the handle tightly and twist it loose from Vinh's head. She couldn't. All she could do at this point was simply turn and run. Run again. And hope the survivor of the four boys didn't catch her.

But Chuckie had the light, and Chuckie had the gun. She had a feeling Chuckie was in no mood to give up. Chuckie would find her. He would make her pay for the loss of his friends.

But if she had to pay, Della thought, the price would be dear.

*   *   *

Prices, she soon discovered, were subject to change without warning.

With only one remaining pursuer, Della thought she ought to be able to get away. Maybe not easily, but now there was no crossfire of spying eyes, no ganging-up of assailants. There was just one boy left, even if he *was* a psychopath carrying a loaded pistol.

Della was shaking. It was fatigue, she realized. The endless epinephrine rush of flight and fight. Probably, too, the letdown from just having killed two other human beings. She didn't want to have to think about the momentary sight of blood flowing off the shining ends of the lug wrench, the sensation of how it *felt* when the slot-headed screwdriver drove up into Vinh's brain. But she couldn't order herself to forget these things. It was akin to someone telling her not, under any circumstances, to think about milking a purple cow.

Della tried. No, she thought. Don't think about it at all. She thought about dismembering the purple cow with a chainsaw. Then she heard Chuckie's voice. The boy was still distant, obviously casting around virtually at random in the pine groves. Della stiffened.

"They're cute, Della-honey. I'll give 'em that." He giggled. "Terri and Tammi. God, didn't you and your husband have any more imagination than that?"

No, Della thought. We each had too much imagination. Tammi and Terri were simply the names we finally could agree on. The names of compromise.

"You know something?" Chuckie raised his voice. "Now that I know where they live, I could drive over there in a while and say howdy. They wouldn't know a thing about what was going on, about what happened to their mom while she was out at the mall."

Oh God! thought Della.

"You want me to pass on any messages?"

"You little bastard!" She cried it out without thinking.

"Touchy, huh?" Chuckie slopped across the wet snow in her direction. "Come on out of the trees, Della-honey."

Della said nothing. She crouched behind a deadfall of brush and dead limbs. She was perfectly still.

Chuckie stood equally still, not more than twenty feet away. He stared directly at her hiding place, as though he could see through the night and brush. "Listen," he said. "This is getting real, you know, *boring*." He waited. "We could be out here all night, you know? All my buddies are gone now, and it's thanks to you, lady. Who the hell you think you are, Clint Eastwood?"

Della assumed that was a rhetorical question.

Chuckie hawked deep in his throat and spat on the ground. He rubbed the base of his throat gingerly with a free hand. "You hurt me, Della-honey. I think you busted my collarbone." He giggled. "But I don't hold grudges. In fact—" He paused contemplatively. "Listen now, I've got an idea. You know about droogs? You know, like in that movie?"

Clockwork Orange, she thought. Della didn't respond.

"Ending was stupid, but the start was pretty cool." Chuckie's personality seemed to have mutated into a manic stage. "Well, me droogs is all gone. I need a new gang, and you're real good, Della-honey. I want you should join me."

"Give me a break," said Della in the darkness.

"No, really," Chuckie said. "You're a born killer. I can tell. You and me, we'd be perfect. We'll blow this popsicle stand and have some real fun. Whaddaya say?"

He's serious, she thought. There was a ring of complete honesty in his voice. She floundered for some answer. "I've got kids," she said.

"We'll take 'em along," said Chuckie. "I like kids, always took care of my brothers and sisters." He paused. "Listen, I'll bet you're on the outs with your old man."

Della said nothing. It would be like running away to be a pirate. Wouldn't it?

Chuckie hawked and spat again. "Yeah, I figured. When we pick up your kids, we can waste him. You like that? I can do it, or you can. Your choice."

You're crazy, she thought. "*I* want to," she found herself saying aloud.

"So come out and we'll talk about it."

"You'll kill me."

"Hey," he said, "I'll kill you if you *don't* come out. I got the light and the gun, remember? This way we can learn to trust each other right from the start. I won't kill you. I won't do nothing. Just talk."

"Okay." Why not, she thought. Sooner or later, he'll find his way in here and put the gun in my mouth and—Della stood up—but maybe, just maybe—Agony lanced through her knees.

Chuckie cocked his head, staring her way. "Leave the tools."

"I already did. The ones I didn't use."

"Yeah," said Chuckie. "The ones you used, you used real good." He lowered the beam of the flashlight. "Here you go. I don't want you stumbling and falling and maybe breaking your neck."

Della stepped around the deadfall and slowly walked toward him. His hands were at his sides. She couldn't see if he was holding the gun. She stopped when she was a few feet away.

"Hell of a night, huh?" said Chuckie. "It'll be really good to go inside where it's warm and get some coffee." He held the flashlight so that the beam speared into the sky between them.

Della could make out his thin, pain-pinched features. She imagined he could see hers. "I was only going out to the mall for a few things," she said.

Chuckie laughed. "Shit happens."

"What now?" Della said.

"Time for the horror show." His teeth showed ferally as his lips drew back in a smile. "Guess maybe I sort of fibbed." He brought up his hand, glinting of metal.

"That's what I thought," she said, feeling a cold and distant sense of loss. "Huey, there, going to help?" She nodded to a point past his shoulder.

"Huey?" Chuckie looked puzzled just for a second as he glanced to the side. "Huey's—"

Della leapt with all the spring left in her legs. Her fingers closed around his wrist and the hand with the gun. "Christ!" Chuckie screamed, as her shoulder crashed against the spongy place where his broken collarbone pushed out against the skin.

They tumbled on the December ground, Chuckie underneath, Della wrapping her legs around him as though pulling a lover tight. She burrowed her chin into the area of his collarbone and he screamed again. Kenneth had always joked about the sharpness of her chin.

The gun went off. The flash was blinding, the report hurt her ears. Wet snow plumped down from the overhanging pine branches, a large chunk plopping into Chuckie's wide-open mouth. He started to choke.

Then the pistol was in Della's hands. She pulled back from him, getting to her feet, back-pedaling furiously to get out of his reach. She stared down at him along the blued-steel barrel. The pirate captain struggled to his knees.

"Back to the original deal," he said. "Okay?"

I wish, she almost said. Della pulled the trigger. Again. And again.

"Where the hell have you been?" said Kenneth as she closed the front door behind her. "You've been gone for close to three hours." He inspected her more closely. "Della, honey, are you all right?"

"Don't call me that," she said. "Please." She had hoped she would look better, more normal. Unruffled. Once Della had pulled the Subaru up to the drive beside the house, she had spent several minutes using spit and Kleenex trying to fix her mascara. Such makeup as she'd had along was in her handbag, and she had no idea where that was. Probably the police had it; three cruisers with lights flashing had passed her, going the other way, as she was driving north of Southeast Plaza.

"Your clothes." Kenneth gestured. He stood where he was.

Della looked down at herself. She'd tried to wash off the mud, using snow and a rag from the trunk. There was blood too, some of it Chuckie's, the rest doubtless from Vinh and Tomas.

"Honey, was there an accident?"

She had looked at the driver's side of the Subaru for a long minute after getting home. At least the car drove; it must just have been flooded before. But the insurance company wouldn't be happy. The entire side would need a new paint job.

"Sort of," she said.

"Are you hurt?"

To top it all off, she had felt the slow stickiness between her legs as she'd come up the walk. Terrific. She could hardly wait for the cramps to intensify.

"Hurt?" She shook her head. No. "How are the twins?"

"Oh, they're in bed. I checked a half hour ago. They're asleep."

"Good." Della heard sirens in the distance, getting louder, nearing the neighborhood. Probably the police had found her driver's license in Chuckie's pocket. She'd forgotten that.

"So," said Kenneth. It was obvious to Della that he didn't know at this point whether to be angry, solicitous or funny. "What'd you bring me from the mall?"

Della's right hand was nestled in her jacket pocket. She felt the solid bulk, the cool grip of the pistol.

Outside, the volume of sirens increased.

She touched the trigger. She withdrew her hand from the pocket and aimed the pistol at Kenneth. He looked back at her strangely.

The sirens went past. Through the window, Della caught a glimpse of a speeding ambulance. The sound Dopplered down to a silence as distant as the dream that flashed through her head.

Della pulled the trigger and the *click* seemed to echo through the entire house.

Shocked, Kenneth stared at the barrel of the gun, then up at her eyes.

It was okay. She'd counted the shots. Just like in the movies.

"I think," Della said to her husband, "that we need to talk."

Every few years, somebody writes an article in one of the review magazines about mystery fiction being in a rut. The remedies proposed always seem to be of two varieties—let's take some of the bold new experimental steps science fiction has been doing; or let's go back to the so-called Golden Age (it's Golden only if you don't try to reread the books produced during that era) and start all over again.

As you may have guessed, I'm not much impressed with rallying cries of this sort and I would use "Horn Man" to demonstrate why.

If you're a reader of hardboiled crime fiction, you have read this story, in one form or another, at least fifty times. There's the sad outsider, the Greyhound bus, the gritty urban setting, the wry turn of events.

You could write it yourself, probably, if you had the time or inclination—or so you might think until you've read a few hundred words of this small masterpiece.

Clark Howard, who spends most of his time writing the fine fat bestsellers, brings a poet's tongue and a judge's eye to the human predicament. In very few words, he gives us full measure of at least two lives, and also tells us something about life in our cities as well.

I look on this story as one of the first and most important contemporary hardboiled stories because of the way it addresses mood and theme and feeling more than plot.

Many other Clark Howard stories are nearly as remarkable, including his often-reprinted tale, "Animals."

Horn Man
CLARK HOWARD

When Dix stepped off the Greyhound bus in New Orleans, old Rainey was waiting for him near the terminal entrance. He looked just the same as Dix remembered him. Old Rainey had always looked old, since Dix had known him, ever since Dix had been a little boy. He had skin like black saddle leather and patches of cotton-white hair, and his shoulders were round and stooped. When he was contemplating something, he chewed on the inside of his cheeks, pushing his pursed lips in and out as if he were revving up for speech. He was doing that when Dix walked up to him.

"Hey, Rainey."

Rainey blinked surprise and then his face split into a wide smile of perfect, gleaming teeth. "Well, now. Well, well, well, now." He looked Dix up and down. "They give you that there suit of clothes?"

Dix nodded. "Everyone gets a suit of clothes if they done more than a year." Dix's eyes, the lightest blue possible without being gray, hardened just enough for Rainey to notice. "And I sure done more than a year," he added.

"That's the truth," Rainey said. He kept the smile on his face and changed the subject as quickly as possible. "I got you a room in the Quarter. Figured that's where you'd want to stay."

Dix shrugged. "It don't matter no more."

"It will," Rainey said with the confidence of years. "It will when you hear the music again."

Dix did not argue the point. He was confident that none of it mattered. Not the music, not the French Quarter, none of it. Only one thing mattered to Dix.

"Where is she, Rainey?" he asked. "Where's Madge?"

"I don't rightly know," Rainey said.

Dix studied him for a moment. He was sure Rainey was lying. But it didn't matter. There were others who would tell him.

They walked out of the terminal, the stooped old black man and the tall, prison-hard white man with a set to his mouth and a canvas zip-bag containing all his worldly possessions. It was late afternoon: the sun was almost gone and the evening coolness was coming in. They walked toward the Quarter, Dix keeping his long-legged pace slow to accommodate old Rainey.

Rainey glanced at Dix several times as they walked, chewing inside his mouth and working up to something. Finally he said, "You been playing at all while you was in?"

Dix shook his head. "Not for a long time. I did a little the first year. Used to dry play, just with my mouthpiece. After a while, though, I gave it up. They got a different kind of music over there in Texas. Stompin' music. Not my style." Dix forced a grin at old Rainey. "I ever kill a man again, I'll be sure I'm on *this* side of the Louisiana line.''

Rainey scowled. "You know you ain't never killed nobody, boy," he said harshly. "You know it wudn't you that done it. It was *her*."

Dix stopped walking and locked eyes with old Rainey. "How long have you knowed me?" he asked.

"Since you was eight months old," Rainey said. "You know that. Me and my sistuh, we worked for your grandmamma, Miz Jessie Du-Chatelier. She had the finest gentlemen's house in the Quarter. Me and my sistuh, we cleaned and cooked for Miz Jessie. And took care of you after your own poor mamma took sick with the consumption and died—"

"Anyway, you've knowed me since I was less than one, and now I'm *forty*-one."

Rainey's eyes widened. "Naw," he said, grinning again, "you ain't that old. Naw."

"Forty-one, Rainey. I been gone sixteen years. I got twenty-five, remember? And I done sixteen."

Sudden worry erased Rainey's grin. "Well, if you forty-one how old that make *me*?"

"About two hundred. I don't know. You must be seventy or eighty. Anyway, listen to me now. In all the time you've knowed me, have I ever let anybody make a fool out of me?"

Rainey shook his head. "Never. No way."

"That's right. And I'm not about to start now. But if word got around that I done sixteen years for a killing that was somebody else's, I'd look like the biggest fool that ever walked the levee, wouldn't I?"

"I reckon so," Rainey allowed.

"Then don't ever say again that I didn't do it. Only one person alive knows for certain positive that I didn't do it. And I'll attend to her myself. Understand?"

Rainey chewed the inside of his cheeks for a moment, then asked, "What you fixin' to do about her?"

Dix's light-blue eyes hardened again. "Whatever I have to do, Rainey," he replied.

Rainey shook his head in slow motion. "Lord, Lord, Lord," he whispered.

Old Rainey went to see Gaston that evening at Tradition Hall, the jazz emporium and restaurant that Gaston owned in the Quarter. Gaston was slick and dapper. For him, time had stopped in 1938. He still wore spats.

"How does he look?" Gaston asked old Rainey.

"He *look* good," Rainey said. "He *talk* bad." Rainey leaned close to the white club-owner. "He fixin' to kill that woman. Sure as God made sundowns."

Gaston stuck a sterling-silver toothpick in his mouth. "He know where she is?"

"I don't think so," said Rainey. "Not yet."

"*You* know where she is?"

"Lastest I heard, she was living over on Burgundy Street with some doper."

Gaston nodded his immaculately shaved and lotioned chin. "Correct. The doper's name is LeBeau. He's young. I think he keeps her around to take care of him when he's sick." Gaston examined his beautifully manicured nails. "Does Dix have a lip?"

Rainey shook his head. "He said he ain't played in a while. But a natural like him, he can get his lip back in no time a'tall."

"Maybe," said Gaston.

"He can," Rainey insisted.

"Has he got a horn?"

"Naw. I watched him unpack his bag and I didn't see no horn. So I axed him about it. He said after a few years of not playing, he just give it away. To some cowboy he was in the Texas pen with."

Gaston sighed. "He should have killed that fellow on this side of the state line. If he'd done the killing in Louisiana, he would have went to the pen at Angola. They play good jazz at Angola. Eddie Lumm is up there. You remember Eddie Lumm? Clarinetist. Learned to play from Frank Teschemacher and Jimmie Noone. Eddie killed his old lady. So now he blows at Angola. They play good jazz at Angola."

Rainey didn't say anything. He wasn't sure if Gaston thought Dix had really done the killing or not. Sometimes Gaston *played* like he didn't know a thing, just to see if somebody *else* knew it. Gaston was smart. Smart enough to help keep Dix out of trouble if he was a mind. Which was what old Rainey was hoping for.

Gaston drummed his fingertips silently on the table where they sat. "So. You think Dix can get his lip back with no problem, is that right?"

"Tha's right. He can."

"He planning to come around and see me?"

"I don't know. He probably set on finding that woman first. Then he might not be *able* to come see you."

"Well, see if you can get him to come see me first. Tell him I've got something for him. Something I've been saving for him. Will you do that?"

"You bet." Rainey got up from the table. "I'll go do it right now."

George Tennell was big and beefy and mean. Rumor had it that he had once killed two men by smashing their heads together with such force that he literally knocked their brains out. He had been a policeman for thirty years, first in the colored section, which was the only place he could work in the old days, and now in the *Vieux Carré,* the Quarter, where he was detailed to keep the peace to whatever extent it was possible. He had no family, claimed no friends. The Quarter was his home as well as his job. The only thing in the world he admitted to loving was jazz.

That was why, every night at seven, he sat at a small corner table in Tradition Hall and ate dinner while he listened to the band tune their instruments and warm up. Most nights, Gaston joined him later for a liqueur. Tonight he joined him before dinner.

"Dix got back today," he told the policeman. "Remember Dix?"

Tennell nodded. "Horn man. Killed a fellow in a motel room just across the Texas line. Over a woman named Madge Noble."

"That's the one. Only there's some around don't think he did it. There's some around think *she* did it."

"Too bad he couldn't have found twelve of those people for his jury."

"He didn't have no jury, George. Quit laying back on me. You remember it as well as I do. One thing you'd *never* forget is a good horn man."

Tennell's jaw shifted to the right a quarter of an inch, making his mouth go crooked. The band members were coming out of the back now and moving around on the bandstand, unsnapping instrument cases, inserting mouthpieces, straightening chairs. They were a mixed lot— black, white, and combinations; clean-shaven and goateed; balding and not; clear-eyed and strung out. None of them was under fifty—the oldest was the trumpet player, Luther Dodd, who was eight-six. Like Louis Armstrong, he had learned to blow at the elbow of Joe "King" Oliver, the great cornetist. His Creole-style trumpet playing was unmatched in New Orleans. Watching him near the age when he would surely die was agony for the jazz purists who frequented Tradition Hall.

Gaston studied George Tennell as the policeman watched Luther Dodd blow out the spit plug of his gleaming Balfour trumpet and loosen up his stick-brittle fingers on the valves. Gaston saw in Tennell's eyes that odd look of a man who truly worshipped traditional jazz music, who felt it down in the pit of himself just like the old men who played it, but who had never learned to play himself. It was a look that had the mix of love and sadness and years gone by. It was the only look that ever turned Tennell's eyes soft.

"You know how long I been looking for a horn man to take Luther's place?" Gaston asked. "A straight year. I've listened to a couple dozen guys from all over. Not a one of them could play traditional. Not a one." He bobbed his chin at Luther Dodd. "His fingers are like old wood, and so's his heart. He could go on me any night. And if he does, I'll have to shut down. Without a horn man, there's no Creole sound, no tradition at all. Without a horn, this place of mine, which is the last of the great jazz emporiums, will just give way to"—Gaston shrugged helplessly, "—whatever. Disco music, I suppose."

A shudder circuited George Tennell's spine, but he gave no outward sign of it. His body was absolutely still, his hands resting motionlessly on the snow-white tablecloth, eyes steadily fixed on Luther Dodd. Momentarily the band went into its first number, *Lafayette,* played Kansas City style after the way of Bennie Moten. The music pulsed out like spurts of water, each burst overlapping the one before it to create an even wave of sound that flooded the big room. Because Kansas City style was so rhythmic and highly danceable, some of the early diners immediately moved onto the dance floor and fell in with the music.

Ordinarily, Tennell liked to watch people dance while he ate; the moving bodies lent emphasis to the music he loved so much, music he had first heard from the window of the St. Pierre Colored Orphanage on Decatur Street when he had been a boy; music he had grown up with and would have made his life a part of if he had not been so completely talentless, so inept that he could not even read sharps and flats. But tonight he paid no attention to the couples out in front of the bandstand. He concentrated only on Luther Dodd and the old horn man's breath intake as he played. It was clear to Tennell that Luther was struggling for breath, fighting for every note he blew, utilizing every cubic inch of lung power that his old body could marshal.

After watching Luther all the way through *Lafayette,* and half-way through *Davenport Blues,* Tennell looked across the table at Gaston and nodded.

"All right," he said simply. "All right."

For the first time ever Tennell left the club without eating dinner.

As Dix walked along with old Rainey toward Gaston's club, Rainey kept pointing out places to him that he had not exactly forgotten, but had not remembered in a long time.

"That house there," Rainey said, "was where Paul Mares was born back in nineteen-and-oh-one. He's the one formed the original New Orleans Rhythm Kings. He only lived to be forty-eight but he was one of the best horn men of all time.''

Dix would remember, not necessarily the person himself but the house and the story of the person and how good he was. He had grown up on those stories, gone to sleep by them as a boy, lived the lives of the men in them many times over as he himself was being taught to blow trumpet by Rozell ''The Lip'' Page when Page was already past sixty and he, Dix was only eight. Later, when Page died, Dix's education was taken over by Shepherd Norden and Blue Johnny Meadows, the two alternating as his teacher between their respective road tours. With Page, Norden, and Meadows in his background, it was no wonder that Dix could blow traditional.

''Right up the street there,'' Rainey said as they walked, ''is where Wingy Manone was born in nineteen-and-oh-four. His given name was Joseph, but after his accident ever'body taken to calling him 'Wingy.' The accident was, he fell under a street car and lost his right arm. But that boy didn't let a little thing like that worry him none, no sir. He learned to play trumpet *left-handed,* and *one-handed.* And he was *good.* Lord he was good.''

They walked along Dauphin and Chartes and Royal. All around them were the French architecture and grillework and statuary and vines and moss that made the *Vieux Carré* a world unto itself, a place of subtle sights, sounds, and smells—black and white and fish and age—that no New Orleans tourist, no Superdome visitor, no casual observer, could ever experience, because to experience was to understand, and understanding of the Quarter could not be acquired, it had to be lived.

''Tommy Ladnier, he used to live right over there,'' Rainey said, ''right up on the second floor. He lived there when he came here from his hometown of Mandeville, Loozey-ana. Poor Tommy, he had a short life too, only thirty-nine years. But it was a good life. He played with King Oliver and Fletcher Henderson and Sidney Bechet. Yessir, he got in some good licks.''

When they got close enough to Tradition Hall to hear the music, at first faintly, then louder, clearer, Rainey stopped talking. He wanted Dix to hear the music, to *feel* the sound of it as it wafted out over Pirate's Alley and the Café du Monde and Congo Square (they called it Beauregard Square now, but Rainey refused to recognize the new name). Instinctively, Rainey knew that it was important for the music to get back into Dix, to saturate his mind and catch in his chest and tickle his stomach. There were some things in Dix that needed to be washed out, some bad things, and Rainey was certain that the music would help. A good purge was always healthy.

Rainey was grateful, as they got near enough to define melody, that *Sweet Georgia Brown* was being played. It was a good melody to come home to.

They walked on, listening, and after a while Dix asked, "Who's on horn?"

"Luther Dodd."

"Don't sound like Luther. What's the matter with him?"

Rainey waved one hand resignedly. "Old. Dying, I 'spect."

They arrived at the Hall and went inside. Gaston met them with a smile. "Dix," he said, genuinely pleased, "it's good to see you." His eyes flickered over Dix. "The years have been good to you. Trim. Lean. No gray hair. How's your lip?"

"I don't have a lip no more, Mr. Gaston," said Dix. "Haven't had for years."

"But he can get it back quick enough," Rainey put in. "He gots a natural lip."

"I don't play no more, Mr. Gaston," Dix told the club owner.

"That's too bad," Gaston said. He bobbed his head toward the stairs. "Come with me. I want to show you something."

Dix and Rainey followed Gaston upstairs to his private office. The office was furnished the way Gaston dressed—old-style, roaring Twenties. There was even a wind-up Victrola in the corner.

Gaston worked the combination of a large, ornate floor vault and pulled its big-tiered door open. From somewhere in its dark recess he withdrew a battered trumpet case, one of the very old kind with heavy brass fittings on the corners and, one knew, real velvet, not felt, for lining. Placing it gently in the center of his desk, Gaston carefully opened the snaplocks and lifted the top. Inside, indeed on real velvet, deep-purple real velvet, was a gleaming, silver, hand-etched trumpet. Dix and Rainey stared at it in unabashed awe.

"Know who it once belonged to?" Gaston asked.

Neither Dix nor Rainey replied. They were mesmerized by the instrument. Rainey had not seen one like it in fifty years. Dix had *never* seen one like it; he had only heard stories about the magnificent silver horns that the quadroons made of contraband silver carefully hidden away after the War Between the States. Because the silver cache had not, as it was supposed to, been given over to the Federal army as part of the reparations levied against the city, the quadroons, during the Union occupation, had to be very careful what they did with it. Selling it for value was out of the question. Using it for silver service, candlesticks, walking canes, or any other of the more obvious uses would have attracted the notice of a Union informer. But letting it lie dormant, even though it was safer as such, was intolerable to the quads, who refused to let a day go by without circumventing one law or another.

So they used the silver to plate trumpets and cornets and slide trombones that belonged to the tabernacle musicians who were just then beginning to experiment with the old *Sammsamounn* tribal music that would eventually mate with work songs and prison songs and gospels, and evolve into traditional blues, which would evolve into traditional, or Dixie-style, jazz.

"Look at the initials," Gaston said, pointing to the top of the bell. Dix and Rainey peered down at three initials etched in the silver: BRB.

"Lord have mercy," Rainey whispered. Dix's lips parted as if he too intended to speak, but no words sounded.

"That's right," Gaston said. "Blind Ray Blount. The first, the best, the *only*. Nobody has ever touched the sounds he created. That man hit notes nobody ever heard before—or since. He was the master."

"Amen," Rainey said. He nodded his head toward Dix. "Can he touch it?"

"Go ahead," Gaston said to Dix.

Like a pilgrim to Mecca touching the holy shroud, Dix ever so lightly placed the tips of three fingers on the silver horn. As he did, he imagined he could feel the touch left there by the hands of the amazing blind horn man who had started the great blues evolution in a patch of town that later became Storyville. He imagined that—

"It's yours if you want it," Gaston said. "All you have to do is pick it up and go downstairs and start blowing."

Dix wet his suddenly dry lips. "Tomorrow I—"

"Not tomorrow," Gaston said. "Tonight. Now."

"Take it, boy," Rainey said urgently.

Dix frowned deeply, his eyes narrowing as if he felt physical pain. He swallowed, trying to push an image out of his mind; an image he had clung to for sixteen years. "I can't tonight—"

"Tonight or never," Gaston said firmly.

"For God's sake, boy, take it!" said old Rainey.

But Dix could not. The image of Madge would not let him.

Dix shook his head violently, as if to rid himself of devils, and hurried from the room.

Rainey ran after him and caught up with him a block from the Hall. "Don't do it," he pleaded. "Hear me now. I'm an old man and I know

I ain't worth nothin' to nobody, but I'm begging you, boy, please, please, please don't do it. I ain't never axed you for nothing in my whole life, but I'm axing you for this: *please* don't do it.''

''I got to,'' Dix said quietly. ''It ain't that I want to; I *got* to.''

''But why, boy? *Why?*''

''Because we made a promise to each other,'' Dix said. ''That night in that Texas motel room, the man Madge was with had told her he was going to marry her. He'd been telling her that for a long time. But he was already married and kept putting off leaving his wife. Finally Madge had enough of it. She asked me to come to her room between sets. I knew she was doing it to make him jealous, but it didn't matter none to me. I'd been crazy about her for so long that I'd do anything she asked me to, and she knew it.

''So between sets I slipped across the highway to where she had her room. But he was already there. I could hear through the transom that he was roughing her up some, but the door was locked and I couldn't get in. Then I heard a shot and everything got quiet. A minute later Madge opened the door and let me in. The man was laying across the bed dying. Madge started bawling and saying how they would put her in the pen and how she wouldn't be able to stand it, she'd go crazy and kill herself.

''It was then I asked her if she'd wait for me if I took the blame for her. She promised me she would. And I promised her I'd come back to her.'' Dix sighed quietly. ''That's what I'm doing, Rainey— keeping my promise.''

''And what going to happen if she ain't kept *hers?*'' Rainey asked.

''Mamma Rulat asked me that same thing this afternoon when I asked her where Madge was at.'' Mamma Rulat was an octaroon fortuneteller who always knew where everyone in the Quarter lived.

''What did you tell her?''

''I told her I'd do what I had to do. That's all a man *can* do, Rainey.''

Dix walked away, up a dark side street. Rainey, watching him go, shook his head in the anguish of the aged and helpless.

''Lord, Lord, Lord—''

The house on Burgundy Street had once been a grand mansion with thirty rooms and a tiled French courtyard with a marble fountain in its center. It had seen nobility and aristocracy and great generals come and go with elegant, genteel ladies on their arms. Now the thirty rooms were rented individually with hotplate burners for light cooking, and the only ladies who crossed the courtyard were those of the New Orleans night.

A red light was flashing atop a police car when Dix got there, and uniformed policemen were blocking the gate into the courtyard. There was a small curious crowd talking about what happened.

"A doper named LeBeau," someone said. "He's been shot."

"I heared it," an old man announced. "I heared the shot."

"That's where it happened, that window right up there—"

Dix looked up, but as he did another voice said, "They're bringing him out now!"

Two morgue attendants wheeled a sheet-covered gurney across the courtyard and lifted it into the back of a black panel truck. Several policemen, led by big beefy George Tennell, brought a woman out and escorted her to the car with the flashing red light. Dix squinted, focusing on her in the inadequate courtyard light. He frowned. Madge's mother, he thought, his mind going back two decades. What's Madge's mother got to do with this?

Then he remembered. Madge's mother was dead. She had died five years after he had gone to the pen.

Then who—?

Madge?

Yes, it *was* her. It was Madge. Older, as he was. Not a girl any more, as he was not a boy any more. For a moment he found it difficult to equate the woman in the courtyard with the memory in his mind. But it was Madge, all right.

Dix tried to push forward, to get past the gate into the courtyard, but two policemen held him back. George Tennell saw the altercation and came over.

"She's under arrest, mister," Tennell told Dix. "Can't nobody talk to her but a lawyer right now."

"What's she done anyhow?" Dix asked.

"Killed her boyfriend," said Tennell. "Shot him with this."

He showed Dix a pearl-handled over-and-under Derringer two-shot.

"Her boyfriend?"

Tennell nodded. "Young feller. 'Bout twenty-five. Neighbors say she was partial to young fellers. Some women are like that."

"Who says she shot him?"

"I do. I was in the building at the time, on another matter. I heard the shot. Matter of fact, I was the first one to reach the body. Few minutes later she come waltzing in. Oh, she put on a good act, all right, like she didn't even know what happened. But I found the gun in her purse myself.''

By now the other officers had Madge Noble in the police car and were waiting for Tennell. He slipped the Derringer into his coat pocket and hitched up his trousers. Jutting his big jaw out an inch, he fixed Dix in a steady gaze.

"If she's a friend of yours, don't count on her being around for a spell. She'll do a long time for this.''

Tennell walked away, leaving Dix still outside the gate. Dix waited there, watching, as the police car came through to the street. He tried to catch a glimpse of Madge as it passed, but there was not enough light in the back seat where they had her. As soon as the car left, the people who had gathered around began to leave too.

Soon Dix was the only one standing there.

At midnight George Tennell was back at his usual table in Tradition Hall for the dinner he had missed earlier. Gaston came over and joined him. For a few minutes they sat in silence, watching Dix up on the bandstand. He was blowing the silver trumpet that had once belonged to Blind Ray Blount; sitting next to the aging Luther Dodd; jumping in whenever he could as they played *Tailspin Blues,* then *Tank Town Bump,* then *Everybody Loves My Baby.*

"Sounds like he'll be able to get his lip back pretty quick,'' Tennell observed.

"Sure,'' said Gaston. "He's a natural. Rozell Page was his first teacher, you know.''

"No, I didn't know that.''

"Sure.'' Gaston adjusted the celluloid collar he wore, and turned the diamond stickpin in his tie. "What about the woman?'' he asked.

Tennell shrugged. "She'll get twenty years. Probably do ten or eleven.''

Gaston thought for a moment, then said, "That should be time enough. After ten or eleven years nothing will matter to him except the music. Don't you think?''

"It won't even take that long,'' Tennell guessed. "Not for him.''

Up on the bandstand the men who played traditional went into *Just a Closer Walk with Thee.*

And sitting on the sawdust floor behind the bandstand, old Rainey listened with happy tears in his eyes.

Faces

F. PAUL WILSON

Bite her face off.

No pain. Her dead already. Kill her quick like others. Not want make pain. Not her fault.

The boyfriend groan but not move. Face way on ground now. Got from behind. Got quick. Never see. He can live.

Girl look me after the boyfriend go down. Gasp first. When see face start scream. Two claws not cut short rip her throat before sound get loud.

Her sick-scared look just like all others. Hate that look. Hate it terrible.

Sorry, girl. Not your fault.

Chew her face skin. Chew all. Chew hard and swallow. Warm wet redness make sickish but chew and chew. Must eat face. Must get all down. Keep down.

Leave the eyes.

The boyfriend groan again. Move arm. Must leave quick. Take last look blood and teeth and stare-eyes that once pretty girlface.

336

Sorry, girl. Not your fault.

Got go. Get way hurry. First take money. Girl money. Take the boyfriend wallet, also too. Always take money. Need money.

Go now. Not too far. Climb wall of near building. Find dark spot where can see and not be seen. Where can wait. Soon the Detective Harrison arrive.

In downbelow can see the boyfriend roll over. Get to knees. Sway. See him look the girlfriend.

The boyfriend scream terrible. Bad to hear. Make so sad. Make cry.

Kevin Harrison heard Jacobi's voice on the other end of the line and wanted to be sick.

"Don't say it," he groaned.

"Sorry," said Jacobi. "It's another one."

"Where?"

"West Forty-ninth, right near—"

"I'll find it." All he had to do was look for the flashing red lights. "I'm on my way. Shouldn't take me too long to get in from Monroe at this hour."

"We've got all night, lieutenant." Unsaid but well understood was an admonishing, *You're the one who wants to live on Long Island.*

Beside him in the bed, Martha spoke form deep in her pillow as he hung up.

"Not another one?"

"Yeah."

"Oh, God! When is it going to stop?"

"When I catch the guy."

Her hand touched his arm, gently. "I know all this responsibility's not easy. I'm here when you need me."

"I know." He leaned over and kissed her. "Thanks."

He left the warm bed and skipped the shower. No time for that. A fresh shirt, yesterday's rumpled suit, a tie shoved into his pocket, and he was off into the winter night.

With his secure little ranch house falling away behind him, Harrison felt naked and vulnerable out here in the dark. As he headed south on Glen Cove Road toward the LIE, he realized that Martha and the kids were all that were holding him together these days. His family had become an island of sanity and stability in a world gone mad.

Everything else was in flux. For reasons he still could not comprehend, he had volunteered to head up the search for this killer. Now his whole future in the department had come to hinge on his success in finding him.

The papers had named the maniac "the Facelift Killer." As apt a name as the tabloids could want, but Harrison resented it. The moniker was callous, trivializing the mutilations perpetrated on the victims. But it had caught on with the public and they were stuck with it, especially with all the ink the story was getting.

Six killings, one a week for six weeks in a row, and eight million people in a panic. Then, for almost two weeks, the city had gone without a new slaying.

Until tonight.

Harrison's stomach pitched and rolled at the thought of having to look at one of those corpses again.

"That's enough," Harrison said, averting his eyes from the face-less thing.

The raw, gouged, bloody flesh, the exposed muscle and bone were bad enough, but it was the eyes—those naked, lidless, staring eyes were the worst.

"This makes seven," Jacobi said at his side. Squat, dark, jowly, the sergeant was chewing a big wad of gum, noisily, aggressively, as if he had a grudge against it.

"I can count. Anything new?"

"Nah. Same m.o. as ever—throat slashed, money stolen, face gnawed off."

Harrison shuddered. He had come in as Special Investigator after the third Facelift killing. He had inspected the first three via coroner's photos. Those had been awful. But nothing could match the effect of the real thing up close and still warm and oozing. This was the fourth fresh victim he had seen. There was no getting used to this kind of mutilation, no matter how many he saw. Jacobi put on a good show, but Harrison sensed the revulsion under the sergeant's armor.

And yet . . .

Beneath all the horror, Harrison sensed something. There was anger here, sick anger and hatred of spectacular proportions. But beyond that, something else, an indefinable something that had drawn him to this case. Whatever it was, that something called to him, and still held him captive.

If he could identify it, maybe he could solve this case and wrap it up. And save his ass.

If he did solve it, it would be all on his own. Because he wasn't getting much help from Jacobi, and even less from his assigned staff. He knew what they all thought—that he had taken the job as a glory grab, a shortcut to the top. Sure, they wanted to see this thing wrapped up, too, but they weren't shedding any tears over the shit he was taking in the press and on TV and from City Hall.

Their attitude was clear: *If you want the spotlight, Harrison, you gotta take the heat that goes with it.*

They were right, of course. He could have been working on a quieter case, like where all the winos were disappearing to. He'd chosen this instead. But he wasn't after the spotlight, dammit! It was this case— something about this case!

He suddenly realized that there was no one around him. The body had been carted off, Jacobi had wandered back to his car. He had been left standing alone at the far end of the alley.

And yet not alone.

Someone was watching him. He could feel it. The realization sent a little chill—one completely unrelated to the cold February wind—trickling down his back. A quick glance around showed no one paying him the slightest bit of attention. He looked up.

There!

Somewhere in the darkness above, someone was watching him. Probably from the roof. He could sense the piercing scrutiny and it made him a little weak. That was no ghoulish neighborhood voyeur, up there. That was the Facelift Killer.

He had to get to Jacobi, have him seal off the building. But he couldn't act spooked. He had to act calm, casual.

See the Detective Harrison's eyes. See from way up in dark. Tall- thin. Hair brown. Nice eyes. Soft brown eyes. Not hard like many- many eyes. Look here. Even from here see eyes make wide. Him know it me.

Watch the Detective Harrison turn slow. Walk slow. Tell inside him want to run. Must leave here. Leave quick.

Bend low. Run cross roof. Jump to next. And next. Again till most block away. Then down wall. Wrap scarf round head. Hide bad-face. Hunch inside big-big coat. Walk through lighted spots.

Hate light. Hate crowds. Theatres here. Movies and plays. Like them. Some night sneak in and see. See one with man in mask. Hang from wall behind big drapes. Make cry.

Wish there mask for me.

Follow street long way to river. See many lights across river. Far past there is place where grew. Never want go back to there. Never.

Catch back of truck. Ride home.

Home. Bright bulb hang ceiling. Not care. The Old Jessi waiting. The Jessi friend. Only friend. The Jessi's eyes not see. Ever. When the Jessi look me, her face not wear sick-scared look. Hate that look.

Come in kitchen window. The Jessi's face wrinkle-black. Smile when hear me come. TV on. Always on. The Jessi can not watch. Say it company for her.

"You're so late tonight."

"Hard work. Get moneys tonight."

Feel sick. Want cry. Hate kill. Wish stop.

"That's nice. Are you going to put it in the drawer?"

"Doing now."

Empty wallets. Put money in slots. Ones first slot. Fives next slot. Then tens and twenties. So the Jessi can pay when boy bring foods. Sometimes eat stolen foods. Mostly the Jessi call for foods.

The Old Jessi hardly walk. Good. Do not want her go out. Bad peoples round here. Many. Hurt one who not see. One bad man try hurt Jessi once. Push through door. Thought only the blind Old Jessi live here.

Lucky the Jessi not alone that day.

Not lucky bad man. Hit the Jessi. Laugh hard. Then look me. Get sick-scared look. Hate that look. Kill him quick. Put in tub. Bleed there. Bad man friend come soon after. Kill him also too. Late at night take both dead bad men out. Go through window. Carry down wall. Throw in river.

No bad men come again. Ever.

"I've been waiting all night for my bath. Do you think you can help me a little?"

Always help. But the Old Jessi always ask. The Jessi very polite.

Sponge the Old Jessi back in tub. Rinse her hair. Think of the Detective Harrison. His kind eyes. Must talk him. Want stop this. Stop now. Maybe will understand. Will. Can feel.

Seven grisly murders in eight weeks.

Kevin Harrison studied a photo of the latest victim, taken before she was mutilated. A nice eight by ten glossy furnished by her agent. A real beauty. A dancer with Broadway dreams.

He tossed the photo aside and pulled the stack of files toward him.

The remnants of six lives in this pile. Somewhere within had to be an answer, the thread that linked each of them to the Facelift Killer.

But what if there was no common link? What if all the killings were at random, linked only by the fact that they were beautiful? Seven deaths, all over the city. All with their faces gnawed off. *Gnawed.*

He flipped through the victims one by one and studied their photos. He had begun to feel he knew each one of them personally.

Mary Detrick, 20, a junior at N.Y.U., killed in Washington Square Park on January 5. She was the first.

Mia Chandler, 25, a secretary at Merrill Lynch, killed January 13 in Battery Park.

Ellen Beasley, 22, a photographer's assistant, killed in an alley in Chelsea on January 22.

Hazel Hauge, 30, artist agent, killed in her Soho loft on January 27.

Elisabeth Paine, 28, housewife, killed on February 2 while jogging late in Central Park.

Joan Perrin, 25, a model from Brooklyn, pulled from her car while stopped at a light on the Upper East Side on February 8.

He picked up the eight by ten again. And the last: Liza Lee, 21, Dancer. Lived across the river in Jersey City. Ducked into an alley for a toot with her boyfriend tonight and never came out.

Three blondes, three brunettes, one redhead. Some stacked, some on the flat side. All caucs except for Perrin. All lookers. But besides that, how in the world could these women be linked? They came from all over town, and they met their respective ends all over town. What could—

"Well, you sure hit the bullseye about that roof!" Jacobi said as he burst into the office.

Harrison straightened in his chair. "What did you find?"

"Blood."

"Whose?"

"The victim's."

"No prints? No hairs? No fibers?"

"We're working on it. But how'd you figure to check the roof top?"

"Lucky guess."

Harrison didn't want to provide Jacobi with more grist for the departmental gossip mill by mentioning his feeling of being watched from up there.

But the killer *had* been watching, hadn't he?

"Any prelims from pathology?"

Jacobi shrugged and stuffed three sticks of gum into his mouth. Then he tried to talk.

"Same as ever. Money gone, throat ripped open by a pair of sharp pointed instruments, not knives, the bite marks on the face are the usual: the teeth that made them aren't human, but the saliva is."

The "non-human" teeth part—more teeth, bigger and sharper than found in any human mouth—had baffled them all from the start. Early on someone remembered a horror novel or movie where the killer used some weird sort of false teeth to bite his victims. That had sent them off on a wild goose chase to all the dental labs looking for records of bizarre bite prostheses. No dice. No one had seen or even heard of teeth that could gnaw off a person's face.

Harrison shuddered. What could explain wounds like that? What were they dealing with here?

The irritating pops, snaps, and cracks of Jacobi's gum filled the office.

"I liked you better when you smoked."

Jacobi's reply was cut off by the phone. The sergeant picked it up.

"Detective Harrison's office!" he said, listened a moment, then, with his hand over the mouthpiece, passed the receiver to Harrison. "Some fairy wants to shpeak to you," he said with an evil grin.

"Fairy?"

"Hey," he said, getting up and walking toward the door. "I don't mind. I'm a liberal kinda guy, y'know?"

Harrison shook his head with disgust. Jacobi was getting less likeable every day.

"Hello. Harrison here."

"Shorry dishturb you, Detective Harrishon."

The voice was soft, pitched somewhere between a man's and a woman's, and sounded as if the speaker had half a mouthful of saliva. Harrison had never heard anything like it. Who could be—?

And then it struck him: It was three a.m. Only a handful of people knew he was here.

"Do I know you?"

"No. Watch you tonight. You almosht shee me in dark."

That same chill from earlier tonight ran down Harrison's back again.

"Are . . . are you who I think you are?"

There was a pause, then one soft word, more sobbed than spoken: "Yesh."

If the reply had been cocky, something along the line of *And just who do you think I am?* Harrison would have looked for much more in the way of corroboration. But that single word, and the soul deep heartbreak that propelled it, banished all doubt.

My God! He looked around frantically. No one in sight. Where the fuck was Jacobi now when he needed him? This was the Facelift Killer! He needed a trace!

Got to keep him on the line!

"I have to ask you something to be sure you are who you say you are."

"Yesh?"

"Do you take anything from the victims—I mean, besides their faces?"

"Money. Take money."

This is him! The department had withheld the money part from the papers. Only the real Facelift Killer could know!

"Can I ask you something else?"

"Yesh."

Harrison was asking this one for himself.

"What do you do with the faces?"

He had to know. The question drove him crazy at night. He dreamed about those faces. Did the killer tack them on the wall, or press them in a book, or freeze them, or did he wear them around the house like that Leatherface character from that chainsaw movie?

On the other end of the line he sensed sudden agitation and panic: "No! Can not shay! Can *not!*"

"Okay, okay. Take it easy."

"You will help shtop?"

"Oh, yes! Oh, God, yes, I'll help you stop!" He prayed his genuine heartfelt desire to end this was coming through. "I'll help you any way I can!"

There was a long pause, then:

"You hate? Hate me?"

Harrison didn't trust himself to answer that right away. He searched his feelings quickly, but carefully.

"No," he said finally. "I think you have done some awful, horrible things but, strangely enough, I don't hate you."

And that was true. Why didn't he hate this murdering maniac? Oh, he wanted to stop him more than anything in the world, and wouldn't hesitate to shoot him dead if the situation required it, but there was no personal hatred for the Facelift Killer.

What is it in you that speaks to me? he wondered.

"Shank you," said the voice, couched once more in a sob.

And then the killer hung up.

Harrison shouted into the dead phone, banged it on his desk, but the line was dead.

"What the hell's the matter with you?" Jacobi said from the office door.

"That so-called 'fairy' on the phone was the Facelift Killer, you idiot! We could have had a trace if you'd stuck around!"

"Bullshit!"

"He knew about taking the money!"

"So why'd he talk like that? That's a dumb-ass way to try to disguise your voice."

And then it suddenly hit Harrison like a sucker punch to the gut. He swallowed hard and said:

"Jacobi, how do you think your voice would sound if you had a jaw crammed full of teeth much larger and sharper than the kind found in the typical human mouth?"

Harrison took genuine pleasure in the way Jacobi's face blanched slowly to yellow-white.

He didn't get home again until after seven the following night. The whole department had been in an uproar all day. This was the first break they had had in the case. It wasn't much, but contact had been made. That was the important part. And although Harrison had done nothing he could think of to deserve any credit, he had accepted the commissioner's compliments and encouragement on the phone shortly before he had left the office tonight.

But what was most important to Harrison was the evidence from the call—*Damn!* he wished it had been taped—that the killer wanted to stop. They didn't have one more goddamn clue tonight than they'd had yesterday, but the call offered hope that soon there might be an end to this horror.

Martha had dinner waiting. The kids were scrubbed and pajamaed and waiting for their goodnight kiss. He gave them each a hug and poured himself a stiff scotch while Martha put them in the sack.

"Do you feel as tired as you look?" she said as she returned from the bedroom wing.

She was a big woman with bright blue eyes and natural dark blond hair. Harrison toasted her with his glass.

"The expression 'dead on his feet' has taken on a whole new meaning for me."

She kissed him, then they sat down to eat.

He had spoken to Martha a couple of times since he had left the house twenty hours ago. She knew about the phone call from the Face-lift Killer, about the new hope in the department about the case, but he was glad she didn't bring it up now. He was sick of talking about it. Instead, he sat in front of his cooling meatloaf and wrestled with the images that had been nibbling at the edges of his consciousness all day.

"What are you daydreaming about?" Martha said.

Without thinking, Harrison said, "Annie."

"Annie who?"

"My sister."

Martha put her fork down. "Your sister? Kevin, you don't have a sister."

"Not any more. But I did."

Her expression was alarmed now. "Kevin, are you all right? I've known your family for ten years. Your mother has never once mentioned—"

"We don't talk about Annie, Mar. We try not to even think about her. She died when she was five."

"Oh. I'm sorry."

"Don't be. Annie was . . . deformed. Terribly deformed. She never really had a chance."

Open trunk from inside. Get out. The Detective Harrison's house here. Cold night. Cold feel good. Trunk air make sick, dizzy.

Light here. Hurry round side of house.

Darker here. No one see. Look in window. Dark but see good. Two little ones there. Sleeping. Move away. Not want them cry.

Go more round. The Detective Harrison with lady. Sit table near window. Must be wife. Pretty but not oh-so-beauty. Not have mom-face. Not like ones who die.

Watch behind tree. Hungry. They not eat food. Talk-talk-talk. Can not hear.

The Detective Harrison do most talk. Kind face. Kind eyes. Some terrible sad there. Hides. Him understands. Heard in phone voice. Understands. Him one can stop kills.

Spent day watch the Detective Harrison car. All day watch at police house. Saw him come-go many times. Soon dark, open trunk with claw. Ride with him. Ride long. Wonder what town this?

The Detective Harrison look this way. Stare like last night. Must not see me! Must *not*!

*   *   *

Harrison stopped in mid-sentence and stared out the window as his skin prickled.

That *watched* feeling again.

It was the same as last night. Something was out in the backyard watching them. He strained to see through the wooded darkness outside the window but saw only shadows within shadows.

But something was *there*! He could feel it!

He got up and turned on the outside spotlights, hoping, *praying* that the backyard would be empty.

It was.

He smiled to hide his relief and glanced at Martha.

"Thought that raccoon was back."

He left the spots on and settled back into his place at the table. But the thoughts racing through his mind made eating unthinkable.

What if that maniac had followed him out here? What if the call had been a ploy to get him off-guard so the Facelift Killer could do to Martha what he had done to the other women?

My God . . .

First thing tomorrow morning he was going to call the local alarm boys and put in a security system. Cost be damned, he had to have it. Immediately!

As for tonight . . .

Tonight he'd keep the .38 under the pillow.

Run away. Run low and fast. Get bushes before light come. Must stay way now. Not come back.

The Detective Harrison *feel* me. Know when watched. Him the one, sure.

Walk in dark, in woods. See back many houses. Come park. Feel strange. See this park before. Can not be—

Then know.

Monroe! This Monroe! Born here! Live here! Hate Monroe! Monroe bad place, bad people! House, home, old home near here! There! Cross park! Old home! New color but same house.

Hate house!

Sit on froze park grass. Cry. Why Monroe? Do not want be in Monroe. The Mom gone. The Sissy gone. The Jimmy very gone. House here.

Dry tears. Watch old home long time till light go out. Wait more. Go to windows. See new folks inside. The Mom took the Sissy and go. Where? Don't know.

Go to back. Push cellar window. Crawl in. See good in dark. New folks make nice cellar. Wood on walls. Rug on floor. No chain.

Sit floor. Remember . . .

Remember hanging on wall. Look little window near ceiling. Watch kids play in park cross street. Want go with kids. Want play there with kids. Want have friends.

But the Mom won't let. Never leave basement. Too strong. Break everything. Have TV. Broke it. Have toys. Broke them. Stay in basement. Chain round waist hold to center pole. Can not leave.

Remember terrible bad things happen.

Run. Run way Monroe. Never come back.

Till now.

Now back. Still hate house! Want hurt house. See cigarettes. With matches. Light all. Burn now!

Watch rug burn. Chair burn. So hot. Run back to cold park. Watch house burn. See new folks run out. Trucks come throw water. House burn and burn.

Glad but tears come anyway.

Hate house. Now house gone. Hate Monroe.

Wonder where the Mom and the Sissy live now.

Leave Monroe for new home and the Old Jessi.

The second call came the next day. And this time they were ready for it. The tape recorders were set, the computers were waiting to begin the tracing protocol. As soon as Harrison recognized the voice, he gave the signal. On the other side of the desk, Jacobi put on a headset and people started running in all directions. Off to the races.

"I'm glad you called," Harrison said. "I've been thinking about you."

"You undershtand?" said the soft voice.

"I'm not sure."

"Musht help shtop."

"I will! I will! Tell me how!"

"Not know."

There was a pause. Harrison wasn't sure what to say next. He didn't want to push, but he had to keep him on the line.

"Did you . . . hurt anyone last night?"

"No. Shaw houshes. Your houshe. Your wife."

Harrison's blood froze. Last night—in the backyard. That had been the Facelift Killer in the dark. He looked up and saw genuine concern in Jacobi's eyes. He forced himself to speak.

"You were at my house? Why didn't you talk to me?"

"No-no! Can not let shee! Run way your house. Go mine!"

"*Yours?* You live in Monroe?"

"No! Hate Monroe! Once lived. Gone long! Burn old houshe. Never go back!"

This could be important. Harrison phrased the next question carefully.

"You burned your old house? When was that?"

If he could just get a date, a year . . .

"Lasht night."

"*Last night?*" Harrison remembered hearing the sirens and fire horns in the early morning darkness.

"Yesh! Hate houshe!"

And then the line went dead.

He looked at Jacobi who had picked up another line.

"Did we get the trace?"

"Waiting to hear. Christ, he sounds retarded, doesn't he?"

Retarded. The word sent ripples across the surface of his brain. Non-human teeth . . . Monroe . . . retarded . . . a picture was forming in the settling sediment, a picture he felt he should avoid.

"Maybe he is."

"You'd think that would make him easy to—"

Jacobi stopped, listened to the receiver, then shook his head disgustedly.

"What?"

"Got as far as the Lower East Side. He was probably calling from somewhere in one of the projects. If we'd had another thirty seconds—"

"We've got something better than a trace to some lousy pay phone," Harrison said. "We've got his old address!" He picked up his suit coat and headed for the door.

"Where we goin'?"

"Not 'we.' Me. I'm going out to Monroe."

Once he reached the town, it took Harrison less than an hour to find the Facelift Killer's last name.

He first checked with the Monroe Fire Department to find the address of last night's house fire. Then he went down to the brick fronted Town Hall and found the lot and block number. After that it was easy to look up its history of ownership. Mr. and Mrs. Elwood Scott were the current owners of the land and the charred shell of a three-bedroom ranch that sat upon it.

There had only been one other set of owners: Mr. and Mrs. Thomas

Baker. He had lived most of his life in Monroe but knew nothing about the Baker family. But he knew where to find out: Captain Jeremy Hall, Chief of Police in the Incorporated Village of Monroe.

Captain Hall hadn't changed much over the years. Still had a big belly, long sideburns, and hair cut bristly short on the sides. That was the "in" look these days, but Hall had been wearing his hair like that for at least thirty years. If not for his Bronx accent, he could have played a redneck sheriff in any one of those southern chain gang movies.

After pleasantries and local-boy-leaves-home-to-become-big-city-cop-and-now-comes-to-question-small-town-cop banter, they got down to business.

"The Bakers from North Park Drive?" Hall said after he had noisily sucked the top layer off his steaming coffee. "Who could forget them? There was the mother, divorced, I believe, and the three kids—two girls and the boy."

Harrison pulled out his note pad. "The boy's name—what was it?"

"Tommy, I believe. Yeah—Tommy. I'm sure of it."

"He's the one I want."

Hall's eyes narrowed. "He is, is he? You're working on that Facelift case aren't you?"

"Right."

"And you think Tommy Baker might be your man?"

"It's a possibility. What do you know about him?"

"I know he's dead."

Harrison froze. "Dead? That can't be!"

"It sure as hell *can* be!" Without rising from his seat, he shouted through his office door. "Murph! Pull out that old file on the Baker case! Nineteen eighty-four, I believe!"

"Eighty-four?" Harrison said. He and Martha had been living in Queens then. They hadn't moved back to Monroe yet.

"Right. A real messy affair. Tommy Baker was thirteen years old when he bought it. And he bought it. *Believe* me, he bought it!"

Harrison sat in glum silence, watching his whole theory go up in smoke.

The Old Jessi sleeps. Stand by mirror near tub. Only mirror have. No like them. The Jessi not need one.

Stare face. Bad face. Teeth, teeth, teeth. And hair. Arms too thin, too long. Claws. None have claws like my. None have face like my.

Face not better. Ate pretty faces but face still same. Still cause sick-scared look. Just like at home.

Remember home. Do not want but thoughts will not go.

Faces.

The Sissy get the Mom-face. Beauty face. The Tommy get the Dad-face. Not see the Dad. Never come home anymore. Who my face? Never see where come. Where my face come? My hands come?

Remember home cellar. Hate home! Hate cellar more! Pull on chain round waist. Pull and pull. Want out. Want play. *Please.* No one let.

One day when the Mom and the Sissy go, the Tommy bring friends. Come down cellar. Bunch on stairs. Stare. First time see sick-scared look. Not understand.

Friends! Play! Throw ball them. They run. Come back with rocks and sticks. Still sick-scared look. Throw me, hit me.

Make cry. Make the Tommy laugh.

Whenever the Mom and the Sissy go, the Tommy come with boys and sticks. Poke and hit. Hurt. Little hurt on skin. Big hurt inside. Sick-scared look hurt most of all. Hate look. Hate hurt. Hate them.

Most hate the Tommy.

One night chain breaks. Wait on wall for the Tommy. Hurt him. Hurt the Tommy outside. Hurt the Tommy inside. Know because pull inside outside. The Tommy quiet. Quiet, wet, red. The Mom and the Sissy get sick-scared look and scream.

Hate that look. Run way. Hide. Never come back. Till last night.

Cry more now. Cry quiet. In tub. So the Jessi not hear.

Harrison flipped through the slim file on the Tommy Baker murder. "This is it?"

"We didn't need to collect much paper," Captain Hall said. "I mean, the mother and sister were witnesses. There's some photos in that manila envelope at the back."

Harrison pulled it free and slipped out some large black and whites. His stomach lurched immediately.

"My *God*!"

"Yeah, he was a mess. Gutted by his older sister."

"His *sister*?"

"Yeah. Apparently she was some sort of freak of nature."

Harrison felt the floor tilt under him, felt as if he were going to slide off the chair.

"Freak?" he said, hoping Hall wouldn't notice the tremor in his voice. "What did she look like?"

"Never saw her. She took off after she killed the brother. No one's seen hide nor hair of her since. But there's a picture of the rest of the family in there."

Harrison shuffled through the file until he came to a large color family portrait. He held it up. Four people: two adults seated in chairs; a boy and a girl, about ten and eight, kneeling on the floor in front of them. A perfectly normal American family. Four smiling faces.

But where's your oldest child. Where's your big sister? Where did you hide that fifth face while posing for this?

"What was her name? The one who's not here?"

"Not sure. Carla, maybe? Look at the front sheet under *Suspect*."

Harrison did: "Carla Baker—called 'Carly,' " he said.

Hall grinned. "Right. Carly. Not bad for a guy getting ready for retirement."

Harrison didn't answer. An ineluctable sadness filled him as he stared at the incomplete family portrait.

Carly Baker . . . poor Carly . . . where did they hide you away? In the cellar? Locked in the attic? How did your brother treat you? Bad enough to deserve killing?

Probably.

"No pictures of Carly, I suppose."

"Not a one."

That figures.

"How about a description?"

"The mother gave us one but it sounded so weird, we threw it out. I mean, the girl sounded like she was half spider or something!" He drained his cup. "Then later on I got into a discussion with Doc Alberts about it. He told me he was doing deliveries back about the time this kid was born. Said they had a whole rash of monsters, all delivered within a few weeks of each other."

The room started to tilt under Harrison again.

"Early December, 1968, by chance?"

"Yeah! How'd you know?"

He felt queasy. "Lucky guess."

"Huh. Anyway, Doc Alberts said they kept it quiet while they looked into a cause, but that little group of freaks—'cluster,' he called them— was all there was. They figured that a bunch of mothers had been exposed to something nine months before, but whatever it had been was long gone. No monsters since. I understand most of them died shortly after birth, anyway."

"Not all of them."

"Not that it matters," Hall said, getting up and pouring himself a refill from the coffee pot. "Someday someone will find her skeleton, probably somewhere out in Haskins' marshes."

"Maybe." *But I wouldn't count on it.* He held up the file. "Can I get a xerox of this?"

"You mean the Facelift Killer is a twenty-year-old girl?" Martha's face clearly registered her disbelief.

"Not just any girl. A freak. Someone so deformed she really doesn't look human. Completely uneducated and probably mentally retarded to boot."

Harrison hadn't returned to Manhattan. Instead, he'd headed straight for home, less than a mile from Town Hall. He knew the kids were at school and that Martha would be there alone. That was what he had wanted. He needed to talk this out with someone a lot more sensitive than Jacobi.

Besides, what he had learned from Captain Hall and the Baker file had dredged up the most painful memories of his life.

"A monster," Martha said.

"Yeah. Born one on the outside, *made* one on the inside. But there's another child monster I want to talk about. Not Carly Baker. Annie . . Ann Harrison."

Martha gasped. "That sister you told me about last night?"

Harrison nodded. He knew this was going to hurt, but he had to do it, had to get it out. He was going to explode into a thousand twitching bloody pieces if he didn't.

"I was nine when she was born. December 2, 1968—a week after Carly Baker. Seven pounds, four ounces of horror. She looked more fish than human."

His sister's image was imprinted on the rear wall of his brain. And it should have been after all those hours he had spent studying her loathsome face. Only her eyes looked human. The rest of her was awful. A lipless mouth, flattened nose, sloping forehead, fingers and toes fused so that they looked more like flippers than hands and feet, a bloated body covered with shiny skin that was a dusky gray-blue. The doctors said she was that color because her heart was bad, had a defect that caused mixing of blue blood and red blood.

A repulsed nine-year-old Kevin Harrison had dubbed her The Tuna— but never within earshot of his parents.

"She wasn't supposed to live long. A few months, they said, and she'd be dead. But she didn't die. Annie lived on and on. One year.

Two. My father and the doctors tried to get my mother to put her into some sort of institution, but Mom wouldn't hear of it. She kept Annie in the third bedroom and talked to her and cooed over her and cleaned up her shit and just hung over her all the time. *All* the time, Martha!''

Martha gripped his hand and nodded for him to go on.

''After a while, it got so there was nothing else in Mom's life. She wouldn't leave Annie. Family trips became a thing of the past. Christ, if she and Dad went out to a movie, *I* had to stay with Annie. No babysitter was trustworthy enough. Our whole lives seemed to center around that freak in the back bedroom. And me? I was forgotten.

''After a while I began to hate my sister.''

''Kevin, you don't have to—''

''Yes, I do! I've got to tell you how it was! By the time I was fourteen—just about Tommy Baker's age when he bought it—I thought I was going to go crazy. I was getting all B's in school but did that matter? Hell, no! 'Annie rolled halfway over today. Isn't that wonderful?' Big deal! She was five years old, for Christ sake! I was starting point guard on the high school junior varsity basketball team as a goddamn freshman, but did anyone come to my games? Hell no!

''I tell you, Martha, after five years of caring for Annie, our house was a powderkeg. Looking back now I can see it was my mother's fault for becoming so obsessed. But back then, at age fourteen, I blamed it all on Annie. I really hated her for being born a freak.''

He paused before going on. This was the really hard part.

''One night, when my dad had managed to drag my mother out to some company banquet that he had to attend, I was left alone to babysit Annie. On those rare occasions, my mother would always tell me to keep Annie company—you know, read her stories and such. But I never did. I'd let her lie back there alone with our old black and white TV while I sat in the living room watching the family set. This time, however, I went into her room.''

He remembered the sight of her, lying there with the covers half way up her fat little tuna body that couldn't have been much more than a yard in length. It was winter, like now, and his mother had dressed her in a flannel nightshirt. The coarse hair that grew off the back of her head had been wound into two braids and fastened with pink bows.

''Annie's eyes brightened as I came into the room. She had never spoken. Couldn't, it seemed. Her face could do virtually nothing in the way of expression, and her flipper-like arms weren't good for much, either. You had to read her eyes, and that wasn't easy. None of us knew how much of a brain Annie had, or how much she understood of what was going on around her. My mother said she was bright, but I think Mom was a little whacko on the subject of Annie.

"Anyway, I stood over her crib and started shouting at her. She quivered at the sound. I called her every dirty name in the book. And as I said each one, I poked her with my fingers—not enough to leave a bruise, but enough to let out some of the violence in me. I called her a lousy goddamn tunafish with feet. I told her how much I hated her and how I wished she had never been born. I told her everybody hated her and the only thing she was good for was a freak show. Then I said, 'I wish you were dead! Why don't you die? You were supposed to die years ago! Why don't you do everyone a favor and do it now!'

"When I ran out of breath, she looked at me with those big eyes of hers and I could see the tears in them and I knew she had understood me. She rolled over and faced the wall. I ran from the room.

"I cried myself to sleep that night. I'd thought I'd feel good telling her off, but all I kept seeing in my mind's eye was this fourteen-year-old bully shouting at a helpless five-year-old. I felt awful. I promised myself that the first opportunity I had to be alone with her the next day I'd apologize, tell her I really didn't mean the hateful things I'd said, promise to read to her and be her best friend, anything to make it up to her.

"I awoke the next morning to the sound of my mother screaming. Annie was dead."

"Oh, my God!" Martha said, her fingers digging into his arm.

"Naturally, I blamed myself."

"But you said she had a heart defect!"

"Yeah. I know. And the autopsy showed that's what killed her—her heart finally gave out. But I've never been able to get it out of my head that my words were what made her heart give up. Sounds sappy and melodramatic, I know, but I've always felt that she was just hanging on to life by the slimmest margin and that I pushed her over the edge."

"Kevin, you shouldn't have to carry that around with you! Nobody should!"

The old grief and guilt were like a slowly expanding balloon in his chest. It was getting hard to breathe.

"In my coolest, calmest, most dispassionate moments I convince myself that it was all a terrible coincidence, that she would have died that night anyway and that I had nothing to do with it."

"That's probably true, so—"

"But that doesn't change the fact that the last memory of her life was of her big brother—the guy she probably thought was the neatest kid on earth, who could run and play basketball, one of the three human beings who made up her whole world, who should have been her champion, her defender against a world that could only greet her with revulsion and rejection—standing over her crib telling her how much he hated her and how he wished she was dead!''

He felt the sobs begin to quake in his chest. He hadn't cried in over a dozen years and he had no intention of allowing himself to start now, but there didn't seem to be any stopping it. It was like running down hill at top speed—if he tried to stop before he reached bottom, he'd go head over heels and break his neck.

"Kevin, you were only fourteen," Martha said soothingly.

"Yeah, I know. But if I could go back in time for just a few seconds, I'd go back to that night and rap that rotten hateful fourteen-year-old in the mouth before he got a chance to say a single word. But I can't. I can't even say I'm sorry to Annie! I never got a chance to take it back, Martha! I never got a chance to make it up to her!''

And then he was blubbering like a goddamn wimp, letting loose half a lifetime's worth of grief and guilt, and Martha's arms were around him and she was telling him everything would be all right, all right, all right . . .

The Detective Harrison understand. Can tell. Want to go kill another face now. Must not. The Detective Harrison not like. Must stop. The Detective Harrison help stop.

Stop for good.

Best way. Only one way stop for good. Not jail. No chain, no little window. Not ever again. Never!

Only one way stop for good. The Detective Harrison will know. Will understand. Will do.

Must call. Call now. Before dark. Before pretty faces come out in night.

Harrison had pulled himself together by the time the kids came home from school. He felt buoyant inside, like he'd been purged in some way. Maybe all those shrinks were right after all: sharing old hurts did help.

He played with the kids for a while, then went into the kitchen to see if Martha needed any help with slicing and dicing. He felt as close to her now as he ever had.

"You okay?" she said with a smile.

"Fine."

She had just started slicing a red pepper for the salad. He took over for her.

"Have you decided what to do?" she asked.

He had been thinking about it a lot, and had come to a decision.

"Well, I've got to inform the department about Carly Baker, but I'm going to keep her out of the papers for a while."

"Why? I'd think if she's that freakish looking, the publicity might turn up someone who's seen her."

"Possibly it will come to that. But this case is sensational enough without tabloids like the *Post* and *The Light* turning it into a circus. Besides, I'm afraid of panic leading to some poor deformed innocent getting lynched. I think I can bring her in. She *wants* to come in."

"You're sure of that?"

"She so much as told me so. Besides, I can sense it in her." He saw Martha giving him a dubious look. "I'm serious. We're somehow connected, like there's an invisible wire between us. Maybe it's because the same thing that deformed her and those other kids deformed Annie, too. And Annie was my sister. Maybe that link is why I volunteered for this case in the first place."

He finished slicing the pepper, then moved on to the mushrooms.

"And after I bring her in, I'm going to track down her mother and start prying into what went on in Monroe in February and March of sixty-eight to cause that so-called 'cluster' of freaks nine months later."

He would do that for Annie. It would be his way of saying goodbye and I'm sorry to his sister.

"But why does she take their faces?" Martha said.

"I don't know. Maybe because theirs were beautiful and hers is no doubt hideous."

"But what does she *do* with them?"

"Who knows? I'm not all that sure I *want* to know. But right now—"

The phone rang. Even before he picked it up, he had an inkling of who it was. The first sibilant syllable left no doubt.

"Ish thish the Detective Harrison?"

"Yes."

Harrison stretched the coiled cord around the corner from the kitchen into the dining room, out of Martha's hearing.

"Will you shtop me tonight?"

"You want to give yourself up?"

"Yesh. Pleashe, yesh."

"Can you meet me at the precinct house?"

"*No!*"

"Okay! Okay!" God, he didn't want to spook her now. "Where? Anywhere you say."

"Jusht you."

"All right."

"Midnight. Plashe where lasht fashe took. Bring gun but not more cop."

"All right."

He was automatically agreeing to everything. He'd work out the details later.

"You undershtand, Detective Harrishon?"

"Oh, Carly, Carly, I understand more than you know!"

There was a sharp intake of breath and then silence at the other end of the line. Finally:

"You know Carly?"

"Yes, Carly. I know you." The sadness welled up in him again and it was all he could do to keep his voice from breaking. "I had a sister like you once. And you . . . you had a brother like me."

"Yesh," said that soft, breathy voice. "You undershtand. Come tonight, Detective Harrishon."

The line went dead.

Wait in shadows. The Detective Harrison will come. Will bring lots cop. Always see on TV show. Always bring lots. Protect him. Many guns.

No need. Only one gun. The Detective Harrison's gun. Him's will shoot. Stop kills. Stop forever.

The Detective Harrison must do. No one else. The Carly can not. Must be the Detective Harrison. Smart. Know the Carly. Understand.

After stop, no more ugly Carly. No more sick-scared look. Bad face will go away. Forever and ever.

Harrison had decided to go it alone.

Not completely alone. He had a van waiting a block and a half away on Seventh Avenue and a walkie-talkie clipped to his belt, but he hadn't told anyone who he was meeting or why. He knew if he did, they'd swarm all over the area and scare Carly off completely. So he had told Jacobi he was meeting an informant and that the van was just a safety measure.

He was on his own here and wanted it that way. Carly Baker wanted to surrender to him and him alone. He understood that. It was part of that strange tenuous bond between them. No one else would do. After he had cuffed her, he would call in the wagon.

After that he would be a hero for a while. He didn't want to be a hero. All he wanted was to end this thing, end the nightmare for the city and for poor Carly Baker. She'd get help, the kind she needed, and he'd use the publicity to springboard an investigation into what had made Annie and Carly and the others in their "cluster" what they were.

It's all going to work out fine, he told himself as he entered the alley.

He walked half its length and stood in the darkness. The brick walls of the buildings on either side soared up into the night. The ceaseless roar of the city echoed dimly behind him. The alley itself was quiet— no sound, no movement. He took out his flashlight and flicked it on.

"Carly?"

No answer.

"Carly Baker—are you here?"

More silence, then, ahead to his left, the sound of a garbage can scraping along the stony floor of the alley. He swung the light that way, and gasped.

A looming figure stood a dozen feet in front of him. It could only be Carly Baker. She stood easily as tall as he—a good six foot two— and looked like a homeless street person, one of those animated rag-piles that live on subway grates in the winter. Her head was wrapped in a dirty scarf, leaving only her glittery dark eyes showing. The rest of her was muffled in a huge, shapeless overcoat, baggy old polyester slacks with dragging cuffs, and torn sneakers.

"Where the Detective Harrishon's gun?" said the voice.

Harrison's mouth was dry but he managed to get his tongue working. "In its holster."

"Take out. Pleashe."

Harrison didn't argue with her. The grip of his heavy Chief Special felt damn good in his hand.

The figure spread its arms; within the folds of her coat those arms seem to bend the wrong way. And were those black hooked claws protruding from the cuffs of the sleeves?

She said, "Shoot."

Harrison gaped in shock.

The Detective Harrison not shoot. Eyes wide. Hands with gun and light shake.

Say again: "Shoot!"

"Carly, no! I'm not here to kill you. I'm here to take you in, just as we agreed."

"*No!*"

Wrong! The Detective Harrison not understand! Must shoot the Carly! Kill the Carly!

"Not jail! Shoot! Shtop the kills! Shtop the Carly!"

"No! I can get you help, Carly. Really, I can! You'll go to a place where no one will hurt you. You'll get medicine to make you feel better!"

Thought him understand! Not understand! Move closer. Put claw out. Him back way. Back to wall.

"Shoot! Kill! Now!"

"No, Annie, please!"

"Not Annie! Carly! Carly!"

"Right. Carly! Don't make me do this!"

Only inches way now. Still not shoot. Other cops hiding not shoot. Why not protect?

"*Shoot!*" Pull scarf off face. Point claw at face. "End! End! *Pleashe!*"

The Detective Harrison face go white. Mouth hang open. Say, "Oh, my *God!*"

Get sick-scared look. Hate that look! Thought him understand! Say he know the Carly! Not! Stop look! *Stop!*

Not think. Claw go out. Rip throat of the Detective Harrison. Blood fly just like others.

No-No-No! Not want hurt!

The Detective Harrison gurgle. Drop gun and light. Fall. Stare.

Wait other cops shoot. Please kill the Carly. Wait.

No shoot. Then know. No cops. Only the poor Detective Harrison. Cry for the Detective Harrison. Then run. Run and climb. Up and down. Back to new home with the Old Jessi.

The Jessi glad hear Carly come. The Jessi try talk. Carly go sit tub. Close door. Cry for the Detective Harrison. Cry long time. Break mirror million piece. Not see face again. Not ever. Never.

The Jessi say, "Carly, I want my bath. Will you scrub my back?"

Stop cry. Do the Old Jessi's black back. Comb the Jessi's hair.

Feel very sad. None ever comb the Carly's hair. Ever.

Author of the book on which the hit film *Single White Female* was based, John Lutz has had a long and notable career in crime writing.

His first novel, the *Truth of the Matter*, remains one of the best psycho-suspense novels of the past quarter century and demonstrates Lutz's way with characters of every stripe. The book also anticipates much of the darker literature of the eighties and early nineties, something for which Lutz has received little credit.

He is presently sustaining two very different series—one about the stomach-troubled Alo Nudger, the other about a failed Floridian dreamer wryly named Carver—and still producing some very important short fiction.

Ride The Lightning
JOHN LUTZ

A slanted sheet of rain swept like a scythe across Placid Cove Trailer Park. For an instant, an intricate web of lightning illuminated the park. The rows of mobile homes loomed square and still and pale against the night, reminding Nudger of tombs with awnings and TV antennas. He held his umbrella at a sharp angle to the wind as he walked, putting a hand in his pocket to pull out a scrap of paper and double-check the address he was trying to find in the maze of trailers. Finally, at the end of Tranquility Lane, he found Number 307 and knocked on its metal door.

"I'm Nudger," he said when the door opened.

For several seconds the woman in the doorway stood staring out at him, rain blowing in beneath the metal awning to spot her cornflower-colored dress and ruffle her straw blond hair. She was tall but very thin, fragile-looking, and appeared at first glance to be about twelve years old. Second glance revealed her to be in her mid-twenties. She

360

had slight crow's feet at the corners of her luminous blue eyes when she winced as a raindrop struck her face, a knowing cast to her over-sized, girlish, full-lipped mouth, and slightly buck teeth. Her looks were hers alone. There was no one who could look much like her, no middle ground with her; men would consider her scrawny and homely, or they would see her as uniquely sensuous. Nudger liked coltish girl-women; he catalogued her as attractive.

"Whoeee!" she said at last, as if seeing for the first time beyond Nudger. "Ain't it raining something terrible?"

"It is," Nudger agreed. "And on me."

Her entire thin body gave a quick, nervous kind of jerk as she smiled apologetically. "I'm Holly Ann Adams, Mr. Nudger. And you are get-ting wet, all right. Come on in."

She moved aside and Nudger stepped up into the trailer. He expected it to be surprisingly spacious; he'd once lived in a trailer and remem-bered them as such. This one was cramped and confining. The furniture was cheap and its upholstery was threadbare; a portable black and white TV on a tiny table near the Scotch-plaid sofa was blaring shouts of ecstasy emitted by "The Price is Right" contestants. The air was thick with the smell of something greasy that had been fried too long.

Holly Ann cleared a stack of *People* magazines from a vinyl chair and motioned for Nudger to sit down. He folded his umbrella, left it by the door, and sat. Holly Ann started to say something, then jerked her body in that peculiar way of hers, almost a twitch, as if she'd just remembered something not only with her mind but with her blood and muscle, and walked over and switched off the noisy television. In the abrupt silence, the rain seemed to beat on the metal roof with added fury. "Now we can talk," Holly Ann proclaimed, sitting opposite Nudger on the undersized sofa. "You a sure-enough private investigator?"

"I'm that," Nudger said. "Did someone recommend me to you, Miss Adams?"

"Gotcha out of the Yellow Pages. And if you're gonna work for me, it might as well be Holly Ann without the Adams."

"Except on the check," Nudger said.

She grinned a devilish twelve-year-old's grin. "Oh, sure, don't worry none about that. I wrote you out a check already, just gotta fill in the amount. That is, if you agree to take the job. You might not."

"Why not?"

"It has to do with my fiancé, Curtis Colt."

Nudger listened for a few seconds to the rain crashing on the roof. "The Curtis Colt who's going to be executed next week?"

"That's the one. Only he didn't kill that liquor store woman; I know it for a fact. It ain't right he should have to ride the lightning."

"Ride the lightning?"

"That's what convicts call dying in the electric chair, Mr. Nudger. They call that chair lotsa things: Old Sparky ... The Lord's Frying Pan. But Curtis don't belong sitting in it wired up, and I can prove it."

"It's a little late for that kind of talk," Nudger said. "Or did you testify for Curtis in court?"

"Nope. Couldn't testify. You'll see why. All them lawyers and the judge and jury don't even know about me. Curtis didn't want them to know, so he never told them." She crossed her legs and swung her right calf jauntily. She was smiling as if trying to flirt him into wanting to know more about the job so he could free Curtis Colt by a governor's reprieve at the last minute, as in an old movie.

Nudger looked at her gauntly pretty, country-girl face and said, "Tell me about Curtis Colt, Holly Ann."

"You mean you didn't read about him in the newspapers or see him on the television?"

"I only scan the media for misinformation. Give me the details."

"Well, they say Curtis was inside the liquor store, sticking it up— him and his partner had done three other places that night, all of 'em gas stations, though—when the old man that owned the place came out of a back room and seen his wife there behind the counter with her hands up and Curtis holding the gun on her. So the old man lost his head and ran at Curtis, and Curtis had to shoot him. Then the woman got mad when she seen that and ran at Curtis, and Curtis shot her. She's the one that died. The old man, he'll live, but he can't talk nor think nor even feed himself."

Nudger remembered more about the case now. Curtis Colt had been found guilty of first degree murder, and because of a debate in the legislature over the merits of cyanide gas versus electricity, the state was breaking out the electric chair to make him its first killer executed by electricity in over a quarter of a century. Those of the back-to-basics school considered that progress.

"They're gonna shoot Curtis full of electricity next Saturday, Mr. Nudger," Holly Ann said plaintively. She sounded like a little girl complaining that the grade on her report card wasn't fair.

"I know," Nudger said. "But I don't see how I can help you. Or, more specifically, help Curtis."

"You know what they say thoughts really are, Mr. Nudger?" Holly Ann said, ignoring his professed helplessness. Her wide blue eyes were vague as she searched for words. "Thoughts ain't really nothing but tiny electrical impulses in the brain. I read that somewheres or other. What I can't help wondering is, when they shoot all that electricity into Curtis, what's it gonna be like to his thinking? How long will it seem like to him before he finally dies? Will there be a big burst of crazy thoughts along with the pain? I know it sounds loony, but I can't help laying awake nights thinking about that, and I feel I just gotta do whatever's left to try and help Curtis."

There was a sort of checkout-line tabloid logic in that, Nudger conceded; if thoughts were actually weak electrical impulses, then high-voltage electrical impulses could become exaggerated, horrible thoughts. Anyway, try to disprove it to Holly Ann.

"They never did catch Curtis's buddy, the driver who sped away and left him in that service station, did they?" Nudger asked.

"Nope. Curtis never told who the driver was, neither, no matter how much he was threatened. Curtis is a stubborn man."

Nudger was getting the idea.

"But you know who was driving the car."

"Yep. And he told me him and Curtis was miles away from that liquor store at the time it was robbed. When he seen the police closing in on Curtis in that gas station where Curtis was buying cigarettes, he hit the accelerator and got out of the parking lot before they could catch him. The police didn't even get the car's license plate number."

Nudger rubbed a hand across his chin, watching Holly Ann swing her leg as if it were a shapely metronome. She was barefoot and wearing no nylon hose. "The jury thought Curtis not only was at the liquor store, but that he shot the old man and woman in cold blood."

"That ain't true, though. Not according to—" she caught herself before uttering the man's name.

"Curtis's friend," Nudger finished.

"That's right. And he ought to know," Holly Ann said righteously, as if that piece of information were the trump card and the argument was over.

"None of this means anything unless the driver comes forward and substantiates that he was with Curtis somewhere other than at the liquor store when it was robbed."

Holly Ann nodded and stopped swinging her leg. "I know. But he won't. He can't. That's where you come in."

"My profession might enjoy a reputation a notch lower than dognap-per," Nudger said, "but I don't hire out to do anything illegal."

"What I want you to do is legal," Holly Ann said in a hurt little voice. Nudger looked past her into the dollhouse kitchen and saw an empty gin bottle. He wondered if she might be slightly drunk. "It's the eyewitness accounts that got Curtis convicted," she went on. "And those people are wrong. I want you to figure out some way to convince them it wasn't Curtis they saw that night."

"Four people, two of them customers in the store, picked Curtis out of a police lineup."

"So what? Ain't eyewitnesses often mistaken?"

Nudger had to admit that they were, though he didn't see how they could be in this case. There were, after all, four of them. And yet, Holly Ann was right; it was amazing how people could sometimes be so certain that the wrong man had committed a crime just five feet in front of them.

"I want you to talk to them witnesses," Holly Ann said. "Find out *why* they think Curtis was the killer. Then show them how they might be wrong and get them to change what they said. We got the truth on our side, Mr. Nudger. At least one witness wil! change his story when he's made to think about it, because Curtis wasn't where they said he was."

"Curtis has exhausted all his appeals," Nudger said. "Even if all the witnesses changed their stories, it wouldn't necessarily mean he'd get a new trial."

"Maybe not, but I betcha they wouldn't kill him. They couldn't stand the publicity if enough witnesses said they was wrong, it was somebody else killed the old woman. Then, just maybe, eventually, he'd get an-other trial and get out of prison."

Nudger was awed. Here was foolish optimism that transcended even his own. He had to admire Holly Ann.

The leg started pumping again beneath the cornflower-colored dress. When Nudger lowered his gaze to stare at it, Holly Ann said, "So will you help me, Mr. Nudger?"

"Sure. It sounds easy."

"Why should I worry about it anymore?" Randy Gantner asked Nudger, leaning on his shovel. He didn't mind talking to Nudger; it meant a break from his construction job on the new Interstate 170 cloverleaf. "Colt's been found guilty and he's going to the chair, ain't he?"

The afternoon sun was hammering down on Nudger, warming the back of his neck and making his stomach queasy. He thumbed an antacid tablet off the roll he kept in his shirt pocket and popped one of the white disks into his mouth. With his other hand, he was holding up a photograph of Curtis Colt for Gantner to see. It was a snapshot Holly Ann had given him of the wiry, shirtless Colt leaning on a fence post and holding a beer can high in a mock toast: this one's for Death!

"This is a photograph you never saw in court. I just want you to look at it closely and tell me again if you're sure the man you saw in the liquor store was Colt. Even if it makes no difference in whether he's executed, it will help ease the mind of somebody who loves him."

"I'd be a fool to change my story about what happened now that the trial's over," Gantner said logically.

"You'd be a murderer if you really weren't sure."

Gantner sighed, dragged a dirty red handkerchief from his jeans pocket, and wiped his beefy, perspiring face. He peered at the photo, then shrugged. "It's him, Colt, the guy I seen shoot the man and woman when I was standing in the back aisle of the liquor store. If he'd known me and Sanders was back there, he'd have probably zapped us along with them old folks."

"You're positive it's the same man?"

Gantner spat off to the side and frowned; Nudger was becoming a pest, and the foreman was staring. "I said it to the police and the jury, Nudger; that little twerp Colt did the old lady in. Ask me, he deserves what he's gonna get."

"Did you actually see the shots fired?"

"Nope. Me and Sanders was in the back aisle looking for some reasonable-priced bourbon when we heard the shots, then looked around to see Curtis Colt back away, turn, and run out to the car. Looked like a black or dark green old Ford. Colt fired another shot as it drove away."

"Did you see the driver?"

"Sort of. Skinny dude with curly black hair and mustache. That's what I told the cops. That's all I seen. That's all I know."

And that was the end of the conversation. The foreman was walking toward them, glaring. *Thunk!* Gantner's shovel sliced deep into the earth, speeding the day when there'd be another place for traffic to get backed up. Nudger thanked him and advised him not to work too hard in the hot sun.

"You wanna help?" Gantner asked, grinning sweatily.

"I'm already doing some digging of my own," Nudger said, walking away before the foreman arrived.

The other witnesses also stood by their identifications. The fourth and last one Nudger talked with, an elderly woman named Iris Langeneckert, who had been walking her dog near the liquor store and had seen Curtis Colt dash out the door and into the getaway car, said something that Gantner had touched on. When she'd described the getaway car driver, like Gantner she said he was a thin man with curly black hair and a beard or mustache, then she had added, "Like Curtis Colt's hair and mustache."

Nudger looked again at the snapshot Holly Ann had given him. Curtis Colt was about five foot nine, skinny, and mean-looking, with a broad bandito mustache and a mop of curly, greasy black hair. Nudger wondered if it was possible that the getaway car driver had been Curtis Colt himself, and his accomplice had killed the shopkeeper. Even Nudger found that one hard to believe.

He drove to his second-floor office in the near suburb of Maplewood and sat behind his desk in the blast of cold air from the window unit, sipping the complimentary paper cup of iced tea he'd brought up from Danny's Donuts directly below. The sweet smell of the doughnuts was heavier than usual in the office; Nudger had never quite gotten used to it and what it did to his sensitive stomach.

When he was cool enough to think clearly again, he decided he needed more information on the holdup, and on Curtis Colt, from a more objective source than Holly Ann Adams. He phoned Lieutenant Jack Hammersmith at home and was told by Hammersmith's son Jed that Hammersmith had just driven away to go to work on the afternoon shift, so it would be awhile before he got to his office.

Nudger checked his answering machine, proving that hope did indeed spring eternal in a fool's breast. There was a terse message from his former wife Eileen demanding last month's alimony payment; a solemn-voiced young man reading an address where Nudger could send a check to help pay to form a watchdog committee that would stop the utilities from continually raising their rates; and a cheerful man informing Nudger that with the labels from ten packages of a brand name hot dog he could get a Cardinals' ballgame ticket at half price. (That meant eating over eighty hot dogs. Nudger calculated that baseball season would be over by the time he did that.) Everyone seemed to want some of Nudger's money. No one wanted to pay Nudger any money. Except for Holly Ann Adams. Nudger decided he'd better step up his efforts on the Curtis Colt case.

He tilted back his head, downed the last dribble of iced tea, then tried to eat what was left of the crushed ice. But the ice clung stubbornly to the bottom of the cup, taunting him. Nudger's life was like that.

He crumpled up the paper cup and tossed it, ice and all, into the wastebasket. Then he went downstairs where his Volkswagen was parked in the shade behind the building and drove east on Manchester, toward downtown and the Third District station house.

Police Lieutenant Jack Hammersmith was in his Third District office, sleek, obese, and cool-looking behind his wide metal desk. He was pounds and years away from the handsome cop who'd been Nudger's partner a decade ago in a two-man patrol car. Nudger could still see traces of a dashing quality in the flesh-upholstered Hammersmith, but he wondered if that was only because he'd known Hammersmith ten years ago.

"Sit down, Nudge," Hammersmith invited, his lips smiling but his slate gray, cop's eyes unreadable. If eyes were the windows to the soul, his shades were always down.

Nudger sat in one of the straight-backed chairs in front of Hammersmith's desk. "I need some help," he said.

"Sure," Hammersmith said, "you never come see me just to trade recipes or to sit and rock." Hammersmith was partial to irony; it was a good thing, in his line of work.

"I need to know more about Curtis Colt," Nudger said.

Hammersmith got one of his vile greenish cigars out of his shirt pocket and stared intently at it, as if its paper ring label might reveal some secret of life and death. "Colt, eh? The guy who's going to ride the lightning?"

"That's the second time in the past few days I've heard that expression. The first time was from Colt's fiancée. She thinks he's innocent."

"Fiancées think along those lines. Is she your client?"

Nudger nodded but didn't volunteer Holly Ann's name.

"Gullibility makes the world go round," Hammersmith said. "I was in charge of the Homicide investigation on that one. There's not a chance Colt is innocent, Nudge."

"Four eyewitness I.D.'s is compelling evidence," Nudger admitted. "What about the getaway car driver? His description is a lot like Colt's. Maybe he's the one who did the shooting and Colt was the driver."

"Colt's lawyer hit on that. The jury didn't buy it. Neither do I. The man is guilty, Nudge."

"You know how inaccurate eyewitness accounts are," Nudger persisted.

That seemed to get Hammersmith mad. He lit the cigar. The office immediately fogged up.

Nudger made his tone more amicable. "Mind if I look at the file on the Colt case?"

Hammersmith gazed thoughtfully at Nudger through a dense greenish haze. He inhaled, exhaled; the haze became a cloud. "How come this fiancée didn't turn up at the trial to testify for Colt? She could have at least lied and said he was with her that night."

"Colt apparently didn't want her subjected to taking the stand."

"How noble," Hammersmith said. "What makes this fiancée think her prince charming is innocent?"

"She knows he was somewhere else when the shopkeepers were shot."

"But not with her?"

"Nope."

"Well, that's refreshing."

Maybe it was refreshing enough to make up Hammersmith's mind. He picked up the phone and asked for the Colt file. Nudger could barely make out what he was saying around the fat cigar, but apparently everyone at the Third was used to Hammersmith and could interpret cigarese.

The file didn't reveal much that Nudger didn't know. Fifteen minutes after the liquor store shooting, officers from a two-man patrol car, acting on the broadcast description of the gunman, approached Curtis Colt inside a service station where he was buying a pack of cigarettes from a vending machine. A car that had been parked near the end of the dimly lighted lot had sped away as they'd entered the station office. The officers had gotten only a glimpse of a dark green old Ford; they hadn't made out the license plate number but thought it might start with the letter "L."

Colt had surrendered without a struggle, and that night at the Third District Station the four eyewitnesses had picked him out of a lineup. Their description of the getaway car matched that of the car the police had seen speeding from the service station. The loot from the holdup, and several gas station holdups committed earlier that night, wasn't on Colt, but probably it was in the car.

"Colt's innocence just jumps out of the file at you, doesn't it, Nudge?" Hammersmith said. He was grinning a fat grin around the fat cigar.

"What about the murder weapon?"

"Colt was unarmed when we picked him up."

"Seems odd."

"Not really," Hammersmith said. "He was planning to pay for the cigarettes. And maybe the gun was still too hot to touch so he left it in the car. Maybe it's still hot; it got a lot of use for one night."

Closing the file folder and laying it on a corner of Hammersmith's desk, Nudger stood up. "Thanks, Jack. I'll keep you tapped in if I learn anything interesting."

"Don't bother keeping me informed on this one, Nudge. It's over. I don't see how even a fiancée can doubt Colt's guilt."

Nudger shrugged, trying not to breathe too deeply in the smoke-hazed office. "Maybe it's an emotional thing. She thinks that because thought waves are tiny electrical impulses, Colt might experience time warp and all sorts of grotesque thoughts when all that voltage shoots through him. She has bad dreams."

"I'll bet she does," Hammersmith said. "I'll bet Colt has bad dreams, too. Only he deserves his. And maybe she's right."

"About what?"

"About all that voltage distorting thought and time. Who's to say?"

"Not Curtis Colt," Nudger said. "Not after they throw the switch."

"It's a nice theory, though," Hammersmith said. "I'll remember it. It might be a comforting thing to tell the murder victim's family."

"Sometimes," Nudger said, "you think just like a cop who's seen too much."

"Any of it's too much, Nudge," Hammersmith said with surprising sadness. He let more greenish smoke drift from his nostrils and the corners of his mouth; he looked like a stone Buddha seated behind the desk, one in which incense burned.

Nudger coughed and said goodbye.

"Only two eyewitnesses are needed to convict," Nudger said to Holly Ann the next day in her trailer, "and in this case there are four. None of them is at all in doubt about their identification of Curtis Colt as the killer. I have to be honest; it's time you should face the fact that Colt is guilty and that you're wasting your money on my services."

"All them witnesses know what's going to happen to Curtis," Holly Ann said. "They'd never want to live with the notion they might have made a mistake, killed an innocent man, so they've got themselves convinced that they're positive it was Curtis they saw that night."

"Your observation on human psychology is sound," Nudger said, "but I don't think it will help us. The witnesses were just as certain three months ago at the trial. I took the time to read the court manuscript; the jury had no choice but to find Colt guilty, and the evidence hasn't changed."

Holly Ann drew her legs up and clasped her knees to her chest with both arms. Her little-girl posture matched her little-girl faith in her lover's innocence. She believed the white knight must arrive at any moment and snatch Curtis Colt from the electrical jaws of death. She believed hard. Nudger could almost hear his armor clank when he walked.

She wanted him to believe just as hard. "I see you need to be convinced of Curtis's innocence," she said wistfully. There was no doubt he'd forced her into some kind of corner. "If you come here tonight at eight, Mr. Nudger, I'll convince you."

"How?"

"I can't say. You'll understand why tonight."

"Why do we have to wait till tonight?"

"Oh, you'll see."

Nudger looked at the waiflike creature curled in the corner of the sofa. He felt as if they were playing a childhood guessing game while Curtis Colt waited his turn in the electric chair. Nudger had never seen an execution; he'd heard it took longer than most people thought for the condemned to die. His stomach actually twitched.

"Can't we do this now with twenty questions?" he asked.

Holly Ann shook her head. "No, Mr. Nudger."

Nudger sighed and stood up, feeling as if he were about to bump his head on the trailer's low ceiling even though he was barely six feet tall.

"Make sure you're on time tonight, Mr. Nudger," Holly Ann said as he went out the door. "It's important.

At eight on the nose that evening Nudger was sitting at the tiny table in Holly Ann's kitchenette. Across from him was a thin, nervous man in his late twenties or early thirties, dressed in a longsleeved shirt despite the heat, and wearing sunglasses with silver mirror lenses. Holly Ann introduced the man as "Len, but that's not his real name," and said he was Curtis Colt's accomplice and the driver of their getaway car on the night of the murder.

"But me and Curtis was nowhere near the liquor store when them folks got shot," Len said vehemently.

Nudger assumed the sunglasses were so he couldn't effectively identify Len if it came to a showdown in court. Len had lank, dark brown hair that fell to below his shoulders, and when he moved his arm

Nudger caught sight of something blue and red on his briefly exposed wrist. A tattoo. Which explained the longsleeved shirt.

"You can understand why Len couldn't come forth and testify for Curtis in court," Holly Ann said.

Nudger said he could understand that. Len would have had to incriminate himself.

"We was way on the other side of town," Len said, "casing another service station, when that liquor store killing went down. Heck, we never held up nothing but service stations. They was our specialty."

Which was true, Nudger had to admit. Colt had done time for armed robbery six years ago after sticking up half a dozen service stations within a week. And all the other holdups he'd been tied to this time around were of service stations. The liquor store was definitely a departure in his M.O., one not noted in court during Curtis Colt's rush to judgment.

"Your hair is in your favor," Nudger said to Len.

"Huh?"

"Your hair didn't grow that long in the three months since the liquor store killing. The witnesses described the getaway car driver as having shorter, curlier hair, like Colt's, and a mustache."

Len shrugged. "I'll be honest with you—it don't help at all. Me and Curtis was kinda the same type. So to confuse any witnesses, in case we got caught, we made each other look even more alike. I'd tuck up my long hair and wear a wig that looked like Curtis's hair. My mustache was real, like Curtis's. I shaved it off a month ago. We did look alike at a glance; sorta like brothers."

Nudger bought that explanation; it wasn't uncommon for a team of holdup men to play tricks to confuse witnesses and the police. Too many lawyers had gotten in the game; the robbers, like the cops, were taking the advice of their attorneys and thinking about a potential trial even before the crime was committed.

"Is there any way, then, to prove you were across town at the time of the murder?" Nudger asked, looking at the two small Nudgers staring back at him from the mirror lenses.

"There's just my word," Len said, rather haughtily.

Nudger didn't bother telling him what that was worth. Why antagonize him?

"I just want you to believe Curtis is innocent," Len said with desperation. "Because he is! And so am I!"

And Nudger understood why Len was here, taking the risk. If Colt was guilty of murder, Len was guilty of being an accessory to the crime.

Once Curtis Colt had ridden the lightning, Len would have hanging over him the possibility of an almost certain life sentence, and perhaps even his own ride on the lightning, if he were ever caught. It wasn't necessary to actually squeeze the trigger to be convicted of murder.

"I need for you to try extra hard to prove Curtis is innocent," Len said. His thin lips quivered; he was near tears.

"Are you giving Holly Ann the money to pay me?" Nudger asked.

"Some of it, yeah. From what Curtis and me stole. And I gave Curtis's share to Holly Ann, too. Me and her are fifty-fifty on this."

Dirty money, Nudger thought. Dirty job. Still, if Curtis Colt happened to be innocent, trying against the clock to prove it was a job that needed to be done.

"Okay. I'll stay on the case."

"Thanks," Len said. His narrow hand moved impulsively across the table and squeezed Nudger's arm in gratitude. Len had the look of an addict; Nudger wondered if the longsleeved shirt was to hide needle tracks as well as the tattoo.

Len stood up. "Stay here with Holly Ann for ten minutes while I make myself scarce. I gotta know I wasn't followed. You understand it ain't that I don't trust you; a man in my position has gotta be sure, is all."

"I understand. Go."

Len gave a spooked smile and went out the door. Nudger heard his running footfalls on the gravel outside the trailer. Nudger was forty-three years old and ten pounds overweight; lean and speedy Len needed a ten minute head start like Sinatra needed singing lessons.

"Is Len a user?" Nudger asked Holly Ann.

"Sometimes. But my Curtis never touched no dope."

"You know I have to tell the police about this conversation, don't you?"

Holly Ann nodded. "That's why we arranged it this way. They won't be any closer to Len than before."

"They might want to talk to you, Holly Ann."

She shrugged. "It don't matter. I don't know where Len is, nor even his real name nor how to get in touch with him. He'll find out all he needs to know about Curtis by reading the papers."

"You have a deceptively devious mind," Nudger told her, "considering that you look like Barbie Doll's country kid cousin."

Holly Ann smiled, surprised and pleased. "Do you find me attractive, Mr. Nudger?"

"Yes. And painfully young."

For just a moment Nudger almost thought of Curtis Colt as a lucky man. Then he looked at his watch, saw that his ten minutes were about up, and said goodbye. If Barbie had a kid cousin, Ken probably had one somewhere, too. And time was something you couldn't deny. Ask Curtis Colt.

"It doesn't wash with me," Hammersmith said from behind his desk, puffing angrily on his cigar. Angrily because it did wash a little bit; he didn't like the possibility, however remote, of sending an innocent man to his death. That was every good homicide cop's nightmare. "This Len character is just trying to keep himself in the clear on a murder charge."

"You could read it that way," Nudger admitted.

"It would help if you gave us a better description of Len," Hammersmith said gruffly, as if Nudger were to blame for Curtis Colt's accomplice still walking around free.

"I gave you what I could," Nudger said. "Len didn't give me much to pass on. He's streetwise and scared and knows what's at stake."

Hammersmith nodded, his fit of pique past. But the glint of weary frustration remained in his eyes.

"Are you going to question Holly Ann?" Nudger said.

"Sure, but it won't do any good. She's probably telling the truth. Len would figure we'd talk to her; he wouldn't tell her how to find him."

"You could stake out her trailer."

"Do you think Holly Ann and Len might be lovers?"

"No."

Hammersmith shook his head. "Then they'll probably never see each other again. Watching her trailer would be a waste of manpower."

Nudger knew Hammersmith was right. He stood up to go.

"What are you going to do now?" Hammersmith asked.

"I'll talk to the witnesses again. I'll read the court transcript again. And I'd like to talk with Curtis Colt."

"They don't allow visitors on Death Row, Nudge, only temporary boarders."

"This case is an exception," Nudger said. "Will you try to arrange it?"

Hammersmith chewed thoughtfully on his cigar. Since he'd been the officer in charge of the murder investigation, he'd been the one who'd nailed Curtis Colt. That carried an obligation.

"I'll phone you soon," he said, "let you know."

Nudger thanked Hammersmith and walked down the hall into the clear, breathable air of the booking area.

That day he managed to talk again to all four eyewitnesses. Two of them got mad at Nudger for badgering them. They all stuck to their stories. Nudger reported this to Holly Ann at the Right-Steer Steakhouse, where she worked as a waitress. Several customers that afternoon got tears with their baked potatoes.

Hammersmith phoned Nudger that evening.

"I managed to get permission for you to talk to Colt," he said, "but don't get excited. Colt won't talk to you. He won't talk to anyone, not even a clergyman. He'll change his mind about the clergyman, but not about you."

"Did you tell him I was working for Holly Ann?"

"I had that information conveyed to him. He wasn't impressed. He's one of the stoic ones on Death Row."

Nudger's stomach kicked up, growled something that sounded like a hopeless obscenity. If even Curtis Colt wouldn't cooperate, how could he be helped? Absently Nudger peeled back the aluminum foil on a roll of antacid tablets and slipped two chalky white disks into his mouth. Hammersmith knew about his nervous stomach and must have heard him chomping the tablets. "Take it easy, Nudge. This isn't your fault."

"Then why do I feel like it is?"

"Because you feel too much of everything. That's why you had to quit the department."

"We've got another day before the execution," Nudger said. "I'm going to go through it all again. I'm going to talk to each of those witnesses even if they try to run when they see me coming. Maybe somebody will say something that will let in some light."

"There's no light out there, Nudge. You're wasting your time. Give up on this one and move on."

"Not yet," Nudger said. "There's something elusive here that I can't quite grab."

"And never will," Hammersmith said. "Forget it, Nudge. Live your life and let Curtis Colt lose his."

Hammersmith was right. Nothing Nudger did helped Curtis Colt in the slightest. At eight o'clock Saturday morning, while Nudger was preparing breakfast in his apartment, Colt was put to death in the electric chair. He'd offered no last words before two thousand volts had turned him from something into nothing.

Nudger heard the news of Colt's death on his kitchen radio. He went ahead and ate his eggs, but he skipped the toast.

That afternoon he consoled a numbed and frequently sobbing Holly

Ann and apologized for being powerless to stop her true love's execution. She was polite, trying to be brave. She preferred to suffer alone. Her boss at the Right-Steer gave her the rest of the day off, and Nudger drove her home.

Nudger slept a total of four hours during the next two nights. On Monday, he felt compelled to attend Curtis Colt's funeral. There were about a dozen people clustered around the grave, including the state-appointed clergyman and pall-bearers. Nudger stood off to one side during the brief service. Holly Ann, looking like a child playing dress-up in black, stood well off to the other side. They didn't exchange words, only glances.

As the coffin was lowered into the earth, Nudger watched Holly Ann walk to where a taxi was waiting by a weathered stone angel. The cab wound its way slowly along the snaking narrow cemetery road to tall iron gates and the busy street. Holly Ann never looked back.

That night Nudger realized what was bothering him, and for the first time since Curtis Colt's death, he slept well.

In the morning he began watching Holly Ann's trailer.

At seven-thirty she emerged, dressed in her yellow waitress uniform, and got into another taxi. Nudger followed in his battered Volkswagen Beetle as the cab drove her the four miles to her job at the Right-Steer Steakhouse. She didn't look around as she paid the driver and walked inside through the molded plastic Old-West-saloon swinging doors.

At six that evening another cab drove her home, making a brief stop at a grocery store.

It went that way for the rest of the week, trailer to work to trailer. Holly Ann had no visitors other than the plain brown paper bag she took home every night.

The temperature got up to around ninety-five and the humidity rose right along with it. It was one of St. Louis's legendary summer heat waves. Sitting melting in the Volkswagen, Nudger wondered if what he was doing was really worthwhile. Curtis Colt was, after all, dead, and had never been his client. Still, there were responsibilities that went beyond the job. Or perhaps they were actually the essence of the job.

The next Monday, after Holly Ann had left for work, Nudger used his Visa card to slip the flimsy lock on her trailer door, and let himself in.

It took him over an hour to find what he was searching for. It had been well hidden, in a cardboard box inside the access panel to the bathroom plumbing. After looking at the box's contents—almost seven hundred dollars in loot from Curtis Colt's brief life of crime, and another object Nudger wasn't surprised to see—Nudger resealed the box and replaced the access panel.

He continued to watch and follow Holly Ann, more confident now.

Two weeks after the funeral, when she left work one evening, she didn't go home.

Instead her taxi turned the opposite way and drove east on Watson Road. Nudger followed the cab along a series of side streets in South St. Louis, then part way down a dead-end alley to a large garage, above the door of which was lettered "Clifford's Auto Body."

Nudger backed out quickly onto the street, then parked the Volkswagen near the mouth of the alley. A few minutes later the cab drove by without a passenger. Within ten minutes, Holly Ann drove past in a shiny red Ford. Its license plate number began with an L.

When Nudger reached Placid Cove Trailer Park, he saw the Ford nosed in next to Holly Ann's trailer.

On the way to the trailer door, he paused and scratched the Ford's hood with a key. Even in the lowering evening light he could see that beneath the new red paint the car's color was dark green.

Holly Ann answered the door right away when he knocked. She tried a smile when she saw it was him, but she couldn't quite manage her facial muscles, as if they'd become rigid and uncoordinated. She appeared ten years older. The little-girl look had deserted her; now she was an emaciated, grief-eroded woman, a country Barbie doll whose features some evil child had lined with dark crayon. The shaded crescents beneath her eyes completely took away their innocence. She was holding a glass that had once been a jelly jar. In it were two fingers of a clear liquid. Behind her on the table was a crumpled brown paper bag and a half-empty bottle of gin.

"I figured it out," Nudger told her.

Now she did smile, but it was fleeting, a sickly bluish shadow crossing her taut features. "You're like a dog with a rag, Mr. Nudger. You surely don't know when to let go." She stepped back and he followed her into the trailer. It was warm in there; something was wrong with the air conditioner. "Hot as hell, ain't it," Holly Ann commented. Nudger thought that was apropos.

He sat down across from her at the tiny Formica table, just as he and Len had sat facing each other two weeks ago. She offered him a drink. He declined. She downed the contents of the jelly jar glass and poured herself another, clumsily striking the neck of the bottle on the glass. It made a sharp, flinty sound, as if sparks might fly.

"Now, what's this you've got figured out, Mr. Nudger?" She didn't want to, but she had to hear it. Had to share it.

"It's almost four miles to the Right-Steer Steakhouse," Nudger told her. "The waitresses there make little more than minimum wage, so cab fare to and from work has to eat a big hole in your salary. But then you seem to go everywhere by cab."

"My car's been in the shop."

"I figured it might be, after I found the money and the wig."

She bowed her head slightly and took a sip of gin. "Wig?"

"In the cardboard box inside the bathroom wall."

"You been snooping, Mr. Nudger." There was more resignation than outrage in her voice.

"You're sort of skinny, but not a short girl," Nudger went on. "With a dark curly wig and a fake mustache, sitting in a car, you'd resemble Curtis Colt enough to fool a dozen eyewitnesses who just caught a glimpse of you. It was a smart precaution for the two of you to take."

Holly Ann looked astounded.

"Are you saying I was driving the getaway car at the liquor store holdup?"

"Maybe. Then maybe you hired someone to play Len and convince me he was Colt's accomplice and that they were far away from the murder scene when the trigger was pulled. After I found the wig, I talked to some of your neighbors, who told me that until recently you'd driven a green Ford sedan."

Holly Ann ran her tongue along the edges of her protruding teeth.

"So Curtis and Len used my car for their holdups."

"I doubt if Len ever met Curtis. He's somebody you paid in stolen money or drugs to sit there where you're sitting now and lie to me."

"If I was driving that getaway car, Mr. Nudger, and *knew* Curtis was guilty, why would I have hired a private investigator to try to find a hole in the eyewitnesses' stories?"

"That's what bothered me at first," Nudger said, "until I realized you weren't interested in clearing Curtis. What you were really worried about was Curtis Colt talking in prison. You didn't want those witnesses' stories changed, you wanted them verified. And you wanted the police to learn about not-his-right-name Len."

Holly Ann raised her head to look directly at him with eyes that begged and dreaded. She asked simply, "Why would I want that?"

"Because you were Curtis Colt's accomplice in all of his robberies. And when you hit the liquor store, he stayed in the car to drive. You fired the shot that killed the old woman. He was the one who fired the wild shot from the speeding car. Colt kept quiet about it because he loved you. He never talked, not to the police, not to his lawyer, not even to a priest. Now that he's dead you can trust him forever, but I have a feeling you could have anyway. He loved you more than you loved him, and you'll have to live knowing he didn't deserve to die.''

She looked down into her glass as if for answers and didn't say anything for a long time. Nudger felt a bead of perspiration trickle crazily down the back of his neck. Then she said, "I didn't want to shoot that old man, but he didn't leave me no choice. Then the old woman came at me.'' She looked up at Nudger and smiled ever so slightly. It was a smile Nudger hadn't seen on her before, one he didn't like. "God help me, Mr. Nudger, I can't quit thinking about shooting that old woman.''

"You murdered her," Nudger said, "and you murdered Curtis Colt by keeping silent and letting him die for you.''

"You can't prove nothing," Holly Ann said, still with her ancient-eyed, eerie smile that had nothing to do with amusement.

"You're right," Nudger told her, "I can't. But I don't think legally proving it is necessary, Holly Ann. You said it: thoughts are actually tiny electrical impulses in the brain. Curtis Colt rode the lightning all at once. With you, it will take years, but the destination is the same. I think you'll come to agree that his way was easier.''

She sat very still. She didn't answer. Wasn't going to.

Nudger stood up and wiped his damp forehead with the back of his hand. He felt sticky, dirty, confined by the low ceiling and near walls of the tiny, stifling trailer. He had to get out of there to escape the sensation of being trapped.

He didn't say goodbye to Holly Ann when he walked out. She didn't say goodbye to him. The last sound Nudger heard as he left the trailer was the clink of the bottle on the glass.

While Nancy Pickard is always a lot of fun to read, and usually gives her readers plenty of scenes and plenty of characters to smile at, she is one of the field's most under-appreciated stylists and social observers.

Fortunately, her readers and her reviewers seem to be catching up with her.

In their quiet, measured way, Nancy Pickard's books are quite serious novels about the consequences of being an intelligent woman of the eighties and nineties. That they are also splendid entertainment only makes them all the more fetching.

Afraid All the Time
NANCY PICKARD

"Ribbon a darkness over me . . ."

Mel Brown, known variously as Pell Mell and Animel, sang the line from the song over and over behind his windshield as he flew from Missouri into Kansas on his old black Harley-Davidson motorcycle.

Already he loved Kansas, because the highway that stretched ahead of him was like a long, flat, dark ribbon unfurled just for him.

"Ribbon a darkness over me . . ."

He flew full throttle into the late-afternoon glare, feeling as if he were soaring gloriously drunk and blind on a skyway to the sun. The clouds in the far distance looked as if they'd rain on him that night, but he didn't worry about it. He'd heard there were plenty of empty farm and ranch houses in Kansas where a man could break in to spend the night. He'd heard it was like having your choice of free motels. Kansas was.

"Ribbon a darkness over me . . ."

Three hundred miles to the southwest, Jane Baum suddenly stopped what she was doing. The fear had hit her again. It was always like that,

379

striking out of nowhere, like a fist against her heart. She dropped her clothes basket from rigid fingers and stood as if paralyzed between the two clotheslines in her yard. There was a wet sheet to her right, another to her left. For once the wind had died down, so the sheets hung as still and silent as walls. She felt enclosed in a narrow, white, sterile room of cloth, and she never wanted to leave it.

Outside of it was danger.

On either side of the sheets lay the endless prairie where she felt like a tiny mouse exposed to every hawk in the sky.

It took all of her willpower not to scream.

She hugged her own shoulders to comfort herself. It didn't help. Within a few moments she was crying, and then shaking with a palsy of terror.

She hadn't known she'd be so afraid.

Eight months ago, before she had moved to this small farm she'd inherited, she'd had romantic notions about it, even about such simple things as hanging clothes on a line. It would feel so good, she had imagined, they would smell so sweet. Instead, everything had seemed strange and threatening to her from the start, and it was getting worse. Now she didn't even feel protected by the house. She was beginning to feel as if it were fear instead of electricity that lighted her lamps, filled her tub, lined her cupboards and covered her bed—fear that she breathed instead of air.

She hated the prairie and everything on it.

The city had never frightened her, not like this. She knew the city, she understood it, she knew how to avoid its dangers and its troubles. In the city there were buildings everywhere, and now she knew why— it was to blot out the true and terrible openness of the earth on which all of the inhabitants were so horribly exposed to danger.

The wind picked up again. It snapped the wet sheets against her body. Janie bolted from her shelter. Like a mouse with a hawk circling overhead, she ran as if she were being chased. She ran out of her yard and then down the highway, racing frantically, breathlessly, for the only other shelter she knew.

When she reached Cissy Johnson's house, she pulled open the side door and flung herself inside without knocking.

"Cissy?"

"I'm afraid all the time."

"I know, Janie."

Cissy Johnson stood at her kitchen sink peeling potatoes for supper

while she listened to Jane Baum's familiar litany of fear. By now Cissy
knew it by heart. Janie was afraid of: being alone in the house she had
inherited from her aunt; the dark; the crack of every twig in the night;
the storm cellar; the horses that might step on her, the cows that might
trample her, the chickens that might peck her, the cats that might bite
her and have rabies, the coyotes that might attack her; the truckers who
drove by her house, especially the flirtatious ones who blasted their
horns when they saw her in the yard; tornadoes, blizzards, electrical
storms; having to drive so far just to get simple groceries and supplies.

At first Cissy had been sympathetic, offering daily doses of coffee
and friendship. But it was getting harder all the time to remain patient
with somebody who just burst in without knocking and who complained
all the time about imaginary problems and who—

"You've lived here all your life," Jane said, as if the woman at the
sink had not previously been alert to that fact. She sat in a kitchen
chair, huddled into herself like a child being punished. Her voice was
low, as if she were talking more to herself than to Cissy. "You're used
to it, that's why it doesn't scare you."

"Um," Cissy murmured, as if agreeing. But out of her neighbor's
sight, she dug viciously at the eye of a potato. She rooted it out—
leaving behind a white, moist, open wound in the vegetable—and
flicked the dead black skin into the sink where the water running from
the faucet washed it down the garbage disposal. She thought how she'd
like to pour Janie's fears down the sink and similarly grind them up
and flush them away. She held the potato to her nose and sniffed,
inhaling the crisp, raw smell.

Then, as if having gained strength from that private moment, she
glanced back over her shoulder at her visitor. Cissy was ashamed of
the fact that the mere sight of Jane Baum now repelled her. It was a
crime, really, how she'd let herself go. She wished Jane would comb
her hair, pull her shoulders back, paint a little coloring onto her pale
face, and wear something else besides that ugly denim jumper that came
nearly to her heels. Cissy's husband, Bob, called Janie "Cissy's pup,"
and he called that jumper the "pup tent." He was right, Cissy thought,
the woman did look like an insecure, spotty adolescent, and not at all
like a grown woman of thirty-five-plus years. And darn it, Janie did
follow Cissy around like a neurotic nuisance of a puppy.

"Is Bob coming back tonight?" Jane asked.

Now she's even invading my mind, Cissy thought. She whacked resentfully at the potato, peeling off more meat than skin. "Tomorrow."
Her shoulders tensed.

"Then can I sleep over here tonight?"

"No." Cissy surprised herself with the shortness of her reply. She could practically feel Janie radiating hurt, and so she tried to make up for it by softening her tone. "I'm sorry, Janie, but I've got too much book work to do, and it's hard to concentrate with people in the house. I've even told the girls they can take their sleeping bags to the barn tonight to give me some peace." The girls were her daughters, Tessie, thirteen, and Mandy, eleven. "They want to spend the night out there 'cause we've got that new little blind calf we're nursing. His mother won't have anything to do with him, poor little thing. Tessie has named him Flopper, because he tries to stand up but he just flops back down. So the girls are bottle-feeding him, and they want to sleep near . . ."

"Oh." It was heavy with reproach.

Cissy stepped away from the sink to turn her oven on to 350°. Her own internal temperature was rising too. God forbid she should talk about her life! God forbid they should ever talk about anything but Janie and all the damned things she was scared of! She could write a book about it: *How Jane Baum Made a Big Mistake by Leaving Kansas City and How Everything About the Country Just Scared Her to Death.*

"Aren't you afraid of anything, Cissy?"

The implied admiration came with a bit of a whine to it—*anything*—like a curve on a fastball.

"Yes." Cissy drew out the word reluctantly.

"You *are*? What?"

Cissy turned around at the sink and laughed self-consciously.

"It's so silly . . . I'm even afraid to mention it."

"Tell me! I'll feel better if I know you're afraid of things, too."

There! Cissy thought. *Even my fears come down to how they affect you!*

"All right." She sighed. "Well, I'm afraid of something happening to Bobby, a wreck on the highway or something, or to one of the girls, or my folks, things like that. I mean, like leukemia or a heart attack or something I can't control. I'm always afraid there won't be enough money and we might have to sell this place. We're so happy here. I guess I'm afraid that might change." She paused, dismayed by the sudden realization that she had not been as happy since Jane Baum moved in down the road. For a moment, she stared accusingly at her neighbor. "I guess that's what I'm afraid of." Then Cissy added deliberately, "But I don't think about it all the time."

"I think about mine all the time," Jane whispered.

"I know."

"I hate it here!"

"You could move back."

Janie stared reproachfully. "You know I can't afford that!"

Cissy closed her eyes momentarily. The idea of having to listen to *this* for who knew how many years ...

"I love coming over here," Janie said wistfully, as if reading Cissy's mind again. "It always makes me feel so much better. This is the only place I feel safe anymore. I just hate going home to the big old house all by myself."

I will not invite you to supper, Cissy thought.

Janie sighed.

Cissy gazed out the big square window behind Janie. It was October, her favorite month, when the grass turned as red as the curly hair on a Hereford's back and the sky turned a steel gray like the highway that ran between their houses. It was as if the whole world blended into itself—the grass into the cattle, the roads into the sky, and she into all of it. There was an electricity in the air, as if something more important than winter were about to happen, as if all the world were one and about to burst apart into something brand-new. Cissy loved the prairie, and it hurt her feelings a little that Janie didn't. How could anyone live in the middle of so much beauty, she puzzled, and be frightened of it?

"We'll never get a better chance." Tess ticked off the rationale for the adventure by holding up the fingers of her right hand, one at a time, an inch from her sister's scared face. "Dad's gone. We're in the barn. Mom'll be asleep. It's a new moon." She ran out of fingers on that hand and lifted her left thumb. "And the dogs know us."

"They'll find out!" Mandy wailed.

"*Who'll* find out?"

"Mom and Daddy will!"

"They won't! Who's gonna tell 'em? The gas-station owner? You think we left a trail of toilet paper he's going to follow from his station to here? And he's gonna call the sheriff and say lock up those Johnson girls, boys, they stole my toilet paper?"

"Yes!"

Together they turned to gaze—one of them with pride and cunning, the other with pride and trepidation—at the small hill of hay that was piled, for no apparent reason, in the shadows of a far corner of the barn. Underneath that pile lay their collection of six rolls of toilet paper—a new one filched from their own linen closet, and five partly used ones (stolen one trip at a time and hidden in their school jackets) from the ladies' bathroom at the gas station in town. Tess's plan was for the two of them to "t.p." their neighbor's house that night, after dark. Tess had lovely visions of how it would look—all ghostly and spooky, with streamers of white hanging down from the tree limbs and waving eerily in the breeze.

"They do it all the time in Kansas City, jerk," Tess proclaimed. "And I'll bet they don't make any big crybaby deal out of it." She wanted to be the first one in her class to do it, and she wasn't about to let her little sister chicken out on her. This plan would, Tess was sure, make her famous in at least a four-county area. No grown-up would ever figure out who had done it, but all the kids would know, even if she had to tell them.

"Mom'll kill us!"

"Nobody'll know!"

"It's gonna rain!"

"It's not gonna rain."

"We shouldn't leave Flopper!"

Now they looked, together, at the baby bull calf in one of the stalls. It stared blindly in the direction of their voices, tried to rise, but was too frail to do it.

"Don't be a dope. We leave him all the time."

Mandy sighed.

Tess, who recognized the sound of surrender when she heard it, smiled magnanimously at her sister.

"You can throw the first roll," she offered.

In a truck stop in Emporia, Mel Brown slopped up his supper gravy with the last third of a cloverleaf roll. He had a table by a window. As he ate, he stared with pleasure at his bike outside. If he moved his head just so, the rays from the setting sun flashed off the handlebars. He thought about how the leather seat and grips would feel soft and warm and supple, the way a woman in leather felt, when he got back on. At the thought he got a warm feeling in his crotch, too, and he smiled.

God, he loved living like this.

When he was hungry, he ate. When he was tired, he slept. When he was horny, he found a woman. When he was thirsty, he stopped at a bar.

Right now Mel felt like not paying the entire $5.46 for this lousy chicken-fried steak dinner and coffee. He pulled four dollar bills out of his wallet and a couple of quarters out of his right front pocket and set it all out on the table, with the money sticking out from under the check.

Mel got up and walked past the waitress.

"It's on the table," he told her.

"No cherry pie?" she asked him.

It sounded like a proposition, so he grinned as he said, "Nah." *If you weren't so ugly,* he thought, *I just might stay for dessert.*

"Come again," she said.

You wish, he thought.

If they called him back, he'd say he couldn't read her handwriting. Her fault. No wonder she didn't get a tip. Smiling, he lifted a toothpick off the cashier's counter and used it to salute the man behind the cash register.

"Thanks," the man said.

"You bet."

Outside, Mel stood in the parking lot and stretched, shoving his arms high in the air, letting anybody who was watching get a good look at him. Nothin' to hide. Eat your heart out, baby. Then he strolled over to his bike and kicked the stand up with his heel. He poked around his mouth with the toothpick, spat out a sliver of meat, then flipped the toothpick onto the ground. He climbed back on his bike, letting out a breath of satisfaction when his butt hit the warm leather seat.

Mel accelerated slowly, savoring the surge of power building between his legs.

Jane Baum was in bed by 10:30 that night, exhausted once again by her own fear. Lying there in her late aunt's double bed, she obsessed on the mistake she had made in moving to this dreadful, empty place in the middle of nowhere. She had expected to feel nervous for a while, as any other city dweller might who moved to the country. But she hadn't counted on being actually phobic about it—of being possessed by a fear so strong that it seemed to inhabit every cell of her body until at night, every night, she felt she could die from it. She hadn't known—how could she have known?—she would be one of those people who is terrified by the vastness of the prairie. She had visited the farm only a few times as a child, and from those visits she had remembered only warm and fuzzy things like caterpillars and chicks. She had only dimly remembered how antlike a human being feels on the prairie.

Her aunt's house had been broken into twice during the period between her aunt's death and her own occupancy. That fact cemented her fantasies in a foundation of terrifying reality. When Cissy said, "It's your imagination," Janie retorted, "But it happened twice before! Twice!" She wasn't making it up! There *were* strange, brutal men—

that's how she imagined them, they were never caught by the police—who broke in and took whatever they wanted—cans in the cupboard, the radio in the kitchen. It could happen again, Janie thought obsessively as she lay in the bed; it could happen over and over. *To me, to me, to me.*

On the prairie, the darkness seemed absolute to her. There were millions of stars but no streetlights. Coyotes howled, or cattle bawled. Occasionally the big night-riding semis whirred by out front. Their tire and engine sounds seemed to come out of nowhere, build to an intolerable whine and then disappear in an uncanny way. She pictured the drivers as big, rough, intense men hopped up on amphetamines; she worried that one night she would hear truck tires turning into her gravel drive, that an engine would switch off, that a truck door would quietly open and then close, that careful footsteps would slur across her gravel.

Her fear had grown so huge, so bad, that she was even frightened of it. It was like a monstrous balloon that inflated every time she breathed. Every night the fear got worse. The balloon got bigger. It nearly filled the bedroom now.

The upstairs bedroom where she lay was hot because she had the windows pulled down and latched, and the curtains drawn. She could have cooled it with a fan on the dressing table, but she was afraid the fan's noise might cover the sound of whatever might break into the first floor and climb the stairs to attack her. She lay with a sheet and a blanket pulled up over her arms and shoulders, to just under her chin. She was sweating, as if her fear-frozen body were melting, but it felt warm and almost comfortable to her. She always wore pajamas and thin wool socks to bed because she felt safer when she was completely dressed. She especially felt more secure in pajama pants, which no dirty hand could shove up onto her belly as it could a nightgown.

Lying in bed like a quadriplegic, unmoving, eyes open, Janie reviewed her precautions. Every door was locked, every window was permanently shut and locked, so that she didn't have to check them every night; all the curtains were drawn; the porch lights were off, and her car was locked in the barn so no trucker would think she was home.

Lately she had taken to sleeping with her aunt's loaded pistol on the pillow beside her head.

Cissy crawled into bed just before midnight, tired from hours of accounting. She had been out to the barn to check on her giggling girls and the blind calf. She had talked to her husband when he called from

Oklahoma City. Now she was thinking about how she would try to start easing Janie Baum out of their lives.

"I'm sorry, Janie, but I'm awfully busy today. I don't think you ought to come over . . ."

Oh, but there would be that meek, martyred little voice, just like a baby mouse needing somebody to mother it. How would she deny that need? She was already feeling guilty about refusing Janie's request to sleep over.

"Well, I will. I just will do it, that's all. If I could say no to the FHA girls when they were selling fruitcakes, I can start saying no more often to Janie Baum. Anyway, she's never going to get over her fears if I indulge them."

Bob had said as much when she'd complained to him long-distance. "Cissy, you're not helping her," he'd said. "You're just letting her get worse." And then he'd said something new that had disturbed her. "Anyway, I don't like the girls being around her so much. She's getting too weird, Cissy."

She thought of her daughters—of fearless Tess and dear little Mandy—and of how *safe* and *nice* it was for children in the country. . . .

"Besides," Bob had said, "she's *got* to do more of her own chores. We need Tess and Mandy to help out around our place more; we can't be having them always running off to mow her grass and plant her flowers and feed her cows and water her horse and get her eggs, just because she's scared to stick her silly hand under a damned hen. . . ."

Counting the chores put Cissy to sleep.

"Tess!" Mandy hissed desperately. "Wait!"

The older girl slowed, to give Mandy time to catch up to her, and then to touch Tess for reassurance. They paused for a moment to catch their breath and to crouch in the shadow of Jane Baum's porch. Tess carried three rolls of toilet paper in a makeshift pouch she'd formed in the belly of her black sweatshirt. ("We gotta wear black, remember!") and Mandy was similarly equipped. Tess decided that now was the right moment to drop her "bomb."

"I've been thinking," she whispered.

Mandy was struck cold to her heart by that familiar and dreaded phrase. She moaned quietly. "What?"

"It might rain."

"I told you."

"So I think we better do it inside."

"Inside?"

"Shh! It'll scare her to death, it'll be great! Nobody else'll ever have the guts to do anything as neat as this! We'll do the kitchen, and if we have time, maybe the dining room."

"Ohhh, noooo."

"*She* thinks she's got all the doors and windows locked, but she doesn't!" Tess giggled. She had it all figured out that when Jane Baum came downstairs in the morning, she'd take one look, scream, faint, and then, when she woke up, call everybody in town. The fact that Jane might also call the sheriff had occurred to her, but since Tess didn't have any faith in the ability of adults to figure out anything important, she wasn't worried about getting caught. "When I took in her eggs, I unlocked the downstairs bathroom window! Come on! This'll be great!"

The ribbon of darkness ahead of Mel Brown was no longer straight. It was now bunched into long, steep hills. He hadn't expected hills. Nobody had told him there was any part of Kansas that wasn't flat. So he wasn't making as good time, and he couldn't run full-bore. But then, he wasn't in a hurry, except for the hell of it. And this was more interesting, more dangerous, and he liked the thrill of that. He started edging closer to the centerline every time he roared up a hill, playing a game of highway roulette in which he was the winner as long as whatever coming from the other direction had its headlights on.

When that got boring, he turned his own headlights off.

Now he roared past cars and trucks like a dark demon.

Mel laughed every time, thinking how surprised they must be, and how frightened. They'd think, *Crazy fool, I could have hit him. . . .*

He supposed he wasn't afraid of anything, except maybe going back to prison, and he didn't think they'd send him down on a speeding ticket. Besides, if Kansas was like most states, it was long on roads and short on highway patrolmen. . . .

Roaring downhill was even more fun, because of the way his stomach dropped out. He felt like a kid, yelling "Fuuuuck," all the way down the other side. What a goddamned roller coaster of a state this was turning out to be.

The rain still looked miles away.

Mel felt as if he could ride all night. Except that his eyes were gritty, the first sign that he'd better start looking for a likely place to spend the night. He wasn't one to sleep under the stars, not if he could find a ceiling.

Tess directed her sister to stack the rolls of toilet paper underneath the bathroom window on the first floor of Jane Baum's house. The six rolls, all white, stacked three in a row, two high, gave Tess the little bit of height and leverage she needed to push up the glass with her palms. She stuck her fingers under the bottom edge and laboriously attempted to raise the window. It was stiff in its coats of paint.

"Damn," she exclaimed, and let her arms slump. Beneath her feet, the toilet paper was getting squashed.

She tried again, and this time she showed her strength from lifting calves and tossing hay. With a crack of paint and a thump of wood on wood, the window slid all the way up.

"Shhh!" Mandy held her fists in front of her face and knocked her knuckles against each other in excitement and agitation. Her ears picked up the sound of a roaring engine on the highway, and she was immediately sure it was the sheriff, coming to arrest her and Tess. She tugged frantically at the calf of her sister's right leg.

Tess jerked her leg out of Mandy's grasp and disappeared through the open window.

The crack of the window and the thunder of the approaching motorcycle confused themselves in Jane's sleeping consciousness, so that when she awoke from dreams full of anxiety—her eyes flying open, the rest of her body frozen—she imagined in a confused, hallucinatory kind of way that somebody was both coming to get her and already there in the house.

Jane then did as she had trained herself to do. She had practiced over and over every night, so that her actions would be instinctive. She turned her face to the pistol on the other pillow and placed her thumb on the trigger.

Her fear—of rape, of torture, of kidnapping, of agony, of death— was a balloon, and she floated horribly in the center of it. There were thumps and other sounds downstairs, and they joined her in the balloon. There was an engine roaring, and then suddenly it was silent, and a slurring of wheels in her gravel drive, and these sounds joined her in her balloon. When she couldn't bear it any longer, she popped the balloon by shooting herself in the forehead.

In the driveway, Mel Brown heard the gun go off.

He slung his leg back onto his motorcycle and roared back out onto the highway. So the place had looked empty. So he'd been wrong. So he'd find someplace else. But holy shit. Get the fuck outta here.

)

*   *   *

Inside the house, in the bathroom, Tess also heard the shot and, being a ranch child, recognized it instantly for what it was, although she wasn't exactly sure where it had come from. Cussing and sobbing, she clambered over the sink and back out the window, falling onto her head and shoulders on the rolls of toilet paper.

"It's the sheriff!" Mandy was hysterical. "He's shooting at us!"

Tess grabbed her little sister by a wrist and pulled her away from the house. They were both crying and stumbling. They ran in the drainage ditch all the way home and flung themselves into the barn.

Mandy ran to lie beside the little blind bull calf. She lay her head on Flopper's side. When he didn't respond, she jerked to her feet. She glared at her sister.

"He's dead!"

"Shut up!"

Cissy Johnson had awakened, too, although she hadn't known why. Something, some noise, had stirred her. And now she sat up in bed, breathing hard, frightened for no good reason she could fathom. If Bob had been home, she'd have sent him out to the barn to check on the girls. But why? The girls were all right, they must be, this was just the result of a bad dream. But she didn't remember having any such dream.

Cissy got out of bed and ran to the window.

No, it wasn't a storm, the rain hadn't come.

A motorcycle!

That's what she'd heard, that's what had awakened her!

Quickly, with nervous fingers, Cissy put on a robe and tennis shoes. Darn you, Janie Baum, she thought, your fears are contagious, that's what they are. The thought popped into her head: If you don't have fears, they can't come true.

Cissy raced out to the barn.

RECOMMENDED READING

Twenty-Five Great Reads

Lawrence Block	*The Burglar in the Closet*
Fredric Brown	*The Fabulous Clipjoint*
Raymond Chandler	*The Lady in the Lake*
Loren D. Estleman	*Peeper*
Stanton Ford	*Grieve for the Past*
Richard Forrest	*A Child's Garden of Death*
Brian Garfield	*Recoil*
Dorothy Gilman	*The Tightrope Walker*
Carolyn G. Hart	*The Christie Caper*
Joan Hess	*Roll Over & Play Dead*
George V. Higgins	*The Friends of Eddie Coyle*
Chester Himes	*The Big Gold Dream*
Dean R. Koontz	*The Vision*
Francis & Richard Lockridge	*Murder Within Murder*
Marie Belloc Lowndes	*The Lodger*
Ross Macdonald	*The Far Side of the Dollar*
Charlotte MacLeod	*The Gladstone Bag*
Ed McBain	*Sadie When She Died*
Margaret Millar	*The Murder of Miranda*
David Morrell	*First Blood*
Barbara Paul	*Liars & Tyrants & People Who Turn Blue*
Elizabeth Peters	*The Last Camel Died at Noon*
Rex Stout	*Some Buried Caesar*
Donald E. Westlake	*Adios, Scheherazade*
Margaret Yorke	*The Come-On*

Twelve "Overlooked" Contemporary Writers

(Note: "Overlooked" and "underrated" are highly relative terms. Though some of these writers are comparatively obscure and others quite well known, none of them has been as highly valued as deserved.)

Harold Adams
James Anderson
Miriam Borgenicht
K. C. Constantine
Warwick Downing
Tony Fennelly

Richard Forrest
Joyce Harrington
William Harrington
Joe L. Hensley
James Sherburne
Tobias Wells (Stanton Forbes)

Fifteen Contemporary Traditional Mystery Novels

(all by living writers and published in the last twenty years)

Barbara D'Amato	*Hard Tack*
William L. DeAndrea	*The Werewolf Murders*
Colin Dexter	*The Wench is Dead*
Peter Dickinson	*One Foot in the Grave*
Susan Dunlap	*A Dinner to Die For*
Aaron Elkins	*Old Bones*
Jane Haddam	*Precious Blood*
P. D. James	*The Black Tower*
Gaylord Larsen	*Atascadero Island*
Francis M. Nevins, Jr.	*Corrupt and Ensnare*
Elizabeth Peters	*The Murders of Richard III*
Herbert Resnicow	*The Hot Place*
John Sladek	*Black Aura*
Scott Turow	*Presumed Innocent*
James Yaffe	*Mom Meets Her Maker*

Twenty-Five Private Eye Novels (all-time)

Andrew Bergman	*The Big Kiss Off of 1944*
Lawrence Block	*When The Sacred Ginmill Closes*
Howard Browne	*The Taste of Ashes*
Robert Campbell	*In La-La Land We Trust*
Raymond Chandler	*Farewell, My Lovely*
Max Allan Collins	*Stolen Away*
Michael Collins	*Minnesota Strip*
Thomas B. Dewey	*The Mean Streets*
Loren D. Estleman	*The Glass Highway*
Erle S. Gardner (as A. A. Fair)	*The Bigger They Come*
William Campbell Gault	*The Convertible Hearse*
Joe Gores	*Interface*
Sue Grafton	*"I" Is for Innocent*
Dashiell Hammett	*The Maltese Falcon*
Joseph Hansen	*Death Claims*
Robert Irvine	*The Angels' Share*
Ed Lacy	*Room to Swing*
Jonathan Latimer	*The Lady in the Morgue*
Ross Macdonald	*Black Money*
L. A. Morse	*The Old Dick*
Walter Mosley	*White Butterfly*
Marcia Muller	*There's Something in a Sunday*
Robert B. Parker	*God Save the Child*
Bill Pronzini	*Shackles*
Paco Ignacio Taibo II	*An Easy Thing*

Twenty-Five Police Procedurals

John Ball	*In the Heat of the Night*
John Creasey (as J. J. Marric)	*Gideon's Fire*
James Ellroy	*The Black Dahlia*
Katherine V. Forrest	*The Beverly Malibu*
Michael Gilbert	*Blood and Judgment*
Reginald Hill	*A Pinch of Snuff*
Tony Hillerman	*The Dark Wind*
Stuart Kaminsky	*A Cold Red Sunrise*
Peter Lovesey	*The Last Detective*
Ed McBain	*Vespers*
James McClure	*The Steam Pig*
William McIlvanney	*Laidlaw*
William Marshall	*Thin Air*
Gerald Petievich	*To Live and Die in L.A.*
Lawrence Sanders	*The Third Deadly Sin*
Dell Shannon	*Case Pending*
Maj Sjöwall and Per Wahlöö	*The Locked Room*
Martin Cruz Smith	*Gorky Park*
Peter Turnbull	*Dead and Crisp and Even*
Dorothy Uhnak	*The Bait*
Janwillem van de Wetering	*The Japanese Corpse*
John Wainwright	*Blayde, R.I.P.*
Joseph Wambaugh	*The Blue Knight*
Hillary Waugh	*Last Seen Wearing*
Collin Wilcox	*A Death Before Dying*

Some Notable Serial-Killer Novels

William Bayer	*Switch*
William Bayer	*Wallflower*
Robert Bloch	*Psycho*
Thomas H. Cook	*Tabernacle*
Bill Crider	*Blood Marks*
Bradley Denton	*Blackburn*
Alison Drake	*Fevered*
Robert Duncan	*In the Blood*
Ed Gorman	*Night Kills*
Brian Harper	*Shiver*
Thomas Harris	*Red Dragon*
Thomas Harris	*The Silence of the Lambs*
William Heffernan	*Ritual*
Dean Koontz	*Whispers*
David Lindsay	*Mercy*
David Martin	*Lie to Me*
Billlie Sue Mosiman	*Night Cruise*
Richard Neely	*The Walter Syndrome*
Bill Pronzini and Barry Malzberg	*The Running of Beasts*
Ellery Queen	*Cat of Many Tails*
Lawrence Sanders	*The First Deadly Sin*
Lawrence Sanders	*The Third Deadly Sin*
Peter Straub	*Koko*
Shane Stevens	*By Reason of Insanity*
David Wiltse	*Prayer for the Dead*
Stuart Woods	*Chiefs*

Twenty-Five Notable *Noir* Novels

Harold Adams	*The Barbed Wire Noose*
Lawrence Block	*After the First Death*
Fredric Brown	*The Wench is Dead*
Tucker Coe (D. Westlake)	*Don't Lie to Me*
Tucker Coe (D. Westlake)	*Murder Among Children*
James Crumley	*The Last Good Kiss*
James Ellroy	*Because the Night*
Thomas Hauser	*Agatha's Friends*
Dean Koontz (Owen West)	*The Fun House*
Dean Koontz	*The Voice of the Night*
Elmore Leonard	*Unknown Man #89*
John Lutz	*The Truth of the Matter*
Ed McBain	*Goldilocks*
Margaret Millar	*How Like an Angel*
Marcia Muller	*The Shape of Dread*
Marcia Muller	*Trophies and Dead Things*
Bill Pronzini	*Shackled*
Lawrence Sanders	*The Anderson Tapes*
Mickey Spillane	*Kiss Me Deadly*
Richard Stark (D. Westlake)	*The Seventh*
Ross Thomas	*Chinaman's Chance*
Teri White	*Triangle*
Charles Willeford	*New Hope for the Dead*
Cornell Woolrich	*The Black Curtain*
Cornell Woolrich	*The Black Path of Fear*

Some Notable Thrillers

Campbell Armstrong
Agents of Darkness

Tom Clancy
Patriot Games

William DeAndrea
Azrael

Len Deighton
Funeral in Berlin

James Frey
Winter of the Wolves

Bill Granger
The Last Good German

Graham Greene
The Third Man

Thomas Gifford
The Wind Chill Factor

David Hagberg
Without Honor

Adam Hall
The Quiller Memorandum

Somerset Maugham
Ashenden

David Morrell
The Fifth Profession

Warren Murphy and Molly Cochran
The Temple Dogs

Trevanian
The Loo Sanction

Twenty Distinguished Mystery Short Stories
(since 1980)

Robert Barnard, **"The Woman in the Wardrobe"** (*EQMM*, December 1987)

Lawrence Block, **"By the Dawn's Early Light"** (*Playboy*, August 1984)

Liza Cody, **"Spasmo"** (*A Classic English Crime*, 1990)

Michael Collins, **"The Oldest Killer"** (*The Thieftaker Journals*, November 1983)

Harlan Ellison, **"Soft Monkey"** (*The Black Lizard Anthology of Crime Fiction*, 1987)

Ed Gorman, **"The Reason Why"** (*Criminal Elements*, 1988)

Linda Grant, **"Last Rites"** (*Sisters in Crime 4*, 1991)

Edward D. Hoch, **"The Problem of the Octagon Room"** (*EQMM*, October 7, 1981)

Wendy Hornsby, **"Nine Sons"** (*Sisters in Crime 4*, 1991)

Clark Howard, **"Horn Man"** (*EQMM*, June 2, 1980)

Peter Lovesey, **"The Crime of Miss Oyster Brown"** (*EQMM*, May 1991)

Susan Moody, **"All's Fair in Love"** (*A Classic English Crime*, 1990)

Elizabeth Peters, **"Liz Peters, P.I."** (*Christmas Stalkings*, 1991)

James Powell, **"A Dirge for Clowntown"** (*EQMM*, November 1989)

Bill Pronzini, **"Incident in a Neighborhood Tavern"** (*An Eye for Justice*, 1988)

Ruth Rendell, **"The Copper Peacock"** (*EQMM*, June 1989)

Jack Ritchie, **"The Absence of Emily"** (*EQMM*, January 1981)

Peter Robinson, **"Innocence"** (*Cold Blood III*, 1991)

Donald E. Westlake, **"Too Many Crooks"** (*Playboy*, August 1989)

Carolyn Wheat, **"Ghost Station"** (*A Woman's Eye*, 1991)

FOURTEEN IMPORTANT MYSTERY REFERENCE BOOKS

Adey, Robert C.S. *Locked Room Murders*, revised ed. Minneapolis: Crossover, 1991.

Albert, Walter. *Detective and Mystery Fiction: An International Bibliography of Secondary Sources.* Madison, IN: Brownstone, 1985.

Barzun, Jacques, and Wendell Hertig Taylor. *A Catalogue of Crime*, revised ed. New York: Harper and Row, 1989.

Conquest, John. *Trouble is Their Business: Private Eyes in Fiction, Film, and Television, 1927–1988.* New York: Garland, 1990.

Contento, William G., with Martin H. Greenberg. *Index to Crime and Mystery Anthologies.* Boston: G.K. Hall, 1990.

Gorman, Ed, Martin H. Greenberg, and Larry Segriff, eds, with Jon L. Breen. *The Fine Art of Murder.* New York: Carroll & Graf, 1993.

Haycraft, Howard. *Murder for Pleasure: The Life and Times of the Detective Story.* New York: Appleton-Century, 1941.

Hubin, Allen J. *Crime Fiction II: A Comprehensive Bibliography, 1749–1990.* New York: Garland, 1994.

Lachman, Marvin. *A Reader's Guide to the American Novel of Detection.* New York: G.K. Hall, 1993.

Pronzini, Bill, and Marcia Muller. *1001 Midnights: The Aficionado's Guide to Mystery and Detective Fiction.* New York: Arbor, 1986.

Queen, Ellery (Frederic Dannay and Manfred B. Lee). *The Detective Short Story: A Bibliography.* Boston: Little, Brown, 1941.

Steinbrunner, Chris, and Otto Penzler. *Encyclopedia of Mystery and Detection.* Marvin Lachman and Charles Shibuk, Senior Editors. New York: McGraw-Hill, 1976.

Strosser, Edward. *The Armchair Detective Book of Lists.* New York: Armchair Detective, 1989. (Note: A revised edition is reportedly in preparation.)

Twentieth-Century Crime and Mystery Writers. Third edition. Chicago: St. James, 1991.

Additional Reference Books

Breen, Jon L. *What About Murder: A Guide to Books About Mystery and Detective Fiction*. Metuchen, NJ: Scarecrow Press, 1981.

McCarty, John. *Thrillers*. New York: Citadel Press, 1992.

Macker, Tasha. *Murder by Category: A Subject Guide to Mystery Fiction*. Metuchen, NJ: Scarecrow Press, 1991.

Nehr, Ellen. *Doubleday Crime Club Compendium*. Martinez, CA: Offspring Press, 1992.

Server, Lee. *Danger is My Business*. San Francisco: Chronicle Books, 1992.

Server, Lee. *Over My Dead Body*. San Francisco: Chronicle Books, 1994.